ALSO BY ELIZABETH KNOX

Dreamhunter: Book One of the Dreamhunter Duet
Dreamquake: Book Two of the Dreamhunter Duet
The Vintner's Luck
Black Oxen
Billie's Kiss
Daylight

ELIZABETH KNOX

MORTAL FIRE

SQUARE
FISH

FARRAR STRAUS GIROUX
NEW YORK

An Imprint of Macmillan
175 Fifth Avenue
New York, NY 10010
macteenbooks.com

Square Fish and the Square Fish logo are trademarks of Macmillan and
are used by Farrar Straus Giroux under license from Macmillan.

Square Fish books may be purchased for business or promotional use.
For information on bulk purchases, please contact the Macmillan
Corporate and Premium Sales Department at (800) 221-7945 x5442
or by e-mail at specialmarkets@macmillan.com.

Library of Congress Cataloging-in-Publication Data
Knox, Elizabeth.
   Mortal fire / Elizabeth Knox.
      p.   cm.
   Summary: When sixteen-year-old Canny of the Pacific island
Southland sets out on a trip with her stepbrother and his girlfriend,
she finds herself drawn into enchanting Zarene Valley, where the
mysterious but dark seventeen-year-old Ghislain helps her to figure
out her origins.
   ISBN 978-1-250-05069-4 (paperback)
   ISBN 978-0-374-38831-7 (e-book)
   [1. Magic—Fiction.   2. Identity—Fiction.   3. Stepbrothers—
Fiction.   4. Islands of the Pacific—Fiction.]   I. Title.

PZ7.K7707Mor 2013   [Fic]—dc23   2012040872

Originally published in the United States by
Frances Foster Books/Farrar Straus Giroux
First Square Fish Edition: 2014
Book designed by Jay Colvin
Square Fish logo designed by Filomena Tuosto

10   9   8   7   6   5   4   3   2   1

LEXILE: 830L

This book was completed with the assistance of a grant from
Creative New Zealand.

To my nieces, Helen Cropp, Bethan Cropp,
and Rachel Barrowman, and my nephews,
Tom, Gus, and Andrew Barrowman

And with thanks to my editor, Frances Foster

So when she speaks, the voice of Heaven I hear
So when we walk, nothing impure comes near;
Each field seems Eden, and each calm retreat;
Each village seems the haunt of holy feet.

But that sweet village where my black-ey'd maid,
Closes her eyes in sleep beneath night's shade:
Whene'er I enter, more than mortal fire
Burns in my soul, and does my song inspire.

—William Blake

AUTHOR'S NOTE

Southland is a large island republic in the South Pacific, in a world very like our own—but not completely. *Mortal Fire* opens in November of 1959, in Southland's southwestern-most city, Castlereagh.

1

CANNY AND HER TEAMMATES stood on platform nine of Castlereagh Station and watched everything they'd seen the night before in Founderston play again in reverse. Passengers from the overnight express were met, kissed, and led away into the concourse—or set off by themselves heads down into the hot wind. Bundles of pillows, sheets, and blankets were removed from the sleeper car, piled into handcarts, and wheeled away by the porters. The only difference was that here, in their hometown, the team's school uniforms were recognized, and several people stepped up to shake their hands. One man even opened his newspaper to their photo and had them sign it, first the three boys, then Canny. The man said that the *Castlereagh Clarion* had finally stopped calling their win an unlikely one.

It was the second year that Castlereagh Tech had carried off the supreme award at the National Mathematics Competition; a contest traditionally won by either

Founderston Collegiate or St. Thomas's—a decades-long rivalry in which the prize simply changed hands between the capital's two best boys' schools. Castlereagh Tech was a coeducational, state-run high school full of "kids of every stripe"—to quote its own principal—and famous for nothing much but disturbances on city buses and the occasional talented rugby player. When, two years before, Castlereagh Tech's junior math team took the prize in their section of the competition, even the *Clarion* reported their win as a surprising result. Last year the same "whiz kids" made the front page in their hometown. This year the *Clarion* was taking their feats a little more for granted.

"Only page two," said one of Canny's teammates, disappointed.

Canny took off her blazer. Mr. Grove, the head of the mathematics department, said, "Agnes Mochrie, you can remove that blazer once you're back in bounds. Until then you must remember you are representing your school."

Canny put her blazer back on. She stared at Mr. Grove, whose favorite pupil she was, and wondered how she could get him to just let her go. Then, because she wanted what she wanted, and was already imagining herself setting off with her suitcase banging on the backs of her legs, Canny just said the first thing that came into her head, without articulating any of the steps that led up to it. "I don't have to wait till visiting time," she said. "I could go now and they'd let me in."

"Please endeavor to make better sense when you speak, Agnes," said Miss Venn—the history teacher who'd had to travel north with the team because Canny couldn't be

4

expected to go on a trip with just three male classmates and the male head of the math department. (This was what the newspapers, and everyone else, failed to remark upon—that the coeducational college that won the National Mathematics Competition was the only coeducational college with a *girl* on its team.)

Mr. Grove was pretty good at following Canny's thinking, even when it wasn't mathematical. He said to Miss Venn, "Agnes visits Marli Vaiu after school every day."

There was a pause of a soft sort that Canny knew was sympathy.

"There's a rehearsal for the end-of-year prize-giving this morning that you're all required to attend," said Miss Venn. "But I'm sure they'll let you go after that."

One of the boys said, "Have our reports gone out?"

"They were put into the mail on Monday."

Canny had nothing to fear from the last report of her school career. She was a good student, and her teachers had always encouraged her. And since it was her last report, there'd be no little improvements she'd be expected to make.

Canny forgot about her report and stared off into space. She was wondering how many of her postcards she might find taped to the mirror above Marli's face, a mirror in which Marli could see the window of the ward and the tops of the trees that the hospital board were planning to cut down to make room for another parking lot. Canny thought about the trees, and their fate, till her mind was full of a green haze as if she were a tree among trees and had just given them the bad news.

Canny was musing, but Mr. Grove thought she was studying the beams of the new roof over the platforms. He asked a question about the roof's construction, one of the casual, fishing questions he liked to ask her. "What makes those beams so strong? Can you guess, Agnes?" he said, and Canny's three teammates abruptly turned away, as if she and Mr. Grove had started taking off their clothes. Canny noticed this disapproval and immediately put it aside without thinking about it. She gave the beams a proper look and, after a moment, told Mr. Grove why exactly they were strong, once meeting his gaze to get him to give her the word she needed, a descriptive word she didn't know but knew must exist.

Mr. Grove smiled. He was proud of her. Canny liked being his favorite, so she attempted a smile and said, "The new bridge in Founderston—"

In his enthusiasm Mr. Grove took off, talking over her. "Yes, the new bridge is built by the same principle. Well observed, Agnes."

Mr. Grove had been an engineer in the army during the Second World War and was passionate about the practical applications of mathematics. He had once famously shouted at a year-nine class that mathematics could save their lives. (He had lost his leg to a badly placed round by a British artillery unit, and his opinions about mortality and mathematics had some weight.)

"But the bridge is stronger than the roof," Canny said.

Founderston's newest bridge had been the best thing about the tour they'd taken of the capital's points of interest. It was a beautiful piece of engineering, and Mr. Grove had helped his pupils to see it with his own loving eyes. But to Canny, the bridge wasn't just beautiful. It had something Extra. It was the first time she'd seen the thing she thought of as her "Extra" attached to an object. She had wondered whether the new bridge's Extra was a property of the river—the mighty Sva—and had only fetched up against the structure in the same way that flotsam collects around the piles of bridges when a river runs high. She couldn't imagine how it might actually be part of the bridge, but it had seemed to be there *for* something.

It was only recently Canny had realized that usually no one else could see this "Extra," though it had at least once appeared in a form visible to others. That was three years before, on a family trip. Canny and her stepbrother, Sholto, had been trailing behind their parents in Founderston's old town when she'd spotted a line scrawled on a smoke-stained brick wall. The chalked letters looked so ordinary that she'd asked Sholto if he could see them too, and whether he knew what they meant.

"I don't know what it says. Perhaps it's Greek. The people in the old town used to speak a kind of Greek. But what do you mean, can I see it too?"

Canny didn't answer Sholto. But when they were home again she looked up the Greek alphabet in an encyclopedia. The Greeks' alpha beta delta was nothing like the chalk writing. And, anyway, why would she see bits of Greek that were invisible to everyone else—letters salted like frost between a certain pair of gate posts, or floating like thistledown above the grandstand when she was at the racetrack with Marli's family?

Canny was very persistent when puzzled and had taken the problem to Sholto again. She asked, "What would you feel if you could see things no one else could see?"

"I expect I'd feel very proud of my powers of perception," Sholto replied. "Though I hope not too proud, because, as sure as eggs are eggs, what no one else sees, no one else cares about."

Canny felt both reassured and put in her place. It was only later that it dawned on her that Sholto had thought she was talking about her flair for math.

Now Mr. Grove was saying, "Of course the worst the station roof has to deal with is a Southerly Buster, whereas a bridge on the Sva—" And he went on to talk about laminar and turbulent flow, and Canny listened because it was interesting, and because she didn't know how to begin to explain that, when she saw the bridge, she thought that someone had *told it* to be strong in the same way that her mother would tell her to be brave. Brave about inoculations, or having her wound cleaned that time she and Marli crashed their homemade go-kart and Canny lost a toenail. Canny wouldn't even be crying, and her mother would say, "Be brave." And sometimes, because she was not just any old mother, but Sisema Mochrie: "Be braver than you are." Canny had looked at the new bridge and thought that someone had told it to be stronger than it was, stronger than its materials and its make.

Mr. Grove was still going on enthusiastically when one of the boys said, "Here's our bus, sir."

The school bus rocked across the potholed asphalt of the drop-off lane, its suspension squeaking. Behind the bus was a car. Canny recognized her stepfather's bulbous beige Austin. Her stepbrother, Sholto, was behind the wheel, and her mother was in the backseat, as if Sholto was her chauffeur.

As soon as she spotted the car, Canny hurried toward it. Her only thought was to cast herself bodily into that suddenly sickeningly narrow gap between her home and school life. She did not want her mother to have any opportunity to emerge from the car and say something her teachers and teammates might overhear. Something typically odd and imperious.

Canny saw that her mother had leaned forward to issue orders—telling Sholto what he should say to her teachers. She jumped off the platform and ran to the Austin, her suitcase pummeling her calves. She heard Miss Venn call out, her voice sharp and angry.

Sholto opened his door and put out a hand to catch her. Her shoulder thudded into his palm, jarring them both. "Hang on a second, mate," he said to her, friendly and casual. He was trying to calm her. "Let me put your bag in the trunk. Then I'll have a quick word with Miss Venn." Sholto removed the bag from Canny's hand, unlocked the trunk, and put it in. He strode off. Miss Venn met him among the potholes—Mr. Grove had only limped to the edge of the platform.

Sholto said, "Hello, Miss Venn. It's good to see you again. Look here—Akanesi's mother has made an appointment with the principal and is anxious about the time. Since we're in a rush, she had better come with me. I'll be able to duck and weave between the trams and get there in good time."

Miss Venn looked mollified. Sholto often had that effect on people, no matter what news he had to deliver. He was a nice-looking, well-spoken young man, and the only time Canny had ever seen him strongly opposed was on the cricket pitch by the other team's bowler. Teachers had always loved Sholto—and he was a graduate of Castlereagh Tech, a former valedictorian, and the son of a university professor, a famously outspoken leftist who had sent both his son and stepdaughter to the Tech out of a conviction that the pursuit of snobbish advantages wasn't really to anyone's advantage.

Miss Venn said, "Certainly, Sholto, don't let us hold you up." She gave Canny a little wave. The only protest permitted Canny was to climb in beside Sholto, leaving her mother alone in the backseat.

Sholto pulled out into traffic and made a U-turn, bumping across the tram lines. Cars tooted. Sholto made apologetic faces and hand gestures. Then they were going with the traffic back along Commercial Street.

Canny glanced at her mother in the rearview mirror.

Sisema Mochrie sat—massive, impassive, and queenly—and watched the shop fronts go by.

"Ma, I'm graduating tomorrow," Canny said. "What can you possibly want to say to the principal?"

"I might want to give her an envelope full of money," said Sisema.

Canny met Sholto's eyes. He pulled a face and then said, "Congratulations, kid. I'm really proud of you. And, honestly, it was seat-of-the-pants stuff, even if I couldn't follow half of it."

Canny remembered the radio microphones and the technician with his portable sound booth set up in the aisle of the magnificent hall at Founderston Girls Academy. She had been told that the competition's final rounds were being broadcast, but had forgotten it completely once she was onstage. For a moment Canny ignored her mother—sitting in the back like an unexploded bomb—and asked Sholto what she'd sounded like on the radio.

"Not at all nervous or triumphant," Sholto said approvingly.

"You've just told me what I *didn't* sound like. But what did I sound like?"

"A sixteen-year-old girl from Castlereagh Tech," Sholto said. Then he grinned. "And a Sybil—as if you might at any moment stray from formula into prophecy."

Sisema snorted. "You're just like your father," she said.

Sholto fell silent. Canny waited. Her mother was going to say "Poetic," or possibly "A flatterer."

"Poetic," said Sisema.

According to Sisema, Sholto was often "just like his father." Whatever Sisema said, it was never wholly insulting, only calculated to make Sholto self-conscious, to make him feel a little quaint and unworldly.

Sholto pushed the Austin past a tram as it jangled through the wide intersection by the steps of the public hospital. They zipped on by the entrance to the steep, oak-lined drive that went up to the parking area behind the hospital. Halfway up the drive was a lane that led into the rear entrance of the ward where Marli was.

Marli Vaiu was Canny's best friend and the only person

to whom she ever tried to explain herself. Marli's family came from the Shackle Islands, like Canny's mother. But Sisema was the daughter of a chief, and Marli's father had come to Southland after the War to work in the fish cannery on Sandfly Point. Sisema and Marli's mother had only met once, at a parent-teacher meeting in the girls' first year at Tech. Marli's mother had instantly recognized Sisema as royalty and treated her with great respect—much to their daughters' astonishment. Marli's mother fawned, and Canny's mother put on an air of polite patronage. It was clear to both girls that the women knew their respective places very well and had carried them intact from the Shackles to Castlereagh, and that they were making the best of a friendship that was to one unfortunate and to the other awkward. Canny and Marli were the only Ma'eu girls at Castlereagh Tech. All other Ma'eu girls were to be found at St. Anne's, a small Catholic school. But Marli's family were Quakers, because the Quakers had been kind to Marli's father when he was a lonely early immigrant. And Sisema, having married a white Southlander, a socialist and atheist, had decided that it was most appropriate for her to accept the faith of her husband's mother and join the Southern Orthodox Church. These choices of worship had thrown Canny and Marli together, two Ma'eu girls in a school that was largely white (though Tech also had a group of Faesu, whose families had begun to drift from their isolated villages on the southeastern archipelago after the War to settle in the southern cities of Canning and Castlereagh).

For the first years of Canny and Marli's friendship, Sisema had made a point of reminding her daughter that there was no need for her to cling to Marli just because they looked and sounded alike. She said she fully expected her daughter to eventually discover that she had much more in common with that girl whose father was the editor of the *Clarion*, or the other, whose grandmother was a stroppy congresswoman. Those two were girls whom Canny could share intellectual interests with. Sisema prodded her daughter now and then about finding a more suitable friend, but when Marli contracted polio and for weeks lay near death in the isolation ward at Castlereagh Hospital, Sisema wordlessly retreated and never tried to part them again.

Canny had visited Marli every day for ten months—only skipping for the math competition, and once when she had a cold, because even mild colds were a threat to Marli's weakened lungs. Canny said "No" to her parents' plans for holidays. They went away, and Canny stayed with Grandma Mochrie and visited the hospital with Marli's family, spreading a flax mat beside the iron lung and singing songs— either to Marli, or with her, at a tempo that suited the rigid regularity of her assisted breathing. Sisema not only stopped trying to separate Canny from her unsuitable friend, she might even have attempted to sympathize. She began once to say to Canny that she understood the attraction of visiting someone who was forced to stay still, sequestered from the world, and would always *be there*. But at "always be there" Canny's head had reared back, her eyes had whitened, and she stalked off, fleeing what her mother was saying because it seemed that her mother was suggesting that her friend would never get better.

· · ·

Sisema told Sholto to wait in the car and bore Canny away to the principal's office.

The hallways of the administrative block were sour and musty. It was an early-summer, end-of-term, teenage boy smell made of sweat and hair oil and tired woolen socks. It was everyday to Canny, but Sisema pressed the back of one of her soft, scented hands against her nose.

When she saw them, the school secretary jumped up and knocked on the principal's door. She opened it, murmured something, and stepped to one side to usher Canny and her mother into the office.

The principal came around her desk and pressed Canny's hand. She congratulated her and made a little speech about how proud the school was of the team's performance. Then she gave Sisema's hand a brief shake and asked them to please take a seat.

Sisema said she'd rather stand. She opened the large bag she was carrying and took out a fan. It was of bleached flax and intricately woven. She used it to fan herself at first— and the principal opened a window. Later Sisema used the fan to gesture, with grace and force and exotic lordliness.

"I have come about my daughter's school report," Sisema began, solemn.

Canny realized that her mother was going to begin by speaking as if English was a hard task she'd mastered only for these occasions. Her whole bearing declared that she was making a great effort and was to be treated accordingly.

The principal said, "It is a very good report. Agnes is one of our top pupils. Not an all-rounder, but I hardly think that today of all days you will find anyone inclined to complain about that."

Sisema didn't say anything. The fan stilled. Canny watched her mother's nostrils flare.

"It is only that—" the principal began, and then swallowed. She asked again whether Mrs. Mochrie wouldn't really rather have a seat.

"It is only that . . . ?" prompted Sisema.

"The school will be required to write Agnes a letter of reference, and it is only fair that Agnes knows what kind of things she might expect that letter to contain."

"Why would you be writing someone a letter about my daughter?"

"Why, for University entrance, of course."

The fan stirred again. The air was allowed to move.

Canny took a breath and said, "Why do you have to talk about me?"

"Akanesi. It is what this appointment is for," Sisema said, "to talk about you."

"But I haven't even had a chance to read my school report."

"I presume your mother has it here with her."

Sisema shook her head.

"Oh dear," said the principal. "I really think you should look at it, Agnes, before we proceed."

"I don't want my daughter to read your report. My daughter does not need to hear those things. Those things that you think," Sisema said, her tone ponderous.

"If the report says something I don't agree with I can defend myself, if I care to," Canny said.

Sisema turned to her. "But you won't care to. You *don't* care."

"Which is part of my point," the principal said. "You must see, Mrs. Mochrie, the qualities in your daughter's makeup that cause her teachers to feel it necessary to raise our concerns with her family."

"What have I done?" said Canny.

The room was silent apart from the twang of a soccer ball on the concrete outside and urgent sporty shouting, all of it ordinary.

"When I came to this country from the islands"— Sisema began—"the government put money in my pocket and gave me a nice government job. I would go out on the town with my paycheck like all the other little government and armed services girls, and I'd try to buy clothes. I'd try to buy shoes. But my feet were too wide for all the pretty shoes in the shops. And the shopgirls would snigger at me as if my big feet meant I was a lewd person."

The principal had gone white. "Mrs. Mochrie—" she pleaded. "It is only that we feel Agnes must do more, for her own sake, to fit in with other young people. That is all we are saying. We're worried about her."

Sisema inhaled, a long slow breath, and at some point in the middle of it, the principal seemed to run out of breath herself as though Sisema had drawn into her lungs all the air in the room. Once the principal was silenced, Sisema said, "*My* point is that you shouldn't make nasty assumptions, like those shopgirls. I would have thought that the differences in Akanesi's background were taken into account." She had stopped pretending that her English was poor.

The principal flushed, and snapped, "We have children from all sorts of backgrounds at this school! Our assessment of Agnes's difficulties has nothing whatsoever to do with her background. Wherever she finds herself there will be requirements."

"I would have thought," Sisema went on, "that the school would shape itself around the needs of its pupils, as my dress shapes itself to my body, not my body to my dress."

Canny watched the principal's gaze flicker, startled, from her mother's swelling bosom to her round hips and disproportionately tiny belted waist. Sisema smirked and shifted her weight and her silk stockings rubbed against each other with a soft hissing noise.

The principal was now quite pink. "We're not saying we expect Agnes to try to win popularity contests. But she doesn't care to try to please anyone."

"Oh. You are making a mistake," Sisema said, her tone flat, as though she were about to tell a lie and the necessity to do so filled her with such scorn that she had to show it. "It is only that Akanesi's face doesn't move. Her muscles are damaged. That's why she doesn't smile like a normal girl. A doctor at her birth had an accident with his forceps when he was trying to deliver her."

The principal looked down at her own fingers, which were tapping on her blotter. She seemed acutely embarrassed. "Whatever the case, surely at least you should discuss this matter with Professor Mochrie."

Sisema flourished the fan. Its sleek white fiber flashed in the light. "My husband, Professor Mochrie, is not Akanesi's father."

Canny was so stunned that her ears were ringing. This dismissal of her stepfather was just about the nearest her mother had come to talking about her real father. She barely had time to catch her breath before the principal said, "Then perhaps Akanesi's father might like to join the discussion?" She had a savage glint in her eye. She'd had enough of being cowed and was fighting back.

Canny's mother was motionless. She seemed not to be breathing at all. Then she said, "Perhaps one day he will." A pause. "But you wouldn't like it."

And then the two women just stared at each other. Finally the principal said, "You should let Akanesi read her report. And then you could actually discuss it with her instead of simply questioning it."

"You write a kind of curse and then tell me to show it to my daughter," Sisema said.

"I'm very sorry you see it that way, Mrs. Mochrie." The principal stood up to signal that the interview was at an end. She looked at Canny, blushed again, and said, "We are terrifically proud of your achievements at the competition, Agnes. And we all believe that you will do something astonishing one day." She offered Canny her cold hand. Canny took it and shook, and then followed her mother out of the office.

BETWEEN THE QUAD AND THE PARKING AREA, where there was less chance of being overheard by either schoolmates or Sholto, Canny took her mother's arm and said, "I hate the way you talk about me."

"But I was there to do that."

"I hate it when you try to explain. What you said about the forceps delivery was a lie."

"I blow smoke in their eyes. They don't deserve explanations. You're a good girl with good marks, and one day you won't have to put up with this testing and examination."

"Mother!" Canny dug in her feet, but Sisema wouldn't stop. She pulled away from her daughter and strolled on, her fan working, and her other hand pressed to her cleavage as though she had heartburn.

Canny ran to catch up with her. "Is my father still alive?"

They had reached the car, and Sholto, whose eyes flew open when he heard Canny's question.

"I only mentioned your father to discomfort that silly woman."

"Really?" Canny was suspicious.

Sholto edged out of Sisema's way and, at the same time, deftly opened the car door for her.

"Yes, of course. Your father is dead. His arms came off. No one could survive their arms coming off."

Sisema glanced at her stepson. "I'll walk into town, Sholto," she said—and then let her suffering show. "Before all my other appointments I think I need to go to church. You can drive your sister to the hospital to visit her friend."

Canny opened her mouth to mention the prize-giving rehearsal, then closed it again. Sisema kissed her on both cheeks, a demonstration of fealty and ownership rather than affection. She ambled off down the hill, her rolling walk turning the heads of a number of senior boys she passed.

Canny got into the car beside Sholto and they sat in

silence for a time, collecting themselves. Finally, "Hell's bells," said Sholto.

"I couldn't get her to say anything more," Canny told him. "She talked about my father as if he was alive."

"Your mother is the slipperiest person there is," Sholto said, meaning that it wasn't Canny's fault that she didn't get any information out of Sisema. "What was her fight with the principal about, anyway?"

"Apparently there's something wrong with me," Canny said.

Sholto started the car and they drove out of the school grounds, and it wasn't until they were nearly at the hospital that Canny realized he hadn't responded to what she'd said. They parked under the oaks, just above the lane at the back of Marli's ward. Sholto said he'd have a little nap. "The day holds more ordeals, I'm afraid, but I won't tell you about them before you've seen Marli." He slid down the seat and jammed one of his big square knees up under the steering wheel.

"Sholto," Canny said. "Did you just forget to be kind?"

"What?"

"When I said that there was something wrong with me, you should have said something nice, like that it takes all sorts."

"It takes all sorts," Sholto said, and closed his eyes.

2

AFTER HOSPITAL VISITING HOURS and getting on toward teatime, Sholto was still sitting slumped in the car. He was resting his eyes, only opening them now and then to check the progress of the afternoon.

Sholto had the knack of letting time go by. He may have had things to worry about, but since he couldn't do anything right that minute about his father's and stepmother's plans, he dropped his shoulders and closed his eyes.

Another ten minutes passed, and Sholto's eyes came idly open. Then he saw something that made him straighten so quickly that the underside of the steering wheel nearly shaved off his kneecap.

Reflected in the round chrome frame of the Austin's wing mirror, Sholto saw Canny hurrying up the hill. Even in the warm light coming through the oak leaves, Canny looked drained, her coffee-colored skin tinged gray. She had pulled the ribbons from the ends of her plaits and they'd unraveled. Her hair, straight but never sleek, was fuming behind her, as black as the smoke from a burning tire. And what had she done with her uniform?

Sholto immediately understood that something must have happened to Marli. If Marli was worse, then Canny's world was in peril—and here he was, the first on hand to help. Sholto jumped out of the car and opened his arms, ready to catch her. He was nervous, but strangely thrilled.

The path under the oaks was empty. Beyond the trees, the windows of the women's medical wing blazed blindly. There was no one in sight. No running girl.

Sholto stood feeling silly. He dropped his arms, put his hands in his pockets, and leaned on the car. He took a slow careful look around, just to make sure. Then, superstitious, he stooped to look into the mirror, which showed him nothing but his own face, his freckles standing stark against his pale skin.

WHEN CANNY ARRIVED ON THE WARD she kissed Marli. She stayed stooped over her friend so that their combined breath misted the mirror directly above the padded leather collar that circled Marli's neck.

The mirror was one of three attached to the head-end of Marli's iron lung. One mirror gave Marli a view of the door, so that she could see who was passing in the corridor. A second was angled up toward the ward's tall windows and the treetops beyond. That mirror was full of sparkling green light. The third, a long rectangle, showed Marli herself, her daily, friendly face. She had to use her mirrors to look around, because the iron lung's bulk took up most of her field of vision.

The collar around Marli's neck created the iron lung's first seal. The seals made the lung airtight and allowed it to do its work. At the top of the machine was an electrical pump and a bellows, which rose and fell, pushing air in and out of the man-size chamber. When the bellows rose, it drew air out of the chamber, creating a vacuum that made Marli's lungs expand. When the bellows depressed, the air pressure in the chamber increased, pushing the breath back out of Marli's lungs again. The machine did what Marli's paralyzed pulmonary muscles could no longer manage. The pump hummed, the bellows clicked and hissed, and Marli said, "Look." She shifted her gaze to the picture taped to the enameled wall of the machine. It was a postcard Canny had sent only two days before—of the cathedral of St. Lazarus, on the Isle of the Temple in Founderston. The postcard was stuck over earlier pictures—drawings in crayon by Marli's little brothers, photographs cut from movie magazines, and a couple of illuminated scripture cards, the kind handed out to the children of Marli's church. Canny thought the quotes weren't very encouraging. One said, "Teach us to number our days," and the other, "We are saved by hope."

Canny found a polishing cloth and cleaned Marli's mirrors. She fetched Marli's hairbrush and smoothed her hair. Then she produced her present, a beautifully wrapped and beribboned box. She began to tear its wrapping off, saying, "It's only fair you open it when I'm here."

Marli laughed, her laugh odd, since it had to work with the regularity of the machine. Marli couldn't open her own present. Her hands were inside the iron lung and could be seen through one of its several portholes. Her left one was clubbed because the muscle had shrunk and contracted. The right one sometimes rose to fiddle with a button, to touch her clothes and herself, her ticking, warm self, no longer visible to her, and trapped.

Canny showed Marli the chocolates, white, milk, and dark, and swirly combinations of the three. "White, please," Marli said, and Canny popped one in her friend's mouth. There was no talk for the next few minutes, only sticky hums of enjoyment.

Once she'd had several chocolates Marli said, "We listened to the broadcast. Even the ward sister sat down."

"I bet it sounded smoother than it was."

"Smoother?"

"Oh, you know," Canny said. She couldn't think of the right word.

"You sounded confident. I mean—you *all* did."

Canny knew Marli would have some idea what it was really like—the silences filled with the reverent murmur of the radio commentator, narrating her team's consultations as if he was talking about a slow patch in a cricket game. Canny hadn't been able to hear him—he was in a glass booth—but she could see his mouth moving. Murmur murmur murmur.

Each team had a captain whose job it was to deliver the answers to the judges, and it was mostly the captains' voices that people heard on the radio. Canny was not her team's captain, though she'd carried her team through the provincial heats and, in the capital, through the play-offs and into the finals. In their semifinal and final rounds, despite the ticking clock, her team had made a show of putting their heads together over every question. They did that because Mr. Grove had sat them down in their hotel on the second day of the competition and said that they had to perform more as a team. Apparently he'd had an uncomfortable conversation with the mathematics mistress of Founderston Girls Academy, whose team was the last of the all-girl teams knocked out of the competition in the quarterfinals. The mathematics mistress had said that she'd been very interested to notice that it was a *girl* who was the power behind his school's great effort.

Canny explained some of this to her friend.

Marli was incredulous. "He made you pretend to have to consult the others?"

"Yes. But to be fair, Jonno was quicker on the plain number questions. Jonno's an adding machine."

A nurse put her head around the door. "I'm just boiling the jug. Do you want a cup of tea, Agnes?"

Canny said no thank you, she wasn't staying long, and the woman left.

Marli said, "Are you in a hurry?"

"Sholto's waiting in the car. I'll walk over tomorrow. Remind me to tell you all about Ma's meeting with the principal. Ma told one of her *stories*. Bald-faced and unblinking."

Marli said she was looking forward to that. They had another chocolate, then Canny found a place for the box on top of the iron lung.

Someone in the corridor had turned on a radio. It was often on and switched to the government-sponsored National Radio with its current affairs and dramas and its big repertoire of inoffensive music.

Canny kissed Marli again. "I'll wait for the news and listen with you, but then I'll have to go," she said, sounding apologetic, as she often would. Then, brighter, "What's the plot for today?"

Marli filled her in on the day's top news stories, which concerned a horse-doping scandal and the mayor of Metternich, who'd been arrested for public indecency.

ONCE THEY WERE HOME Sholto wheeled out the push-mower to mow the lawn. This was usually his Saturday afternoon chore.

Canny asked him why he was doing that now and he told her to go upstairs, take off her uniform, and unpack her bags. "Put your laundry in the basket," he added.

She went upstairs and did everything he asked. Then she came and sat on the porch.

Sholto was kneeling on the newly mown grass, his shirt off and the sun already reddening his shoulders. He was using clippers to trim the grass left around the legs of the immovable outdoor bench.

Canny saw that there were a couple of long, thick canvas bags leaning on the porch railing. "What are these?"

"They're tents," he said.

"What for?"

"Camping."

"Who for?"

"That depends."

One bag was bigger than the other—both smelled of damp and the dust of basements.

Sholto scattered the clippings back into the lawn. He rinsed the clippers at the outdoor tap and came to sit beside her. He told her that her mother and the Professor were going on a trip. When he was speaking to Canny, Sholto often called his father "the Professor."

Canny was trying to imagine her mother camping, putting up a tent, building a fireplace, boiling a billy. "It's the holidays," she said. "I'd forgotten."

"They crept up on you."

The study break before her exams had felt like a holiday. The exams were quite easy, except in English comprehension and French dictation where she was resigned to disappointing results. With those subjects, no amount of study helped. She'd sat University-level mathematics and already had a start on her degree. Biology and chemistry were rote learning, and easy for her. She did well in history even though she knew she was only a solid history student, but her teachers were dazzled by the name Mochrie. Canny finished early in every exam and would sit looking at the back of the head of the boy or girl in front of her, or at dust motes in the light coming through the stained glass of the war memorial window. It seemed to Canny that the exams were over before she'd even gotten into the swing of them. Other seniors went on to plan the senior ball and leavers' dinner. Canny hadn't gone to the ball. Nor did she intend to go to the dinner. She'd had her rite of passage—the math competition.

Now, suddenly, tomorrow was the last day of school.

During the break the previous summer Canny and Marli had met every day at the saltwater baths near the ferry terminal. They'd swim and sunbathe, or huddle in their towels on blustery days. They were together all day, every day. Every day but Christmas, which Sisema would insist was a day for family only. Canny's family hadn't gone away because the Professor was finishing a book. In mid-summer the saltwater baths closed because of the polio epidemic. Marli and Canny had taken to catching the ferry to Westbourne, where they swam off the shingle beach. February came, and the primary schools stayed closed. All the little children had red sun bonnets—the disease was said to mind the color red. In mid-February Canny had a stomach bug. She phoned Marli, who said she felt unwell too. Two days later Canny was eating again, and Marli's big brother phoned to say that Marli was in the hospital, in the isolation ward. She had polio, and it was touch and go.

Canny hadn't considered yet what she was going to do to fill her time this summer. Study maybe—the Professor had insisted she do at least two arts subjects. She'd chosen Middle English and Shakespeare. She'd need to do a bit of reading. And she'd visit Marli of course. Spend longer on the ward every day. Perhaps they could embark on a series of books together—there was a horse series Marli was interested in. *My Friend Flicka. Thunderhead. The Green Grass of Wyoming.* The equinoctial gales might keep blowing till late December. The city would be dusty; the rain warm. Last summer seemed perfect now, and sealed away, with everything that belonged to it—the smell of wet bodies on hot concrete, a steamy scent seasoned by dust; the sight of Marli's rat-tailed hair, her gleaming back; the smell of the sun-struck butter in the apple pastries sold at the West-bourne kiosk; and the taste of lemon ice. Last summer was preserved like an everlasting daisy in a glass paperweight. Or perhaps like Marli's body in that steel box.

"Canny?" Sholto said. He put a hot, grassy hand on her foot and gave it a friendly squeeze. "Are you all right?"

"Yes. I was just—" Remembering. But it had felt more active than that. "I was feeling for cracks," she said.

Sholto tilted his head and looked expectant.

"Sometimes it's as if there are cracks in things. Seams in unexpected places. Like that join in Grandma's Japanese cabinet, that one that isn't really a join, but a secret com-partment, with a spring mechanism."

Sholto said, "I like it when you bother to explain things to me. Though usually it's math concepts I haven't a hope of understanding."

She said, "This is the opposite of math."

"Math has an opposite?"

"Maybe 'opposite' isn't the right word. The Professor is right about me needing more English. So, what I mean is that sometimes it's like *if only* I can get my fingernails in the right place things will crack open and reveal a secret compartment, and inside the compartment there will be something, some new language just as descriptive as math."

"I don't think of math as descriptive."

"Well, it is. For example, in cartography numbers de-scribe objects with real dimensions—oceans, continents, islands."

"What about dates?"

"Calendars are just agreed-on systems. Ours has a year zero—the birth of Christ. Other people's calendars start counting from different dates. In math and physics, numbers are precisely descriptive."

"In law, *words* are precisely descriptive."

"But only of agreed-on systems."

"What about poetry?" Sholto quoted: "'Thou still unravish'd bride of quietness, Thou foster child of silence and slow time . . .' That's precise, and ambiguous." He added, "Those lines are from Keats's 'Ode on a Grecian Urn.'"

Canny didn't know the poem, but she'd seen Greek earthenware in the antiquities room at Founderston's museum—plates decorated with pictures of boys playing pan pipes and girls in pleated gowns garlanded with vine leaves. At Canny's school, they were taught to write business letters, but only how to "appreciate" poetry. Sholto's two lines of Keats sounded better than the poet her class had to "appreciate" this year—Walter de la Mare. "Those words have cracks and secret compartments," she said, then frowned. "Sholto, why did the poet call the Grecian urn a bride and a foster child? I mean, marriage is a contract, and fostering is too. It's an undertaking, not a blood fact. Someone undertakes to look after someone else's child."

"Like the Professor and you."

"Yes."

"And the urn's 'blood facts' would be the potter, the clay, and the fire?" Sholto said.

Canny touched her own face and said, "I wonder what *I'm* made of."

Sholto looked at his own hands, which were grass-stained. He wiped them on the legs of his pants. "When you go to University you should pick up at least one poetry paper. I don't think you're going to find any cracks in the math."

"If they're not there, then they're nearby," she said dreamily.

"It'll turn out you mean love," Sholto said. "At the moment math is the only thing that excites you, so you're nosing around numbers as if numbers are life. But in two years you'll be telling me about some boy." He scrambled up. "And speaking of love—I'd better jump in the shower. Susan's coming to dinner."

THE PROFESSOR WAS CARVING THE ROAST. It was Wednesday and they usually had roast only on Saturday—itself a departure from the traditional Sunday roast. The Professor was a vocal and principled atheist, but wasn't going to let that stop him enjoying a weekly leg of lamb. When Canny asked why they were having their roast midweek, her mother said, "The Professor and I are going on a trip."

"You're really going camping?"

The Professor said, "Camping? What an odd thought, Agnes. No, we're going to the Shackle Islands. Your mother is getting a medal."

When Canny was small it seemed that only a few people knew what her mother had done. Now, though the War was longer ago, more fuss was made of Sisema Afa's war story. A couple of years back Canny had been surprised (and embarrassed) to find her mother in an illustration on her school stationery—part of the "Heroes and History Makers of Southland" series. (In other years Canny had had stationery featuring the navigator Vasco da Gama, who first mapped Southland, and Scott of the Antarctic, and the dreamhunter Tziga Hame.) Canny remembered the murmuring in the school stationery room as her class filed through gathering their exercise books, pens, and slide rules. The murmuring got louder, and then Jonno from her math team thrust his notepad under her nose. On its cover was a picture of a girl not much older than Canny was then. A dark-skinned girl with sleek black hair and bare muscular arms, wearing only a lavalava. The girl was paddling an outrigger. In the outrigger, lying top to tail, were two men from the Southland Air Force, their faces pale under bloodstained bandages. The outrigger was on rough dark blue water, the white line of breakers behind it.

Susan began to gush. "An investiture! That's marvelous, Mrs. Mochrie. You must be so proud of your wife, Professor."

The Professor looked a little startled. "Naturally," he said.

Sisema was making her demure face, her lips pursed and eyes cast down.

Susan turned to her again. "Do you feel that you're still the same person as the girl who did those things?"

Canny's mother liked to tell her story. She enjoyed her fame, but Canny knew that Sisema intensely disliked questions of this sort. Her eyelids lifted, but only to half-mast. "What a silly question—how can someone be *another* person?"

"Oh dear, of course I didn't mean literally," Susan said, and laughed.

Canny held her breath. She'd once overheard Susan talking to Sholto about her folklore studies and "sophisticated and unsophisticated approaches to story." Canny guessed that Susan thought her mother was having an unsophisticated reaction to the idea that people change over time and are more "a series of identities than a person," which was also something Canny had overheard Susan saying. Canny watched her mother and waited to see Susan punished.

"You are very young," Sisema said, cold.

The Professor went pink, then said, simpering, "Yes. You young people must have trouble imagining how we keep our youthful ideals alive in our practical middle-aged bodies. Well, let me tell you, Susan dear, we middle-aged people like to think we haven't changed at all."

"I was only being curious," Susan said. She sounded wounded.

"Where is the ceremony?" Canny asked, to change the subject.

"Calvary, on the South Shackle," said the professor. "We've booked a berth on the *Pacific Queen*. She sails the day after tomorrow."

"I remembered to have your tuxedo dry-cleaned," Sisema told her husband. "And I bought myself a new hat."

"Capital." The Professor passed the meat plate to Sholto, who helped himself to four slices, then glanced around the table, making the calculations of quantity that even dogs can. He put one slice back.

For the next little while everyone dedicated themselves to their food. Canny could see that Susan was upset—and that Sisema was pleased to have had an opportunity to make Sholto's girlfriend feel her power. During the remainder of the dinner Sisema spoke once or twice to Sholto's girlfriend, but only in response to questions, and never looked at her.

Sholto bolted his food and then looked bilious. Susan kept throwing him fiery glances. Her looks said, "Do something to defend me!" After a time Canny remarked that Sholto would have to give her a lift to Grandma Mochrie's because she had a lot of books she wanted to take with her.

Sisema said, "You won't be staying with your grandmother."

The Professor explained. "Grandma has an ulcerated foot. The doctor has instructed her to keep off it."

"Couldn't I help her?"

"How?" said Sisema, skeptical. "She has her housekeeper. And a nurse comes daily."

"I could keep her company. Read to her." Canny experienced a spurt of panic. "Where are you going to send me?"

Susan began smoothing nonexistent wrinkles out of the tablecloth.

"You're going with Sholto and Susan to Massenfer," said the Professor.

Massenfer was a coal-mining town on the Peninsula. Thirty years ago there had been an explosion in Massenfer's Bull Mine. The Professor was writing a book about the changes in labor laws that resulted from the disaster.

Sholto said, "I'm doing some research for Da. Actually I have a proper research assistant's position, with pay."

"Sholto is doing interviews for an oral history," Susan said. "And there's some work I can do in the area. Some stories I'd like to collect. The history department has borrowed the anthropology department's recording equipment. Sholto and I are to share it." She put her hand on his. "Plus it's a summer holiday."

"Then you can't want me with you," Canny said.

Susan carefully maintained her cheerful expression.

"We are very grateful to you young people," the Professor muttered. "It's wonderful that you've been able to adjust your plans at such short notice."

"Akanesi will not be any trouble," Sisema said to Sholto. "And, by the way, the Professor and I are telling people that you and Susan are engaged to be married."

Susan's eyes flew wide.

The Professor began fluttering his hands—they looked like a pair of butterflies blown out over a wide lake by a great gust of wind.

"Please don't do that, Mother," Sholto said. "Our friends might decide to throw us a party. Think how embarrassing that would be."

"The Professor and I think it's important for you to maintain some appearance of decency."

"Sholto told me that you both have very liberal outlooks." Susan sounded puzzled.

"Maybe. But we understand that other people don't." Sisema was imperturbable.

form

"I would have thought that you of all people—" Susan began, and Canny saw Sholto jab his girlfriend with his elbow.

Sisema continued. "While you are in the southwest sharing a tent you will be engaged to be married. You can break the engagement once you come home to Castlereagh, if that's what suits you. Sholto, I don't know why you can't just manage people by telling them what they expect to hear. It would make your life easier."

When Sisema insisted that people do things her way, the insistence usually came with some advice on how to get on in the world.

Sholto and Susan gazed at Sisema, their mouths open.

Sisema turned to Canny. "I think we're ready for dessert. Could you bring in the trifle, dear? It's in the refrigerator."

AFTER COFFEE SHOLTO WALKED SUSAN HOME, forty minutes each way in the blue dusk, by way of the zigzag steps and pedestrian pathways that linked the streets winding around University Hill.

Castlereagh was all hills, ridges around the harbor, and steep-sided valleys where the desirable houses were built up high to catch either the morning or afternoon sun. Much of the inner city dated from the time when cars were rare, so roads were narrow and steep and many lacked footpaths. Instead there were dozens of these official and unofficial shortcuts, steps and paths, some with safety rails, some without. The citizens of Castlereagh had strong hearts and big calf muscles.

Susan complained to Sholto whenever she could spare

the breath. What had she done to get on the wrong side of Sholto's stepmother? Didn't Sisema understand that they were doing her a big favor by taking Canny? "Does she not want us to enjoy ourselves, or get to know each other better?"

"I don't really like to speculate about people," Sholto said. "What they're thinking and so forth."

"Come on, Sholto! You can't say that. You want to be a historian."

Sholto thought of telling Susan that, actually, historians weren't supposed to speculate. But she did have a point. "Look, it's just convenient for them that we take Canny with us. She'd be staying with Grandma if Grandma was on her feet."

Susan subsided. Then, at her gate, she kissed him, her lips lingering and being generally clever.

Sholto moaned.

"Ha!" said Susan. "Take that." She went through the gate, closed it between them, smirked, and went on up her front path.

Sholto tried to retire without talking to anyone, but Canny came and knocked on his door.

He opened it and stood barring it. "No, you're not coming in."

"What can we do, Sholto? We have to think of something."

"Okay—*you* think."

Canny's brows pulled together so that a tiny rumple formed between them—this, for Canny, was an expression of great perplexity. "I can't come up with anything."

"There you go then," he said. "You can't think of anything because we're out of alternatives. Anyway, it'll be fine. We have two tents. We can pitch them far apart. The car journey isn't too long. And I promise we'll make room for plenty of books."

Canny clutched the doorframe and leaned in so that her nose was nearly touching his chin. "You could just *pretend* to take me," she said. "You could drive me over to Marli's house. Marli's family would be happy to have me."

Sholto thought of the Vaiu household in Congress Valley. The Vaius' front path was edged with river stones painted red, yellow, teal, and white—the family's idea of a garden. There were two old cars up on blocks on the lawn. Marli's brothers were cannibalizing the wrecks for parts for the one car that worked. Sholto said, "Do you think I have a death wish?"

"I don't know what that is."

"Psychology. Freud. A useful idea." He spread his hands. "If I left you at the Vaius', Sisema would kill me."

"You and Susan are going to end up hating me, and it won't be my fault."

"Canny, if you keep out of our hair and do the little jobs we give you and don't get into any trouble, then we'll all get along fine."

She was about to protest again but he said, "Good night," and poked her in the chest. She swayed back and her fingers lost their grip on the doorframe. He slammed his door.

IN THE DARK OF NIGHT SHOLTO CAME AWAKE with the impression that he'd heard someone knocking. He lay still

38

and listened. The night was hushed. There was no wind, and no little native owls calling in the nearby cathedral gardens. From far off, in the port, came the sound of rail freight rolling into the booming interior of the late, freight-only, Westport-bound ferry.

Perhaps there had been an earthquake, one of those little shivers that were always followed by a more solid silence.

Sholto got out of bed. The air was cold on his bare chest, and the floorboards cool on the soles of his feet. He went to his door and pressed his ear to its panels to listen, as if there were something fearful out there. The hallway was quiet. He pulled the door open. The first thing he saw was a bright white object at his feet. It seemed to float an inch from the carpet but was, he saw, balanced on several of its twisted prongs. He had no idea what it was. It looked a little like a drop of hot homemade toffee shaken off a stirring spoon into a glass of cold water to test its readiness to set. The object was swirly, complex, and graceful—and it was sitting on the hall carpet, burning, and radioactively white.

Sholto looked up at his sister. She was leaning on the wall opposite his door, her hands hidden behind her body. She was wearing an old-fashioned, full-length, white cotton nightdress. Her hair was loose and full of static, and seemed to make a hood and cloak of black smoke around her. "Sholto," she said. She gave him a little smile. And, since she never smiled, Sholto was, for a minute, shocked into speechlessness. What could she want? She looked quite peaceful, but she made him wary. She was so poised, so womanly. It was very confusing. "What is this?" he said. It came out as a grumpy whine.

"An artwork."

"You're giving me an artwork?"

"Yes."

"Why are you giving me an artwork?"

"So you can look after it for me."

"In the middle of the night you're giving me an artwork so I can look after it for you?"

"Yes."

"And does this mean I'm supposed to take it with us? Do you think I should put it in the back window of the car, with our sun hats?"

"No, that wouldn't do at all. I want you to keep it here, at home."

Sholto regarded the artwork. It seemed to smolder and float in the dark—though there was moonlight coming through the stained-glass window on the landing. The moon was so bright that the window's colors were visible—dark red and amber and lilac. Sholto wondered whether he was dreaming. "Where am I?" Sholto said.

"Home," said his sister. "It's Thursday morning, on the day before we set out, and I've brought you this artwork. It's a papier-mâché sculpture made of chicken wire, and strips of newspaper, and the tissue used to wrap apples. I want you to put it away somewhere and keep it safe for me." She didn't move. She didn't take her artwork and place it in his hands. She only spoke—calmly and coaxingly.

Sholto stooped and picked up the sculpture. It was

papery, surprisingly heavy, and smelled of corn flour paste. And of apples.

Canny stayed where she was, leaning on her hidden hands. "Thank you," she said. "I know I can rely on you."

"You can go back to bed now," he said, "I'll take this— Lady Senator's fancy hat—and find a corner for it." He pushed the door closed with his foot and rolled the artwork onto the top of his wardrobe. Then—because it was too burningly visible—he threw an old shirt over it.

He went back to bed and fell asleep as soon as he'd pulled up the covers.

3

CANNY CLIMBED OVER THE FARM GATE and set off toward an open-sided barn packed with hay bales. The barn stood beside a sheep drafting yard, a rigid structure of silvered timber.

Back on the road, Sholto was nursing the Austin's radiator. It was boiling, water spluttering out through the chrome grille. He covered his hand with his sleeve to get the cap off the radiator, but still burned himself. He shook his fingers and swore. The landscape swallowed his curses and what Susan said in reply—her sympathetic words delivered in a curt tone.

The road was unpaved, though the map said it was the main route onto the Peninsula. They'd been driving for over an hour since the last turnoff and had met no other traffic. They'd seen hawks, and swamp hens, and sheep of course—the land on both sides of the road was part of the vast Mount Ruth Run.

Canny jumped over the green crease of a water race. Apart from the water race everything else was dusty dry. The pasture had been grazed down to nubs. Most of the sheep had been moved on. But there were rabbits, and as Canny went up the slope it came alive in front of her. The rabbits were the same color as the ground, beige brown, and they only became visible when they moved, bolting this way and that, some surging up over the nearest hill, others disappearing into a bank honeycombed with burrows.

She glanced up the valley toward the pass. The mountain range had a few patches of snow along its crest. The mountains were dark, both their rock and vegetation—thorn bushes and thyme. All afternoon the Palisades had presented the same even profile, a near black wall, crests rippled rather than peaking. There was a wind, but Canny could only hear it teasing her ears, for there was no foliage near her for it to sing, or sough, through.

Susan and Sholto were now at the water race, pressing the turf and then dipping his felt hat into the brackish puddle they'd made. Canny watched this, heaved a sigh, and turned back to the car to fetch her soap-holder from her bathroom bag. She offered it to Sholto, who frowned at her but took it.

"I hope it's not going to be all like this," Canny said.

"Could be. Sholto's no Boy Scout," Susan said. "We should have been carrying a can of water."

"You didn't think of it either," Sholto said.

Canny said, "I don't mean the trip, I mean the landscape. I hope it's not all like this." There was so much air between the valleys, they felt airless.

43

"It's dry this side of the mountains, and rain forests the other, and the two valleys in the arms of the range are just right apparently, like Baby Bear's porridge."

"You didn't tell me it would take three days to get to Massenfer," Canny said. "Every time I repack my tent it seems to have swelled."

Sholto headed back to the car, carrying the two full halves of the soap dish carefully level. But then of course he discovered he could only tip one at a time into the radiator while the other half spilled.

"You should tear that in two," Canny said.

"I didn't know I was allowed to," he said, but Canny knew he hadn't thought of it. She was always being surprised at the many more steps it took other people to do things, just because they didn't think them through first.

Sholto tore the container in half and thrust one half into her hands. "Get on with it," he said.

Susan said to Canny, in a mild, inquiring tone, "Are you going to continue to be surly?"

"Can I ride up in front with Sholto?"

"No," said Susan and Sholto together.

They had gotten the radiator a third full when a stock truck pulled up behind them and its driver came to their aid. He had a water can. While he was filling their radiator, he told them that they might want to stay this side of the pass tonight. "It's raining the other. Quite heavily." He drove away. They all climbed back into the hot car. Susan said, "We'd have room for a water can if Canny hadn't brought so many books."

"Leave it, Sue." Sholto started the car and they rattled off.

CANNY HAD SPENT THE NIGHT before they left making phone calls. She rang the girls from her school who had been with her on the day Marli first came up from the isolation ward. The girls who had stood with her by the iron lung, their faces filled with pity and polite terror. She said the same thing to each girl; that she was being made to leave town for four weeks. She'd got some Mary O'Hara books out of the library and had left them on Marli's ward. Could they take turns to go in and read to Marli?

The first girl said of course she would. Her family wasn't going away till after Christmas. The second sounded reluctant but said she'd try to find the time, and wouldn't Marli rather listen to *Peyton Place*? The third said sorry but she'd started a job at the switchboard of Southland Mutual Assurance. The fourth was silent for a time then said, "Agnes, I hope you know that Marli isn't going to get better." She didn't pause for a reaction, but forged on. "My mother is a physiotherapist and she says that if Marli had any chance of recovery she'd be out of that iron lung by now for at least part of the day. Almost every patient from the epidemic is in rehabilitation. You know—massage, hydrotherapy, that stuff. Or they're being measured for calipers. Didn't you wonder when the polio ward slowly emptied, and then they shifted Marli to a room of her own?"

Canny was silent. The girl finally responded to that. "Someone had to tell you," she said. "I know being faithful is your thing, but you can't blackmail other people into it. We have lives to get on with. And you've got to get on with your own life."

Canny bit her lip. She thought of things she'd like to shout, but nothing to simply *say*. Then, suddenly, she had it. She said, "Well, if it's inconvenient, of course you shouldn't bother. I just thought I'd ask." She sounded grand and placid. She sounded like her mother.

"Be like that then," said the girl, and hung up on her.

THAT NIGHT A FARMER let them pitch their tents by the hawthorn hedge in his home paddock. Sholto built a campfire. Canny peeled potatoes. Susan cut up some limp carrots and then dumped them, the potatoes, and a can of corned beef into the billy. The stones of the fireplace had only just come out of the stream and were still steaming. The fire sulked and complained.

After dinner Canny went to scour the billy at the farmhouse water tank and fetch water for their tea. There were ducks near the water tank waiting for someone to run the tap. When Canny turned it on, they came and stood under the stream and slapped their wet wings. Ducklings gathered and pecked in the mud. Canny returned to the fire. "There are ducks," she told the others. "Various stages of duck."

Susan laughed. "You have odd ways of putting things."

"She means little ducklings, big ducklings, and ducks," said Sholto.

"Did you see the rooster?" Susan said. "I want his tail for a fascinator to stick in my hair."

Canny quite liked Susan when she said things like that.

Sholto brewed up some faintly greasy tea. They drank it very hot, then Sholto and Susan had a whispered argument about who would have the only lamp. Sholto said, "We stopped so late that there's no light to read by." He glanced at his sister.

"I'd rather imagine she was asleep, even if she isn't," whispered Susan.

"Oh please! Do you think I want to imagine her lying awake listening to us? Thank you for putting that thought into my head."

"Sholto, I want that lamp." Susan was definite.

"But we don't need it."

"Darling, I might want to look at you."

That settled it. Sholto went back to his sister and announced that he and Susan would have the lamp. After all, their tent was the one with a lamp hook on its pole.

"I curl up around it," Canny said. Then, "It's only eight-thirty."

"If you want to read, you can use your flashlight."

Sholto picked up the lamp and went to the big tent. He crouched, passed it to Susan, and climbed through the flap. The tent became a yellow pavilion. The lamp was lifted and suspended, the shadows flattened. Arms rose and fell as sweaters and T-shirts were pulled off over heads. Clothes lost volume and were laid aside. The remaining solid shadows came together and lay down.

Canny took her flashlight but didn't switch it on. She walked away into the dark. The hawthorn was in blossom, and when she looked back it showed, foaming in the dark like a long line of surf. Canny walked on. Sholto's tent became a little blister of lamplight. The lights in the farm-house were off. The farm dogs must not have heard her moving, because they remained silent.

There was a crack of blacker dark before Canny's feet—another water race. She slid her bare toes forward and felt the wet bristles of grass, nibbled down to the roots. She jumped over it, landed safely on the far side, and walked on. She couldn't see where she was going, only the ranges humped solidly black against churning heaps of cloud. The yellow lantern of the tent shrank and shrank. The shadows inside it shuddered like blades of grass. Canny turned away from the tents and peered into the night. There was some-thing there she felt she belonged to—not the night, or space, but some other immensity. She leaned forward, and her lips parted.

Someone slapped her—a sharp openhanded slap across her right cheek. The blow turned her head and knocked her off balance.

She yelped in shock and reeled back. She was pursued, slapped once again, a hot, singeing blow. It felled her.

The next thing she knew someone was lifting her head into their lap. Her mouth was full of blood. "It's okay," said Sholto. He brushed her hair from her face. He was sit-ting on the turf, her head resting on his knees. "Raise the lamp," he said. The light moved, and Canny saw Susan, holding the lantern and hunched inside Sholto's flannel shirt. Its buttons were unfastened, and her legs were bare. Susan said to Sholto, "What was she doing walking about in the dark?"

Canny felt more embarrassed than frightened. She muttered that she'd had her flashlight. "It must be around here somewhere."

"We heard you cry out," Sholto said. "You seem to have knocked yourself silly."

Canny went cold. She remembered her teammate Jonno's description of how he'd feel before his fits came on—Jonno suffered from epilepsy, though his doctor said he might grow out of it. He'd said, "I feel as if God has put a hand down through the clouds and cupped the top of my head, to bless me, and make adjustments. Then, next thing I know, I wake up with a sore mouth—all tired and confused."

Canny had bitten one side of her tongue. Her lips were tacky with blood, and blood was all she could smell.

"I'm fine," she said, slurring. "The sheep droppings are so dry they're like ball bearings. I lost my footing."

"I think she's all right," Susan said, impatient.

Sholto got up, helping Canny to her feet. Susan stepped back and lifted the lamp. She pointed at Canny's flashlight, which had landed beside a tussock.

Sholto picked it up and switched it on, but only for a moment. He pointed it at the tents—two grayish igloos—and then switched it off and handed it to Canny. Susan walked away, the lantern at her side casting its light back. She was scolding, "If you stumble about stargazing of course you're going to trip over."

Canny looked up. There were no stars—but there were embers, as if Susan were carrying a pitch pine torch rather than a hurricane lamp. Flakes of brightness swarmed up through the air, some of them the size of silver dollars. They were filmy, and some even seemed to reflect things, as if they were bits of torn cellophane. Canny saw fragments of writing—her Extra—flowing upward and curling away, all in one place, like dead leaves in water flowing over a weir, only in the air. "Look!" she breathed. She couldn't help herself. She'd never seen her Extra that clearly before. Surely it was visible to everyone.

She didn't know whether they even looked. Susan's light continued to move away. Sholto's grip tightened. "Let's get you wrapped up snug in your sleeping bag," he said.

THE FARMER GAVE THEM a jerry can full of water and they tackled the pass in the cool of the morning. They went slowly, pulling over every time they spotted a plume of dust from a vehicle coming up behind them.

Canny was quiet. She felt weak and tender, as if she was convalescing after a bout of food poisoning.

Susan asked to hear Sisema's story. When Sholto began to tell it, Canny realized she hadn't known all of it. She'd almost certainly heard it told before, but she hadn't managed to keep the details in her head. She'd probably been resisting her mother's story because, lately, she'd begun to hear it as a countdown. *"In two years Agnes will be the same age I was when . . ."*

LOST LINK WAS AN OUTLYING ISLAND of the Shackle chain, a volcano, though the original cone was submerged and long extinct. Over millennia coral had built up along the remnant of the crater rim, and the island was ringed in a continuous reef with only seven passages where streams let out into the ocean. Lost Link lay ten sea miles northwest of Calvary on the South Shackle. Calvary was the only sizable town on the Shackle Island chain. (There had been another, Gethsemane, but it was destroyed by a cataclysmic eruption in 1919.) The Shackle Islands produced sugar and, lately, copper. The islands were peopled by their original inhabitants, the Ma'eu; by the descendants of cane cutters brought to the island by blackbirders in the late eighteenth century; and by the descendants of colonial settlers, most of whom had originally come from Southland. But on Lost Link there were only the original people, plus a few whites, the owners of pineapple plantations.

One quiet Sunday in July 1942, a couple of boatloads of Japanese soldiers appeared and promptly and systematically removed every white person on the island, and every gun they could find. The news Lost Link could have done with arrived afterward. It appeared that the same thing had happened in Calvary, but on a much larger scale. Some Southlander Shackle Island families had been able to flee ahead of the invasion, but there were many people and only a few berths. The ships had stopped coming; then, after two days of silence, Zeros had been spotted overhead, then Japanese warships sailed into Calvary Harbor. The remaining Shackle Island Southlanders were immediately rounded up and impounded, then shipped off somewhere—no one knew where. The Japanese then looked for people who could go on running the town and would treat the invaders with the proper fearful respect.

Sisema's father was the head of one of the three chiefly

families of Lost Link. He called a meeting in one of the island's churches and told the people about the Japanese officer who had come to speak to him, and what conditions the officer had given for their safety. "He said that we must treat their enemies as our own," said Sisema's father. "And I asked him whether he was a Christian. And he said to me that he was not, and that his duty lay with his emperor and his admirals." This was all that Sisema's father said. He then took a seat and folded his arms. The church filled with murmuring. Sisema's father listened to the murmuring and remained impassive. Then the priest got up and raised his hands for a hush and began to say, "It is clearly our duty—"

He was interrupted by Sisema's father, who heaved himself to his feet again and said, "We know how much God loves our singing, but he also loves our silent prayers."

Again there was that murmur.

"God knows what's in our hearts," Sisema's father finished, and looked meaningfully at the congregation. The priest gestured for the congregation to stand. He told them what hymn they should all have, and the rest of the meeting was spent in song.

A month later, in August, when the migratory humpback whales were passing by the island, a man turned up at Sisema's father's house, pale with excitement and still carrying his fishing spear and his catch—a brilliant green parrot fish. Sisema's mother told him off about his wet feet on her dry mats and took the fish from him, though it wasn't a gift, it was his dinner, and he looked sadly after it when Sisema's mother handed it to her and asked her to go down to the shore to gut and scale it. The fisherman said he had to speak to his chief, urgently. He was invited in to do so.

When Sisema came back with the gutted fish, her hands smelling of tangy iron, she discovered that her father had gone out. She didn't see him till the next day. He seemed preoccupied. Her uncles and older male cousins kept coming and going. There were whispered conversations. And, in the evening, Sisema's mother and grandmother hauled her father out into the pawpaw grove some distance from the house. There was a spectacular shouting match. Sisema's father stalked back indoors with his mother trailing after him weeping, wringing her hands, and begging him to "think again."

It was Sisema's little brother who finally filled her in. Apparently the priest was hiding two airmen—Southlanders—whom the fisherman had spotted clinging to the wreckage of their downed plane. They had been adrift for days and were both blistered by sunburn. One had a concussion, and the other a festering wound on his scalp. The airmen had to be gotten off Lost Link. It would be no good taking them to the Shackles, because the main islands were full of Japanese. The plan was for Sisema's older brother, Benemani, to take the best outrigger and carry the men off to Port Morrison, far to the southwest, a journey of nearly five hundred miles. Sisema's grandmother was furious that her son would even consider sending his firstborn son. And the rest of the family thought that the whole idea couldn't possibly work anyway.

Every Sunday, Japanese soldiers would appear at the

morning church services. They'd make a count of the youths and grown men. If Benemani went, he'd be missed. If he waited till after the count he'd have seven days—but every day the airmen were on the island they were putting people in danger. So, the plan was that Benemani would go immediately, and then, on Sunday, Sisema's tearful family would show the Japanese a fresh grave.

"But funerals last three days," Sisema said. "The Japanese will know that by now. And if Benemani was to die, everyone would come to his funeral. He's not a by-the-way person. Someone less important should go."

"Father can't ask anyone else to send their son. And Benemani has offered," Sisema's little brother said. "I'd do it, but I'm not strong enough."

It was then that it came to Sisema that she was strong enough. And she wouldn't be missed since the Japanese never bothered to count the women. She went to her father and said she'd go; she'd take the Southlanders to Port Morrison. And her father looked at her, and she could tell he was thinking that, with her, the airmen would have a good chance of a safe landfall. Her father knew that his sons were all good, God-fearing boys, but, for years, he had been calling his daughter life-heart, not after life or hearts but after the hardwood tree the people made their spears and oars from. And he said, "Yes, daughter, I will send you. You should follow the whales. Their long path passes within fifty miles of Port Morrison. You must watch for the appearance of smaller seabirds. Then you'll know you're near to land. Watch to see where they fly at sundown, and go after them. Port Morrison has a reef, so you'll know what to listen for, even if it's very dark."

That night Sisema set out in her father's best outrigger. She had green coconuts and breadfruit, pawpaw and pineapple. She had dried fish, and fishing tackle, and bait in a jar. She had blankets, and a big finely woven flax mat that would be more use against wind and rain than a tarpaulin. She had a knife. She had gourds full of fresh water. She had limes and oranges. She had her father's compass, the one he was given when he retired from his job as harbormaster. And she had the men in her care—Captain Young and Flight Lieutenant Stopes.

Before she set out she kissed her family, and they all knelt on the sand while the priest said a prayer. Then she climbed into the outrigger, and her brothers pushed her out into the lagoon. She paddled quietly to the Oloi Passage, waited for the right break in the surf, and sent the outrigger surging into the open water. She paddled away from Lost Link and didn't put up her sail till the island was a little bump on the horizon, the long coast of the Shackles beyond it, under cloud.

Sisema followed the whales, sailing among them for six days and nights. Then a contrary wind came up and she had to tack. The whales went on without her. The wind died, and the sail lay slack on the mast.

Sisema had been eating the fruit, and sometimes baiting her hook and trailing a line behind in the water. She'd had some luck, but, becalmed, she decided to fish for a while in earnest and maybe catch enough to restore her strength.

One of the airmen—the concussed captain—had by that time improved. He took a line too and they both sat, twitching their lines on either side of the bow. He caught a fish. She gutted, scaled, split and boned it, ate one fillet herself and gave the other to the captain. She kept its head for bait, and they tried again. They fished and gorged. Then he took the paddle while she watched the stars and worked out where they were. She used her father's compass to set a course, then retrieved her paddle and forged on.

A wind found them again at dawn and they sailed on till, after another day, she saw five frigate birds flying toward a patch of mounded white cloud. Sisema was sure that land was there. She and the airman paddled furiously as the day darkened.

It was full dark when Sisema first heard the reef—a sound she'd lived with most of her life and had missed so much when she was at school in Calvary that, for a long time, she hadn't been able to sleep without it. Eventually she and the airman could both see the reef, its line of white.

Sisema turned the outrigger, and they paddled along the reef till she thought she discerned a break in the surf. She put her hand over the side and tasted the water—there was fresh mixed with the salt. That meant she had found a passage. She turned the outrigger again and brought it in close. She waited, and had the captain wait, till at a word from her they both paddled madly. The boat hit a big reflected wave, and its stern dropped, then its bow slewed around and, for just a moment, Sisema saw the reef below them, phosphorescence combing through its corals. Then a wave came under the hulls, the outrigger accelerated, and shot forward into the lagoon.

They beached the boat. The airman carried his mate up to the tree line, then returned to help Sisema haul the outrigger up onto the dry sand. They lay down to wait for morning. They couldn't sleep. Their bodies were full of fear. Fear like venom. They were both afraid that they'd find that the Japanese had gotten to Port Morrison ahead of them.

The beach would not settle down, all night it rocked and heaved, as the boat had. To pass the hours the captain told Sisema something about himself. He talked about his brother who was in the coastal watch, his sister who was a nurse on a hospital ship now stationed off North Africa. He talked about his father, who had died many years ago in the explosion at the Bull Mine in Massenfer. And then the sun came out, and they saw a PT boat heading in toward some port just around the next headland—a port whose lights they would have been able to see the night before, if it wasn't for the wartime blackout.

Sisema put the outrigger back in the water, the captain laid his feverish friend down between them. Together they paddled around the headland and into the harbor. By the time they reached the wharf, the ships they'd paddled past—two American PT boats and one frigate—had sent signals to the shore. A crowd had gathered on the wharf. The airman called out his name, "Captain Alan Young of 22 squadron, SAF. We were shot down off the South Shackle, fifteen days ago."

Someone said, "The Shackles? But that's five hundred miles away. How did you get here?" And then they all fell silent. The captain pointed with one blistered hand at Sisema. "This is Miss Sisema Afa of Lost Link Island. She brought us all the way here."

Miss Sisema Afa. Eighteen years of age. A tall, dark, powerful girl, who was a hero from that moment on.

Sisema left Port Morrison for Southland two weeks later, strapped into nets in the belly of a transport plane. She was wearing a dress the head of Port Morrison's USAMC nurses had run up for her on someone's sewing machine, standard-issue white leather shoes, also courtesy of the USAMC, her own salt-burned flax hat, and her father's gold compass, all polished up.

A big black car was waiting for her at the airstrip in Southland. There was a short ride through green farmland, where Sisema saw cows, whole herds of them, tall trees, houses with clay tile roofs, then Founderston's somber greenish-white stone buildings, and a sinuous, silvery river— the Sva. The car passed through gates into the inner courtyard of a vast building, and Sisema was ushered through a succession of grand and cavernous rooms before finally hearing herself announced. "Miss Sisema Afa." She was ushered in to meet the president of Southland, who took her hand in his two warm ones, and called her "My dear girl."

"IT WAS AFTER THEN THAT SISEMA'S TROUBLE started," Sholto told Susan. "The stuff no one talks about, though people keep telling the story, with relish. Before Da met Sisema, I heard him tell her story. And when he told it, he had tears in his eyes. But back then, during the war, Sisema was forbidden to tell it herself. She was congratulated, and was taken into the president's own household until she was ready to decide what she wanted to do. But there were no ceremonies, or dinners in her honor, or newspaper stories. So long as the Shackles and Lost Link were occupied by Japanese, Sisema couldn't even explain to people she met how she came to be in Southland, who she was, and what she'd done. Because, if it got back to the occupation forces, her family and village would have been in danger."

"So what *did* she do?" Susan said.

"Lived in Founderston with a Methodist minister's family. She was Catholic of course, but she made it pretty clear that, after her convent schooling, she'd had enough of living with nuns. She enrolled in a secretarial school and set off every day to learn shorthand and typing. She went out in the evenings and had some nice party dresses. Air force wives and ladies from the foreign office had taken her shopping. They'd take her out to tea. She had a generous allowance. She was always being asked over for dinner by various people who only knew that she had rendered their country some great service. She was spoiled and cosseted— and desperately lonely. She's admitted as much to me. But she doesn't elaborate. For instance, I asked her if the other girls at the secretarial school were nice to her. And she just shrugged."

"Like Canny," Susan said, and laughed.

"It always means 'No,'" Sholto said. "If Sisema or Canny shrugs, it's not noncommittal. It's not skeptical. It means

'No,' and, 'Now you're going to have to show me that you have wit enough to understand that I just said no to you.'"

"Oh dear," Susan said, still laughing.

"That's not true," Canny protested.

Susan said, "When were the Japanese driven out of the Shackles?"

"June 1943."

Susan fell quiet, but Canny could still hear her slow, idiot calculations. And still she had to ask, "So when was Canny born?"

"September 1943."

"Is this the summit of the pass?" Canny asked, to change the subject.

"The summit is about two hundred feet up, and over there," Sholto pointed to one side of the road.

"Oh look!" Susan breathed in wonder. Sholto pulled over so quickly that the Austin slid in a drift of gravel and rocked to a standstill. Canny was about to tell him off for nearly losing the exhaust pipe, but stayed quiet once she'd looked too.

Sholto said, "I've heard about this. It's famous. There's a hiking track up to it through the Zarene Valley."

There was a rock formation on the summit of the pass through the Palisades. It was made of limestone, stacked like blocks of hand-hewn masonry. Some of the rock was pale, fawn and beige, some gray, and some was the rich color of olivine, and as smooth as marble. There were turrets and columns of one kind of stone capped by balancing big blocks of another.

They got out of the car and walked past a sign that read

"Fort Rock." They went up a path worn through the turf of the pasture. Now and then one of them would stumble. Sholto once came down hard on his knees, and Susan, snatching at a thorn bush to steady herself, pierced her fingers but didn't swear, only sucked them and continued to stare at the astonishing formation.

They couldn't take their eyes off it.

The summit of the Palisade Range was completely dry, but there must have been a spring under Fort Rock, because the illusory castle seemed to be surrounded by a real garden, a rock garden with heathers, and hebes, and mats of carnations in shades from white to cerise.

They skirted the formation, stumbling through its garden, gazing and gazing.

"Apparently it is almost impossible to photograph," Sholto said. "Look at those colors!"

They feasted their eyes. Canny's started to water. She wiped them and gazed some more.

"We should have a picnic here," Sholto said. "I'll go get everything." He turned his body first, then his head followed, his eyes lingering on the spectacle. Then he sighed and bounded away downhill to the car. Susan felt around behind her and found a boulder to sit on.

"Is this one of your folklore things?" Canny asked.

Susan looked perplexed but didn't turn to her. Canny thought there was something strange about the fact that Susan didn't look at her. Susan wasn't angry. She was just riveted by Fort Rock.

Susan said, "No. Why do you ask?"

Canny heard the car trunk slam but didn't look. She

could scarcely take her eyes off the rock formation. It was like an entity. It exhibited grace and majesty. It was like a tiger stretching in the sun, untamed and self-satisfied. "Susan," she said, "why is there a special walk up to Fort Rock when the road goes so near?"

"It's supposed to be more beautiful when you come on it gradually. The walk is some kind of secular pilgrimage, I think. The Zarene Valley doesn't have roads, only walking tracks. It's all apiaries and orchards. They sell honey and honeycomb, apples, cider, jams and jellies, cherries, apricots—the fruit from the valley is famous."

Sholto arrived, out of breath. He had the remainder of the farmwife's loaf of bread and the eggs he'd boiled in the billy last night—before putting in the tea leaves, so that their tea had been a little sulphurous from the eggshells.

Sholto sat down facing the rock. He spent another few minutes admiring it, then looked away to saw off several rough slices of bread. They peeled their eggs by touch, munched, and stared.

A skylark was singing. Its shadow passed overhead. Canny looked up and followed its flight with her eyes. Then she saw the Extra. The air over Fort Rock was thick with it, long strips like blown ribbons. It was clearer than ever, though semitransparent or, at least, the same color as the sky. Canny could see the rock through it, and the clouds, and the blue air. The Extra went up in billowing banners, long lines of calligraphy flowing up, renewed constantly, like the tape flowing out of a telex machine, full of information, endlessly complex, but still only a long calculation with a sum. And the sum said one thing. "Look at me," it said. "LOOK," it implored, "AT ME."

"Can you see that?" Canny said.

Sholto said, "I'd fetch my camera, but the film is only black-and-white." He sounded mournful.

Shakespeare had all these sonnets where what he said came down to this: *Youth is fleeting and you'd better get married and have children and make a copy of the beauty you own because the world owns it too.* Canny had been reading a selection of those sonnets and had noticed how the poet didn't so much elaborate on a simple idea as demonstrate it over and over, with proof after proof made of observations about changing fashions, or the seasons, or the frailty of memory. Fort Rock's Extra worked in the same way—it described something striking, over and over. It said it was worth taking time to really *look* at some things. It said, "You may never come here again." It promised, "This will one day be your castle, your refuge in some moment of lonely pain."

Canny could read it—or at least get the gist of it. And she was pretty sure that even if Sholto and Susan could see the Extra they wouldn't be able to read it any more than they could find a solution to a complex math problem.

Canny handed her crusts to Sholto, who ate them. She asked Susan, "If the folktale you want to hear isn't about Fort Rock, what is it about?"

"Magic," Susan said. "Supposed local witches."

Canny laughed happily.

Susan, misinterpreting the laugh, said, "I know you pride yourself on your scientific worldview, but I'm an anthropologist, and anthropology is the study of how people live, and their stories and beliefs."

"Look, look, look," sang Fort Rock.

Canny got up and brushed crumbs from her skirt. She walked away around the formation. She made a point of watching where she was putting her feet. Everything before, and behind, and beside her was beautiful. She walked till she was on the side of the formation opposite to where the path climbed from the road. She closed her eyes. The colors swarmed through her head, singing, as if she were falling headlong through a flight of angels with rainbow-colored wings. At any moment she really would fall—she'd be facedown on the springy turf, enveloped in its earthy perfume.

Canny raised her head to face the valley and opened her eyes. There was wind, and green vagueness. There was nothing worth looking at. Canny felt bereft. She closed her eyes again and felt hot tears run down her cheeks and meet beneath her chin, where they turned cold in the wind. And then that thread of cold began to threaten to solidify and tie up her jaw so that she wouldn't be able to open her mouth. She didn't try to open her mouth. Instead she clenched her teeth and opened her eyes again.

The Zarene Valley lay before her. There was a long fall of slopes, covered first in thick tussock, then in forest. The forest climbed again at a humped hill, which sat by itself at the head of the valley. The hill was a glacial moraine, an aeons-long accumulation of boulders left by a glacier that had long ago disappeared. Canny recognized what the moraine was from her geography lessons, although its rocky bones were well covered in trees. A river appeared beyond the hill as if emerging from underground. It flowed on, tur-quoise in the sunlight and green in the shade of trees, mak-ing a big lazy S between the gently sloped hills to either side of the valley. Canny could see orchards and several clusters of box beehives. And she could see, on the very top of the moraine, in a clearing in the forest, a large white-painted timber house. The house was perched on a lawn at the top of a terraced garden.

As soon as she spotted the house, Canny relaxed. She stopped falling and threatening to dissolve. She no longer felt that she was foolishly turning her back on the most beautiful thing she had ever seen. The billowing banners of Extra had subsided into a very proper silence, as if she'd just said something to shut them up. Canny saw the house—and the command to look the other way immedi-ately relented. "So," she thought. "This is what nobody is supposed to see. What no one would want to spare a glance—this hidden house."

4

CYRUS HAD COME UP through the forest to the house on Terminal Hill to help Ghislain shift his single beehive. Ghislain kept a hive so that its bees could pollinate the fruit and flowers on his garden's immaculate top terraces. Every six months he and his cousin would shift the hive between the east and west sides of the second-to-top terrace, always moving it clockwise for luck. They'd move it in the early morning when the bees were still waking up, and would carry the stacked boxes—the whole little tower—all in one go.

The plan was the same today, but Ghislain noticed that his cousin was getting older and would need to watch his feet when he walked. He asked, "Is it easier for you to go forward or backward?" And Cyrus only gave him a keen look and said, "How thoughtful you are," then didn't express a preference, wouldn't even give Ghislain that much. Of course this was a family trait. Ghislain's father had been just the same. If he was in a bad mood sometimes he wouldn't even answer when you asked him if he wanted a pickle with his sliced ham.

Cyrus picked up the smoke blower.

Ghislain said, "Do you really need that?" He wasn't expecting an answer. He was expecting the usual barely concealed impatience, the silence that said that this was a very big thing Cyrus was doing for Ghislain—that *anything* was.

But, to Ghislain's surprise, Cyrus did reply. "We don't want them to swarm."

"Even if they haven't anywhere to go?" Ghislain said. He was trying to keep the conversation going.

Cyrus held out his arms. His sleeves were rolled up. Ghislain could see the warm sign moving like ant trails along the paths of sinew on Cyrus's tanned and freckled skin. "I'm not about to let myself be stung," Cyrus said. Then he passed Ghislain the hat and veil he'd brought along. Ghislain took them and then put them down on the grass.

"I'm going to open the hive and inspect it first," Cyrus said. "You might want to step back, or put those on."

Ghislain told him to go ahead.

Cyrus picked up his smoke blower and opened its lid. He took some dried sumac berries from his pocket and dropped them on top of the smoldering pine needles. Then he closed the lid and pumped the bellows, blowing smoke into the gaps in the hive and over the hidden frames. The smoke would prevent the worker bees from being roused by the hive guards. It would make them sleepy, and encourage them to go and feed. They'd fill themselves with nectar and, fat and stupefied, wouldn't put up a fight when the hive was opened.

Cyrus blew a cloud above the hive and then raised his hand to scribble his calming runes in the hovering smoke.

Doodling and noodling, Ghislain thought. He was offended by the fussiness of Cyrus's magic, though one part of him knew that this scorn wasn't his own feeling. After all this time he was so attuned to the Great Spell on the house—the massive, static spell that was everywhere, in the brilliant green of the close-clipped and rolled lawn, and the sharp edges of the timber trim around the windows, and the impossibly stainless brightness of the brass plate on the front doorsill—that, when Cyrus made his signs, Ghislain could feel the house lift an eyebrow and look down its nose. So he too lifted an eyebrow and looked down his nose at the hive and told it, "Be quiet."

The humming tapered off, then stopped. The hive was silent.

"If you've killed them, I'm not giving you another one," Cyrus said. Then, "I don't know how you do that—without even lifting a finger."

Ghislain said he didn't know either. He was happy that his cousin had actually said something real to him. But he could see that Cyrus didn't believe him, and for the next few minutes, while he raised the lid and removed a couple of frames and brushed the bees off them, Cyrus didn't speak to Ghislain, or look at him.

THE BEES WERE CRAWLING STILL, but their wings were immobile. Cyrus could see that the hive looked healthy despite Ghislain's having quelled it with a single phrase. He ran his finger down the dripping honeycomb that filled one frame to taste the honey. Cyrus's bees made honey from the clover and blue borage that grew on the lower slopes of the hills, and from parrot's beak, and honeydew creepers and other forest flowers. Ghislain's bees only worked his garden—the lavender and roses, the stocks, sweet peas, pansies, and carnations. Ghislain's honey didn't have a particular flavor, it was only sweet.

Cyrus closed the hive. They bent their knees and picked it up and began their slow shuffle through the rows of lettuces, then behind the bean frame, then through the squash patch. They finally set the hive down between Ghislain's two pear trees.

Cyrus straightened and flexed his back. He said, "What other people feel when you lie to them is shame. I feel ashamed that you're trying to fool me, and ashamed *for* you."

"Thanks for the sermon, Cyrus. But I think you spend too much time talking to children. You're sounding stuffy." Ghislain looked at Cyrus's hands and added, "Old and stuffy." One of the bees then roused and stung him. He clapped his hand to the place, but by that time the bee was crawling away, a line of internal membrane stretching from its torn abdomen to the throbbing sting. The barb pulsed, pumping venom; Ghislain used his thumbnail to scrape it from his skin. The bee fell onto the grass and clenched up in its death throes.

The hive began to hum again.

Cyrus unhooked his blower from his belt and filled the air with smoke. He scribbled more soothing symbols. The smoke dissipated. The little spell became invisible and then began quietly to degrade. Cyrus walked to the edge of the terrace and emptied the smoldering pine needles into a wet compost of old apple cores, potato peelings, melon rinds, rabbit bones, and the ash from the house's hearths. Cyrus could see that, though the compost was breaking down, the heap would eventually reach the top of the terrace wall. He said to Ghislain, "You should start dumping your scraps somewhere else."

"So that in three hundred years, when I'm filling in the last chink in the wall of compost surrounding my house, I'll be able to console myself by saying, 'Think how bad things would be now if I hadn't followed my cousin's advice.'"

"Now you're just being melodramatic," Cyrus said.

"I'm a teenager," Ghislain said. "Teenagers are sometimes melodramatic. It says so on the radio."

Cyrus looked at Ghislain—his smooth skin and strong shoulders and the flag of bright black hair flowing back from the widow's peak in the center of his forehead. He shook his head and walked away again.

He went up the steps to the top terrace, climbing into the concentrated stillness there. He passed between rosebushes whose blooms were all perfect, as if each one had a deity's attention focused solely on it. The air on the top terrace was as clear and shining and *slow* as the gelatin they used in the movies to make the heroine's tears brilliant and lingering in close-up—Cyrus had read that somewhere. Cyrus picked some roses and wove them around the crown of his straw hat.

Ghislain went by him and jumped up onto the veranda. He said, "I still have some cider. Would you like some?"

Cyrus moved the hat and flowers into a patch of shade and absentmindedly started up the steps after Ghislain. He was thirsty. It would be nice to sit down with his cousin and—

—he got to the top of the steps and looked at Ghislain—who was beyond the shining brass doorsill, standing in the hallway and looking back with eyes that glinted with mirth.

Cyrus stopped.

"I'll get you one day," Ghislain said, and disappeared indoors.

Cyrus retrieved his hat and blower and climbed down Terminal Hill, descending from perfection to an ordinary orderly garden, then a scruffy garden, then a wilderness of weeds and brambles. Finally he went into the forest.

CYRUS FOUND HIS COUSIN LEALAND in the big kitchen at Orchard House, labeling jars of apple jelly. The jars were ranged along the table and bench tops, gleaming and jewel-like. These were the early apples and the jelly was pale pink. The jelly's color deepened as the season went on. The big pans had been washed and put away, but the sugar and apple smell was still in the air, mixed with that of the paste used to stick labels to each jar. Half the jars were labeled. A girl was helping Lealand, slotting jars into crates painted "Zarene Valley Apple Jelly." The kitchen was warm; there was yeast rising in a bowl on the range top, and wisps of steam showed at the vent in the lid of the big soup pot.

The back door was open and Cyrus could see several of

the older boys out in the home orchard trying to fashion a prop for the drooping branches of an ancient apple tree.

Cyrus took a look at all the industry and pitched in. He carried the full crate out to the back porch and brought in an empty one. He and Lealand filled it. They cleared the end of the table. Then Lealand poured them both a glass of cider and they carried their glasses out to the side porch. Lealand told the two big girls he found there to put down their knitting and get the bread on. One went straight in, the other clapped her hands to summon the nine-year-olds, who were playing in a puddle by the tank stand.

The Zarene children were evenly divided between Orchard House and Cyrus's sister Iris's place, which had a compound of bunk rooms one field away from the guesthouse. Iris managed the guesthouse. She had the older girls to help with the cooking and cleaning, and two big boys as general handymen. The rest of her charges were all five to eight and tended to run wild. She'd say their contribution was to keep the valley's walkways clear by trampling along them in shoes all winter and barefoot all summer. Sometimes Cyrus or Lealand would call on Iris's eight-year-olds if they needed more hands in the apiary or orchard, or in the vegetable gardens. But Lealand had his own permanent charges. They all had their jobs and were obliged to spend some of their time passing on their skills to the younger ones. So it was normal, for instance, to see twelve-year-old Bonnie showing a couple of nine-year-olds how to beat the rugs draped over the clothesline, or twelve-year-old Lonnie encouraging several wiry ten-year-olds to tackle the wheel on the cider press.

Iris's charges all came to Orchard House for lessons. Every morning of the week the big schoolroom upstairs was full of kids. Like many country children, the Zarenes were correspondence students. Their weekday mornings might be spent listening to the school's broadcast from Founderston, or filling in correspondence school worksheets, ready for the Thursday post. But two hours each afternoon the lessons were devoted to the Alphabet—or at least the Alphabet in the first two of its three forms, Basic for the five- to nine-year-olds, and Tabular for the older children. Cyrus was occasionally called on to give a lesson, or to host some of the older children at the apiary, but only the stolid, untalented ones. Anyone with ability tended to be too sensitive to the go-and-wander-and-gather-and-come-back-at-sundown spell he had on his worker bees. At the apiary, children could never be counted on to stay and finish anything. But Cyrus was a conscientious man, so rather than have kids at the apiary, he'd go along to the gardens and help the boys and girls with their work there. The kids could manage to plant and hoe, but needed adult help with the heavy spadework. With that, and the little workings that discouraged aphids and caterpillars.

Everyone in Zarene Valley worked—and only Iris's little ones didn't work all the time. The Zarenes had their way of life, and they were used to it. But it was a make-do way of life, and they hadn't exactly chosen it.

The cider was chilled and the glass sweating. Cyrus sipped then wiped his hands on his pants. "I thought you might want to see me," he said. "You did, didn't you?"

Lealand nodded. He didn't speak for a bit—then, when he did, it was only to call to the boys that they'd need a sturdier prop, and they should stop trying to use what was on the farm and go to the forest at the top of the valley and cut a branch of tea tree. "Take the mule. You have an hour before dinner."

Once the boys were off along the trail, Lealand looked at Cyrus and said, "Last night the remnant of the old ward activated."

Cyrus was surprised he hadn't felt it. "Don't you get twinges from it now and then?"

"I won't anymore. It ignited, and then every remaining bit of it was extinguished. I was out of bed and at the window in time to see the fragment over the home orchard catch fire and float up like burning paper."

"Could you read any of it?"

"Bits," Lealand said. He pulled a notebook from his shirt pocket and handed it to Cyrus.

Cyrus looked at the curls and angles of sign and the dotted lines running between them. Lealand had been trying to figure out the original form of each sign from the trajectory of the fragments as they flew apart, which was a task less like trying to figure the center of a bomb blast from the distribution of debris, than trying to reconstruct the charge inside a bomb by putting the molecules of its detonating chemical back together again. Lealand could make an attempt, but Cyrus knew he wouldn't be able to do it.

When the family first settled the valley, the Zarene forefathers had put up wards beyond the mountains encircling it. Those forefathers—Aron and Elek Zarene—were very powerful and insightful men. The old wards had simply *worked*. And unlike the newer great magic, they hadn't cost anyone anything.

Cyrus asked Lealand whether he'd told Iris what had happened.

"Last night, straight afterward. Since I was up, I went over to the guesthouse and spoke to her. Then I went down to my favorite fishing spot and put a line in the river. I was there at eight when a couple of Iris's guests hiked past. I heard them talking about their crazy hostess, so I suppose they'd had some exhaustive genealogical interrogation with their full cooked breakfast."

Cyrus laughed.

"It isn't funny," Lealand said. Which only made Cyrus laugh more. Lealand had an amusing turn of phrase and anyone would think he found things amusing—but he didn't. He was stern and grim, and had been for thirty years.

"Lealand, are the old wards any great loss? They were only remnants."

"They were meant to keep certain people out of the valley. But I guess nowadays Iris's registration process filters out any direct descendants of the other four of the Five Families."

"When the wards activated, do you think it was because they recognized a threat? Or did they just finally collapse?"

"I couldn't tell. But don't worry—anyone recognized by the old wards won't disturb our spells. The old ones and ours have opposite purposes. The old ones were to keep things out, ours are to keep them in."

Cyrus nodded. "You're right. But we should keep an eye out."

They sipped their cider.

5

THE AUSTIN HAD A COOL run down the far side of Fort
Pass and they reached Massenfer in the late afternoon.
There was no camping ground near the town. Massenfer
wasn't a vacation destination. It was all industry—coal
mines, quarries, and a rail yard. It had a town hall, a library, two movie houses, and a street of shops including
one humble department store. It had an ice cream parlor, a
couple of tearooms, two restaurants, and two hotels—one
converted from an old dream palace and now sporting a
large circular dance hall on its first floor. The hotels served
farmers coming to the railhead to sell livestock. Everything else was for the residents—so cheap and battered. The
mining company had built the first houses, timber cot-
tages that were all on the east bank of the Taskmaster River
and near the long black tailings that glittered on the slopes
around the original mine. That mine was long since closed;
the more recent diggings were all farther from town.

Sholto sensibly stopped at the sheriff's office to ask where they could pitch a tent and not be moved on in the middle of the night. A deputy showed Sholto a map and pointed to a gravel flat by the river, between the willows lining the water and the stop bank that protected the low-lying streets of company houses.

Susan and Sholto decided that they'd have a hot meal and put up their tents when dusk fell, rather than put them up and leave them unattended near those houses. "They aren't people of means," Susan said, "and we don't want to expose them to temptation."

Massenfer's main street was cold, windy, and gray. It was a Monday night and the restaurants had signs saying that their kitchens closed at eight. The Chinese restaurant was full, so they went to a place called Maisie's, which advertised "wholesome home-cooked food." They took their seats and were handed menus in limp leather covers, and once the waitress had gone, Sholto leaned across the table and whispered, "You have to imagine Maisie wheeling a tea trolley stacked with stew pots through the night-cart lanes to the back entrance of the restaurant."

"Yes. It should say *home-style* cooking," Susan said, pedantic.

Canny watched her stepbrother and his girlfriend as they frowned over their menus. They looked perfectly normal. She said, "So, you don't feel bereft?"

"You mean because they're not offering *Îles Flottantes?*" Sholto said, gesturing at his menu.

"No. Because you had to leave Fort Rock."

"Fort Rock. Roquefort. Mmmmm," said Susan, then, "I'm so hungry I'm obsessing."

Canny stared at her, disbelieving. "You couldn't take your eyes off it."

"Fort Rock was spectacular," Susan conceded. "Worth a detour, just like they said in the guidebooks." Then, "I'm going to have the stroganoff."

"I'll have the goulash," Sholto said, and shut his menu.

"You were bewitched," Canny said.

"Weren't you?" Sholto said. "It was nature really putting on a show."

"But what did you think of the view?"

They looked at her blankly.

"The view of the valley below Fort Rock."

Sholto shook his head. "Missed it."

Canny knew that just because Sholto and Susan hadn't seen the house, that wasn't proof that magic was hiding it from them. Canny might be imagining things. Seeing the symbols, seeing the house as special, seeing Sholto and Susan's behavior as strange. She needed some independent proof, and she had no idea how to get it.

The stroganoff and goulash weren't hot enough. They had skins on their surfaces as if they'd been drying out in a pie warmer. Their bread rolls were still frozen in the middle. Susan complained, but when it was time to pay, the place shamelessly charged them the advertised price. Susan stubbornly withheld part of what they owed, and words were exchanged over the register.

Canny escaped into the street. It was drizzling. The hills

were halved by low cloud. Sholto joined her. Canny said to him, "If Susan doesn't hurry we'll be putting up our tents by torchlight."

"Don't you start. I can't put up with both of you complaining about each other. I'm afraid you've got to be the one who has to bite her tongue."

"Why do I have to?" Canny was outraged.

"There are things about Susan that aren't perfect, but you can't change people."

Canny put her finger in her ear, the one facing Sholto, and scratched it vigorously, as if she were digging out his words before they had a chance to settle and lay their eggs. "People do change," she said. "Marli used to be all noisiness and bounce, and now she's thoughtful."

"That's just a lack of vitality."

"It isn't just. Time is different for her. And she's always talking to nurses, who look after people, instead of other schoolgirls, some of whom don't even make their own beds."

"Okay, people do change, but that doesn't mean you can change people."

"If people can change, then people can change people," Canny said. "It's simply logic."

"People aren't logical," Sholto said with smug finality.

Susan appeared, flushed with triumph. She said she had worn the woman down. Then, "We'd better get those tents up before it pours on us."

IN THE MIDDLE OF THE NIGHT the light rain turned into a downpour. Canny woke to the sound of solid drops blown into the canvas and the tent fly flapping wildly. She lay listening, worrying that the fly would come loose. But it stayed in place, and after a time, though the rain continued, the wind seemed to decide it had fulfilled all its heraldic duties and would now let the storm get on with it. Canny couldn't do anything about the weather, and she was draggingly tired, her head still sore from last night's slaps. She pulled her sleeping sheet up under her chin and drifted off again.

Sometime later—it was still dark—she felt something clammy pat her cheek. She twitched away from it, only to feel the clammy something cover her face, cupping her mouth and nose. She freed her arms and batted at it. It made a sodden gulping noise. Her fingers found her flashlight and she switched it on.

Her tent had subsided; the two wet cheeks of yellow canvas were poised above her head as if about to sit on her.

Canny scrambled out of her sleeping bag, unable to do so without touching the walls of the tent. Wherever the bag touched it immediately sponged up big blots of water. Canny climbed out of the tent and shone her light around. She saw that the tent pegs had all come loose. They'd been far too easy to hammer in—they were camping well above the river, but the ground was river gravel. Canny was soaked. She pointed her light at the car. Its windows were white with mist. She squelched over to it and tried its door.

Susan was curled in the backseat in her coat, with her wet hair plastered to her forehead. Sholto was in the front. He'd made a cushion of his coat and put it on top of the handbrake so he could stretch across both seats.

Canny prodded Sholto till he shifted off the passenger

seat, then she climbed in and sat, dripping and shivering. Sholto scarcely looked at her. He unrolled his coat, handed it over to her, then leaned on the driver's window and closed his eyes again. Canny pulled the coat on, its silk lining sticking to her wet legs.

It was a long time till she was warm enough to doze off, and she was only able to sleep fitfully, finally opening her eyes on gray morning light and the water-distorted sight of Sholto and Susan collapsing the tents.

The tents wouldn't fit in the tent bags—and couldn't go in the trunk. The recording equipment was in the trunk and couldn't get wet. Canny ended up sitting in the backseat next to the sodden bundles of canvas, with the equally sodden sleeping bags piled around her.

They drove back into the middle of town and had a breakfast of tea and toast. When they leaned on the tabletop their sleeves left damp patches.

"Let's go home," Canny said.

Sholto told her to shut up.

A man at another table turned around and said it was only raining this side of the ranges. They could go all the way back over the Palisades, or try Zarene Valley. "It's only an hour's drive, and it's in the rain shadow."

Sholto asked for directions.

The man came across to their table and sat next to Canny. He pressed his leg along hers and she scooted over till she was crammed against the streaming window.

The man drew on a paper napkin with a squared carpenter's pencil. "You go downriver out of town, till you see the turnoff to the mine. There's a bridge. You go over that, turn up the mine road, and keep on going till you go right back past the town on the other side of the river. You'll reach a fork. Turn left there. The bigger, right-hand road goes up to the pits. The small road will take you into Zarene Valley. It meets up with the Lazuli River at Pike's Landing and goes on through the gorge."

The man looked up at Sholto, who nodded.

"The road comes to an end about here," the man said, making an X on his paper napkin map.

"It's a private road after that?" Susan said. "Or are there really no roads in Zarene Valley?"

"None, only walking tracks. It's very pretty there. And there are good places to pitch a tent without having to go too far in. If you do go in, well, they're friendly enough, but they'll ask you questions."

"What kind of questions?"

"Your names. Who your people are. The Zarenes put a lot of stock in names. Theirs all rhyme. They've all got brothers and sisters called John, Don, Yvonne, Leon, and so on."

Susan looked thrilled. "I've heard about this."

Sholto said to Susan, "If we have to spend more on gas coming and going from the Zarene Valley, then at least we'll save on camping fees."

"Is there a store?" Susan asked the man.

The man shook his head. "You can just ask the farms for food. Eggs, fruit, vegetables, cider. They'll sell you it, unless they want you to leave, in which case they won't. There's a guesthouse; people stay there when they're hiking up to Fort Rock."

"So the Zarenes will be able to explain Fort Rock," Canny said, thinking aloud.

The man gave her a sharply speculative look.

Canny looked back at him. "Geologically," she said.

"Sure," the guy said, and shrugged.

"Thanks." Sholto pocketed the map.

The man said good day and left them.

Susan looked out at their car, which was standing in a curb-high puddle. "Shall we scratch today? Come back later. When's your first appointment, Sholto?"

"Thursday. With the mine safety manager, George Mews. He was a draegerman in 1929."

"Thursday, then," said Susan.

THEY CROSSED THE TASKMASTER ON THE BRIDGE that served the mine. It was a two-tiered construction, with a single car lane above a train track. The road was only a layer of thick ironwood planks between crisscrossed girders, and when they were on it, Canny could see through the gaps in the planks to coal trucks sliding by below her. The road to the mine ran alongside the rail line, both gradually climbing above the river. The road was black and glittering with coal dust. The Taskmaster was gray and opaque, smooth, with small faults of current near the middle of its channel.

They reached the turnoff to the mine and took the smaller road. Its surface was greasy and corrugated by runoff. But there was no more coal dust. They went slowly, and met no other traffic—only one boy on a mule going the other way. He, his mount, and his saddlebags were covered by a huge army-issue rain poncho.

Canny pressed her face to the rain-spotted window. She watched the edge of the road. The river was a long way below. For a time she couldn't see the water, only the bluffs opposite, bare but for the odd tenacious tree. The river broadened—or rather they reached the confluence of the two rivers, where the graveled road they were on dipped down to a pier and landing. The road sign said "Pike's Landing."

The Taskmaster disappeared from sight around a spur of land. The road veered to cross the Lazuli on a high trestle bridge, then followed the river up through its gorge.

The Lazuli was a very different river—smooth like the Taskmaster, but milky with snowmelt in the shade of the forested gorge. Then, as the forest dwindled and the road dropped closer to the river, the river began to broaden, brighten, and clarify.

The rain turned to drizzle, and then they drove around the corner and into sunshine. Everything sparkled. The bank by the road wasn't bare rock anymore but covered in ferns and dotted with tiny pink and white orchids. Then, around the next bend, the road was damp and steaming. A few minutes later they were driving in full sunshine, with a blue sky overhead.

The road began to look more like a cart track—with a strip of green grass down its center. Then it came to an end. Before them was a field of sleek green grass and the river, brilliant turquoise in color and lined with willows and ash trees.

Sholto stopped the car and they all got out. They gathered their drenched tents and damp sleeping bags and followed a path to the water. Susan and Sholto draped the sleeping bags over the limbs of willows and spread the tents over some bushes covered in rolls of cloyingly sweet purple flowers.

Sholto lay down on the grass. Susan joined him and nestled close. They were soon asleep.

6

CANNY WAS LIGHT-HEADED with tiredness. She tried lying down, but when she closed her eyes the peach-colored screen on the inside of her eyelids filled with the billowing streamers of Extra she had seen over Fort Rock.

Canny was usually able to remember whatever she gazed at with real attention. On those rare occasions when they got to discuss a novel in her English class—as opposed to writing business letters and working on public speaking projects—Canny would always be saying, "But on page 41 it says . . ." or "The author uses the exact same odd word in the second paragraph of page 90 . . ." Her classmates would ask her, "How do you do that?" Canny's only answer was that she'd just remember. But she'd given up offering that answer, since she was tired of hearing other kids tell people, "Canny has a brain like flypaper. She's good at rote learning and math." As if different kinds of intelligence were mutually exclusive, so that a person couldn't have a memory *and* an imagination, in the same way that someone couldn't be short and tall, or thin and fat. And besides, noticing two significant uses of an odd word in a book wasn't a feat of memory—it was seeing a pattern.

Canny's flypaper brain was keeping her awake, so she got up and wandered back to the parked car. She clambered onto its roof to see if she could look up the valley to the forested hill and the house no one was supposed to see.

The valley curved, and only the edge of the hill showed. She couldn't see the house, and she suspected that it was visible from nowhere in the valley or even the hills on either side. She decided that, despite her light head, she'd walk a little way along the river. She jumped down, grabbed her change purse, put it in her pocket, and set off.

THE PATH CONTINUED BESIDE THE RIVER, passing between willows with fronds hanging in the water—drowned leaves, yellowing and furred with algae—and a gentle slope covered in young birches and elderflower bushes. The uphill scrub was filmy, and Canny could see through it. Before long, she saw the path was going past orchards, long disciplined rows of trees that marched across the level ground and partway along the slopes on one side of the river. On the other side was rough pasture. She heard a distant clatter of bells, then saw a flock of goats flowing over a stony slope.

The valley went on like that, with cultivation on one side and livestock on the other, where there was less flat land.

Canny passed some vegetable gardens sheltered by hedges of lemon and feijoa trees. In one garden three dark-haired children were hoeing between rows of squash plants. Canny hurried by. She felt shy, as if she was trespassing. One boy stopped work and stood watching her, his hand shading his eyes, till she was out of sight.

The river was sinuous and blue green. Its surface was smooth. Canny glimpsed some trout hanging in its transparent depths, perhaps ten feet underwater. It was only when Canny saw the fish, but no sign of the river bottom— not even the shadow of it—did she understand how deep the river was. A little farther on, there was another break in the trees, and she looked out into the middle of the stream to watch a turn in the current, water torquing around some deeply submerged rock.

Canny's head was spinning, so she left the clearing and followed the river path into a stand of high poplar. The ground was white there, as if it had been snowing. When her eyes adjusted she saw that the snow was a creamy drift of fallen poplar seed, inches deep, a semitransparent film with last year's dead leaves caught up in it.

Canny was standing, staring stupidly at the suspended leaves as if their wizened brown curls were writing she could read, when she was surprised by a cavalcade of children. They came running around a twist in the path, all barefoot, and in shorts and shifts and worn shirts, all tangled-haired, and surprisingly silent. There were fifteen of them. (Canny never had to count—she'd always just see the number, another little peculiarity that made her classmates say "How do you do that?")

The children pattered to a halt and stood staring. It seemed as if they had been playing some game that involved writing in ink on the inside of their right arms. Canny glimpsed the ink, then really looked at the marks. She thought she saw her Extra, only—

The arm she was staring at fixedly was tucked behind its owner's back.

Canny stepped off the path and into an ankle-deep drift of poplar fluff. She waited for the kids to go by.

One of the little ones took the hand of a girl who looked to be about twelve and said in a loud whisper, "She's very brown."

The older child said, "Shhhh." Then, "Hello."

The loudly whispering child went on. "She is a big, big girl. And very, very brown."

Canny said, "I may not be a normal shade in these parts, but I am a perfectly normal size."

"Sorry about my cousin. She doesn't mean any harm." The girl stooped, gave the child's hand a fierce little shake, and whispered, "You remember the big kids, don't you?"

The little girl shook her head, said, "She is the same size as my mummy. But Mummy wasn't brown."

The big girl shoved the little one ahead of her and said, "You go on," to the rest.

"Where are we going?" said a boy.

"I don't care. I'm going to stay here a moment and make peace with this visitor. You go and entertain yourselves." The girl then hid her right hand and wrist in her apron pocket and turned to Canny. The others hesitated a moment, then hurried on, picking up their pace till, as they passed out of sight, they were sprinting again.

The girl was thin and tan. Her clothes were clean—or probably had been in the morning.

Canny held out her hand. "My name is Agnes, but everyone calls me Canny."

The girl took Canny's right hand awkwardly with her left, and shook. "Bonnie," she said, "though I'm going to call myself by my middle name—Yvette—when I go to school next year." Then she pointed up the valley. "You were going this way."

Canny moved back onto the path and they went on together, sometimes stepping sideways to stay together, swerving a nettle or tree root. Bonnie now and then glanced up, her look one of admiration, which was a new experience for Canny.

Canny asked the girl where she was going to go to school.

"Founderston. My mother and father live there. I'm starting at Founderston Girls."

Of course there was no telling what kind of school any barefoot country kid might go to, but Canny was a little surprised. She thought of that school's tree-lined, bowling-green-smooth playing fields and dark wood-paneled classrooms. She said, "That will be a shock to you."

"I know."

"You're here for the summer?" Canny asked.

"No, I live here. Zarenes all get raised in the valley between five and twelve."

"Even if their mother and father live somewhere else?"

Bonnie nodded.

Canny was thinking that this was a very strange

arrangement. But then again plenty of Islander girls and boys in Castlereagh schools had come from the Shackles for their education and were living with aunts and uncles. Of course those kids were usually sent away from home at thirteen, not five.

"But you're living with aunties, I guess?" Canny said.

"I've been living with Uncle Lealand. The little ones you saw, they live with Aunt Iris." Bonnie gathered her tangled ringlets and pulled them all over one shoulder and started twisting them. "You have very long hair," she said. "Is that the fashion?"

"You've been out, haven't you? You've seen the fashions."

"Sometimes I stay for weeks in Massenfer with my parents. We have long visits. And they're always sending me nice dresses and shoes. Mother is a buyer for a department store. She has very good taste." Then, "Are you from Castlereagh?"

"Yes."

"There are lots of Islanders in Castlereagh. Because of the canneries." Bonnie said this quite bluntly, as if recalling some lesson.

Canny asked her if she ever got to wear her pretty dresses and shoes.

Bonnie stopped twisting her hair. "I do when I go to Massenfer, to the movies. Us big ones go every Sunday."

"What's that on your arm?" Canny asked, hoping Bonnie would hold still and show her.

Bonnie covered the blue symbols with her other hand.

"It looks like a tattoo."

Bonnie laughed. "Children don't have tattoos, do they?"

Canny said that her mother was tattooed from her hips to her knees. "When she was full-grown though, otherwise the patterns would stretch out of shape. She had it done when I was a little girl, when we lived on Lost Link Island." Canny could still remember the long hours when she was supposed to be napping. She'd lie with her cheek pressed to the woven mat, listening to the tapping of the block on the hardwood tattooing comb. Sweat ran down her mother's face, and blood down her flanks. Canny remembered the tattooist's stained fingers rubbing dye into the little perforations that, day by day, built up into patterns—palm leaves, sharks' teeth, woven sails.

She said to Bonnie, "Women aren't generally tattooed either, I suppose." She wanted the girl's confidence so she made an effort to smile. "So, I guess that mark can't be a tattoo."

"You don't believe me," Bonnie said.

"Well—it does look like a tattoo. But I'm glad it isn't, because this summer, girls are wearing sleeves to here"— Canny touched the place on her arm where her cap-sleeved blouse ended, then her wrist—"and gloves ending here."

The younger girl's lip quivered. She stopped and stared balefully at Canny. Then she held out her arm.

Canny took it and turned it to the glow coming off the sunlit river. The symbols were in tattooing ink, and immobile, but they were like simpler creatures from the same environment as the great creature of Extra over Fort Rock. She said, "What do they mean?"

"Nothing," Bonnie said, and withdrew her arm.

They walked on. They passed a group of houses with

boarded-up windows and sagging porches covered in passion fruit vines. The houses may have been derelict, but they were surrounded by regular rows of cherry trees full of heavy fruit. As soon as Canny saw the cherries she recognized them as the most prized kind that always appeared in the Castlereagh fruit shops at Christmastime.

"How does your mother get on with her tattoo?" Bonnie asked. "Do people stare?"

"Well, for a start, people only see it when she's in a bathing suit. When she got it she didn't know she'd be coming back to Southland. She didn't know she'd be living in two worlds."

Bonnie looked eager for more, so Canny told her Sisema's story about the hermit crab.

"Mother was pretty miserable on Lost Link. After her time in Southland during the War, the island seemed too small. And she wasn't completely accepted when she came home—for instance, she was banned from the body of the church. That was because of me. Because I didn't have a dad. Anyway, what she says is that she got sick of all the nonsense and decided she wanted to go back to Southland. But she couldn't bear to think she'd end up somewhere ugly or untidy. That's the word she uses—'untidy.' You see, Lost Link's towns might have rusty, shabby buildings, but everything is covered in flowers, and all the trees are—" Canny made shapes in the air, trying to describe what she remembered. "They're sort of solid, and definite, and symmetrical. Like new furniture. Except furniture with leaves and flowers on it. And it rains a lot on the island, so everything is always clean. Then the sea is"—Canny looked at the river; it was a very similar color to that of the sea inside Lost Link's reef—"turquoise, like your river.

"Anyway, Mother didn't want to give up any of that. Or never being cold. And she thought that if she left she wouldn't be anybody anymore. That without her family she wouldn't know who she was. They were being stern with her, but they weren't strangers.

"One night she was sitting on a curb in Arahura, the town with the port. It was a high curb, for storm water. She was sitting with her feet in the gutter. There was a park behind her, and palms, hissing in the wind. The beach was just beyond the palms, and she could hear the reef over the sough of the wind in the palms, sounds that filled everything up so there wasn't a speck of silence. She was feeling like someone in limbo. Then she noticed a hermit crab. One of those crabs that lives in an empty sea snail shell. It was walking along the edge of the curb looking for a place to step down. It would try and try, but the curb was too high. This was a cautious crab. Anyway, this undecided walk along the edge made my mother think of herself, and the decision she had to make, and then she suddenly thought, 'If I go, I won't be leaving my home. I can be like that hermit crab and carry my home with me.' "

Bonnie looked fascinated. She said she thought she'd heard a song like that on the radio, sung by a singer with a ukulele.

"Someone wrote a song about my mother's story. Or a song with her hermit crab in it. It's mostly about the Shackle Islanders in Castlereagh."

Bonnie did a little skip. She stopped hiding her tattoo.

Canny could hear children—maybe the same group on another path. They were shouting in some competitive childish excitement. A dog had joined them, and they'd stirred it up so that it was barking, that bark with a little whine at the end. An anxious bark.

Bonnie wanted to know if Canny was staying in the valley.

"If it keeps raining in Massenfer. We got rained out. Our tents and sleeping bags are wet. I thought I'd take a walk to see if I could buy some eggs and fruit. Could you tell me where to go for that?"

"You could have at the gardens back there. But there's a stall by the guesthouse. I'd take you all the way, only I'd better go fetch those kids to their dinners."

"Is there a map of the valley anywhere?" Canny asked.

"In the guesthouse there's a map of walking tracks. It has on it everything you might want, the stalls, the swimming holes—"

"How about the house on the little hill at the head of the valley? Is there a track up to it?"

Bonnie stumbled and then stopped still, her mouth open.

Canny had partly expected some sign of surprise. But not one quite this dramatic. Only the day before she hadn't really known there were such things as spells outside of stories—though every time she saw her Extra she had felt, vaguely, that she might be living in one of those stories. But she was *sure* there was a spell on Fort Rock. It might be there to create a tourist attraction, rather than to distract people from the view. But when Bonnie stumbled, Canny was sure that the spell on the rock formation was *about* the house—was all about the house. "Are you okay? What is it?" she said innocently.

"There isn't a track," Bonnie said. Her eyes flicked left and right, as if she were looking for a cue card in order to answer a question she'd never expected to hear asked. Then she gave the only answer she knew. "It's out of bounds."

"You mean it's private property?"

Bonnie flushed. "The whole valley is private property. But we like visitors. Only—that hill isn't safe. It's unstable. There are sinkholes. And gobs deep underground. A gob is a void left in the ground after the coal's been taken out. Terminal Hill is above the end of the coalfield, and over part of Bull Mine. The Bull is closed and flooded. No one goes up the hill. There isn't a path anymore. And the house is—no one lives there."

Canny just nodded and turned to stroll casually on. The girl fell into step beside her. Her head was lowered, her hair hiding her face. "It's derelict," she murmured. "That's the word." They came to a branch in the path. Bonnie said, "Aunt Iris's guesthouse is up that way." She flipped her hair back and turned her face up to Canny's and gazed at her, but all she said was "Bye," then she waved and ran off.

Canny left the river and followed the path to the guesthouse. It intersected other paths, but there was always a sign pointing the way to the Zarene Valley guesthouse. The path went along the edge of an orchard. The ripening pears were not the pretty pinkish sort that Castlereagh's fruit stands would display in glowing mounds; they were the kind that bottled well but grew skins speckled like the worn gilt on old picture frames. The fruit was abundant, but the tree limbs were bearded with lichen, and very old. The trees seem to hum, though since the blossom was over, it was too late for the bees, and too early for wasps to come and feast on ripe fruit. But Canny could see insects among the leaves. Or rather at first she saw insects, because she expected insects. But it was more Extra, an insectile cloud of symbols that shimmered into filmy visibility when she looked at it straight on. She stopped and tried to read it. But it wasn't words, only letters. *Maybe* letters. And then she saw it—many words, changing momentarily with the dance of their letters, and she couldn't read them any more than she could read an ordinary sentence if she knew only the vowels.

The sun made the top of her head hot, so she went on into the shade of a stand of native trees. She walked along thinking about the Extra and feeling sad—because it was now clear to her that, though she'd been calling it hers for years, someone else had made it, for their own purposes. People who knew how to use it, whereas she only help-lessly noticed it. The sadness Canny felt was similar to the feeling she had when her teachers talked about "our European Heritage," and she went on for a time, head down, scuffing her feet, and whispering, *"Not mine, not mine."*

When she came out of the trees, the guesthouse was in front of her. It was a big building, with a wraparound ve-randa. An ancient woody wisteria grew along its front, so that the veranda was festooned with tassels of pink blos-som. The garden was cared for, but not designed. It was a children's garden, sectioned into little plots of flowers grown from seed and salad vegetables. At the end of each plot were tall stakes with two hooks, one for a sunhat and the other for a watering can.

A youngish man and woman were sitting on the front steps doing up the laces on their hiking boots. "Morning," said the man. "Great day for it."

Canny said, "Is this place nice?"

"It's lovely," said the woman. "Really restful."

"And the food's great," said the man.

"Very reasonable," said the woman.

"Thanks," said Canny, and went past them indoors.

SHOLTO WOKE TO DISCOVER that Canny had disappeared while he and Susan were asleep and wasn't now in calling distance. He was worried, especially after he went down to take a look at the river and discovered what sort of river it was. He found a fallen tree, its big trunk still buried in the riverbank. The tree was totally stripped of bark by the current. Its branch and crown were submerged and being played on like some giant drum by that deep current, so powerfully that the loud, bass knocking made the riverbank quiver.

For some time, Sholto walked up and down calling, till Susan joined him and told him to stop being a wet hen. "She's a big girl. You're being overprotective."

"This river flows into the Taskmaster, and as you know the Taskmaster once washed away a whole bridge, which demolished another bridge miles downstream—after reaching it in minutes."

"Yes, and a bus full of people went into it in 1938, and

neither bus nor bodies were ever seen again. You've already told me the stories."

"The Taskmaster flows out to sea and eventually becomes an ocean trench. And it doesn't really become the river it is till this one joins it," Sholto said. "It's *serious*, Susan."

"But we aren't talking about the river, Sholto. We're talking about your sister."

"Canny can't take on a river."

"No, I don't mean that, I mean she's too sensible to go paddling in this," Susan said. "And we have other problems. Our tents are nearly dry but our sleeping bags are still sopping."

It was then that Canny arrived, breathless and waving a business card. She shoved it into Sholto's hand. It was a list of room tariffs rates, mealtimes, and a helpful little map showing where to find the Zarene Valley guesthouse. "One night," Canny said. "Please, Sholto, we can carry our sleeping bags there and hang them on the clothesline. The boy I spoke to at the guesthouse said our stuff will be perfectly safe. We can even leave the car unlocked."

"Not with the department's recording equipment in it," Susan said. "But well done, Canny, let's go there. Sholto?"

Sholto muttered, "What say they expect us to take three rooms?"

"Canny and I can share if it's one night. And we can ask them where we can camp."

Canny looked very happy. She was bouncing up and down. She did that sometimes. But her face was, for once, almost animated. Sholto gazed at his stepsister. She didn't look like herself at all. It was as if she'd been wearing a mask—something beautiful, and finely wrought—as if for a masked ball, and midnight had finally come and she had taken it off. He was quite moved by the change, but his feelings came out as surliness. "Well, it's good to see you happy for once."

"So, is that yes?"

"Yes."

Both girls squealed.

"One night," he reminded them.

Susan ran back up the meadow shouting that she'd bundle the bags.

"Get your wash things and a change of clothes," Sholto said to Canny.

He got what he needed then they locked the car and, burdened by bags, set out up the river path, leaving their almost dry tents draped on the lilac bushes.

THE RECEPTION DESK WAS TUCKED into the angle under the stairs. There was a seat in front of it and, on the wall above, a board with room numbers and keys. A sign on the desk read: "Ring the bell on the porch." Sholto and Susan waited for several minutes before overcoming their—Canny thought—very adult timidity and going to find the bell. It was a school bell, and when Sholto swung it, Canny almost expected a jostle of kids to arrive and line up at the base of the steps.

A boy darted around the side of the house and said, "I'll get Aunt Iris," and rushed off again.

Canny followed him.

There was a belt of trees behind the guesthouse, and a

track that led through them to a field. On its far side were
four long, low buildings with bricked terraces and many
doors. The doors were all open, and children's shoes were
lined up by each doorsill. There was a large outdoor oven
under a shelter by the building and a long table set with
many places. The children were waiting. A tall woman
with a mass of gray-streaked black hair bunched in a bun
was serving from a large pot. Each child took a filled plate
and carried it carefully to its place at the table.

The boy spoke to the woman, who glanced down the
slope then said something that called the boy's attention
to the fact he'd been followed. He came running back.
"Aunt Iris will be down in a minute. Once she's done serving the orphans."

He scampered past, and Canny had to chase him. "Are
they?" she said.

He vaulted up the steps before he responded. "Are they
what?"

"Orphans?"

"That's the Orphans' Dormitory back there."

Canny knew there had once been a fund for war widows
and orphans, but the War had been over for fourteen years.
She wanted to know what had orphaned those twenty children. She hurried to catch up and seized the boy's collar.
The boy stopped abruptly and gave a strangled squawk.

Then Sholto was there. He grabbed Canny's wrist.
"What the hell are you doing? Leave the kid alone."

Canny let the boy go and Sholto smoothed him down
and apologized. The boy went ahead of them into the house
and Sholto rounded on Canny, glaring. "I have never, in my

life, seen you lay hands on another child," he said. "What's wrong with you? No wonder your school called in Sisema for a talk! Do you want to know what they said? 'Canny isn't a good mixer'—which is a politely coded way of saying you don't give a *stuff* about people. They called you 'impervious to the point of rudeness' and 'full of secretive habits.' Shall I go on?"

"Just shut up!" Canny shouted.

Susan stepped in. "I know you're tired, pet. We all are. Let's just all simmer down."

Canny opened her mouth to tell Susan to shut up too and then felt the cloud of pressure that she'd not been consciously aware of suddenly burst apart and yield. Her head had been in a vise—but wasn't anymore.

She looked about the dark hallway and saw the boy. He was perched partway up the stairs and smirking at her. When she held his gaze, his smirk twitched and disappeared. Canny looked away and began to massage her temples. She told Susan she had a headache. "Lack of sleep," she said.

"We'll have a room soon. And you can lie down."

"We skipped lunch. And you have a small fuel tank." Sholto touched her arm. "Sorry I was sharp with you."

SHOLTO FELT BAD. His sister was sometimes stubborn, but she almost always argued using logic and remained reasonably polite. Everyone was entitled to lose their temper occasionally only—

—only there was a second there, when his sister had hold of the kid by the back of his shirt, that Sholto was really afraid for him. Canny's face had been calm, as usual. And she really did seem only to want her question answered. But still, she'd reached and taken hold and wasn't even scowling, but something black and adamant was there inside her, or *behind* her—

—"Or in my imagination," Sholto told himself. He didn't know why he was all of a sudden having these weird apprehensions about Canny. It was true that he'd never actually been in the position of having day-to-day responsibility for his sister, but why would his worry manifest as hallucinations, like imagining that something sinister was standing behind her right now, or, only the other day, seeing her hurrying toward his parked car when she wasn't actually there?

The sunlight in the door was blocked momentarily as their hostess came in. She was a very tall woman, taller than Sholto. She was big and womanly like Sisema, but whereas Sisema even in her most majestic moments had something theatrical in her grandeur, something even of comic theater, this woman was simply grand. A plain, bony country woman who stood drying her hands on her apron—and looking like an empress. "I'm sorry to keep you waiting." She offered her hand. "Iris Zarene."

"Sholto Mochrie," said Sholto. He took her hand and felt both its strength and the thick pads of scar tissue on the back of it. "This is my fiancée, Susan Miller, and my sister, Agnes. We'd very much like to stay a night. Do you have two rooms?"

"One double," said Susan, then had a nervous outbreak of French. "A *chambre matrimoniale*."

The woman didn't answer immediately. She edged between the desk and stairs and took a seat on the too-small chair. She opened the register. "Let me see."

Sholto glanced at the row of hooks above the desk. There were five keys hanging there, and one empty hook. "Or I suppose we could all squeeze into one room, if you have bookings already," he said.

The woman looked up at him. She had large, clear, slightly protruding brown eyes. "So—your name is Mochrie. Mochrie of where?"

"Castlereagh," said Sholto.

"Sholto's father is Professor Mochrie," said Susan, "who wrote the new general history of Southland."

"And Sholto's mother?" asked the woman, in a light and playful way. "What was her pedigree?"

Susan laughed. "That I don't know. And I should." She turned to Sholto. "What was your mother's maiden name?"

"Tiebold."

The woman went still. She said, "Not those Tiebolds who married Hames?"

"No, the Tiebolds of the navy. My grandfather was an admiral. Even my mother served in the women's auxiliary during the War."

"Fascinating," said the woman, neither sarcastic nor sincere. She looked at Susan. "Are you also of Castlereagh?"

"Yes. My father is the Miller who is moderator of the Methodist Church, and my mother, whose maiden name was Berry, was a radio broadcaster."

"Janet Berry?"

"Yes!" Susan smiled. She was enjoying the game. She

turned and pulled Canny forward too till they were all standing crammed and slightly hunched under the angle of the stairs. "But Canny here has the finest pedigree of us all. Her dad is Professor Mochrie—very respectable. But her mother is Sisema Afa."

Sholto looked at Canny. He supposed she must be used to this, but he did feel for her every time the veil of her mother's fame dropped down over her own real person.

"Goodness," said Iris Zarene. She was now only being polite. She had lost interest. She turned the register toward Sholto, put a pen down on the page, and selected two room keys. Sholto stooped and wrote their names, and his and Canny's address. He handed the pen to Susan to sign.

"Lonnie!" Iris called. The boy thumped down the stairs and stood, still smirking.

Iris Zarene frowned at him. "Lonnie. I remind you of the rules of my house."

He pouted.

Iris went on. "Now, be a good boy, and show our guests to their rooms." Then, to Sholto, "Dinner will be in the dining room in forty minutes."

AFTER DINNER SHOLTO CAME into Canny's room to show her how to light her oil lamp and how to shut it off when she was ready for bed.

"It's a bit different than our hurricane lamp."

"We had these in Lost Link when I was little," Canny said. "Though I wasn't allowed to touch."

Sholto lit the wick and replaced the chimney. The room

filled with pinkish radiance. "All right, are you comfortable?" said Sholto, already halfway out the door.

"Perfectly."

"Well, enjoy that bed, because we'll be back in our tents tomorrow night."

"Here? Or Massenfer?"

"Massenfer makes more sense. Tent sites are free in both places but we'll save on gas by staying there. And apparently there are no phone lines here, and Sue and I have interviews to arrange."

Sholto left, and Canny immediately emptied her bag onto the bed and found a pen and paper. She knew she should be writing to Marli. She'd only written one letter so far and had dropped it into a mailbox that morning on their way out of Massenfer. She'd written the letter after she was slapped in the paddock on the far side of Fort Pass, and had reported that, but only in haste and on the last page. The rest of the letter was complaints about the heat, and Susan's putting on airs, and Sholto's pandering to Susan's airs. Canny knew that the longer she went without trying to explain Fort Rock, the bewitched Sholto and Susan, and the streamers of Extra, the harder it would be to start. But as soon as she had her pen in hand she realized that she wasn't going to write to Marli. What she was going to do instead was try to formulate her own spell. A spell made up of the order "Look at me!" and the discouragement she thought she'd read in the swarm of symbols in the pear tree—"Stay away" or "Don't settle here," probably directed at codling moths, whose larvae would burrow into the cores of apples and pears and grow there in soft nests of gray mildew.

Canny didn't know how long she sat and thought, and figured, and tried different formulations of the signs. When she finally had something she thought would work—something much simpler than the components she'd used, a scribble that seemed to blaze at her—she discovered that hours had gone by. She was stiff and sore. She got up and stretched her back. Then she washed her face. She was going to go back down to the end of the valley and write her formula on their tents. She would try it and see if anything happened.

Canny got her flashlight and returned to the dresser where she'd left the paper with all its crossings-out and the final successful line.

The paper had vanished.

She checked the floor. Got down on her knees and peered under the dresser. There was no sign of the paper. Then she had a thought. She shut her eyes and put her hands on the top of the dresser. She ran her palms along it, searching. Her hand met the edge of a sheet of paper, and she picked it up. But, even then, when she had it in her hand, she found she couldn't look at it. The feeling was like when she was angry at someone—someone she cared about and expected not to hurt her, like Sholto, with whom she sometimes quarreled. When Canny was angry with Sholto she couldn't look at him. She'd have to make a real effort. This was like that. She tried to look, but she felt too uncomfortable. It was like acute embarrassment. Then, as she tried harder, it was like disgust—piteous disgust—as if the paper were one of the blind, pink, trembling nestlings her old cat used to bring in and leave on her bedroom floor.

Canny crumpled the paper and tucked it under her pillow. She didn't need it. She was pretty sure she remembered how the line ran.

IN THE MORNING, when Sholto came out of the guest bathroom, he noticed his sister's door was open. He put his head around it and saw her neatly made bed. It didn't occur to him that the bed hadn't been slept in at all. He spotted a note sitting on top of her bag:

Sholto—I've gone for an early-morning walk. I'll be back by nine. I'm sure you don't mean to leave before then.

Sholto went to tell Susan that the bathroom was free. And that Canny was going to miss breakfast.

7

It was about one in the morning when Canny wrote her spell on the tents, with the same fountain pen she'd used for her figuring. She couldn't begin to imagine how someone might write a spell on the air, or on something airy that was then set free to collect somewhere, like the signs in the old pear trees. A good downpour and her spell would wash out and the tents would be apparent again. But it *had* worked. She hadn't been able to look at the tents once she'd written on them. She'd think she was looking straight at them, but all she could see was the purple lilac. But when she glanced down at herself she could see the color of her shirt and shorts. The nearly full moon was behind her, but the canvas of the tents was before her, throwing back the light of the moon.

Canny stretched out her hand and touched the cold cloth. She found she couldn't bring her own hand into focus while it was in contact with the tent.

"It shouldn't be this easy," she thought. She was more troubled that it had worked at all, than that it had worked on her as well—though surely you'd think the person who produces a charm should be immune to it. It had been hours of work, and she'd had to concentrate more fiercely than she had on anything, ever. But somehow it still seemed too easy; as if it was something she could simply turn around and teach the next person who came along. Mr. Grove always said, "There is nothing so difficult that it can't be taught to someone willing to learn." But how could that be true of this—this *magic*?

When Canny got back to the guesthouse she discovered she was hungry but not tired. She'd had very little sleep the night before, and this night was rapidly shading toward morning. The sky was pink behind the Palisades. There would soon be enough light to see under the trees on that forested hill. Canny went inside, wrote a note to Sholto, then set off up the valley.

The path Canny followed veered left once it reached the base of the forested glacial moraine. Canny continued along it. After a time she saw that the path was going to circle the hill, without at any point heading up its slope. Still, Canny kept on walking till she reached the east-facing base of the hill, where she sat down and waited for the sun to come up. When it appeared, it lit the crowns of the trees and threw rays of light—golden and filmy with morning mist—into the forest.

Canny stepped off the path and into the trees. She began to clamber straight up the slope, clutching at ferns and stepping over tree roots. At first, the ground beneath each woody root would make a solid step. Then the shadows thickened, and the hollows between the roots became treacherous. Eventually, Canny's foot broke through a crust of dead leaves and plunged into a deadfall. Her ankle turned, and a branch scored a long scratch on her calf. She struggled out and looked at her leg, saw blood trickling through the black scabs of leaf mold.

After her fall, Canny abandoned her straight course for one that took her along and up, and not quite so close to the tree trunks. The forest was dark, the day not yet warm. Her palms burned from cold and being scraped. The going was still difficult, but easier than it had been. She began to have the impression that she was on a path, or what was left of one. She stopped using her hands and was now ascending a series of natural terraces, probably formed by the retreat of prehistoric ice. It was an easy climb, and she had a pleasant progressive sense that she was going the right way.

The sun was climbing the sky, so there was more light. It struck the broad-leaved epiphytes on the tree trunks and green ribbons of vines.

Canny paused and took her bearings. When she'd begun up the hill, the rising sun had been shining directly on the back of her head. Now it was on her right. She realized she was still circling the hill, not going up it. Or, she was going up it, but at such a shallow angle that she'd have to wind around it ten times before reaching the summit. She'd be well and truly tired by then, and the day would be over.

Canny took a good slow look around. She continued to feel that, yes, this was the way. That she would achieve her goal. That this was a nice walk. That she was safe on this path.

Canny closed her eyes and cleared her mind by calculating pi to a challenging number of places. Then she opened her eyes again and took a proper look around. And there it was, shining like ground mist, Extra, around her ankles and tugging at her like the current of a gentle stream.

Canny stepped straight out of it and, once again, began to forge her way directly up the slope. It was very hard going; her hair caught on branches, her feet slipped, and her shins were scraped; handholds and footholds kept giving way. Once she pulled out a whole kidney fern and brought a log the size of her own torso rolling down on her. She only just twisted aside in time to avoid injury. She waited till the forest was quiet again and continued on up, shunning every easy passage that presented itself. Her hands were savaged by hanging on for dear life as the bank crumbled behind her, but she forged on, tenacious and bloody-minded.

A heavy body crashed through the bush near her, past her, downhill. Canny glimpsed a boar, its bristly hide, and the breath smoking white through its jagged tusks. She stayed motionless as it rushed away through the undergrowth—a real thing, and a real danger.

It took her some time to muster her courage to go on. She was exhausted and her limbs were trembling. She crept, scared she'd startle another boar or bring the first back her way. Wild pigs had paths, she knew that. She must be near a pig path.

Then Canny had a thought. The pig was real, and pigs had paths, so perhaps rather than avoiding it she should try to find its path, and see if that would offer her an easier way up the hill. She made her way back to the place where she'd spotted the animal. Going downhill was surprisingly easy, as if, in her struggle, she'd beaten a proper path. To test this she tried turning back momentarily, but as soon as the upward slope was before her again, it was as gnarled an obstacle course as ever.

Canny couldn't locate the exact place she had been when the boar blundered by her. Instead, she struck out from the general area, looking carefully at the ground and the trunks of trees. Eventually she found a trunk where all the bark was splintered down to pith. A boar had sharpened its tusks there. Under the tree was a muddy slot—a track that rambled away uphill. It was partly concealed; ferns curled over it. But it was deep, packed down, and printed by sharp trotters.

Canny followed it. She crept along, looking behind her all the time, her ears attuned to the scuffling, thumps, and grunts of pigs.

The pig path wriggled its way up and around the hill, shaped by obvious obstacles, like a vine-hung escarpment and a very old fallen tree. But then, all of a sudden, it swept out in a long curve, deviating from its general course, which was counterclockwise around the hill. There was no obstacle to explain the path's deviation, or the shape of it, a perfect half circle. Canny stopped and stared. Her heart sped up. She looked through the trees the track had skirted and saw sunlight on ferns and fallen leaves—a clearing.

Canny left the boar path and pushed through the branches. Before long she heard the sound of a lamb calling to its mother. She realized she'd been hearing the sound for a few minutes, but had assumed it came from a pasture down the valley and was bouncing back from one of the rock faces on the hill's southern slope. But when she broke into the clearing she found the sheep, up to its belly in bracken. It plunged away from her and then abruptly turned, as if yanked back by a rope it wore. But it wasn't tied; it was only unable to leave its lamb.

The lamb was bright-eyed, urgent, bleating—and half-buried in a slip. The clearing was part of a man-made terrace. The roots of trees had rotted and displaced the terrace's boulder wall, and that wall had ruptured, letting out a flow of thick, wet clay. The slip had caught the lamb, which must have been grazing there. The lamb lay, its front legs bent, the clay beneath it marked where its hooves had cut grooves. It had been trying and trying to drag itself free. Its neck was stretched out, face turned to its mother. The fleece on its back, chest, and chin was clotted with clay slip.

Canny hurried to help it. It was frightened of her and tried to twist itself away, scrabbling toward its mother. Canny dropped onto her knees beside it. She jammed her fingers into the slip above it and tried to scoop the clay away. But the clay was dense, heavy, and sticky. Grit jammed under Canny's fingernails, and when she pulled her hand free it was with a painful tugging in her nail beds. She got up, found a stick, and tried again. The stick bent uselessly and only made a smooth conical hole in the clay. When she pulled it out, the hole filled with water. The clay might be pliable, but she could only mold it, not move it.

The ewe seemed to understand she meant to help. It

came up to her and jostled against her, then licked the lamb's head, melting the dried clay with grassy spittle.

Canny got a grip on the lamb's fleece and tried, tentatively, to pull it free, only gently testing the grip of the clay. The lamb cried out—an almost human scream. The ewe pattered away, bleating in distress, then immediately returned and pushed between Canny and her lamb.

Canny got up and backed off, then she plunged into the forest and ran as fast as she could downhill, in search of help.

BECAUSE THE KIDS TENDED TO GET GLUE all over themselves whenever he asked them to mend the irrigation hoses, Lealand had taken his bicycle repair kit out among the Golden Queen peach trees to do it himself. He was working on a section near the river trail when the girl came into sight, stumbling with tiredness, scratched, and sweat-soaked right up into the roots of her hair.

She left the trail and headed straight for him. He got up and hurried to meet her.

She stopped at the orchard gate and hung over it, taking great whooping breaths.

Lealand waited for her. "Just take a moment," he said.

She gestured behind her, then turned to properly direct her gesture. She was pointing to the hill at the head of the valley.

Lealand relaxed, because there was no real trouble. But he continued to regard her attentively, because that was what she'd expect.

The girl was tall and slender, but not willowy. He wasn't

sure how old she was, somewhere between fifteen and eighteen. A hiker.

Since this hiker had hurried to get help, she must have gotten a long way up the hill. To have gone so far she must have meant to climb—though Lealand couldn't imagine why she would want to. The last person turned back by The Injured Animal was a geologist, who had been interested in the hill itself, the composition of its soils and stones. The geologist was a highly motivated adult. That was almost six years ago now, and the spells on Terminal Hill got stronger every year.

The girl finally caught her breath. "There's a lamb buried in a slip—halfway up the hill, on the southeastern side, about fifteen degrees above the rock face."

There were a number of remarkable things about the girl's news and directions. How specific she was, just for starters. The clearing on the old overgrown road was, come to think of it, fifteen degrees above the rock face. But since when did girls give directions like gunners aiming an artillery piece? There was that—and that she said *a lamb*. She said *buried in a slip*.

Lealand said, "I'll have to get some tools." He took her arm. "Come along with me. You're exhausted."

She followed him, and then overtook him, hurrying him on toward Orchard House.

The big boys were busy in the home orchard cementing stones around the base of the tea tree branch they'd cut to prop the leaning apple tree. Lealand told one to run and fetch Cyrus. The boy took off, his bare heels raising dust once he reached the track. Lealand continued on to the house. He led the girl up onto the porch and told her to take a seat. She did and was immediately surrounded by fascinated youngsters, one of whom thought to ask her if she'd like a drink of water.

Lealand went to get tools. He always kept the tools for this task ready at hand. He gathered up an awl, bailing twine, a brush, and Stockholm tar, then, after some thought, collected a shovel and a big canvas bucket as well.

THAT BOY LONNIE WAS LYING on a wicker sofa on the porch when Canny arrived. He had a cold flannel on his forehead and a jug of juice beside him.

The smaller children claimed Canny's full attention for a time. They wouldn't stop asking her questions—though none about what kind of emergency had brought her to Orchard House. They had no idea how to talk to strangers. They kept firing off random and disconnected questions as if she were an exhibit in a classroom and their teacher hadn't properly prepared them for her visit.

Lonnie got up, came over, and thrust a few kids aside. He sat next to Canny. "Leave her alone," he told them.

They ignored him till he raised his hand, then they shrank back and fell silent.

Lonnie said, "I'm the one who should be asking questions about the world outside the valley. I'm being packed off on Saturday, even though school doesn't start till summer is over."

"Where are you going?" Canny said.

"Middleton, on the plains. My mother's there." He made shooing motions at the kids and they melted away, most setting off along the path the messenger had followed. Lonnie said they were heading over to the guesthouse to get their lunch. "We had classes here this morning."

Canny said, "I went for a walk."

"I gather you found an injured animal?"

Canny nodded.

"Our uncles will take care of it."

"Its mother was so distressed."

Lonnie frowned. *"Mother?"* he said. Then he looked away for a time. Canny watched his face change. He began to look sly. "Farming folk don't like to let city folk know what they usually have to do with injured animals," he said. "City folk like to think they're helping when they come running in asking someone to rescue some poor beast."

"I'm not soft. I know the lamb's back is probably broken. But there's no need for it to go on crying. Or for its mother to have to listen to it. And I couldn't kill it. It's not mine," Canny said. "I don't have the right to make that decision."

"I wasn't trying to shock you. I thought you'd like some plain facts."

"The facts I'm most fond of aren't plain ones," Canny said.

Lealand came across from the barn and put the tools and bucket on the steps. He told Lonnie to go lie down again.

"The kids were bothering Miss Mochrie," said Lonnie.

Lealand pointed at the couch and Lonnie went back to it.

"Are you staying at the guesthouse, Miss Mochrie?"

"We were last night," she said. "My brother wants to go back to Massenfer."

"The bright lights of Massenfer," said Lealand.

Canny laughed. "We went to a restaurant, and our bread rolls were still frozen in the middle. The place is a bit dismal, but Sholto is supposed to be doing some work there. And Susan."

"And Susan's doing some work?" Lealand said, and Canny saw that she'd said that Sholto was doing Susan. She blushed. "Yes. Research. Both of them. Susan is Sholto's fiancée."

The wind chimes on the porch stirred and tinkled, though there wasn't any wind.

Lealand said, "The forest is very thick on the hill. If you're right about the place then you were a good way up. What on earth were you doing?"

"I was lost," Canny said.

Again the wind chimes stirred in the still air. Canny looked at them, then carefully down at her hands. She turned them over. "I'm so dirty. I tried to pull the poor animal out."

"You'll want to wash."

"Yes, thank you." She finished her water and looked at the clay prints left on the glass. "I followed a path," she said. "I think pigs had made it. I saw a wild boar. A big beast with a broken tusk. I was frightened. So I stopped going the way I was going and went a different way." All of this was true. The chimes were silent. Canny thought of something to test them. "I hurt my hand," she said. It was her leg that was sore—the one with the scratch. The chimes made only one faint, bright correction. Canny wondered whether, if she was to shout out that she *wasn't* looking for a way up to the house on the hill, the chimes would erupt in an unholy clamor as if about to be ripped from their hooks by a hurricane. And, anyway, what did these people do on windy days when someone came to the house and lied?

A tall man was coming back through the orchard, accompanied by the boy sent to fetch him. He had extraordinarily thick white hair, as glassy as the hair on a ninety-year-old but of a youthful texture, springy, and flowing. He was spry, but had a slight limp.

Lealand pick up his tools. Then he stayed a moment to introduce them. "Cy, this is Miss Agnes Mochrie. Miss Mochrie, this is my cousin Mr. Cyrus Zarene."

Canny asked Cyrus whether he was a brother to the Iris who ran the guesthouse. He nodded.

"Like Bonnie is a sister to Lonnie, I suppose?" she said.

"Bonnie and Lonnie are cousins," said Lealand, regarding her closely.

"Don't you get confused?"

"We don't," said Cyrus. Then he gave her a friendly wave and set off toward the forested hill. Lealand told the girl at the other end of the veranda, the one reading a book while pressing the treadle of a butter churn, that she should show Miss Mochrie where she might wash up.

The girl was very conscientious. She took Canny to a large upstairs bathroom and ran a bath for her. She put some cotton balls and iodine on the floor by the bath and said Canny might like to disinfect her scratch. She unlocked a big linen press and handed Canny a towel, then left her to it.

Canny opened one of the bathroom leadlights and looked out. She glimpsed the two men through a gap in the trees, then lost them again. Canny wondered about them. There was something old-manish about them—and old-womanish about Iris Zarene. But they were indeterminately middle-aged in the way they spoke and stood and moved. They were sleek and healthy and scarcely wrinkled— but they had a kind of placid gravity that middle-aged people didn't generally have, as if they were older. The kids seemed normal, though their weird rhyming names and their living arrangements certainly weren't. But the adults were somehow strange in themselves, in a way that alarmed Canny but that she also found attractive. People were often a slippery challenge to her, but at least these people didn't make her feel awkward and misshapen.

Canny turned off the taps, removed her clothes, and eased herself into the bath. Her scratches smarted. She washed quickly. The door was locked, but she was in a strange house. The rooms around her sounded empty, but she could hear voices out the back, and in the orchard. Someone was hammering. Someone else was beating a rug. And there was the gentle thump of the butter churn.

Canny finally washed her face and then got out and let the bath drain while she toweled herself dry. She put her dirty clothes back on. When the bath was empty, Canny could once again listen and track the movements in and around the house. She opened the door a crack and peered through. The hallway was empty. She crept out, holding her sandals.

She went along the hall, looking into each room. There

was a bedroom with four bunks, and then another, the same. Then she found a schoolroom. The desks were in inward-facing groups, like those in the friendly and informal city primary school Canny had attended, though there were none of that school's drying lines hung with paintings on cheap wrinkled paper, or murals with leaves collected from nature walks pasted onto them.

The blackboard was wiped clean but was cloudy with chalk dust. There was a big old radio on the teacher's desk and a stack of textbooks from the correspondence school. But the thing that really drew Canny's eye were the friezes around the top of the wall. There were the numerals and examples—one nose, two eyes, three hanks of hair to make a braid, four fingers, five toes. There was the alphabet, from A for Apple to Z for Zipper. And there was *another* alphabet, without illustrations. Two hundred symbols, rendered in black paint on yellowing white cards.

Canny walked into the room and went close. Under each symbol was a line of small print, also in symbols. The same line on every card. It took Canny only a few moments to work it out. She didn't read it, but got its meaning intuitively as she had with the other signs she'd encountered. She understood the small print negated any magical effect each letter of this alphabet might have. Part of the small print looked like the spell she'd put on the tents. It said something like "Disregard." But if it had only said "Disregard" Canny wouldn't have been able to see the alphabet at all, and the pupils who studied in this classroom couldn't have looked at the letters to learn them. Canny guessed that what the whole line of small print said was

"For demonstration purposes only," or something very like it.

She stepped back and her eyes went around the walls. The signs were inactive—rendered so—but as she studied them, something lit inside her. Each symbol smote her. If she ever had a chance to tell Marli what had happened to her, that was how she would put it. She was smitten. She was assaulted, and in love. These were *her* things—her very own. But also each recognition was like the stroke of a bell, a long sad tolling, as if at the death of a monarch.

Canny was pulled out of her reverie by the sound of children running up the stairs. She realized that she didn't have time to get out of the schoolroom. She was going to be caught snooping. The curtains on the room's windows were thick and floor-length. Canny ran lightly across the room and plunged into their dusty folds. She pinched her nose and tried to breathe only through her mouth.

The kids stopped at the bathroom door, which Canny had closed behind her. They whispered to one another for a time, then came on into the schoolroom.

Canny couldn't guess how many of them there were. They were obviously trained to habitual quietness in-doors.

"How big is *big*?" one was saying softly as he came in.

"You know. Whenever you go to Massenfer to the movies you see them in the streets. Like the ones who hang around the milk bar."

"Does she have . . . ?"

"Yes. But little ones."

"Pointy?"

"Rounded. Quite nice."

A giggle.

"Boys!" This was said in disgust.

A desk lid creaked.

"Why do you think Uncle Lealand sent for Uncle Cyrus?"

"How should I know?"

"She was telling lies. Do you think that's why?"

"No, silly. That was later. On the veranda. I was there, making butter. If she was lying, Uncle wouldn't have known till she got to the house."

A new voice. "People lie all the time. Everybody does. I even forget sometimes and lie here, the usual little stuff that everyone politely ignores."

"Uncle Lealand never lies. He just says, 'You don't need to know.'"

"What say we did need to? Have you ever thought of that? Or—what say Orchard House disagreed with Uncle Lealand? Would the chimes sound?"

"It's Uncle Lealand's spell. It has to have the same opinions as he does. It isn't for when people are mistaken and say something that isn't true. It's to catch deliberate falsehoods. Uncle Cyrus says that the Wards are philosophers, not machines. He means that they sort of think about things and make their own judgments."

It was Bonnie who was speaking now—Canny was sure of it. She breathed shallowly and tried to ignore the tickle in her throat.

A desk lid banged. Footsteps pattered back out into the hall.

"But, Bon," said the first kid, her voice farther off now, "*why* did Uncle Lea call Uncle Cy?"

FIVE TIMES OVER THE LAST THIRTEEN YEARS Lealand had had to set off toward the hill at the head of the valley carrying his rifle and a bag of tools—the awl, the bailing twine, the brush, and the little pot of Stockholm tar. Of all the people who had gone far enough up the hill, somehow defying its difficulties to encounter The Injured Animal, only one of them had wanted to go back with Lealand and help him. The geologist, six years ago now, hadn't defied anything to climb the hill. He'd had his own powerful magic—the ordinary magic that extraordinarily interested people always have. He had suffered tumbles and scratches, but hadn't felt the spells themselves because he was so absorbed in his own pursuits. The soil here, the bare bones of rock there, all the different minerals the glacier had disgorged and piled up over hundreds of thousands of years. The Injured Animal had stopped him though. It was as far as anyone ever got. It was a horror: a creature that needed help and probably couldn't be helped. It was a pity. It was the worst that happens. The worst that always eventually happens. The Injured Animal sent absolutely everyone back down the hill. Only the geologist had insisted on returning to the clearing on the course of the old road, to see for himself whether something could be done for the poor cow who had blundered onto the stake of a snapped sapling and had torn her abdomen open. And, because The

Injured Animal was a Great Spell, the greatest its maker
had ever cast, it wasn't just a spectacle—a sweating, trembling, bloodied, distressed cow with intestines bulging and
threatening to pour right out of the gash in her belly. It
wasn't just sounds—grunts, labored breathing, the way the
cow stamped her feet, goaded by pain to move, and then
punished by pain for having moved. It was a Great Spell,
so when Lealand had the geologist hold the cow's head
while he pushed her intestines back into her, the geologist
had felt the cow's whiskers, and her slobber, and her strength.
And Lealand had felt the heat in the wet entrails, and the
tension on the skin he pulled together and punched
with the old sailmaker's awl and threaded closed with
binder's twine. And when he'd finished sewing up, and had
sealed the wound with a thick paste of tar, his hands were
sticky with blood, and the geologist was tired, and his foot
was sore because the cow had stepped on it.

This time Lealand carried the bag as well as his rifle up
the hill because the spell was a story and required him to
honor its truth. The cow could be mended, or the cow could
be put down. But whatever he did, the cow would be there,
ruptured and suffering, for whoever next happened along.

Lealand also took Cyrus with him because it was Cyrus's
spell, and the girl had reported seeing not a cow, but a lamb
buried in a mud slip and still alive, under the helpless eye of
its mother.

They took the pig path uphill, Lealand pushing his own
personal warning ward ahead of him so that the pigs would
steer clear of them. Cyrus stopped to use his knife to cut a
leafy branch from a whitey wood sapling so he could use it

as a walking stick. He complained that this was the second time in a week he'd had to climb this hill, and his leg was giving him trouble. Before they got to the clearing they heard the distressed lowing. They found the cow, trampling her own blood into the mossy turf, the ball of glistening guts bulging out of her side. She was noisy, so Lealand placed the muzzle of the rifle against her head and pulled the trigger. The shot echoed all over the hill. The cow dropped onto her knees, then slumped sideways, kicked once, and was still.

The clearing was silent.

"Are you sure the girl said a lamb and a ewe?"

"She was descriptive and filled with compassion. Can you think why the spell would show itself differently to her?"

Cyrus shook his head. "It's not designed to take anything from the imagination of its witnesses. It's something I saw—one of Uncle Colvin's cows. We did fix her, and she lived."

"This girl, Agnes Mochrie, she saw the spell differently." Lealand was tired and troubled. "That *means* something."

Cyrus put a hand on his arm. "You've told me yourself that none of our spells are running down, that they're getting stronger. Maybe it changed to be more effective. *I'd* be in even more of a hurry to help a trapped lamb than a gutted cow."

"You know as well as I do that a spell can't change itself. Only we can change it."

"Hmmm," said Cyrus.

Lealand gestured at the corpse of the cow. "It didn't change."

"Apparently not," said Cyrus, thoughtful.

Lealand frowned at him. "Even if this girl was a descendant of Lazarus she couldn't have altered your strongest spell without decades of training. And she's a Shackle Islander from Castlereagh. She might have some Zarene ancestor, or the blood of one of the other five families. She might have magic in her. But she is completely ignorant, innocent, and unformed. She couldn't do it. So, it's not her, it's the spell."

"Lea, let's just go back and explain to her very gently that we had to destroy the lamb because its back was broken. Let me explain. I'll hold her hands and take a good long look at her."

They were only ten paces down in the darkness of the forest when they heard the cow start up again, its low moans of pain.

WHEN THEY GOT BACK TO ORCHARD HOUSE they found the girl sitting on the steps. Her grazes and scratches were clean but angry on her smooth limbs. She got up, eager for news—but her face didn't move. It was like the face of a delicate doll, wide-eyed, smooth, blankly beautiful. Her hair seemed alive, a rippling black smoke around her head and upper body. Cyrus looked her in the eye and shook his head sadly.

"I heard the shot," she said.

He took her hands. "Its back was broken, I'm afraid. There wasn't anything we could do. Lea buried it."

"What about its mother?"

"She has some grazing there. We'll go back for her when she's calmer."

"The poor thing," the girl said, about the lamb or ewe, Cyrus wasn't sure. "Isn't the world hard," she said, pulled her hands from his grasp and stretched hands and forearms, like a cat luxuriously extending its claws. The gesture was out of keeping with her tone of pity and reminded Cyrus forcibly of Ghislain. The world might be hard, but something in her was stepping away from that hardness, stepping out of the blood and shaking its feet. He said, "There are no tracks up that hill because it's geologically unstable. There are hidden sinkholes. We welcome walkers, but where there aren't tracks there's a good reason for it."

"There was a pig path."

"Did you mistake it for a track?"

"I just went up it," she said, then cocked her head slightly as if listening for something.

The wind chimes! She was listening for the wind chimes and picking her way carefully around the edge of a lie. Cyrus wanted to shout at her, *Who the hell are you?* But instead he asked politely, "Will you be staying long in the valley?"

"My brother thought we might camp here while he does business in Massenfer. It's not very nice in the town. The police told us to pitch our tent by the river, but the ground is all gravel and won't hold our tent pegs."

"Massenfer isn't a place people visit. It doesn't know how to be visited."

"My brother's here to record the stories of the survivors of the 1929 mining disaster."

"Why?" Cyrus couldn't help sounding incredulous and outraged.

She blinked at him, surprised. "Because they're getting older," she said. "It's for a book. The book isn't about the disaster; it's about the Industrial Safety Act of 1932. Very boring. Sholto's doing the background, which is the interesting bit."

Cyrus considered for a moment, then said, "I survived the 1929 explosion. And Lealand was a draegerman and went in afterward to search for survivors."

The girl stared at him. Her mouth stayed a little open. Then she blushed. "I don't know whether Sholto has you on his list."

"Cyrus Zarene."

"I'll ask him. He wrote to all the people he planned to interview. Did you not get a letter?"

Cyrus shook his head, smiling.

"What?" she said. "Don't you ever get letters?"

Cyrus laughed. He decided he liked this girl, even if she did present problems.

"Would you mind being interviewed?" she asked. "If I bring Sholto an interviewee then he might not be too mad at me for being late. We were supposed to go back to Massenfer today to look at the library."

"You're at the guesthouse?"

She nodded.

"I'll walk you back, give your brother your excuses, and then offer myself. Do you think that would do?"

She jumped up. "Yes! Thank you." She turned to Bonnie, who was at the other end of the veranda, scouring out the butter churn. "Tell the others thank you very much for the bath."

"Sure," said Bonnie.

"See you," said Canny, and followed Cyrus through the orchard to the path by the Lazuli.

CANNY ARRIVED BACK AT THE GUESTHOUSE in time to witness Sholto's confrontation with Iris Zarene. She could hear raised voices as she climbed the porch steps. Cyrus, coming up behind her, said, "Perhaps we should wait outside."

She ignored him and hurried in.

Iris was three steps up the staircase, and Sholto was having to tilt his head to look at her. His fists were balled at his sides and he was quivering with indignation. Susan was standing behind him. She looked angry too, but also embarrassed.

"I demand an explanation!" Sholto was saying.

Iris Zarene gave a very provoking shrug. Then she looked over Sholto's head at Cyrus. She said, "Mr. Mochrie is missing two tents."

Susan leaned toward Canny and whispered, "We went to pack up the car. We figured you'd turn up eventually. Anyway, we discovered the tents weren't there anymore."

"How about everything else?" Canny asked. She thought she sounded very plausible—anxious, and a bit inhibited by the scene Sholto was making.

"That pack of kids roam up and down the river all the time—" Sholto said, and was cut off.

"True," said Iris. "They might have noticed something. We should ask them." She gave Sholto a smug look.

"That's not what I meant. I meant a bunch of unsupervised kids can get up to all sorts of mischief."

"I suppose you want me to line them up so that you can interrogate them?"

Sholto's flush deepened. "If you would, please."

Iris Zarene's nostrils flared and her eyes narrowed. "I will not subject my children to the humiliation of being treated as dishonest."

"I won't be treating them as dishonest if they fess up and tell me where they've stashed our tents!" Sholto said. "I'm not calling them thieves, I'm calling them pranksters, and you can't want them doing things like this."

"How kind of you to say that. How good to know that you don't think I'm like Fagin in *Oliver Twist*—some villain with an organized gang of child thieves!"

"I didn't suggest anything of the sort. You're purposely misunderstanding me in order to get on your high horse and gallop off out of trouble!" Sholto shouted.

Iris burst out laughing.

"Oh, I'm glad you're amused!" Sholto said.

Cyrus took Sholto's arm. "Where were your tents? If you don't mind me asking."

"At the end of the road. In the field, hung on some bushes to dry. They're heavy canvas. The wind couldn't carry them off. And, anyway, there hasn't been any wind."

"I'm sure we can get this settled amicably," Cyrus said.

"My brother is a peacemaker," said Iris, in her dry,

contemptuous way. Then, in an insinuating tone, "Mr. Mochrie, have you asked your sister about your tents?"

Sholto looked at Canny. "Where have you been?"

Canny said she'd been for a walk. "I found a lamb stuck in a slip. I went to Orchard House to get help, and I waited for news." She looked at Susan, who seemed properly sympathetic and concerned. "Mr. Lealand had to put it down."

Susan patted her shoulder. "That's rough."

Sholto said, "You're all right?"

Canny nodded. Then added, "I haven't seen the tents." The chimes of Orchard House would not have sounded—though it wasn't strictly true, since she *had* seen them before she made herself, and everyone else, unable to see them.

Susan said, "Sholto, maybe someone came along the road to the valley, saw our tents, and decided they were just what they needed. Other travelers. Or somebody from Massenfer."

Cyrus said, "I hear you're researching the history of the 1929 explosion."

"So?" said Sholto, still riled up. "How is that relevant?"

"It was merely a question."

"Mr. Zarene is a survivor," Canny said.

Sholto fell silent. Canny could see him mentally reviewing something—either the list of survivors, or of casualties. He would, of course, know the names. "There were two Zarenes who were survivors," he said.

"Myself and a cousin."

"We all counted ourselves survivors," said Iris. "We women too. So many died. Twenty-two men from Massenfer, and nine from the valley."

A silence came into the room and, like a cat, turned in a circle a few times, trampling down all arguments to make itself comfortable before settling. Sholto was staring at Iris Zarene in dumb embarrassment.

She took a deep breath then said, "How about if I extend you several days of my hospitality free of charge. And please leave it to me to investigate the whereabouts of your tents."

"And how about I speak to my cousin Lealand about your interviewing the two of us?" Cyrus offered.

Sholto blushed and shuffled.

"That's very good of you," Susan said quickly. "Thank you." She elbowed Sholto.

"Thank you," Sholto muttered. He glanced at Canny. "Sue and I will get ourselves to Massenfer and make some phone calls to set up more appointments this afternoon. You can stay here. Just keep out of trouble, okay?"

"I'm going to write a letter to Marli," Canny said. She'd try. She was very, very tired—from missed sleep, and walking, and from taking in too much information, and from using what she'd learned. However natural that was to her, it seemed it was also natural that she was exhausted.

"Come on, Sue," Sholto said.

Iris, very grand, asked Sholto's retreating back, "Will you want dinner, Mr. Mochrie?"

Susan smiled very winningly and said, "Yes, thank you. That would be lovely." Then she winked at Canny and whispered, "It's your turn to be the shining Mochrie. I know you can do it."

Then they were out the door.

8

THE FOLLOWING MORNING CANNY woke early, and with an innovative thought. She knew how she could get up the hill. She could follow the wild pigs' path without fear of meeting one. She could go unnoticed.

Under the shower she figured out how to write the "disregard" symbol on herself. She decided that she should probably write it somewhere central and visible, like her forehead.

Canny dashed back to her room, got dressed, then, standing in front of the dresser in the grayish morning light, she tried for some time to transcribe the line she remembered so that it scrolled neatly above her eyebrows. She was using the only pen she had, a fountain pen, and it was hard to hold the nib at the right angle so that the ink flowed freely.

Try as she might, she couldn't get it right. Eventually,

she wrote the line out on a piece of paper, closing her eyes before she finished so that she wouldn't lose sight of it. She then used a lead pencil to coat the reverse side of the strip of paper with a thick layer of graphite. Next, she held the smudged side of the paper tightly to her forehead, and, looking into the mirror, she traced over the inked signs with the point of her pencil. That was easy to do because, of course, the signs in the mirror were reversed and, reversed, they didn't work on her. Canny removed the paper and used her fountain pen to ink over the faint graphite marks.

But, once the signs were sharp and clear, Canny haplessly found herself doing what she was always able to do with mirror-writing—she flipped the letters right-way-round in her mind and read them. Her eyes watered, then she saw double. The room began to spin.

Canny squeezed her eyes shut, gripped the edge of the dresser, and concentrated on staying upright. After a time, the vertigo went away.

Canny opened her eyes again. She didn't look into the mirror, where she could still see herself out of the corner of her eye. Instead she looked down at her own hands. Or she tried to. But she found that she couldn't *make* herself look. Nor could she watch her right hand reach for the bedroom door handle. She had to take deliberate note of the handle's position, look away, then grasp it. Canny made her way downstairs holding the banister. She couldn't even check where she was putting her feet. Her progress was that of a very shortsighted person making their way around without the aid of glasses.

She took an apple from the fruit bowl in the dining room, then went carefully out into the day.

THE PIG TRACK WAS NOT MUCH MORE THAN A GREASY slot that Canny could only climb by walking heel to toe. She had to find handholds with her eyes, take note of their position, and look away as she reached for them. She'd always had very good coordination—her physical education wasn't one of the things her teachers had worried about. So she could do that—look, take note, look away, take hold—but she was quickly exhausted by the relentless need to concentrate.

When she finally came on the pigs, she was glad of the spell. They had their heads down, snuffling and plowing up the earth at the base of a rotten log. Preoccupied, and in the dappled sunlight, they seemed happy and handsome animals, but they were huge.

She left the path and circled out a short way through the trees. The pigs heard her and raised their heads. Their wet black snouts flexed, nostrils flaring. One bristled and trotted forward, but then he stopped and swung his head, his eyes flicking and seeking but not finding her. He gave a low, anxious-sounding squeal, turned, blundered past his mate and away into the bush. The sow gave a shriek and followed him. Canny thought, "I've made myself invisible. Even to animals!"

And then all of it finally hit her, crashed into her, and knocked her down. She sat on the turf with her head on her knees. The world swooped and spun like a witch's hat roundabout, pushed so hard it was nearly tipping off its pole. Canny yanked her knees apart and threw up between her feet. She felt hot bile hit her ankle but couldn't see her foot. She could see the small pile of partly digested apple, though. It steamed. By the time she'd recovered enough to go on, the vomit had stopped steaming.

The next trial she faced was more frightening than the pigs, which she'd planned for. She was moving away from the sun. The path wound around toward the northwest face of the hill. A gap in the tree showed her a view down the valley, of Orchard House, and another house with fewer outbuildings, but surrounded by meadows of wildflowers full of box beehives. Farther away she saw the gables of the guesthouse and the roof of the dormitories. The guest-house's kitchen chimney was smoking. Breakfast was on. Canny's stomach rumbled. Then, overlapping that low internal sound, there came a moan, a grunt of distress. It was answered by bleating—a distressed lamb, exhausted, but renewing its cries for help.

Canny went cold all over. It was several minutes before she was able to force herself to go on.

The ewe was at the edge of the clearing, trembling, ready to flee. She looked at Canny, timid, but mutely appealing. The lamb looked at her too. It struggled, and its four hooves made lines in the clay slip before it. Its wool was draggled, its chin wet with mud. But it was no worse, and no better, than it had been the day before.

For a short time Canny tried to fathom how treacherous and heartless and bone lazy Lealand and Cyrus Zarene must have been to have not bothered to climb the hill and see to their own livestock. To fail at that, then to come back and lie about what they'd had to do. She imagined them standing on the river trail only a short distance from Orchard House. She imagined their look of smiling complicity—then Lealand raising the gun and firing into the air. *There, that will appease the softhearted city girl.*

Then Canny took a harder look at the lamb and she saw that there was no sign in the slip above its back of the four clear grooves where her fingers had scooped at the clay. There was no sign anyone had been here in the clearing at all. And then it struck her—the ewe and lamb were looking at her. The pigs hadn't been able to see her. They'd run from her as if she were a phantom. The lamb and ewe seemed to be able to see her, only because *she could see them* and that was the point of them, that she should see them, regard their horrible plight, feel pity, and act on it by turning around and going back down the hill in search of help.

It must have been that the back of Canny's mind was still occupied by a gnawing worry about how on earth she could explain any of this to Marli—it must have been— because as she stood staring at the lamb and ewe, Canny suddenly heard Marli's voice. It was as if her friend were there beside her. Marli asked in her gentle, straightforward way, "Don't you have sense enough to be afraid?"

Canny opened her mouth to answer, then remembered she was alone. And she was. Alone—despite the two animals in front of her, the sight and sounds of them, and the gusting emotion she had about them.

In the course of her life, she'd had moments of fright. There was the time she'd run out between two parked cars and her mother had grabbed her by the hood of her rain jacket and pulled her back out of the path of a truck. And there was the time she missed the second step on a flight of stairs and fell. She remembered the spurt of fright, the feeling of calamity, and cursing herself for clumsiness and the pain when she landed, and how surprised she was to find herself bruised but not broken. She remembered all that, but hadn't there been something cold sitting behind her animal fright? Something sitting scornfully in the very next moment and saying, as her mother always said, *"This isn't something we have to bother with."* Come to think of it, maybe she only felt really truly afraid when she was with Marli and properly looked at her friend's twisted body behind the greenish glass of the iron lung's portholes. That separation always seemed to promise the next one, when the lung would be replaced with a coffin, and the coffin with a grave. *That* frightened Canny—it terrified her.

Canny did speak then to her absent friend. "Yes, I am scared, really scared. But this is magic, Marli, and who knows what magic can do?"

She took a deep breath and walked past the lamb and ewe and went on up through the forest.

THE NEXT CLEARING CANNY REACHED she recognized as part of an overgrown road, one that had once climbed, zigzagging, up the hill. Of course if there was a house, there must have been a road.

The ground had bits of gravel on it, under moss and saplings. Canny turned to follow the road and, thereafter, her climb was fairly easy; she had only to contend with the scrub. There were no misdirection spells, no injured animals to ambush her. The slope became shallower and the road wound back into the sunlight. The day was hot—and Canny nearly made the mistake of mopping her brow with her arm. She stopped herself just in time; after all, she'd still want to be invisible to the wild pigs on her way down.

The road became clearer and clearer, then suddenly terminated at a vine-covered, tumbledown garage. On the downhill side of this garage there was a partial break in the forest, and Canny glimpsed what looked like the bumper and back wheels of a vehicle, hood down in the undergrowth, run off the road. After all her trouble Canny didn't like to go even ten paces downhill; still, the wreck made her curious, so she slid down far enough to see that there were letters stenciled in white paint on the driver's door. She lifted the curtaining vines and read: "USMC." After a moment her mind supplied "United States Marine Corps." There were no other clues as to why a Marine Corps jeep should be abandoned, front bumper down, in a trackless forest.

Canny returned to the slumped garage. Cracked cement steps went up beside it. She climbed them, passed through some overgrown rhododendrons, and came out on a terrace covered in the remnants of a garden; plum trees, a thicket of raspberry canes, and blackcurrant bushes so old that only their tops were in leaf. It looked to Canny as if someone had recently cleared a path through the tangle, for the cut stalks were still leaking sap, and there were broken branches whose leaves had only just begun to wilt.

"So," she thought, "someone comes here."

She followed the roughly hacked path. It took her to

another set of steps that led to a higher terrace. These steps were less dilapidated, and the flight was edged in red bricks with frothy alyssum planted in their cracks.

The next terrace was light and sunny,-the sky almost open above it. There were more trees, peaches and pears and cherries, all full of fruit and tended. There were vegetable beds, recently watered, the water taken from rain barrels that stood at intervals along the wall of a higher terrace. The garden curved to follow the conical top of the hill. Canny looked left and right, but couldn't see another set of steps, one that would take her to the top. She chose to go left and keep the sun on her back. She picked a cape gooseberry, eased it out of its origami envelope, and ate it—then stopped and ate several more. They were delicious, sweet, and powerfully aromatic. She went on. Eventually she came to a flight up. She did pause to wonder about people who'd want to make their way from a parked car to a house by such an indirect route. It was so nonsensical. Canny was sure it would turn out that it was another crazy Zarene Valley contrivance meant to baffle, like the lack of signposts on the tracks or, come to think of it, the kids' strange rhyming names.

These steps were perfect, as if they'd never been walked on before. Canny peered up them. She could see the crown of a black beech tree some distance off. The beech was darkening already and would be deep red, almost black, by the summer's end. Now its leaves were green below, red above, overlapping, rich, stirring colors. There was another tree, a golden ash, cascading green-yellow. Perhaps it was just that she'd been down in the tangles of the native forest so long that her eyes couldn't adjust, but there was something terrifying about the intensity of the color in the crowns of those trees. They were too brilliant, too lovely, and Canny had the momentary mad impression that it wasn't she who was looking at them, but someone infinitely more alive, and great, like a god.

She swallowed and began up the steps, touching each one, feeling the cold brick, as smooth as marble.

The roof of the house came into view. A clay tile roof in perfect condition, white weatherboard walls, white gingerbread work on the veranda, beveled window frames and veranda posts—every angle perfectly sharp as if a master carpenter had only just finished, and the house had had its first three coats of paint and hadn't even been rained on yet. The windows were all bright and clean.

The house was set on a lawn. The grass was freshly mown, and the lawn was in that state of natural perfection achieved a few days after mowing in early summer when the buttercups and daisies come up faster than the grass and cover the lawn. This lawn was a galaxy of daisies, and the air was filled with their light perfume. There were shrubs around the house—lavender, roses, rosemary, sage, thyme. All the shadows were still, and blue-black. The roses were perfect. Everything was perfect.

A white grit path skirted the edge of the lawn to approach the house. Canny stepped onto it. The grit made a satisfactory noise under her sandals. Two monarch butterflies appeared before her, tumbling over one another. They flew away over the grass. Canny followed them with her eyes—and caught sight of someone.

It must have been seven in the morning, and the boy, or young man, was only just up. He looked sleepy and disheveled and underdressed, in a pair of clean striped cotton pajama pants and nothing else. He had the same haircut as just about every other man Canny knew—short back and sides, long on top—but just about every man Canny knew (barring a few of Sholto's friends who were growing their hair longer and sporting youthful, moth-eaten-looking beards) used hair cream to keep the long bit on top firmly in place. The young man's fall of hair was a sleek black flag. It was currently hanging down toward the ground because he was stooped over, feeding cut carrots and beetroot tops through the wire of a cage full of white, lop-eared rabbits.

Canny, embarrassed to catch sight of a man in his pajamas, took a couple of steps back down so that only her head showed. The young man didn't notice her. He finished pushing the vegetables into the cage and stood up, watching the rabbits eat. It was a quiet, tender sight, and very reassuring. Surely a man in his pajamas feeding rabbits couldn't be a dangerous person.

He went indoors through some side door. The house had a grand entrance with double doors and stained glass, but Canny guessed the man had gone from the side veranda into a kitchen. She took off her sandals and left them under a rosebush, then ran lightly up the steps and across the lawn. The grass was very soft. She gingerly crossed the graveled path and climbed up onto the veranda. She ducked down under each window and made her way around the side of the house. The rabbits stopped nibbling and turned her way, their eyes seeking and noses quivering. One sat back on its hind legs, grabbed the wire and began plucking at it with its claws. Canny put her finger to her lips—though the gesture would be as invisible to the animals as she was. She then took a quick careful look into the kitchen—a big room with black-and-white floor tiles and a long timber table, scrubbed white. The room was empty. She crept inside.

There was a loaf of bread on the table and a plate filled with oozing honeycomb. There were crumbs on the table-top, and a trail of them leading out the kitchen door.

Canny followed.

The man was upstairs. Canny could hear drawers open-ing and closing, and the sticky sound of bare feet moving on polished floorboards.

Canny listened for a moment, then realized that he was on his way back down.

She bolted aimlessly, then took a quick look around and dashed into the darkness beside the staircase. There was a cupboard under the stairs. She tried its handle, but it wouldn't budge. The man was on the last flight. Canny saw his hand above her, running along the banister. She crammed herself into a gloomy corner and froze.

He didn't see her—and probably should have when he turned to walk into a room to one side of the front door. She could see him clearly, his handsome profile against the light. He'd combed his hair, but hadn't tamed it with cream. He was wearing a grandpa collar shirt and baggy tweed pants. The clothes were old-fashioned, but looked brand-new. Canny's own clothes were light-colored. She should have been seen. But it seemed that her spell worked on people as well as pigs and rabbits.

The man went from view. A voice faded in—a radio. The announcer's smooth, woody tones swooped in, as if he'd slid a distance down the sky bodily on a wire and had come in through the window. The radio's valves warmed, and the announcer was there, talking about an air crash in Brussels.

It was then that Canny saw the spells. They were in the woodwork, signs that wove around one another, carved in large motifs and small, on the banister, the newel post, the lintel and doorsill, and a decorative strip that ran above the wall panel just below where the wallpaper started. The signs were even on the timber picture rail, and in each panel of the stained glass. The only patterns that were merely patterns were the embossed geometries of the pressed paper ceiling and the leafy swirls on the wool rug, both of which had been manufactured outside the valley.

The house's glass and woodwork were speaking to Canny—placidly, profoundly—in a language she couldn't understand. Everything gleamed, there was no dust any-where, or sign of wear. The woodwork looked as if it had been carved yesterday, or maybe even *tomorrow*, as if the house were still a dream, or an ideal place, as perfect as carvings were in a craftsman's imagination before he took a saw, or plane, or chisel to seasoned timber.

The man who reared rabbits and wandered about in pajama bottoms or his granddad's clothes—he seemed harmless. The house, now that Canny had really looked at just this bit of it, seemed utterly terrifying.

So she very sensibly decided to creep away, to go somewhere and think about what she'd seen. But once she came near to the door of the room the man and radio were in, curiosity got the better of her. She eased around the door frame.

The man was sitting at a desk covered in neat piles of paper and books. He was writing. He didn't look up when she came in, and she was at liberty to stare. He really was good-looking. His setting was cultivated—the books, the polished teak desk—but he struck Canny as being like some rare wild animal, as beautiful as some young people are, but more graceful than anyone she'd ever seen.

Canny gazed at him, and a hard lump formed at the base of her throat. The last thing she wanted was to be noticed by him, but she hated to go away without speaking to him.

What could she say? It suddenly struck her that she had nothing much inside her—no good stories, no fun games, no jokes or chatter or forceful opinions about movies or music, like the kids in her class. She had Marli, nursed very close to her heart but somehow encased and concealed in Canny's love for her—and immobilized, as she was in the iron lung. People were always saying, or at least implying, that there was something wrong with Canny, and she at last understood that those people were right, and that it *mattered*.

Canny crept forward to get a better look at what the man was working on. Some of it was mathematical. Vectors. And some of it was recognizably the Zarene Alphabet, and some, she saw after a moment, was made of only bits of Zarene symbols in layers. It looked a little like Chinese writing.

The man sighed, put his hands behind his head, and tilted his chair. He stayed like that for a long time. Then the chair dropped back onto four feet. He got up to sharpen his pencils, leaving the curled shavings on the spotless rug. Then he sat down again, pressed his thumb between his eyebrows to massage away a headache, and bent over his pages.

Canny slowly dropped into a crouch and then sat down. She stayed to watch him work. Gradually the sunlight moved till it was coming in the window behind him. He got up and opened that window, then went right back to work.

It was several hours before he stopped, stood up, and left the room.

Canny took her time following him, not wanting to be heard. She took note of where he put his feet, but none of the floorboards made noise.

The man went into a downstairs bathroom, and she heard a flush and water running. He came out with a wet face and hair spiked at the nape of his neck.

Once he'd gone back into the kitchen, Canny used the bathroom herself, positioning herself to pee on the side of the bowl so it didn't make any noise. The water in the bowl was now yellow and Canny hoped the man would imagine he'd just forgotten to flush. She checked her reflection in the mirror, careful not to look too closely at the inked signs on her forehead. It was reassuring to see herself, a bright-eyed girl, not the bodiless ghost who had been steering her body about all day—inside it, but blind to it.

Canny left the bathroom and continued the way the man had been headed. As she went, she fingered the long strip of signs at the top of the panels. There were whole sentences there, with full stops but without capitals. The words—if they were words—all ran together, and Canny got the feeling she was looking at whole stories that amounted to a single instruction. She had no idea what that instruction was, or why it would take such exhaustive exactitude, such persuasion, to turn it from a request into a law.

Canny went through the kitchen. The honey and bread had been put away. She hurried out the back door and was confronted by a startling sight.

The young man had strung up one of the rabbits by a thong tied around its back legs. Its head wobbled on its broken neck. Its eyes were still bright, but the spark of life was falling away from them. As Canny appeared, the man had just finished making a series of deft incisions around the rabbit's bound legs. He then clamped the bloody knife in his teeth, grimacing to keep his lips off its sharp edges. He fiddled with the insertion, got purchase, and stripped the rabbit's skin off, like someone pulling off a very tight sock. Then he spat the knife back into his hand and cut the rabbit down. All this was done within sight of the other rabbits. They were staring, and utterly still. They were transfixed; and so was Canny, so much so that when the man turned to the kitchen door and came on, knife in one hand and rabbit in the other, Canny drew a startled breath and dodged out of his way.

The man broke stride and stopped completely still. Canny froze. Only a foot separated the two of them. When he'd stopped the rabbit had swung, and several drops of blood splashed Canny's ankle. She saw that the rabbit's ears still had fur on them. Droplets of blood were beaded on the fur.

The man's head swiveled away from Canny, then back toward her. His nostrils flared and his mouth opened. His eyes were unfocused—they flicked back and forth. Then he dropped the knife and the rabbit and lunged forward. He pushed Canny back into the wall, and his sticky palm slapped her forehead and started scrubbing—wiping away her spell.

9

"**Iris sent you,** didn't she?" His hand stayed on her brow, pressing her head against the door frame. Her shoulders were bent into the right angle of wall and door, the tips of her shoulder blades smarting where they had struck. His knee was between her legs, and she couldn't move. His hand stank of blood. It was smothering her. She could only say, muffled, "No. No."

He shook her, and she let out a squeal of fear.

"That's Iris," he said, and jabbed his fingernail into the flesh of her forehead.

Canny could see her own hands now—or she was finally able to look at them properly. They were bunched on his chest. She was too intimidated to grab his shirt or to hit him. The muscles her hands rested on were springy. His skin radiated warmth through the fabric of his shirt. She was too shaken even to make her hands into fists.

His eyes were a vivid black, softened by long thick

lashes. The way he was looking at her, it was as if he still couldn't see her, or she wasn't quite real to him.

Canny managed to say, "You're hurting me."

He let go, stepped back, and she came up off the wall, not meaning to make a break for it, only to relieve the tortured tendons of her neck and shoulders. He put up a hand, palm out toward her, and she was pressed back again. He didn't lay the hand on her, instead the air between them seemed to compress and solidify, and she was held painfully in place.

"Iris can't care about you," he said. "I hope you understand that." He flexed the fingers of the raised hand and inscribed a series of graceful symbols in the air. Semitransparent sparks of sign appeared around his hand. They formed a kind of ghostly chain, and then he cast the chain toward her. It lashed out and wrapped itself around her, pinning her arms to her sides.

Canny toppled over, hit the boards of the porch hard with her arm and knees and head. Her sight went black, and then filled with silvery sparks. For a time she went away. She was swimming in the dark. Then she was looking at stepping-stones made of patches of moss. The ewe hurried toward her over the moss, her flanks heaving. There was a deep roaring, and the ewe was swallowed by a wall of fire—or perhaps turned into one—flame, blue at its edges, and orange-white at its heart.

Canny came back to herself and yelled.

"Go on. Relieve your feelings," said the man.

She found herself in the front hallway, lying in a splash of colored light. He was standing over her. He put his fingers in his ears and waited, looking fastidious, while she shouted for help. She gave up only when she finally got hold of herself.

He unblocked his ears and said, "Finished?"

Canny nodded.

"You just lie there," he said. "I have some work I want to get on with."

"I was watching you working before," she said.

"I don't want to have a conversation with you, girlie."

He left her. After a time she could hear him in the kitchen. There was the sound of a shovel chopping into a coal bin. The iron doors of the range opened and closed, handles squeaking and locking with a metallic bite. A little later she heard him at the kitchen bench, jointing the rabbit—heard knife, chopping board, gristly resistance. He went outside for a time and then returned. A tap ran. He cut carrots and shelled peas—she could hear the pop and unzip of the pods. He'd switched off the radio in the parlor and switched on another in the kitchen. He was listening to a radio play on the National Program—two fruity-sounding people having a brittle argument.

Canny rolled over to check something. Yes, all the light fittings on the walls of the house were gas. Brass fittings, with woven asbestos mantles, and a wing nut to raise and lower the flame.

Canny heard water coming to the boil and then the hollow splash of stuff dropped into a pot. These were all orderly, purposeful, domestic noises. Noises she should have been reassured by. And just because she'd happened on him skinning a rabbit he'd been tenderly feeding a few hours before, that didn't mean he was dangerous. People raised rabbits to eat. It was a frugal thing to do, particularly for a country person who couldn't just dash down to the local butcher. He had blood on his hands, but everything else he did was civilized in a countrified way—except tying her up and leaving her lying in the hallway.

After an hour he reappeared. He asked whether she was comfortable.

"No."

"Good." He opened the front door. The sun was past the zenith and sinking toward the horizon. It came at an angle into the hall.

"If there's no electricity, how do your radios work?" she asked.

"How indeed," he said.

"And there's no evidence of a gas line up the hill."

"There's a gas house behind the main house. It's carbide gas, made of carbide and water."

"Of course," she said.

He looked at her and lifted an eyebrow. "A girl who is good at chemistry," he said. Then, "Electric light is cold. I prefer gaslight."

He had a couple of pencils in his hand. He put one on the floor and straightened to face the wall. He looked at the shape his shadow made, and, with practiced movements, he sketched around its outline. He even drew his drawing hand. Then he sat down and made a beginning at the skirting board. He began to fill in the life-size shape of his shadow, very slowly, with little blocks made of six vertical strokes of the pencil, with a seventh, horizontal, running through them.

Canny had twisted herself around to watch. She recognized these marks from the movies as a prisoner's calendar, each block representing a week. Monday, Tuesday, Wednesday, Thursday, Friday, Saturday—all crossed by Sunday.

"Are you doing that for my benefit?" she asked.

"In what way would it benefit you?"

"I mean, are you doing it to scare me?"

"Does it scare you?"

Canny didn't answer.

He was quiet for a time, and then finally said, "I do this every day."

Of course he didn't. The wall showed no sign of having been drawn on before, or painted over. She didn't believe him but still asked, "Why do you do it?"

"How about you tell me why the spell on your forehead has such lousy grammar? Is Iris finally going senile?"

She didn't know how to answer.

He went on drawing, his back turned to her, his pencil scratching and scratching. He said softly, "I sketch around my shadow because my shadow tells me I'm still here. I like to keep a count of how long."

The sun coming through the doorway moved onto Canny's face. She closed her eyes and dozed for a time. When she woke up the sun had set and the gas was lit, giving off a soft yellow-white light. Moths were circling the incandescent mantle. The man was still working on the figure, which was filled in all the way up to its chin. He seemed to sense that Canny was awake. He didn't look at her, but said, "So they brought you back to the valley to spy on me. Didn't they tell you what would happen?"

"That you'd catch me?"

"I might not have. But you've mastered the Alphabet, so you should know as well as they do that since the second Great Spell is theirs, not yours, you've no protection against it. The longer you spend here the more likely it is that the spell will suck all your skill out of you—your skill, and your life force, maybe beyond recovery."

"They didn't tell me that," she said, wondering how she could get him to tell her exactly who "they" were.

"Whose are you? A niece of Iris's perhaps?"

"I don't exactly know who I am," she said. "But I have a brother here. Sholto. He'll be terribly worried about me. You have to let me go."

"I don't have to do anything. My quota of things I have to do is filled up for life. It's like I'm in a rest home, and incapable. I don't actually have to do anything else—ever."

"You said you had work."

He glanced over her shoulder, and Canny shivered at the sight of the white reflected points of light in the center of his black eyes. "I have put on a stew, which you will have none of," he said. "I've performed my little ritual with the shadow calendar."

"My brother will be looking for me."

The man put down his pencil and sat beside her. He left the figure incompletely filled in. She tilted her head at it and said, "It's not finished."

"No," he said. "It's not full of days." Then, in a tone of musing anticipation, "I hope your brother will come looking for you. Then he can join us. It's nice to have company. And it's fun to test people's professed loyalties. It's a good game, I seem to remember." He put his head on one side, remembering. His face was blank and innocent as he mused, and more beautiful than ever. He seemed to go away, and come back, and then notice her again. Without ceremony he picked her up and carried her into a dark room and deposited her on a couch. When he turned up the gas and pressed the flint striker that lit the flame, Canny saw that the sofa was made of cow's hide, with hair still on it. The room was a library. Its shelves had glass doors. The books were old, leather- and cloth-bound, though there were piles of magazines on the short counter where the shelves for large books ended and the smaller shelves went on up the wall.

The man left the room for a moment and came back with a steaming plate of stew, which he ate, with great enjoyment, in front of her.

Canny's stomach rumbled and her mouth filled with saliva.

He sucked the little rabbit bones, relishing them, then he licked his fingers and leaned back in his chair. He sighed with satisfaction.

"I don't suppose you have many guests," Canny said.

He laughed. "You're so funny. Very cool. That was a very polite, prissy question."

"I am cool. Quite famously—though, to tell the truth, I haven't appreciated it before now." She wriggled, but the nothing visible binding her wouldn't relent.

He slid off the couch and shuffled across the floor to her. He bent close and stroked her cheek with a tacky, rabbity finger. "But you are scared?" he said, as if he needed her to reassure him she was.

"Yes. I'd be stupid not to be. Though mostly I'm worried about Sholto. He's kind of bossy, but I don't like to cause him anxiety."

"So Iris didn't tell you not to use names?"

"Oh," said Canny.

"That's one of the first lessons. No names. I know everything is pared back to basics, but surely they must still teach that?"

Canny thought. It was hard to think because his stroking finger had moved from her cheek to her mouth. She liked the feeling of his finger passing across her lips—and, at the same time, she wanted to bite him.

"You don't look scared," he said.

"My face doesn't move. Bad forceps delivery. Damaged nerves." Canny silently thanked her lying mother.

For a moment she thought she detected a look of delicate sympathy on his face. That made her wonder whether some of his craziness was put on. He had her tied up and wouldn't feed her, but was sorry to hear she had damaged facial nerves. "Um," she said stupidly, "about the names— they do rhyme. That's a kind of camouflage, isn't it?"

"It makes it hard to address ill will to any one person if there's several of them with same-sounding names. Curses are dim-witted and have a poor sense of direction. So—I suppose if there is a Sholto, there's a Waldo?"

Canny snorted.

He frowned at her and said, "Having several names is better, but it isn't something anyone can arrange. You can't deliberately change your name. The differences have to evolve naturally, so that they represent slightly different identities."

Canny thought of her own names. She was Akanesi Afa as a child. Then Agnes Mochrie when she came to Castlereagh and the Professor adopted her. Her teachers called her either Akanesi or Agnes. Her classmates and Sholto called her Canny. Marli called her Canny or Akanesi. If anyone wanted to address something malicious to her, the names probably would serve as a baffle.

"What's so funny?" he asked.

"I don't know *your* name," she told him.

"Of course you do." He looked scornful, as if he didn't know why she'd bother to lie.

"I know some things about you, but not your name."

He linked his fingers, wrapped them around his knee and leaned back. He looked like someone waiting to be entertained. "Do tell."

"I know you're pretending to be crazy to scare me. And I know you're a prisoner. There's a spell on Fort Rock that makes people unable to tear their eyes from it so that they won't look at the view of the Zarene Valley. Because Fort Rock is the only place from which it's possible to see this house."

He took a deep breath and said, "That last part— everyone knows that."

"By 'everyone' you mean Zarenes?"

"Only Zarenes count."

"Naturally." Canny was disgusted.

"As for the first part. I have been crazy. I could easily be crazy again. In fact, once you've been crazy the possibility of slippage feels like the only real certainty. The odds are short."

"Do I get any credit for having worked it out?"

"Even Iris wouldn't keep her creatures in such dark ignorance. I'm sure you were briefed."

"I'm not Iris's creature."

This time he didn't jab her forehead, only pressed a fingertip there. "Iris's spell equals Iris's creature."

Canny decided to start telling the truth—or at least some of it. She was hesitant, particularly since he'd made that remark about only Zarenes counting. She had felt that already about those Zarenes she'd met—their exclusivity. Bonnie was curious, but Canny had felt when she was talking to the girl that she was being taken not as herself but as representative, and what she represented to Bonnie was *other people*. People who weren't quite as good as the Zarenes. Lonnie had given her a headache, and then smirked at her in an unpleasant anticipatory way, as if she were a frog and he had just poked a firecracker into her backside. She was sure her headache was supposed to get much worse, only she'd thrown it off. Iris was superior, and had played games with Sholto when he was upset. Lealand was frosty. In fact only Cyrus Zarene seemed okay. So the Zarenes were insular, and tribal, and in possession of great power, and only they counted. She got that. And that was why she'd only tell some of the truth.

"I copied part of one of Iris's spells and added it to part

of another. It was the 'Look at me' spell from Fort Rock with a kind of 'Don't' added to it."

"You can't copy part of one of Iris's spells. They don't come in parts," he said, disbelieving.

"I did though," she said. "Everything is divisible."

"Except zero."

"Well—yes," Canny muttered, surprised to encounter someone who spoke mathematics.

He regarded her for a time. Then he made a little gesture, and the soft nothingness that had held her melted away.

She sat up and rubbed her wrists like some movie heroine who had just been untied, though the bonds hadn't constrained her wrists or ankles, or chafed her skin.

He looked at this playacting and raised an eyebrow. Then he got up and helped her to her feet. He pushed the swiveling wall lamp beside the fireplace so that instead of shining out of the big mirror above the mantelpiece it shone hard on the decorative molding of the mantelpiece itself. "All right," he said. "Make something different out of some of that."

Canny peered at the long line of symbols, of sign overlapping sign. She said, "It's like Chinese writing."

"It's like everything of Iris's—ideogrammatic."

"Yes," said Canny, who hadn't remembered the word but knew that was right, that Chinese was in ideograms.

"Yes *what?*" he said. Then, very exasperated, "I can't tell whether you're pretending to know more than you do, or less than you do."

Canny laughed.

His jaw dropped slightly. He was still for a moment, then

said in a very different tone from any he'd used so far, "Your face moves. Do you really think it doesn't?"

Her face heated up. She put her hands on her cheeks to cool them. Perhaps it looked to him as if she was feeling for movement—surprised by it herself.

"Maybe you're getting better," he said.

Canny felt awkward and embarrassed, so returned her attention to the carvings. She felt as if she was peeling them apart layer by layer to study their component parts. The young man kept quiet and let her look.

"Is this Iris's?" she asked.

"Hardly," he said, dismissive.

Canny touched the carvings, followed them with her eyes and finger. She followed them along the mantel, and onto the wall, and along the carved strip at the top of the panel. The big shouting syllables of the stained-glass window were part of it too. It wove around the room and out the door. It wound through the house, putting a mark on every immovable surface, and some movable—like doors and windows. Finally, as she followed it, it seemed to leave the walls and swim before her, like whitebait in a river at dawn—alive, transparent, multitudinous.

Once she lost it, as if the river had vanished underground, but it was only because she'd lost the light when she walked crabwise into a dark room. Then he was there, behind her with a candle, lighting her way.

Canny read on. Her ears began to ring—and then all the signs were melting, and coming apart, and flying upward like sparks. She closed her eyes and watched them, tearing at the inside of her eyelids, burning, ceaselessly moving, and ceaselessly *meaning something she couldn't understand*.

She cried out and fell. He caught her. He held her and she heard him saying, "Sorry. I'm sorry." Then her brain mercifully shut down into nothing more than the pain and nausea and animal misery of the worst migraine of her life.

HE SEEMED TO UNDERSTAND HER PLIGHT. He got her into a dark room, and lying down. The bed was fresh and sweet and comfortable—not unused or stale. Maybe it was his room, but it didn't smell occupied either. He put a shaded candle on a table on the far side of the room and a bowl by the bed, and a cold cloth on her head.

She managed to tell him to go away. She didn't want him to see her vomiting.

He did leave her, and she was alone with it—the horrible sensation that someone had washed her face and scalp in hot water, and both were drying, shrinking, and tightening around her skull. If she didn't move, not even her eyelids, the pain was almost bearable.

She was grieving too. She'd seen something, but hadn't been able to hold it in her head long enough for a recognition—the kind of recognition that wasn't just her understanding something, but the something coming to life when she looked at it and looking back at her. Very complicated equations did that when she solved them. They came to life. The universe came to life and looked back at her.

WHEN SHE WOKE UP THERE WAS SUNLIGHT filtering through the curtains. The bowl by the bed had been emptied and rinsed. The door was open, and the air smelled of beeswax.

How could someone hope to pass as a madman when they were such an accomplished housekeeper? Canny would have laughed if she'd dared move her jaw. She lay still for a long time, drifting, exhausted, and simply grateful that the pain had gone. She was finally roused by the sound of voices. The young man's first. From his tone he was asking a question, though she didn't hear what. Then someone else answered, tersely. "I think the customary greeting is 'Hello,' Ghislain. You're supposed to say, 'Hello, how are you?'"

"Come on—two visits in one week? Of course I'm surprised," said the young man, whose name was Ghislain.

Canny sat bolt upright. She swung her legs out of bed. Her scalp felt threateningly tender, but she persisted. She glanced out the window.

It was Cyrus Zarene. He was standing on the lawn, by the hedge of roses and lavender at the edge of the terrace. She couldn't see Ghislain, who was beneath her on the veranda.

Cyrus said, "There's a girl missing. A guest. Sixteen years of age. From Castlereagh. We wondered if she'd come up here."

"How would she manage that?" said Ghislain.

"It's happened before. People have found their way up here."

"Not for a long time. The road is overgrown."

"You haven't seen anyone?"

"I saw you. Six days ago."

"No girl?"

"What would I do with a girl?"

There was a silence. Cyrus Zarene looked up at the house, and Canny stepped back out of view. She did it without thinking. She didn't want to be seen by Cyrus—or found again by Ghislain. Which meant she had best leave by another door, or window, while the two of them were occupied.

She went out along the hall to the head of the stairs. The front door was open. She could see the young man's shadow on the perfectly sanded boards of the veranda. But she couldn't see the drawing, the silhouette on the wall. There was no sign of last night's prisoner's calendar.

She heard: "If you don't believe me, you could always come indoors and conduct a search." Then, after a pause, "I thought not."

Canny ran back the way she'd come. In big old houses like this there was often a servants' staircase. It would lead off the upper hall, where she was. There would be a passage off the hall, with servants' little rooms and back stairs.

But she didn't find what she was looking for—and of course she didn't, how could such secretive people ever have lived with servants, outsiders, in their houses?

Canny was cursing herself for stupidly losing time. She darted into a bedroom. It was unused, the mattress was doubled up on the bare springs of the bed. Canny threw up the sash and poked her head out. There was no sign of a fire escape on the back of the house. It was an eight-foot drop from the windowsill to the veranda roof. Canny didn't hesitate. She climbed over the sill and briefly dangled by her hands, then let go.

Her feet hit the tiles and promptly slid out from under her. The roof was too steeply sloped for anyone to stand on it comfortably. Canny came down on her knees and her chin hit the weatherboard wall. She bit her tongue. But there wasn't any time to pause and nurse it. She had to keep moving. She dropped onto her belly and slid down the roof till her feet hit the gutter. Then she gathered herself to look back. It was at least eighteen feet to the ground. Perhaps she could shimmy down a veranda post. She turned herself around and hung her head over to locate one, and then she turned back around and edged along the veranda roof till she was above it. She took hold of the gutter and swung herself out into space. The gutter creaked loudly as the bands fastening it popped open. It sagged away from the roof. Canny kicked out and hooked one leg around the post she was aiming for. Then the other leg. She gripped the post with her thighs and then with the soles of her feet, using them as her older boy cousins had when they were climbing coconut palms back on Lost Link.

The gutter was still protesting, but she'd taken most of her weight off it. She let go with one hand and snatched for the post. Her legs had it, but her hand hit the fancy woodwork along the eaves. Her knuckles crunched. She got a grip on the woodwork and let go of the gutter. Her bare legs squeaked on the freshly painted post. Its surface clung to her skin and burned as she slid.

Then a hand closed on her right ankle. Another moved under her left foot. The hands took part of her weight.

Canny found another handhold on the woodwork. She dropped lower and he moved his grip to hold her behind the knee. He didn't say, "Let go," but she did let go. She had no choice but to trust him. She dropped, and he opened his arms so that she slid through them, his hands on her thighs, then her back, then her shoulders. He set her feet on the boards of the veranda. For a minute she gazed into hard, mineral-black eyes. She couldn't read anything there—no amusement, or displeasure—nothing at all. His face was masklike. And there was something else wrong with him—something missing.

She struggled out of his arms and took off. She ran, waiting for the soft rope of signs and air to trip her and tie her up again. She sprinted across the lawn and jumped over the roses and lavender, forgetting that they marked the edge of the terrace. She jumped up three feet and sailed over the lavender, its flags brushing her feet. Before she could do anything about it she was out over the ten-foot drop to the terrace below, with a bamboo bean frame directly below her. Then something scooped her up and threw her sideways, so that her fall became a leisurely arc to the right of where she'd jumped. She fell like a badminton shuttlecock rather than a body. She dropped into a compost heap and was enveloped in its heat and thick vegetable stink.

Canny lay stunned and, once again, waited to be recaptured. She waited for the young man to appear at the edge of the terrace. But no one came. She got up and peeled some black fibrous mats made of turnip tops, lettuce leaves, and eggshells off her clothes. And it was while she was doing this that she realized what had been missing. The young man had been holding her tight. She'd been pressed against him, and his body had had no scent. He had smelled of nothing at all.

Canny climbed off the heap of compost and went looking for the steps to the lower, overgrown terrace. She had to go all the way around the front, where she heard voices again. It appeared that, after helping her down from the veranda roof, Ghislain had gone back to Cyrus. Perhaps Cyrus had been in the house searching while the young man had come to help her.

Ghislain had come to her assistance, and Cyrus meant her no harm—so why was she hiding from them? Why did she feel that, no matter what, she must get away unseen? It was inexplicable, this urgent need to stay hidden.

She reached the steps and ran down them, then found her way to the pig path and slid and scrambled her way down it, her eyes out for wild boar and her heart pressing painfully under her collarbone.

10

SHOLTO GOT UP that Thursday shortly after Canny had left the guesthouse. He didn't look in on her, so wasn't to know all day that she was missing. He too took an apple from the fruit bowl in Iris Zarene's kitchen and ate it as he walked down the valley to the meadow where they'd left the Austin. He drove to Massenfer and, at eight in the morning, reported at the gate of Massenfer colliery. He gave his name and waited in the custodian's little shelter for George Mews, the mine safety manager.

It was a bit of a wait. The custodian stirred several teaspoons of condensed milk into his coffee and sat back on the stool with his belly in his lap. He didn't look at Sholto again. The corrugated tin roof popped as if a large bird had landed on it. It was the sun, coming out from behind the clouds. Before long the little shelter was stifling.

George Mews, mine safety manager at the Cleverly Mine, had, thirty years before, gone into the Massenfer's

Bull Mine after the explosion to search for survivors. Mr. Mews's condition for letting Sholto interview him had been that Sholto first take a tour of the Cleverly to see how things had improved in the intervening years.

Sholto waited twenty-five minutes, and then Mews appeared. Mews was a squat, powerfully built, balding man. He handed Sholto a clean pair of overalls, a helmet, and a belt onto which was clipped a self-rescue breather. Sholto put everything on. Mews said, "We'll walk up to the portal, Mr. Mochrie, and I'll give you a quick lesson with the breather before we go underground. But I won't do to you what we do with the new lads. *Them* we walk up and down the gateway till they're stinking hot and sick of sucking air through the filters—all so they can get some idea of what they'd have to do in an emergency."

"The men in '29 didn't have these," Sholto said, getting right down to it. After all, the man hadn't even wanted to shake his hand.

"You're wrong about that, Mr. Mochrie. They did. But they were all still clipped to their belts." Mews tapped the box. "Theirs were a bit more primitive. But the Draeger Rebreathers that rescuers wear nowadays have hardly changed at all from the one I was wearing when I entered the mine after the explosion in '29."

The portal to the mine was huge and square and framed by steel. There was one big old axle-and-gear winch nearby, and two vast ventilation outlets, both apparently pulling atmosphere out.

Mews took Sholto through the drill. The filters on the mask made Sholto's breathing into a business that required real effort. He was glad when the lesson was over and he was allowed to take the mask off again.

Then, without any further ceremony, Mews led Sholto underground. About thirty yards in they met the shift manager. "This young man is here for a history professor," Mews shouted, flipped his eyebrows at the other man, and then drew Sholto farther in.

They walked alongside the conveyor that carried the coal from the distant diggings to the surface. It was noisy. Mews leaned in to ask Sholto to please notice how wet the coal was. "A safety measure, of course." The conveyor dripped and the ground squelched underfoot.

After a few minutes of steady downhill trudging they stopped at a crosscut. The conveyor was farther off, and Mews could speak. He asked what Sholto thought of the gateway. "The gateway is what you might call the mineshaft."

"It's quite steep," Sholto said. He'd been looking back at the portal now and then as they walked. They hadn't gone very far before the floor had come up to close off the daylight, like the inverted eyelid of some giant, mythical creature.

Mews took Sholto's arm again and they angled back toward the conveyor and continued along beside it. Neither they nor it were going very fast, but their combined speeds, going different directions, made Sholto's head spin. He was very nervous and painfully alert. He couldn't seem to keep his head still. He kept looking about and casting his helmet lamp over everything.

Mews stopped to point out the blocks of timber mortared into the wall of the mine. He explained that beyond that was a sealed void. "What we call a gob. It'll be full of methane. The gas keeps coming out of the coal that's left when the seam has been mined. Now, at Bull what happened is that they probably accidentally broke through into an old gob. The gas escaped and spread, and there was a spark somewhere. They had a machine like our continuous miner at their working face. A kind of digger with steel belts covered in fist-size picks that claw at the face, ripping coal from the seam. The men at the machine had reported seeing sparks running on the back of its picks."

Sholto knew that this was the front-running theory: that there was a breakthrough into an old void, the methane level went up, and despite all the water on the machinery, there was a spark. He said to Mews, "I've read that the whole shaft was shut off after it flooded in '26. And the mine had a safety review—and yet there was still an accident."

"That's right. Though you have to remember that, in 1926, it was the *company* in charge of safety and the safety review, not the government. The government didn't get involved until after the disaster. That's what your da's book is about—the changes in labor laws. In '26, when the mine flooded, thirteen men were trapped. Nine were saved, after being underground for three days. Four drowned. One of the draegermen who went with me into the mine in '29 after the explosion had been in Bull when it flooded in '26. He'd been trapped and rescued. He was working as a chain runner in '29. Chain runners take care of the conveyors, or rail carts. We had carts and horses in the Bull. In '29 this man was on the night shift, so he wasn't underground when it happened. When we went down after the explosion he was all for keeping going, because he'd been saved himself against terrible odds. But the deeper we penetrated, the less there was left to find." Mews paused and stared off into the dark. "Of course none of us wanted to leave the eleven men we had to leave. They're still there today. Anyway—this fellow—the sheriff's deputies had to drag him away from the pit."

"He had family down there?"

"Yes. He was a Zarene, from the valley. Lealand Zarene. Many of us had family trapped. And we all had mates. I lost my sister's husband. He's still down there."

After the explosion the coal seam in Bull Mine caught fire and hadn't stopped burning until the lower shaft was flooded. They pumped the water out again, but the strata had been fatally weakened, and the mine was too unsafe to reopen, even to look for whatever remained of the men who couldn't be reached. The pit was closed, there was a final memorial service, and a monument was unveiled. Sholto had seen photographs of the service.

Mews was quiet for a time. Sholto didn't want to break in on the man's memories so didn't immediately go on with his questions—like, why was the mine shaft so white? There was rock dust everywhere, coating the walls and floor, and there were bags of it at every crosscut. Eventually he said, "The mine is white."

"Yes," said Mews. "The floor of the gateway in the Bull was very soft underfoot. And black. I remember that. The stone dust here—they throw it around pretty liberally. The proportion has to be more than half stone dust to coal dust before the coal dust is rendered noninflammable. They had only just started stone-dusting back then. They were stone-dusting at the working face, but not the length of the gateway. It was burning coal dust ignited by exploding methane that produced the carbon monoxide that killed most of the men who died in '29."

"Afterdamp," Sholto said.

"That's what it's called, or chokedamp. Take your pick."

"If I was to take a pick down here I'd only embarrass myself," Sholto said, and was pleased to hear Mews laugh. Then the man asked, "How old are you, Mr. Mochrie?"

"Twenty-three," said Sholto.

"The youngest man in the mine today is seventeen. In '29 the youngest was fourteen, a kid called Felix Zarene."

Sholto was sweating. He was having a hard time keeping his eyes on Mews's face. The headlamps made any direct eye contact almost impossible, and Mews had a habitual sidelong glance, his head tilted down so that his helmet lamp lit where his feet would go, while his eyes turned up. This up-under-the-brows scrutiny made Mews look very shrewd, and a bit skeptical too. "You keep looking at the ceiling, Mr. Mochrie," he said, sounding amused. "Those arches up there are steel and timber. We timber as we go." He pointed at the steel that studded sections of the ceiling. "Those are rock bolts. They pin together the layers of rock."

"They're holding the roof up?"

"Yes. Perhaps you should have taken a tour of the

Westport Mine. Westport is a roof and pillar mine. They're much more roomy, and not as deep."

"I wasn't planning to go down a mine at all, but I see now that I had to."

"I'm pleased to hear that."

They stopped under a huge vertical shaft. Mews called it a downcast. Sholto could see a flicker of daylight through a giant fan, far above. There was a ladder too, an escape ladder. Sholto couldn't help but think how hard it would be to climb if the shaft was full of smoke.

They went on, trudging downhill for some minutes till they reached the place where coal was being torn from the face of the seam by a big, steel-toothed machine.

"This is the inbye," shouted Mews. "That's what we call the working face. We are now a mile underground." Mews showed Sholto into the flame-proof enclosure of the gate-end box, where all the equipment was. The continuous miner was clawing at the face and feeding broken coal back onto the conveyor.

Sholto saw that there were bags of stone dust everywhere, apparently waiting to be spread. He asked if the equipment was stopped so that that could be done.

"No, these bags are what are called a passive barrier. If there's an explosion the force of it throws the stone dust up into the air and the stone dust suppresses the fire. We use stone dust and barrels of water as passive barriers. You will have noticed the bags and barrels everywhere."

Sholto didn't quite get it. He said, "Sorry, but isn't that shutting the stable door after the horse has bolted?"

Mews patiently explained that explosions were made of a shock wave and fire. It was the shock wave that dispersed the water or dust, and the shock wave moved ahead of the fire. "The shock wave throws up the stone dust and water, then the fire hits the barrier and flames out. The fire flamed out in the Bull when it hit the wet patch that was the result of a continuing leak after the flooding in '26. But the men above the wet patch didn't survive, because there were two fires."

"What?" Sholto thought he mustn't have caught that right. Did Mews say *two* fires?

There were three miners working under the drill canopy, keeping a close eye on the machine and the coal face. Lumps of coal were sometimes shaken down from the ceiling by the vibrations. They bounced off the canopy. Sholto could see them rolling and flashing in air that glittered with dust. There was a breeze in his face. It was breezier at the working face than anywhere he'd been so far, except the ventilation shaft. The air was being pulled their way by a huge, wet canvas curtain. Mews saw Sholto looking at the contraption and said, "That's a brattice, auxiliary ventilation. The seam is very gassy this week."

"Oh," said Sholto.

And then it happened. One of the miners craned and peered, then flung up a hand. Several people—including Mews—shouted, "Shut her down! Shut her down!" But not before a plume of flame shot out of an invisible fissure in the face and rolled, blue, across the ceiling.

The men at the hoses hit the fissure with jets of water.

Sholto had dropped into a crouch, his hands over his ears. Water rained down on him. The continuous miner had stopped. The conveyor rattled into silence.

Then the flame was gone. Spray continued to wash the fissure. Mews called out to the men with the hoses, "Stop for a minute, would you?"

He tugged Sholto's arm, then stepped up onto the continuous miner. The machine had pulled back from the face and its steel claws could be climbed. "Come on," Mews said.

Sholto was terrified, his arms and legs stiff and reluctant, but he followed the man. The picks were dripping and cold, but sharp, and Sholto was glad of his gloves. But once he was perched up by the fissure, Mews made him remove one glove. Mews pressed Sholto's fingers to the fissure. "That's a blower," he said.

Sholto felt the warm, silky pressure of the gas against his palm. He nodded to Mews to show he felt it, and they climbed down again.

Mews checked the three gasometers. Everyone stood about in the silence, Sholto watching the glowing filaments of the electric lightbulbs—a source of fire behind a shell of fragile glass. He was grateful for the light, and afraid of it. His heart was pounding. The only sound was the ventilation, and the hiss and splash of the hoses. Mews sat Sholto down on the conveyor and got settled himself. "When it starts up again we can ride it out," he said.

"Won't they need you here?"

"Once they can start up again they won't want me breathing down their necks. The blower will exhaust itself. The gas will dissipate. There is much less already. I can scarcely smell it."

"I could smell it up there."

"Yes. Gas gathers against the roof. The week before the explosion in '29 the mine definitely smelled of gas. But it wasn't one leak. It wasn't just the breakthrough to the gassy void, no matter what you hear said. Look, there were things we didn't know then that we know now. Now we have barometers in mines. Did you know that coal leaks gas when the barometric pressure goes down? Bet you didn't. In '29 there was a storm, a nasty one. It hung over the western arm of the Palisades for three days. We miners were quite glad to be underground and out of it. It was mostly wind, not rain, or we'd have been worried about flooding. But the whole mine was bleeding methane."

"I'd never heard any of that before," Sholto said.

"Look it up, kid. The meteorological records. The county council road reports. There was a huge slip in the Lazuli Gorge. The scar has grown over, but it's still visible."

Sholto realized he'd come for eyewitness stories—not scientific analysis. For his father, the Bull Mine disaster was the story of the inquiry and the labor law changes. It was the story of the disaster's impact on the growth of the unions. How it changed all the government's plans for the southwest. And how all that related to the stock market crash. The Professor was always talking about material realities, but Sholto was beginning to see that the Professor's view of what was material, and real, was perhaps a little limited.

Mews was sitting on the still conveyor, picking up lumps

of coal, looking at them and putting them back like someone holding up eggs to a bright light to check for the shadowy patch that would show they were fertilized (and unsalable. City people didn't like to find the red spots or little blobs of dark fiber that reminded them that eggs came from chickens and might sometimes contain the beginnings of an embryo). As he studied the coal, Mews said, "Of course at Bull we had rail tracks and horse carts instead of a conveyor. The horses were unshod. Had to be. Horseshoes can cause sparks. They had leather bits and tackle too. The Bull had a narrow point on its gateway, what's called a convergence, where the walls are forced inward, because of rock pressure. The engineers kept reinforcing it, and it kept closing very gradually. The afternoon of the explosion the horses wouldn't go past the convergence. One of the chain runners took note of that and went all the way down to the working face to pull his son out in the middle of his shift. They were both sacked for it. They went off home, and five hours later their teacups rattled. The explosion was at six p.m. and most of the town was sitting down to eat. Everyone knew what it meant when their crockery rattled."

Sholto's family had dinner at eight. Dinner at eight—and an imperfect grasp of material reality. Sholto was feeling ashamed of himself and his comfortable, white-collar life.

The conveyor started up again abruptly and began to carry them away from the coal face. The continuous miner started too and resumed its shrieking rattle when its picks touched the coal seam. Sholto looked back and watched the bright nexus of the inbye recede. After the sound of the continuous miner the conveyor seemed quiet. Still, Sholto had to lean close to Mews when the man started to talk again.

"That man I was telling you about, the one who was all for going back into the mine after the explosion—you're going to want to talk to him. Lealand Zarene. Nine of the thirty-one who died were Zarenes. The Zarenes weren't a mining family, though. Lealand, his father, Colvin, and uncle Talbot had been in the Bull for a good six years, but the rest of them were newbies. The family had land, but not much else, and they were trying to raise money to pay lawyers to fight the Lazuli Dam project. You will have heard about the Lazuli Dam?"

"Yes," Sholto said. He knew that the dam was first planned in the mid-1920s. If it had been built it would have flooded the Zarene Valley and drowned all the orchards. The plans were shelved after the stock market crash, resurrected in 1938, and shelved again when Southland went to war in 1941.

Mews said, "The road up the gorge to the Zarene Valley was built for the dam. It's not exactly a country road. And had the Zarenes ever wanted it a road would have been built through the valley to join the road across the Palisades at Fort Rock."

"They didn't want a road?"

"Not a proper one. There was a narrow dirt road from Fort Rock, but they let that grow over. Anyway, the Zarenes would tell people that they were down the mine to raise money for legal fees. But there's the matter of the life insurance policies."

"Life insurance policies?"

"You should ask the Zarenes about that. Anyway—as I understand it, the whole Lazuli Dam idea is back on the table. This government is very big on hydroelectricity."

Sholto was tired of trying to hear over the sound of the machinery. Also, since he was safely on his way out of the mine he felt he should take a good look around and get impressions, make the most of the experience. He hated the place. Hated the bolted roof over his head. Hated the timber brickwork behind which the gas lay like a sleeping dragon. And the moment the white slot of the mine's mouth appeared, he had to suppress the urge to jump off the conveyor and run up the incline and back into the light.

They dismounted from the conveyor at the portal. Mews stopped to talk to some workers. Sholto walked out under the open sky. He wanted to remove his helmet, but knew that it wasn't permitted till he was back on the far side of the colliery gates.

Mews joined him. "I'm afraid I've complicated your story."

He had. Sholto's story was to have been all eyewitness accounts. The ordeal. The sorrow. The words of the men who'd had to front up to newspapers and the government inquiry. Sholto had loved all the color of the tale and appreciated the politics. But from Mews he'd gotten geology and engineering and economics. Plus a storm, insurance policies, and *two fires*. He was being asked to consider—actually, he wasn't entirely sure what he was being asked to consider. He said, "Is there anyone I can talk to about the plans to dam the Lazuli?"

"The historical plans, or the recent ones? Your girl-friend will have found things in the newspaper archive in the Massenfer library."

"She's not researching this."

"But she is researching?"

"Folklore. Stories about witchcraft."

"Oh," said Mews. He looked hard at Sholto. A moment passed, and then he said, "I've been working in coal mines for thirty-five years now. I know what is and isn't possible. When there are accidents in mines, there are always people wanting a miracle. And when a miracle happens, they thank God and don't think too hard about the odds. One man walked out of Bull Mine after the explosion in '29, and one was carried out. The man who was carried out was a chain runner working the shift opposite Lealand Zarene—his cousin Cyrus. Cyrus Zarene was with his horse team, riding a car near the top of the gate. He was blown up the gateway, and when we went in we found him almost straight-away, unconscious, and with a busted leg. The other survi-vor claimed he was around the corner of the crosscut at South Main, having a cup of tea. He said the fire went right on past him, up the shaft. But that isn't possible. Fire goes anywhere there's air. Some people will tell you that the pattern of burns on the debris showed that a fire had gone *down* the shaft from the crosscut at South Main. It came up from the working face where the explosion was, flamed out at the wet patch, then a *second fire* came down from the crosscut at South Main. A second fire that *started* there. People will tell you that. Of course I think the rea-son the other survivor—Ghislain Zarene—walked out of the mine with scarcely any soot on him, when everyone else was dead, was because he hadn't been down the shaft at all when it happened. He can't have been. The only possible explanation is that he clocked on, then climbed out the Bull's downcast—except I can't say why he would have, except that he knew the mine would explode. So there's that. And there's the life insurance policies, of which he was one of the beneficiaries—though he couldn't have set them up himself because he was only seventeen and too young to sign a legal document. But there are those who will tell you that of course it was a Zarene who survived. And of course it was that one."

Sholto frowned at the mine safety manager, who had spent the last hours challenging his ignorance, but who had been otherwise very helpful. Why was Mews now spinning this strange story?

Mews caught Sholto's look of skepticism, and his face cooled. He looked away. He said, "The barbershop in Massenfer has local historical photos on its walls. Go in and have a look. There's a photograph there that people say is of that Zarene lad, taken about four years before he went down the mine. It was taken at a school picnic in the Zarene Valley. The Zarene children used to ride over on their horses to go to the school in Massenfer. I had a couple in my class. Anyway, have a look at that picture and make up your own mind."

THE BARBER TOLD Sholto he'd be with him shortly. There was a man already in the chair. The barber gestured with his scissors at a bench by the door.

Sholto said he'd amuse himself by having a look at the historical photographs.

"All my uncle Jim's," said the barber. "He worked for the *Messenger*, 1907 to 1927."

"An institution in himself," said the man in the chair. "Jim Bindle."

"He opened a studio after that and photographed just about every wedding on the Peninsula for the next fifteen years."

"My wedding too," said the man in the chair.

"That's him as a young fellow," the barber said, and pointed with his scissors again.

Sholto had been so busy attending to the history of Jim Bindle that his perusal of the photos had stuck at a panoramic picture of the massed employees of the timber mill. He crossed the room to give Bindle's portrait a few moments of polite inspection. It showed a thin, tanned young man in a white duster coat, leaning on a small cairn. "He was a dreamhunter!" said Sholto.

"Ranger," said the barber. "He was making photographic landmark maps for the Dream Regulatory Body."

The silence of loss came into the room.

As an undergraduate Sholto had once tried to write an essay about this. The Professor said that it was very interesting, but was Sholto trying to invent a new kind of history? One without historical references and facts? Sholto's essay argued something like this: Southland was a big country, with a population that was sufficiently large but not too large; with industry and a wealth of minerals; with scientifically developed agriculture, good roads and rail, three deepwater harbors, some fine universities—so why wasn't it more of a player on the world stage? Sholto's answer to his essay's question was that Southlanders were in a sense a sad and defeated people. They were people who had once lived in a beautiful house, which had burned down. They had a way of life that vanished overnight. There were remnants—like Massenfer's oddly shaped hotel, once a dream palace. But all the remnants were reminders. Of the great twenty-year boom, a boom that had elevated ordinary people into great wealth and fame, nothing remained. Southlanders had had something irreplaceable—the Place, a mysterious territory where some could go and catch dreams that they could perform for others—they had that miraculous thing, and they lost it.

Sholto's father's generation were raised by parents baffled by loss and defeated by grief. The Professor said that Sholto's essay's conclusion—that Southlanders were people who had everything going for them, but were spoiled—was the kind of thesis that only a glib young man could come up with. Susan had read that essay too. She and Sholto had only just met. Susan admired it, which had made Sholto warm to her. She said it was brilliant and quite right. "People get over things," she said, "even families do. But cultures don't. Or maybe cultures are made up of the things that people don't get over."

Sholto gazed at the energetic young Bindle and sighed. He moved on to a picture of the Massenfer road rail bridge under construction. A picture of a school theatrical performance, the boys wearing beards drawn on with burnt cork. A picture of a landslide, and one of loggers crowded on the stump of a vast tree. Then he came to a series of pictures of the school picnic, 1925, with women in striped cotton frocks sitting in cars or pony traps stuffed with picnic baskets and holding infants in sailor suits. Men in shirtsleeves having a tug of war with three times their number of boys. There was the usual rag tied on the rope between them. It was a humorous photo. It looked like a woman had dashed forward to move the long ruler that marked the place the rag must not cross. She was helping the boys to win. Sholto took a closer look. She was beautiful, with sleek dark hair and the smooth brow and half-circle eyelids of an Italian Madonna. Sholto was sure it was Iris Zarene.

The last photo in the series was a great surprise. Its background was the same field spread with picnic rugs and baskets. It was late in the day. The well-dressed children were now barefoot and sunburned. The shadows were long and low—including the shadows of the stones floating above the boy's head, one that looked as if it was a bird about to alight on his shoulder and one hanging by his face and throwing a slash of shadow across his smiling mouth. The boy was kneeling, one hand on the grass. His other hand was about to touch down too, and the blades of grass beneath it seemed to bristle up toward his fingers. There were seven rocks in the air. The boy's pose was not a juggler's—hands up, having tossed something and waiting for something else to come down—he seemed not to be looking at what he was up to. Sholto knew that pictures like this had been contrived. There was a famous one of the artist Salvador Dalí, apparently suspended in the air, his brush and easel suspended too, and a black cat, a chair, a glassy arc of water. Of course Dalí had lifted his easel, jumped, let go easel and brush and—at the same time— some unseen people out of the photo's frame had tossed a chair, a cat, a pitcher full of water, all on cue, and the photographer had snapped off his shot. That's what this must be. It was Jim Bindle's arty surrealist photograph, circa 1925. That's how it must have been done. But still, Sholto felt uneasy. The trick didn't explain the energetic bristle of grass on that tired picnic ground, or the look on the boy's face. It was the expression of someone too proud to be proud of what he was doing. Sholto read the expression because he'd seen it before. It was how Canny had looked when her team was in the finals of the junior section of the National Mathematics Competition, her first, before her teachers began trying to hide who in Castlereagh Tech's team was answering most of the questions. Sholto had been in the audience. He hadn't understood any of the math, so instead of listening, he watched everyone's faces. Canny kept pressing her bell and producing answers. She looked embarrassed and formidably patient. Sholto was reminded of a cart horse he'd seen standing in its stall with a whole litter of puppies around its still hooves—the stupid mother dog had gone and given birth and left them there, and the horse hadn't dared move his feet for fear of crushing a puppy. Canny had looked like that—patient, proud, irritable, restrained. And so did the boy in the photo.

"Who is this?" Sholto asked the barber.

"Hmmm," said the barber.

Sholto waited.

"People usually ask me how my uncle did it."

"Well, yes, it's very cleverly done," Sholto said, to get that out of the way.

"That is Ghislain Zarene," the barber said.

"One of the two survivors of the Bull Mine disaster?"

The barber was silent. But after a moment the man in the chair said, "He may have survived, but after the memorial service he wasn't seen again."

Sholto turned back to the picture. He saw it had a caption, in Jim Bindle's neat printing. The caption read: "Boy levitating rocks."

IN THE CAR ON THE WAY BACK from Massenfer, Sholto told Susan about his visit to the mine. He decided to leave the story of his visit to the barbershop for later, after dinner. But after dinner he and Susan were looking for Canny, who hadn't been seen that day by anyone.

11

WHEN CANNY GOT to the bottom of the hill her feet were muddy, her ankles and calves were covered in scratches, and she was impossibly tired. The only thing that kept her from lying down in a field and falling asleep was the thought that someone might find her. She didn't want to be carried back to Orchard House and its telltale wind chimes. She knew she'd have to explain her overnight absence, and that her explanation would have to include how she'd come to lose her sandals, which were still where she'd left them, under a rosebush beside the lawn of the hidden house. She needed a plausible story, and Sholto should be the first to hear it. Sholto had to believe her story, and then keep telling it for her.

She must get to the guesthouse without being seen and wait near it till Sholto appeared.

There was a game Canny used to play with Marli and Marli's little brothers when she'd stay over. The kids had to make their way around the streets of their suburb at night avoiding the lights of passing cars. They were pretending to be escaped prisoners of war. They'd spent a lot of time pressed into hedges.

That's what Canny did. She left the path and went around the edges of fields, creeping along on the shady side of hedges and windbreaks. It was a long, crooked course, and it took her past several derelict houses, all weathered and windowless. The houses were at a similar stage of decay, as if the families who had owned them had left the valley around the same time. The sight was sad and made Canny think that the hidden house was like one of those big flourishing trees that stand in a circle of bare ground because nothing is able to grow in its shade.

Canny finally settled in a stand of trees about half a mile from the guesthouse. She kept watch, but for over an hour she saw only Zarene children coming and going. One group of older kids trailed in looking very tired. Canny recognized Lonnie among them. He had a pair of binoculars around his neck.

A few minutes later Canny spotted Susan, standing by the children's garden beds gazing up the river path, her hand shading her eyes.

Susan wasn't Sholto, but she'd have to do. Canny got up and hurried through the field. She went as fast as she could. Her heels were bruised from walking a long way barefoot, and each footfall jarred her sore head.

Some kid looking out a back window of the guesthouse was the first to see her. Canny heard a cry, and then a moment later a woman ran up to Susan and turned her. The woman was one half of the hiking couple. Susan started toward Canny. They met by the children's dormitories. Canny let Susan enfold her. She pressed her head into Susan's shoulder, only wanting to hide her face and collect her thoughts—but it was nice to be held, and she was so very tired.

SUSAN KNELT ON THE FLOOR of Iris Zarene's kitchen and lifted Canny's feet into an enamel basin Iris had filled with warm water. Susan covered her hands with soap suds and washed Canny's legs. She dried them and applied iodine to all the scratches, and Band-Aids to the worst of them. She took a seat beside Canny, reached out and tucked Canny's hair back behind her ear so that she could see Canny's grubby cheek and downcast eyes.

Iris Zarene removed the basin and put it on the bench. The light hit the slivers of Canny's eyes as she raised their lids a little to glance sidelong at the bench. When Iris left the room, Canny got up and emptied and rinsed the basin.

"I hardly think little gestures of tidying up after yourself are going to get you out of trouble," Susan said. "Sholto will be back soon with someone from the sheriff's department in Massenfer—unless Mr. Cyrus manages to turn them away." Iris had sent her brother off to the bottom of the valley and start of the road to wait for Sholto.

"I'm all right," Canny said. "Sholto didn't need to get the sheriff."

"At first light we were out searching the riverbank, Canny. We were looking into all the underwater willow branches."

Iris Zarene said from the doorway, "She must have wanted her brother to worry. It must *please* her to worry him."

Canny dropped her head and kept her mouth closed.

Susan said, "We're sorry for all the trouble, Miss Zarene. But I think this is a private family matter."

Iris Zarene gave a derisive snort and went out again.

Susan turned back to Canny. "Is this your way of making us take you back to Castlereagh and your friend?"

"No, Susan. I like it here."

"That's what I thought. So, what happened to you?" Susan paused, then added, "Did something bad happen to you?"

SHOLTO CAME IN WITH THE OTHER HALF of the hiking couple. They'd gone together to Massenfer to talk to the sheriff. A deputy followed Sholto's Austin back into the valley, but their cars were met at the end of the road by Cyrus, who explained that the girl had been found and was all right. Sholto asked the deputy whether he'd like to talk to Canny, just to make sure. Sholto really wanted to scare his sister and impress upon her how seriously he took his responsibility for her—seriously enough to summon the law if she went missing overnight. Sholto also hoped that the deputy might bring up the matter of the missing tents with Iris Zarene. Sholto had told the Massenfer Sheriff's Department about the tents.

But the deputy had accepted Cyrus Zarene's story. He and Cyrus shook hands, and Sholto watched the deputy's gaze flicker down to the marks tattooed on Cyrus Zarene's left forearm.

The deputy set off back the way he'd come, only saying in passing that Sholto should from now on probably keep his sister under his eye at all times.

SHOLTO DREW CANNY OUTSIDE and sat beside her on the steps. He said, "Look at me."

She was pale and drawn. Her clothes smelled of compost and had big blotches of rotted vegetable matter on them. There was eggshell in her hair, as well as leaves and twigs, and a wilted sprig of lavender. Sholto pulled out the lavender. She took it from him and began to rip it into crumbs.

"Okay—spill," Sholto said.

"I didn't want to talk to any of them."

"Zarenes?"

She nodded. "I'm mad at them."

"All of them?"

"No. But—how can you trust people who . . ." She trailed off and lowered her head. The black curtains of hair closed around her face.

"Come on, Canny. Before I leap up and start throttling Zarenes indiscriminately. At least tell me which one I have to throttle, and why."

She was quiet, collecting herself, Sholto thought, so he stayed still and chewed his lower lip.

"You know how I found that trapped lamb?" Canny said. Her voice quavered.

"Yes?" said Sholto.

"Mr. Cyrus and Mr. Lealand said they went up and dealt with it."

"Yes?"

"They didn't. They're horrible, heartless, lazy people. They just wandered a little bit off along the river trail and shot the rifle into the air and then sniggered at one another about the silly, sensitive city girl. I should have known. That boy Lonnie, he was sitting with me on the porch of Orchard House and *he* knew what they were going to do. He was teasing me about being a sentimental city girl."

"Okay, okay," Sholto said. "You're leaving the important things out—like why you vanished!"

"I'm trying to explain why I was so upset," Canny said, raising her voice.

Sholto was very distracted by the gushing floods of relief pouring through him. His sister was angry. And she had a cause. But nothing terrible had happened to her. "All right, just tell it your way," Sholto said. "Take your time."

"I waited till I saw Susan before I came back."

"Didn't you hear me calling last night? I went up and down the valley."

"I hiked all the way up to Fort Rock," Canny said. "Then, when I was only partway down it got dark. I stayed put because there were ravines, and I thought it was safer to stay put. I saw your lanterns. I felt terrible, Sholto, but I think it was the right thing to do. That it was better to worry you than break a leg."

"But it's two p.m. now. Sunrise was five a.m."

"I was cold all night. Shivering. I went to sleep as soon as the sun came up. Sorry."

"You haven't told me why you ran off."

"They didn't shoot the lamb!" Canny shouted. "I was walking up that way and I could hear the lamb and its mother. I didn't believe it, but I went to look anyway."

She clapped her hands over her face and put her head down on her knees. Her hair tumbled to cover her lower legs, so that all Sholto could see of her was her back and shoulders and the nape of her neck, and her toes peeping out from the shawl of hair.

"It was still alive," she said indistinctly. Then she moaned. "I had to hit it on the head with a rock." She moaned again. "I had to hit it over and over." Then, "Oh, Sholto!" she cried, and threw herself against him and burrowed her head into his chest.

THE NEXT MORNING Susan and Sholto hurried Canny out of the guesthouse at seven. She barely had time to brush her teeth. She wasn't even properly awake till they got to the car. She sat in the back of the Austin, her stomach growling. As the car wound through the gorge, she had to concentrate on looking past Susan and Sholto's shoulders at the road ahead, because she always felt carsick when she traveled on an empty stomach. Her brother and his girl-friend were murmuring at one another, but she still managed to catch some of what they said.

Sholto was saying that it was somewhat inconvenient that the Zarenes he had to interview were the same lazy brutes who had neglected to see to a suffering animal, then lied about it.

Susan leaned so that her head was between Canny and

that vital view of the road. Susan whispered, "Just because you promised Canny to have a word with them doesn't mean you have to straightaway."

"I should postpone it?"

"I don't see why not. Canny has spent the night out. Hopefully she learned a lesson about not letting emotional turmoil get in the way of sensible self-preservation. So what's the harm in waiting?"

"I can hear you," Canny said.

"You have very sharp ears, miss," said Susan. She sat back and kept quiet. Canny concentrated on quelling her nausea and no one spoke again till they were in town.

Sholto pulled in by a small stucco building just before the center of town.

"Why are we stopping?" Susan asked. "Isn't this a Scout hall?"

"It's not open," Sholto said. "I was wondering whether we could borrow some tents from the Scouts."

"That's a thought," said Susan.

"No," Canny said.

Sholto swung around, hooked his elbow over the seat, and stared at her. "I don't want to make you feel bad, Canny, but you must see how awkward all this is. We skipped breakfast to avoid Miss Zarene. We've accused them of stealing from us. We've had them out searching for you. We've brought a Massenfer deputy into the valley. And I'd arranged to be around at Mr. Cyrus's this afternoon with the recording equipment—and you expect me to tell him off!"

"Don't then!" Canny said.

There was a moment of shimmering silence, then Sholto turned back, let out the clutch, and they drove on.

They stopped at a café for breakfast, during which no one said much more than "Please pass the salt." Sholto and Susan kept their eyes cast down. Canny understood that they were angry with her—Sholto because she wouldn't make any effort to make him feel more comfortable about failing her, and Susan because she resented having to babysit Canny and had from the start. But they seemed to be angry at each other too, and Canny was having a hard time figuring out why. She looked at them and felt her resolve soften. She had meant to keep on lying. She wanted freedom—freedom to do what she wanted, and the way she saw it, keeping those three Zarene adults on the back foot was the best way of securing that freedom. She wanted Sholto to confront them, be indignant, accuse them of putting his sister in a position of having to euthanize livestock because they were too bone lazy to walk up the hill and do it themselves. It wasn't as if they could explain that the buried lamb was only an illusion. And they'd have no reason to believe she was lying. By talking to them, Sholto was supposed to make her story seem completely credible: how she killed the lamb then ran off weeping and wringing her hands, away from people—heartless, untrustworthy adults. How she'd sat alone on the hill, crying and nursing a bruised heart. How she'd been caught out in the dark and had huddled shivering all night. Sholto believed her story, so he'd be convincing. His fury, his protectiveness, his performance of her story, all of it was Canny's free pass to come and go as she pleased. To climb the hill. To visit the hidden house. To talk to its prisoner again.

Now that Sholto wasn't going to perform his part in her play, Canny no longer felt guilty about deceiving him. She glowered across the table at him. So her feelings were inconvenient? How dare he think that, even if she was lying about them.

Sholto got up to pay and went outside and waited, leaning on the car.

"Bugger him," Susan muttered, and tipped the last brackish brown dribbles of tea into Canny's cup. "He can just bloody wait for us to finish."

"Why are you mad at him?" Canny asked.

"Well," Susan said, then paused and thought for a time. "I guess because he stops short all the time. Sholto is great at managing people whenever it doesn't matter much, but once he's opposed, he caves in and then starts going on about other people's unreasonable demands. It's all because he can't please the Professor."

"But the Professor is mild. He never makes a fuss."

Susan snorted. "The Professor is a man who likes being disappointed. He'd rather feel let down and long-suffering than actually ask for what he wants or argue with anyone. Which, I have to say, isn't very *manly* of him."

Canny gazed at Susan in wonder. "You can't be right."

"You wouldn't notice because you spend all your time worrying about your mother. Splitting icebergs off her ice floe and floating off on them waving your little Canny flag, a flag with some kind of math symbol on it—nothing pretentious like the infinity symbol but, say, that proportionality one that looks like a fish. You're so busy trying to figure out how to be Sisema Afa's daughter that you never think about Sholto being his father's son."

"The Professor is *nice*," Canny said.

"To you. You he doesn't take personally. If you ever get married and ask the Professor to give you away he won't be able to, because he *already has*."

Canny covered her mouth with her hand.

"Oh God!" Susan said, "Don't mind me. I'm only trying to help. I really care about Sholto, but it drives me crazy that he can't stand up to his dad, or any other man. To me—yes. To your mother—in a pinch. To you—every time. But all men are like the Professor, and Sholto's nuts try to climb into his stomach every time he has to stand up to one."

Canny uncovered her mouth and just stared at Susan till the woman reached out and gently pushed her jaw up so that her teeth met with a click.

"I keep forgetting you're a schoolgirl," Susan said. "You're so tough-minded."

They were startled then because Sholto came and banged on the window by their heads.

"Hey!" said the man behind the counter. "Cut that out!"

Susan apologized, not very convincingly, and as a nice gesture cleared their table for him.

Canny went out to her brother, who opened the car door for her and waited to do the same for Susan.

CANNY SPENT MOST OF THE MORNING sharing a long library table with Sholto, Susan, and two giant binders of yellowed newspapers—the *Massenfer Messenger* for the year

1929. She sat with her shoulders hunched and one arm curled protectively around her writing set. She used up almost her whole store of fancy paper writing to Marli. She told Marli everything that had happened in the last three days, starting with Fort Rock and her first glimpse of the hidden house. She wrote about the valley with its few adults and many children, and how the children were tattooed, and how she'd seen spells in a tree, like a gathering swarm. She told Marli about her own experimentations and the invisible tents. She wrote about the forested hill, the illusion of the trapped lamb and its miserable mother, the strange alphabet in the schoolroom at Orchard House. Finally she told Marli about the prisoner in the house on the hill.

Canny felt as if she were making a dash over some dangerous ground—like an ice floe, the ice floe Susan had talked about. Only momentum would get her safely across.

She left off only when she'd finished the story. She put her pen down and shook her cramping hand.

"That can't all be complaints about Sue and me or nasty Zarenes," Sholto said. Then, "If you want to stretch your legs you could go get me a newspaper."

"I'd have thought you had enough newspapers."

Sholto fished in his pants pocket and tossed her a coin. "I want a copy of today's *Clarion*," he said.

Susan said, "He wants to see what bands are playing at the Honeypot. What we're missing."

"Go. And come back," Sholto said, and followed this with a stern look.

The newsagent had sold out of the *Castlereagh Clarion*

but sent Canny on to the railway station, which had a vending box.

The station was possibly the grandest building in Massenfer. It had a huge portico, decorated cornices and pilasters, and tall ornamental urns on the roof, everything constructed of cement made to look like masonry. There were several cars parked by the grand steps and one pony and trap. Canny patted the pony, and it huffed into its nosebag, blowing oat dust up into its eyelashes. Canny hurried into the station's cool, tiled interior and looked around, squinting as her eyes adjusted. She couldn't see where she was going and ran into Lealand Zarene. He put a hand on her shoulder to steady her. She hadn't seen him partly because he was moving so fast—striding through from the platform. And she hadn't recognized him because he was wearing a suit and hat.

"Sorry," she said, before remembering she was supposed to be treating him like a villain.

"Agnes," he said, stepped around her, and went on his way. She heard him talking to the horse, his normal terse voice warmed and softened.

Canny located the *Clarion*'s vending box and fed Sholto's coin into it. She grabbed a newspaper and tucked it under her arm. She wasn't going to leave the building till Lealand Zarene had gone. She sidled out of sight of the main entrance then, skirting its walls, went onto the platform.

There were a number of people waiting. The board said the Westport Express was due in half an hour. It was families waiting, and they'd already piled their luggage into the porters' cart. School was out, so they were mostly men seeing off wives and kids and handing over last-minute presents—comics and coloring books and money to spend on the train. There were a few solitary businessmen; a grandma who was being kissed and hugged by a very large family; and one boy, on his own already, sitting on the farthest bench, stooped over with a cardboard suitcase between his feet and his knuckles pressed into his eye sockets. It was Lonnie Zarene, who, it seemed, had been left with half an hour to wait and no loving fuss of farewell.

Canny went and sat on the far end of the bench from him. She laid the newspaper down between them.

Lonnie's head snapped up, and he glared at her with reddened eyes, then turned his head and wiped his tears. "Piss off," he muttered.

She waited while he pulled himself together, then said, "You don't want to go?"

"To Middleton?" He sniffed. "Who would?" Then he rounded on her. "I didn't take you for a busybody."

"No? The other day I grabbed hold of you because I wanted to ask you about the so-called orphans. That was busybodying."

"I mean I didn't think you'd pry about a person's feelings."

"It's sympathy, not prying."

"How can I tell? Your face is blank." He was glowering at her, but the stare wasn't just to push her away, it was a hard scrutiny too.

"When I grabbed you, you gave me a headache," Canny said. "You got sick afterward and were lying about on the veranda of Orchard House, being babied. I figure you're the family darling. So I'm surprised your uncle has just left you to wait all by yourself."

Lonnie looked wary.

"How did you give me the headache?"

Lonnie held his breath a moment then let it out in a huff. He said, "Didn't you feel me scribble on your hand?"

"No. Sholto was grappling me."

Lonnie laughed. "Yes."

"So there are sigils for headaches?"

Lonnie stopped laughing. The wariness returned, doubled. "What do you mean by 'sigils'?"

"You tell me."

"Why should I tell you anything?"

Canny looked away. The air was wriggling over the steel rail lines. It was going to be a scorching day. The sun was striking up from the rust-brown concrete beneath the bench and her legs were uncomfortably warm. But on her right side, the side opposite where Lonnie sat, Canny's arm and shoulder and cheek were cool, as if in shadow. But there was no shade there, nor anything to cast one. Canny probed the moment. The moment was strange for a reason. It was like other moments so far back in her life that she couldn't remember them properly. For some reason her mother's story about the hermit crab came into her mind, and she started to look about her for a sign—some real thing that was also a sign.

But there were only the people waiting for the train, and Lonnie waiting on what she had to say, and the newspaper lying between them, so fresh its ink was still sleek.

It was one of those skinny holiday editions they'd get in

the weeks around Christmas, when editors favored happy stories. The main headline said, "Heroine Honored." Below the caption was a grainy wire photo of the prime minister of the Shackle Islands standing by watching the vice president of Southland pinning a medal onto her mother's impressive chest.

Canny gave a little laugh, then said to Lonnie, "You don't want to leave Zarene Valley, and they're making you go. That's why you should tell me. You should talk because it seems you don't get to have a say."

"As if you're going to be able to change anything."

"I might."

Lonnie made an explosive, scornful noise. Then he leaned forward to look past her. Canny saw he was reading the clock.

"All right," she said. "You gave me a headache for about forty seconds. It was meant to settle in and make me sick for hours."

"Days. I'm good at pain." Lonnie was boasting.

None of it made much sense to Canny, but she didn't expect it to—she just waited for more pieces. She wondered how many pieces she'd need before she saw the pattern.

Lonnie slumped. "But when I get on that train none of it is going to be any good to me. I leave most of my magic behind. I'm the strongest Zarene in fifteen years—Iris says. But I can't keep what's mine."

"Why won't they let you stay if your talent only works here? Did your parents say you had to go?"

Lonnie snorted. "Whenever my parents came to visit

me they'd never come any farther than Massenfer. They never dared to set foot anywhere near the valley. They'd get a room in the Palace Hotel, and we'd go for walks and sit in that nasty little park behind the library and watch the poor birds in the aviary plucking the wire. Or they'd take me to the diner and they'd always sit opposite me in our booth—and they're not small people. They'd sit with their mammaries on the tabletop and take turns to touch my hands and say, 'How nice it is to see you, son.'" Lonnie perfectly imitated his parents' forced warmth—and their fear. "My parents don't want me. But they don't have any say. No one respects them. Bonnie's ma and da have some claims by showing they care. They'd do things like get the steamer to tow a houseboat all the way up the Taskmaster to Pike's Landing. They move into it for the summer holiday and she gets to live with them."

Canny suddenly understood what Lonnie was telling her. He was saying that once Zarenes were adults, they couldn't come back into the valley. This was the bit of information inside Lonnie's story that it was vital for her to know. To test that she'd got it right, she said, "So that's why there are no teenagers or younger adults in the valley."

"No one over thirteen. Puberty used to be when we Zarenes got strong—if we were ever going to, that is. Now it just means we get sent away."

The crossing bells began to clang.

Lonnie jumped and looked at her, wide-eyed.

"Go on," she said. "Quickly."

But he didn't. He went back to an earlier subject. "I scribbled the pain ideogram on your elbow when you grabbed me. The pain went to your head because that must be the part of you most prone to pain."

Canny thought of the migraine she'd endured in the hidden house. Perhaps when Lonnie cast his spell he had made a suggestion to her whole system, weakening something, or opening a door.

"I didn't realize right away that you'd thrown it off. I can't think how you did."

"Show me what you wrote," Canny said. She tapped the newspaper. Her fingernail made a dent in its surface, and a little crescent of shadow on her mother's cheek.

Lonnie hesitated. Then, with his right index finger, he slowly inscribed a series of signs.

"Do it again," she said.

He repeated the gesture.

The train slid into the station and made a wall of shadow before them.

"Again," Canny said.

Lonnie repeated his gesture once more. It took six seconds to complete. There were seventeen separate movements.

"They're not letters," she muttered.

"They're combinations. They blend," Lonnie said. "We call it the Ideogrammatic form of the Alphabet. It's very advanced. Hardly anyone gets taught it."

He got up and grabbed his cardboard suitcase. He asked her whether he could take the newspaper, he had nothing to read on the train.

Canny nodded. She probably looked gormless. Her jaw felt loose.

"I'd better get on."

"They have to load up the luggage," Canny said.

The porter on the platform was making a great show of carefully passing bags to the man in the baggage car. They went about it as if they were moving egg cartons.

"I can't believe I'm leaving," Lonnie said. His eyes and nose grew red again.

"What has to happen to make it possible for you to come back?"

He shook his head. "It's too hard."

Give me something, she said.

"Uncle Lealand, Uncle Cyrus, and Aunt Iris put a very powerful spell—an imprisonment spell—around an older and even more powerful spell, and the two spells changed each other. Now they suck up all our magic. Cyrus, Lealand, and Iris are immune because the imprisonment spell is their work. Do you see?"

"Yes, but . . ."

Lonnie backed away toward the train. The last of the other passengers bounded up the steps, kissed his hand, and threw the kiss to his wife. He went on in to find his seat, and the porter, suddenly possessed by a demon of spite, began hurling the remainder of the bags onto the train.

Canny followed Lonnie. He mounted the steps and turned around. "Oh, that's what I should ask," he said. "Can you see sign?"

"Yes."

"How?" he asked. His face twisted. "I can't, unless it's properly written out in chalk or ink."

"I don't know how I do it."

"How good is your memory?"

Canny laughed.

"What's that supposed to mean?"

The train guard came up beside Canny. He'd obviously chosen to board by that door so that he could herd Lonnie safely into the carriage. "The train's about to depart, so stand back, miss," the guard said to Canny.

Lonnie looked thunderous. He put his suitcase down and flicked his right arm so that a long smooth length of bare skin slid from his too-short cuff. He showed the guard his tattoos. To Canny it looked like a reflex—something the boy might do in the schoolyard or the streets of Massenfer if some other kid was giving him trouble.

The guard glanced at the marks, looked bemused, and said, "Go on, son. Best to find your seat now."

Lonnie seemed shocked. Then he said, more to himself than Canny, "Oh God—how will I be able to do this?"

The newspaper slid off his suitcase and Canny caught it and returned it to him. The guard picked up the suitcase and stepped onto the train. He planted the bag firmly against Lonnie till the boy took it. Lonnie looked gray and defeated. He turned around and went into the carriage.

The guard blew his whistle, waved, and the train began to move off.

Canny hurried along beside the carriage. She saw Lonnie take a seat and bump his head on the window. She sped up, came alongside, and slapped the glass. He looked at her, then picked up the newspaper and brandished it—saying, "Thanks for this." Then he glanced at it—frowned—and held it up, tapping on the picture of Mrs. Sisema Mochrie. His mouth made words. "Is this your mother?"

Canny mouthed, "Yes."

The train picked up speed, and Lonnie's pale face and the pale rectangle of the newspaper glided away, then were wiped out by a reflection of the blue sky.

SHOLTO FORGAVE CANNY FOR GIVING AWAY his newspaper when she told him who she'd given it to. He said, "That was a thoughtful thing to do." And Canny realized that Sholto thought she'd given Lonnie Zarene a peace offering. She let him think it.

They had lunch in Massenfer then headed back to the valley. On the way, Canny mentioned that her mother was on the front page of the *Clarion*.

"We should have picked up another copy," Susan said.

"I'm going to have to put in a call to Sisema and the Professor anyway," Sholto said.

Canny was astonished. Toll calls were a great trouble and expense. Sholto would have to make his call from one of the private phone booths in the Massenfer post office.

"I was told to call collect if anything happened."

"But nothing has happened," Canny said.

"I think if your mother discovers you were outdoors overnight in a strange place and that I didn't tell her about it, she'd have my guts for garters. If I confess she'll just be delighted to have my incompetence confirmed." Sholto grinned at Susan and waggled his eyebrows. "Confession is good for the soul, you know."

"When will you call?" Canny asked.

"Soon. I have to do it before they start back. Tomorrow maybe."

WHEN IRIS'S GUESTS, the two young scholars from Castlereagh, arrived at the apiary, Cyrus was changing the frames in one of his beehives. The young people were carrying a big box—the recording equipment. Fortunately it had two handles, and they were about the same height, the woman tall, the young man average. The girl, Agnes, trailed after them with a bag Cyrus learned later held the tapes, power cords, microphones, and junction box.

Cyrus waved to let them know he'd seen them and would be along shortly. They didn't need his help setting up the equipment—they'd soon see there was only one place that would work. For the next little while he concentrated on soothing the hive, getting the bees to voluntarily abandon the dripping frames. He never had to brush them off. He only wrote in the smoke, "Sleepy. Go down. Wait. Patience." The smoke eddied around his gloved fingers.

What the family called "warm sign"—signs meant to act in the moment—would never work for Cyrus unless he amplified them with something like smoke. The molecules of smoke carried the magic, momentarily, and lent it some strength or staying power. Without smoke, or steam, or dust, Cyrus had to be in contact with what he wished to spell. The best of the younger Zarenes—two women who lived in Westport, and one man who lived in Founderston, and Lonnie of course—all of them had needed to be in contact with what they spelled. They'd needed to write on the thing, indelibly if possible, to get the results Cyrus could get by inscribing messages in smoke. They couldn't do what he could, and Cyrus was never quite sure why. Perhaps it was because they were too clumsy and left too much space, too many seconds, between one series of movements and the next. Certainly one of the women in Westport had written to him saying that she'd realized that what was required of them when he was teaching them was like the grace of the Balinese dancers she'd seen. The dancers' gestures were just about as intricate, though not nearly as speedy. It was as if Cyrus's best pupils were always making a translation in their minds from the sign they knew, the layers of Tabular Alphabet that, knitted together in different ways, made up the Ideogrammatic form of the magic. His pupils' fingers just wouldn't dance. Signs for them were always planned, pondered upon, double- and triple-checked. Even Lonnie, who remembered what he was shown once he'd been shown it only half a dozen times, still hadn't mastered warm signing without contact. He and Lealand and Iris had all done their very best for Lonnie. They'd given him every possible advantage. Lealand had even thought to send Lonnie to tap dancing classes in Massenfer to—as Lealand put it—"shake his memory out of his brain and into his limbs." Two years of dance had done nothing for Lonnie's magic. And five years of piano lessons. None of Lonnie's teachers' efforts had produced someone who could help them with the spell—the spell they'd put together thirty years before, one that, at first, they'd had to pour all their strength into and constantly repair. A spell that finally settled and ran itself, but that was now so faultlessly strong that it'd begun to wind away into itself all the magic in the valley.

Cyrus put the full frames in the honey box. It was a warm day and honey oozed out of the wax cells of the combs to pool in the bottom of the box. Cyrus blew more smoke and once again inscribed calming signs before slotting in fresh frames. As he eased the last one into place, he happened to glance up.

The dark girl was standing a short distance away, watching him.

Cyrus finished up and went over to her. "Hello, Agnes," he said.

"They sent me to ask if it was okay to set up the recording equipment in the parlor. It seems to be the only room with two power points."

"Tell them the parlor is fine, and I'll be with them as soon as I've put the honey in my cool store."

She gave a little nod and took off. Her hair fanned out in a dark, static cloud and, without touching Cyrus, threw a waft of warmer air against his face. He blinked in surprise and watched her lope back to the house.

"WHERE SHOULD I BEGIN?" Cyrus said, and peered at the microphone. It looked like the hood ornament of a fancy car.

"A bit of background, I thought." The young historian settled back, clutching his notepad. He squared his jaw and then flushed up to the roots of his gingery hair. "So— why did you choose to go and work in the coal mine?"

"Money," Cyrus said.

Sholto made a come-hither gesture, asking for more.

Cyrus watched the light moving silky on the big reel of tape in Sholto's machine. "Zarenes generally give short answers," he said.

"For the purposes of this interview you might like to give longer ones," Sholto said. "It's better if I don't keep directing you. I don't want you only telling me what I already know. I want you to expand a bit. Though you'll find I can persist with questions. Believe me, my sister has trained me to reel in whatever is behind any short answer."

"Because she gives them?" Cyrus said, and glanced at the girl.

Her brother had posted her at the door so she could listen for the whistle of Cyrus's kettle and get to it before too much whistling ended up on the audiotape. She was making tea. She'd asked him if she could pick a lemon off his lemon tree. Apparently the girl student—Susan—didn't take her tea with milk. Agnes had explained all this to Cyrus when he was in the kitchen washing his hands, so he wasn't at all sure about this description of her giving short answers. What she gave was a series of peacefully ordinary requests and explanations, all framed in short sentences. She was simple and civil but there was an alertness burning out of her, as if everybody she ever was, from infancy till now, and everybody she ever would be, from now until her death, was looking at Cyrus out of her warm brown eyes.

The kettle began to whistle and the girl hurried off to silence it.

Cyrus said to Sholto, "But she's not your sister, is she?"

"She's my stepsister."

"Canny's mother is Sisema Afa," Susan said. "The war hero."

"So she's not a Southlander."

The young man looked irritated. "The Shackles are a protectorate of Southland."

Cyrus thought, "Any minute now he'll accuse me of bigotry."

"Shackle Islanders have citizenship," Sholto went on, then added, "whether you like it or not."

Cyrus laughed. "I didn't mean any offense. I was only curious. I hope my amateur curiosity is acceptable to you, as opposed to your professional one."

Sholto flushed again. Then he apologized. "I'm sorry, Mr. Zarene. I realize that this interview is going to touch on personal tragedy."

"Yes," said Cyrus. Then he began to talk.

THE FAMILY HAD TO MARSHAL THEIR FORCES against the Lazuli Dam project. They had to hire lawyers. And, though they had land, they didn't have much money.

"We were only farming to feed ourselves back then, and producing a little surplus to sell so that we could buy what we weren't able to make ourselves. Back then people didn't need so many *things*. Anyway, the government offered to buy out all the families in the valley. They went house to house—sweating men in suits with attaché cases and blistered feet. It was summer and no one had told them that the road into the Zarene Valley only went as far as Terminal Hill."

"The gorge road is more recent?"

"Yes. It's a construction road built for the dam project. The dam was meant to go at the Zarene Valley end of the Lazuli Gorge, so they cut a road that far. There used to be a road that wound down from the summit of the Palisades. It ran from Fort Rock to Terminal Hill, the glacial moraine at the top of the valley. Its traces are still there, covered in thorn bushes and grass."

"So the government men walked in and went house to house offering to buy out the valley piecemeal?"

"Yes. But the land was—and is—owned in common. So every house they knocked at, people would say, 'I can't sell you anything.' So—we gave them the runaround. Eventually they sent a letter to every house, citing the Resource Management Act. You do know that there is no such thing as private property in Southland once the government decides there's not?"

"I've never been entirely sure that private property is a good thing," Sholto said.

"You're not counting tents then, Mr. Mochrie?" Cyrus said.

The young historian looked as if he was being confronted rather than teased. Cyrus laughed and went on with his story. "My father, Talbot Zarene, decided that we needed a lawyer to fight the government. And we needed money to pay for a lawyer—real money, to pay a really good lawyer. So the men of the family got together and drew lots, and those with the short straw went and signed on at Bull Mine. You see, after it flooded in 1926, the mine was having a bit of a problem with labor. Some of the families who'd lost men just upped and left the district, went to Westport to work in the mills."

"So Lealand Zarene was already a miner before the ballot? Because he was one of the men trapped by the flood."

"Lealand's father, Colvin, planned to build a bottling plant. Father and son were both underground raising capital for that. But the plant was never built. We're still home-brewing cider. And we don't produce enough of it for it to be seen any farther north than Castlereagh. The Zarene Valley apple orchards were mostly planted by Colvin, for cider. But Lealand has done a lot of grafting over the past twenty years, and now half our apples are export quality. Come picking season we strip the trees, wrap the apples in tissue, crate them in straw, and send them off to Europe."

"But you went down the mine because you drew the short straw?"

"Pretty much."

Agnes came in with a tray. Her brother jumped up to shift Cyrus's big old Columbia radio off the coffee table, where he'd moved it to make room for the recording equipment. The girl knelt down on the floor beside the coffee table. She said, "I'll pour it in a moment." Then, "Sholto, you said I should check out the swimming hole."

"Is it safe?" Sholto asked Cyrus.

"It's deep. But from the bank there are fifteen yards of calm water till you hit the current, and even if you get caught in the current it'll just carry you along to the shingle bank on the next bend. Some of the older children will probably be there now."

"All right," Sholto said to his sister. "But be back at the guesthouse before dinner."

She fixed her gaze on the steam at the spout of the pot. Her fingers twitched, and she twined them together in her lap.

Cyrus had a thought. If she'd written his calming runes in the steam from the kettle the tea would be cool. So she hadn't. Of course she hadn't.

Smoke and steam weren't the same. Smoke talked to by sign would then talk to the air, and to things that lived in the air. Steam only talked to water. The teapot was steaming at its spout, so she hadn't tried writing his bee-calming sign. Besides, watching him once wouldn't tell her anything except that he was making funny gestures above a beehive. She could see what he was doing, but she wouldn't be able to interpret or remember it. So why was he so sure she *had* been dabbling her fingers in the steam and accidentally communicating something to the water?

"You took your time," Sholto said to her.

"I forgot the lemon. I had to reboil the jug," she said smoothly. To Cyrus she sounded like someone who always had an excuse at hand, and who was rather disgusted at having to produce excuses. Perhaps one of her parents was a bully. That was one way in which bullied children and spoiled ones were alike—their ability to fend people off with an excuse. For a second time the girl reminded Cyrus of Ghislain, who'd been both bullied and fearfully spoiled. It was most disconcerting to be reminded of Ghislain.

Sholto consulted his notes, then said, "When did you start in the mine?"

"It would have been March, 1927. I was twenty-three."

"And a farmworker?"

"A beekeeper, as I am now. And I started as a chain runner, working with the coal carts and horses."

"Are you good with animals?" Sholto asked, then
smirked and glanced at his sister.

Cyrus was baffled by this, but answered yes.

"Were you aware of any problems with the mine's
safety?"

"Nothing I didn't expect. It was a coal mine. Coal mines
are dangerous, and there are always precautions in place.
For instance, the horses were all unshod, the carts had
wooden wheels and ran on wooden rails. But if you're asking whether I personally saw trouble coming—no, I didn't.
That day my shift started at eight in the morning and
ended at seven in the evening. Shortly after six, I was taking my last load up the gateway when the explosion happened. The explosion was at the working face, so I was
nearly a mile from it. I didn't hear it. The ground didn't
tremble. The shock wave was funneled up through the mine
and reached me before I knew anything had happened. It
picked me up and threw me nearly sixty yards. I woke up
two days later at the hospital in Massenfer."

"Okay," Sholto said, and began riffling through his
notes. Cyrus supposed the young man was looking for a
question he might ask to which he—Cyrus—would have
an answer. He was aware that he was telling the story very
badly.

"So you had an ordinary day, then you woke up in the
hospital?" Susan said, clearly hoping for more details.

"That's right."

Sholto gave a small satisfied grunt then smoothed the page in front of him. "Did you notice any unusual behavior in those horses of yours?"

Mid-afternoon, when Cyrus was on his third run of the day, his horses had shied at the narrow place in the mine's main shaft. He had grabbed a handful of stone dust from a bag standing at a crosscut, tossed it into the air in front of the leader's nose, and quickly inscribed the calming runes he'd mastered as a beekeeper. The horses had settled and gone on without complaint. A chain runner an hour afterward had had the same problem—and didn't have a remedy for it. That man left his idle team and went all the way down to the inbye to pull his son off shift and walk him out of the mine. The narrow place was clear when Cyrus came back through it on his last run. The other chain runner's disobedient team had been taken back out into the light—and they lived. Cyrus's horses were in harness and were hauling several hundred pounds of coal. The shock wave that carried Cyrus up the gateway had wrenched the coal carts off their rails, slammed them into the horses, and shunted them forward. The explosion didn't so much sweep them off their feet as snap all their legs at the ankle. Cyrus didn't see what had happened to his horses, but Lealand had, and had told him about it later.

Cyrus said, "It was the chain runner after me who had trouble with his horses. That was later in the day."

The girl poured the tea. She asked Cyrus how he took it.

"With lemon," he said, since she'd gone to the effort of offering it.

She did everything quickly and unobtrusively, handed everyone their cups, then said, "I'll be off now."

"Be sensible," her brother said without looking up. He was flicking through his notes again. The girl went out the door, and Cyrus turned his attention back to Sholto, who had found what he wanted. The young man looked up at Cyrus, met his eyes, and reddened slightly. "Tell me about the insurance policies," he said.

12

THE CORN FLOUR PASTE that Canny had mixed up in
Cyrus Zarene's kitchen was still good and tacky when she
produced the paper on which it was smeared from her
pocket, unfolded it, and slapped it onto her forehead. In-
visibility spell in place, she set off at a run for the river path
and, eventually, the forested hill.

Forty minutes later she arrived on the immaculate lawn,
sweating and out of breath. She paused, lifted the hem of
her shirt to mop her face. The strip of paper rustled. She
peeled it off.

The doors of one room were open onto the veranda.
There was a contraption just outside the room, a series of
wooden trays not unlike the frames from one of the beehives. One tray was propped up on its side. It was filled
with a grid of metal squares.

Drawn by this curious contraption, Canny set off across
the lawn. When she got closer she saw that the grid in the

frame was made of inch-wide slices through average-size tin cans—rounds that had been hammered into squares and then slotted together into the frame. Behind the frame was an upended apple box with a lump of clay on it, sticky potter's clay with fingerprints all over it.

Canny didn't see Ghislain Zarene till he moved. He was indoors, at a table, with his back to her. When she stepped onto the veranda, he leaped to his feet and quickly pulled a sheet across the work surface before him, hiding what was there. Only then did he turn—then froze, and remained very still.

Canny scrubbed off the dried corn flour paste on her forehead, then took the paper from her pocket and showed it to him. "I passed right by the wild pigs this time. They sure do look dangerous close up."

Ghislain pointed at the floor by the open door. Her sandals were sitting there, toes pointing indoors as if they too were coming rather than going.

"I went past where I'd left them and forgot to look," she said. She went in and picked up the sandals by their straps. She fastened the buckle of one to the strap of the other and hung them around her neck.

Ghislain said, "Why are you back here? What purpose does it serve?"

"At least you're not saying *whose* purpose." She smiled at him.

"No," Ghislain said. "These visits are your own idea. I know that now."

The sheet Ghislain had thrown over the table began to convulse, as if it covered a whole litter of kittens who had just woken up and were looking for a way out. Ghislain jumped back as the sheet flung up into the air and tore itself into perfectly even strips. The strips of cloth then formed speedy granny knots and dropped down, inert again.

Canny stood with her mouth open long enough for spit to pool behind her lower lip and spill over. She clapped her mouth closed and wiped her chin. Ghislain watched this, then burst out laughing. She laughed too. Then she asked him whether he'd known that was going to happen.

"No!" he said, still laughing.

She came all the way in to take a look at what he had been doing.

"It doesn't matter if I see, does it? It's only Zarenes you're hiding from."

"And you can't really read sign yet," he said.

"If I can see what the sign is doing I can read it, and remember it, and adapt it too."

The table was covered in squares of wet clay, each around three by three inches and perhaps half an inch thick. The tiles were incised with Ideogrammatic sign, some hand-cut into the clay, and some channels so evenly formed they must have been stamped rather than cut. Canny saw the stamps were nearby. They were made of number eight wire, the kind used for farm fences, formed into calligraphic twists with the help of pliers. The pliers were lying beside the stamps.

There was a fire in the hearth, now only a heap of hot coals. The day was warm, and the room was stifling. Ghislain had his shirtsleeves rolled up and shirt unbuttoned.

There was clay on his skin, clothes, and even in his hair. "I can't stop what I'm doing," he explained, then impatiently gathered up the knotted strips of cloth from the tabletop and flung them into a corner of the room.

"Why did the sheet do that?"

Ghislain brushed his hand over the clay tiles. "These say 'go away,' but 'go away' in an organized way. I guess the sheet tried to go, organizing itself differently as it did."

Canny looked around and took in the tongs on the hearth and the rough-walled, semi-opaque glass bowl with a lid that stood beside a box full of lead soldiers—grenadiers, and one medieval knight minus horse. Canny pointed at the glass container on the hearth. "Is that a crucible?"

"Yes. I made it from a big quartz boulder my great-aunt Rowan used as a doorstop."

The crucible must have taken Ghislain quite some time to carve, Canny thought.

"Don't go near it. If it's broken it won't mend itself."

"I guess not," Canny said, a little surprised by this schoolmarmish bit of telling off. "So. You roll clay flat, then cut it into tiles with those bits of tin can inside the frame. Then you either stamp the tiles with sign, or carve sign into them. Then you melt down the lead soldiers in your crucible, and you pour the melted lead into the grooves in the tiles."

Ghislain just stared at her.

"You're making lead sign. What for?"

He didn't answer, but did say, "You can give me a hand by rolling that ball of clay into a sheet more or less the same thickness as the other tiles." He pointed at the marble rolling pin that was soaking in a bucket of water. "Then use my cookie cutter thing to cut tiles for me."

Canny put down her sandals and then knelt by the apple box to knead the lump of clay. She flattened and folded it several times then rolled it out and used her wet hands to smooth its surface. She placed the frame over the doughy rectangle and pressed down hard. The squares of tin sliced the clay into eight ripply-edged tiles. Canny picked them up and put them on the table by Ghislain, who was busy cutting sign into a tile with a steel knitting needle. He pulled up a chair for her and moved his own to make room.

She sat down. "What do I do now?"

Ghislain's left arm was inches from her own. Even in the warm room she imagined she could feel the heat coming off him. Human heat. He smelled good, a faint fresh sweat smell over something innocent, a little like oatmeal and brown sugar.

"Grab the 'go' sign and stamp the tiles you've cut. Keep well within the edges. And don't press too hard." He slid a stamp across the table. Then he tilted his head and watched her sidelong.

Canny had a moment of uncertainty. The wire stamp in front of her did not say "go." It said something about *when*. It was a "when" not a "what" sign. "Go" would be a "what" sign. "What should I do?" "Go." "When should I go?" was a different question.

"Oh," Canny said. "This stamp says 'now,' not 'go.' Which is why none of the 'go' tiles are getting up and going, I guess.

Because they need to be told when to go. Signs aren't re-sistible, are they?"

"You've resisted a whole lot already. And you're a sign reader. A real sign reader." He sounded awed. He'd been testing her.

Canny gazed at the stamped tiles and stamps, then se-lected one stamp and met Ghislain's black gaze. He reached out, tentative, and wrapped one of his hands around her bare arm—then just held on. His hand was smooth with dried clay slip, and warm.

Canny closed her eyes and dropped her head. She in-clined very slowly till her brow bone touched his shoulder. She wasn't thinking about anything, but then she sur-prised herself by asking how often he killed a rabbit.

"Did that frighten you?"

"Yes."

"I breed them, and that takes time. So I guess I'm hav-ing meat six or so times a month at this time of year. Less in winter. I don't kill my chickens unless they stop laying. Cyrus brings me a box of little chicks once a year. I'm not allowed a rooster. Cyrus brings flour too, and oats. But I usually eat corn and potatoes rather than bread, because I grow them."

He really was a prisoner. Canny wasn't going to ask why his family had him confined, not if the answer would make her stop wanting to be here with him.

He said, his voice slightly muffled, "You don't actually *read* sign, you just understand it." Canny felt his breath stir-ring her hair. That's why his voice was muffled—he had his mouth against her hair. Canny stayed still and breathed shallowly till she thought she'd faint. Then she sat upright again, pushing herself off from him but maintaining her contact with him. It seemed to be the only hope she had of keeping her head—holding him off, but leaving her hands on him.

Canny didn't know how to explain what she did do with the Zarene Alphabet. The night he had her follow the carvings she'd tried to take in the sum of it, the spell in total, and the fireworks of her migraine had partly consisted of glowing squiggles of ideogrammatic sign flying apart into their component pieces and reassembling again. And there were clues, things she'd see and her brain would put aside for a time, and then present to her sometime later, once a place to put them appeared. That's the way her mind had always worked. So she'd recognized that the tile had said "Now" because there was a big case clock in Ghislain's library that didn't have hands, but only a blank cover over its face, a cover that revolved and had one tiny window in it that showed only the hour. The other day, when she'd been lying tied up, the number the window revealed was a 7, then an 8, then a 9. Under each numeral there was an ideogram, one with a kind of "Don't" built into it, like the fine print on the Alphabet in the schoolroom at Orchard House. Canny was absolutely sure that when the library clock struck midnight and the number 12 showed in its little window, the sign with the 12 would say "Now." Canny deduced the "Now" from the "Don't," which was actually a "Not now." She'd looked at the clock and figured that something was supposed to happen at midnight, and at no other time.

She said to Ghislain, "I remember all the pieces, and I move them around in my head till I understand the pattern."

A look of beatific happiness filled Ghislain's face and he said, in wonder, "You're not a Zarene at all, are you?"

"That's what I keep telling you! I'm Canny Mochrie from Castlereagh," she said. Then, more formal, "I am Canny and Agnes and Akanesi—just to give you all my names."

"You shouldn't."

"I want to."

She still felt flustered, but less so. She was calm enough now to take her hands off him. She pulled back as if his shirtsleeves were sticky or magnetic and she had to tug to break free. He gave a faint gasp and they both rocked in their chairs. Then they were just two people sitting side by side at a worktable. She picked up the correct stamp. The one that said "Go"—

—like the signs stenciled on Cyrus Zarene's beehives, which said, "Go, gather, and return." She was seeing it all now—the patterns.

Canny carefully pressed the twisted wire into a clay tile. Then she did another. Ghislain stooped over his work again, first dabbing his fingers in a muddy water glass and wetting the surface of the tile he was working on.

"I think I'm cleverer when I'm here with you," Canny said.

"I'm sure I'm not the necessary ingredient."

"No. You make me stupid too."

"I'll take that as a compliment."

Canny shifted another limp, printed tile into a patch of sunlight to dry. She asked him how many he had to make. She wanted him to explain what he was up to.

"This is the last of the day. I'm running out of clay." He kept working quietly. When he wet his fingers and ran them over the tile, Canny would watch, mesmerized. He didn't acknowledge this, but said, "Do you know what this one says?"

She stared. "No." She just liked watching his busy, stroking hand.

"It's a refinement. With any large, complex, enduring spell there has to be one or two powerful instructions."

"Like, 'Go now,'" Canny said.

"Exactly. And the rest are refinements like, 'Not that way, or *that* way, or even this'—so that every possibility is closed off, except the one you want."

Ghislain picked up a dried grass stem and blew through it, cleaning the water from the intricate symbol he'd fashioned. "It's the refinements that take the most time."

"Do you fire these tiles?"

"It isn't necessary. Which is just as well, since I don't have a kiln. When I pour the molten lead there are always some that shatter." He got up. "Are you finished? Come and wash your hands."

They stood side by side at the big basin in the immaculate black-and-white bathroom. Canny rinsed her hands, then looked up to catch him watching her in the mirror. She blushed. He said, "Come on, you can help me water the garden."

They went down to the second terrace, where the orderly

vegetable beds were. He gave her a watering can and took a zinc bucket himself. They plunged these vessels into the nearest rain barrel, which was full of wriggling mosquito larvae. They filled the channels by the cabbages and broccoli then went on to other rain barrels around the conical hillside. They watered carrots, onions, garlic, and radishes.

Ghislain stopped beside one caterpillar-ravished bed of lettuce and upended his bucket so Canny could sit on it. He knelt among the plants and began writing sign over them. His fingers flashed. After a time he stopped, and they both watched till Canny saw the caterpillars curl up and drop from the leaves onto the soil—not to die, but to each uncurl and set off, inching their way to the stones that edged the drop to the next terrace. The caterpillars all crawled over the edge of the terrace and out of sight.

Ghislain said, "Did you pick that up?"

"The signs? Yes. That was another 'Go.'"

"You're a prodigy."

"Aren't you?"

"No. I was always a strong signer. There were some things I could do very, *very* well. But I was never intelligent, or thorough, or imaginative, like my cousins."

"You made a rope out of air," Canny said.

Ghislain looked at her. "I'm much stronger than I once was. Stronger than *everybody*. I don't know why. If anyone asks me—and by anyone I mean Cyrus, since he's the only person I ever see—then I pretend I *do* know, because it worries him."

He got up and gave her his hand. They left the watering can but took the bucket and continued on and he showed her the little spring where he'd dug the clay. She helped him scoop some out. Cold water bubbling out of the waxy ooze washed over her chilled hands. They filled the bucket with clay, and he carried it. They stopped to wash at the first rain barrel. Seized by an impulse, Canny tried Lonnie's pain rune on the wriggling mosquito larvae. Perhaps it would kill them, she thought. She wrote the rune over and over, making little splashes on the surface of the water. But the larvae continue to rise and fall, flicking their happy bodies. "Damn," she said.

"What are you doing?"

She kept trying, and then was pleased to see the larvae begin to wriggle more convulsively.

Then the water began to steam. Canny snatched back her scalded fingers. The water in the barrel started to boil. Ghislain pulled her away from it—he put his arms around her and held her still. Her ears were ringing. She watched the water boil for a minute, then turned her face to surreptitiously sniff his neck.

"Are you hurt?"

"Mmmm. No." Canny's throat seemed to have turned to wood, while her legs were milk pudding.

"Are you crying?"

"No."

"Water doesn't know pain," Ghislain said reassuringly. "It only knows dissolution. So if you tell it to feel pain, it only tries to evaporate the quickest way it can."

"Oh."

"You just boiled ten gallons of water in thirty seconds."

"Oh. Yes." There was a silence, then Canny said, "I should open a bathhouse."

That made him laugh, and they were off, giggling again.

Eventually he let go of her, picked up the dropped bucket, and walked on. They went up the steps.

"Why is the garden a wilderness one terrace down, normal in the vegetable beds, and perfect up here?"

"The spell is on the house. Its influence flows out like ripples on a pond. When I was a boy, the spell just kept things neat and tidy, spick and span."

Spick and Span were characters in a radio advertisement from the sponsor of a popular radio serial. Ghislain had said "Spick" in falsetto and "Span" big and gruff like the radio voices. This reminded Canny that he was in her world as well as this one, a world with a kind of paradise at the top of it.

"If you're here at midnight I can show you the spell in action."

So, she was right, something did happen at midnight. But she wouldn't be here. She should be on her way already.

"I have to put in an appearance at dinner," she said. "With damp hair. I'm supposed to be at the swimming hole." She sighed. "Sholto is going to watch me like a hawk all evening. I promised him I'd transcribe Mr. Cyrus's interview tonight. Though I don't see how I can since there's no electricity at the guesthouse."

"What interview?"

"My brother is researching the 1929 mining disaster of which your Cyrus is a survivor."

Ghislain averted his head. Canny was sure that he was hiding his face. She said, "I've been telling lies to keep my freedom. But I'm going to have to do some of what Sholto wants so that he thinks I'm being good. Good and reliable."

They got back to the house. Canny draped her sandals around her neck again. She produced the spell paper from her pocket, dipped it in some clay slip, and pressed it onto her forehead. Ghislain stopped fussing with stuff on the table and said, "Oh fine. Do that then."

"Can't you see me?"

He squinted in her direction. "I can't *look* at you. That's how it works."

She put a tentative hand on his arm. "Here I am."

"There you are," he said. Then, "Don't go."

Canny thought of Marli, who'd never say "Don't go," only, sometimes, "Can't you stay a little longer?" She removed her hand. A clammy, shrinking feeling came over her, not about Ghislain, but herself. She remembered her mother saying, of Marli, that it must be nice for Canny to visit someone who she could always know would be *there*, waiting for her. Was the warmth she felt toward Ghislain, her excitement about him, only a reflection of her feelings for Marli—for someone else who couldn't follow her if she walked away from them? What was wrong with her? Or, perhaps she should rather ask, what *else* was wrong with her, apart from her detachment, her frozen face, her secretive habits. "You can't want me to stay!" she said, passionate. But what she was thinking was: "You can't want *me*."

She clapped her hands over her ears and hurried off.

She could hear Ghislain calling her name all the way down to the wrecked jeep and beginning of the forest.

BY THE TIME CANNY ARRIVED BACK at the apiary she was out of breath, but calmer. She found Susan and Sholto packing up the recording equipment. She told them she'd decided to check out the swimming hole before getting her swimsuit. "It seemed too much bother going back for it. Instead of swimming I had a nap on the grass," then, blithely, "There's always tomorrow."

"Tomorrow you're transcribing today's interviews for me," Sholto reminded her. "Sue and I are going over to Orchard House to see if Mr. Lealand can spare us an hour. We'll bring the equipment back here tomorrow. Mr. Cyrus says it's okay for you to work here, but you should ask him what time tomorrow would suit him. You'll find him in the kitchen."

Cyrus Zarene was pasting labels onto slender bottles of something honey-colored and wholly liquid. The bottles didn't have crown caps, like the cider, but corks. Canny favored Cyrus Zarene with the gloomiest look she could muster. "Why did you have to be so helpful?"

"About?"

"Me coming here to transcribe interviews."

"I was more helpful than you know. I even offered to keep the equipment here overnight, but apparently the department of anthropology at Castlereagh University is full of ogres."

"They're certainly full of themselves," Canny said, and rolled her eyes. "The university's anthropologists want to be seen as a science, but they're a social science, like psychology, and it's not the same thing. But they reckon that since history is only an arts subject, it's even lower in the pecking order. The kids I go to school with—university is a mystery to them. I wish it was more of one to me."

The labels on the bottles said "Zarene Valley Mead." Canny suddenly had an idea. She asked whether she could buy a bottle. "As a present for Sholto and Susan. I've given them a lot of trouble, and I want to say sorry."

"That's a nice thought."

"I'll run and get my purse."

"Tell you what, Agnes, I'll let you have a bottle if you give me a hand with the hives in the home paddock."

"Okay.

Cyrus dried his hands and began slotting the bottles into a wooden crate. Canny made to help. "Leave that," he said. "Go tell your brother that you're assisting me with something, and that, in payment, I'm giving you some mead. Just so as I know the drink will end up in their bellies, not yours. It's strong stuff and you're a bit young for it. Sorry if you planned to surprise them, but you must see what I mean."

"Fair enough," Canny said. She went to tell Sholto she'd be busy for a bit, and to reassure him that she'd be back at the guesthouse by dinnertime. She didn't mention the mead.

CYRUS TOOK THE GIRL OUT TO THE HIVES. It was late afternoon and the low sun made the chalky paint of the frames glow—Nile green, white, ochre, melon pink. Each hive was wreathed with circling bees. The home paddock hummed. Canny carried the honey box and wore a hat with a veil. Cyrus had a bare head, and his sleeves were rolled up. He paused to drop dried juniper berries on top of the mix of smoldering moss and pine needles in the smoke blower. Canny thought that the smoke smelled like Grandma Mochrie's parlor at five in the evening when Grandma would say "The sun is over the yardarm" before fixing herself a gin and tonic.

Cyrus blew smoke into the hive. He picked up the heavy stone used to keep its tin top in place, and then lifted the lid.

The bees rose in a cloud. They darted around Cyrus and Canny. They seemed sullen and insecure. One settled on Canny's hand and stung her. She gave a yelp and made to break away. Cyrus grabbed her arm and held her in place. She watched several bees settle on the pale hairs of his forearm and scramble around like people trying to wade through long bracken. The abdomen of one bee dipped, thrust, and deposited its sting in Cyrus's skin. The bee crawled away, while the sting stayed where it had lodged, pulsing.

Bees were crawling on Canny's veil, before her eyes.

Cyrus released her—he needed both hands for the blower. He blew a thick cloud, like another veil. He flicked two bees off his neck.

Another bee stung Canny's leg, then, straight afterward, her elbow. Again Cyrus seized her arm to prevent her from running. She didn't dare struggle. The bees were around them now, not tens, *hundreds*—and the tone of the hum had changed from musing to electrical.

"What are you doing?" Canny whispered. She suppressed her urge to shout and flail. There were dozens of bees crawling along the tops of the frames, tapping the timber and one another with their tiny feelers, passing on some terrible rumor. Canny didn't know what the bees were saying, but what she imagined was: "There's a stranger at the hives." It was a call to arms. Why wouldn't Cyrus work his magic? Why didn't he scrawl his signs in the smoke?

Another bee stung her neck—it had crawled under her veil.

Cyrus let go and again blew smoke, then lunged after her and grabbed her once more. She had managed to retreat three careful paces. Sparks—a series of stings—touched her, and fire ran into her bones. Her heart was pounding. Before her eyes the smoke was growing thin and increasingly ineffectual. Abruptly Canny raised her free hand and wrote on the air. "Calm. Calm. Calm. Calm," she wrote.

Cyrus released her other arm and she used that hand to sign in counterpoint, "Go down."

The bees sank through the smoke. It was as if the air in the home paddock was a pot on the stove, and she'd just turned off the flame.

CYRUS'S BEES RELIED ON BEING SOOTHED. They became tense and apprehensive if smoke surrounded them but was empty of information. Cyrus's spells were part of the weather of their lives. He knew that if he opened a hive, blew smoke, and didn't inscribe the signs, his bees would react. He knew he and the girl would be stung, and that, with the bees swarming so menacingly, it wouldn't be too hard to make her hold still for long enough for what he hoped to happen—that she'd break down and beg him to do what she'd watched him doing, settle the hive by writing signs in the smoke. Cyrus wanted the girl to show him that she'd understood he was using magic. But instead of begging him to intervene, her free hand flew up and her fingers flashed the nine separate signs of the spell to soothe. She performed the movements without fault or hesitation and, because he was surprised, Cyrus let her go, and she thrust her other hand into the smoke and improvised. For a moment she was making two separate series of movements. One of nine and one of eleven.

Cyrus had been told that his great-aunts, Joanne and Rowan Zarene, had worked together to do this—what two Zarenes together could seldom manage, no matter how long they practiced, because the character of their magics would never match. The old aunties were identical twins, so they matched. The old aunties had been the most accomplished members of the family in living history. It was Joanne and Rowan who'd laid the foundations of the house on Terminal Hill, who'd composed the great "Renew, Restore, Repair" spell and carved it into the house's woodwork, who'd made the house what it was by working together.

But this girl, her skin blotched with bee stings, performed *by herself* two very complex spells. And she performed them simultaneously, as if that was the way it was always done.

The insidious, ever-present humming of the hives in the home paddock had died away, and a breeze could now be heard jostling the leaves of the apricot tree near where they stood.

Cyrus took a couple of deep breaths, then said, "Now you've shown your hand." In fact she'd shown both of them.

The girl looked at him, wide-eyed, but her face was frozen. He didn't understand how much pain she was in till her eyes filled and tears spilled down her cheeks. He touched her arm and drew her well away from the hives, then got her to stand still while he pinched the stings from the red patches on her arms and legs, to stop the venom spreading. She let him do that. But then, when he was rising creakily out of his crouch, she spoke. Her voice was toneless and low-pitched. "It hurts," she said. Then she bounded backward away from him, fleet-footed. She paused only to shout at him, accusingly. "You kept hold of me! You wouldn't let me get away!" Then she turned on her heel and took off.

Cyrus was alarmed. He was right to think she'd been watching him and studying his every move. She might have only supposed he was blessing his beehives, but she hadn't. She'd watched and seen magic—that was Cyrus's belief. But she'd also learned how to copy what he did. That was extraordinary in itself. She was very alert, and her memory was capacious. She recognized that what he was doing was more than merely ceremonial. When she wanted the bees to calm down she asked them, as he had asked them. She'd performed a spell. She was completely within her rights to be angry at him for how he chose to flush her out. But he was right, and she could hardly pretend that what he'd done was crazy.

But Cyrus feared that was exactly what she would do. She'd tell her brother only what Cyrus had done, not why he did it, or the experiment's final result. She was going to say that Mr. Zarene grabbed on to her and held her still in a cloud of angry bees, and Sholto Mochrie would rush off and fetch a deputy from Massenfer—again.

Cyrus put the tin lid back on the open hive and replaced the rock that weighed it down. He walked back to his house, holding his head in both hands as if to stop his skull from flying apart. "What a calamity," he thought.

Indoors, he made himself some tea, but he didn't ice his stings. He accepted his pain as penance for his stupidity.

Once he was sitting down with his cup of tea, he felt less frightened, but no less amazed. What was amazing wasn't that the girl had watched him, understood what he was doing, and copied him. That was just *asking*. Asking was only part of the magic. Any clever person could pick up a spell, given time. So, asking was one thing, being answered quite another. When Agnes Mochrie's dark fingers flashed, the bees calmed and time itself seemed to slow till the late afternoon sunlight was as thick, lucent, and golden as honey.

Zarenes, perhaps half of them, once they had a grasp of the Alphabet in its Basic and Tabular forms, would be able to ask something of the magic and have it reply, "Oh, all right," grudgingly. To some it said, plainly, "Yes." To very few, it answered, "Yes, I will!" joyous, like a bride or groom. It had sometimes said, "Yes! I will!" to Cyrus. And always to Ghislain—the magic had doted on Ghislain like it was his mother and father. But now and then, throughout the centuries, it would do more. It would consolidate itself and

say, like the genie of stories, *"Your wish is my command."*
And when the bees sank out of the air and a balm fell over
the afternoon, it had said that to Agnes Mochrie.

Cyrus was sitting over his empty cup with his head in
his hands, when he heard a back step creak. Agnes Mochrie came in the door. Her hair was sopping and stuck to
her, and her shorts were soaked. Her shirt was only blotted
with water—she must have taken it off before going into
the river to cool her bee stings. She glared at Cyrus, and
then her gaze moved to the bench and the bottles of mead.
"You owe me," she said savagely.

"I could give you the mead then walk you back to the
guesthouse. I think we should both have a talk with Iris—"

"I'm not talking to any of you!"

He got up, and she backed off. He picked up one slender
bottle and offered it to her.

"Put it down on the end of the table," she said.

He did, and stepped back.

She darted forward, snatched the bottle, and ran from
the room.

CANNY SNEAKED INTO THE GUESTHOUSE and put on her
slacks and a cardigan. She knotted a scarf around her neck
and checked herself in the mirror. Most of her stings were
covered.

She took the bottle of mead to Sholto and Susan, who
were sitting on the porch swing. They were very pleased by
her gift, and touched. Susan went to find a corkscrew and
three glasses, and they opened the bottle. Canny had a little. The mead was sweet and fragrant, and the small buzz

she got from it was a distraction. Discomfort was taking up most of her attention. Her consciousness seemed to be running a relay race from sting to sting, pausing at each and then carrying amplified pain along to the next.

At dinner she was silent and droopy. Susan and Sholto didn't notice. They were flirting, leaning together and laughing. Canny watched their behavior and realized that the way she saw it had changed. It no longer looked embarrassing and exclusive, but kind of sweet. They were tipsy, and funny. There were new guests—a family with two children, one five, the other two. The two-year-old was being fussed over by Iris's older girls, who were serving that night. The parents were clearly charmed by the fussing, by Susan and Sholto's laughter, and the way they were showing one another off in conversation. The five-year-old was perky and kept saying smart things to get attention, and was getting plenty. The food was excellent, as always, and everyone at the table seemed comfortable and content.

Canny didn't feel left out. She didn't feel like a leper. Her arms and legs and neck were smarting, and she felt light-headed, but she had plans, and she liked her plans and knew where she wanted them to take her.

THE GUESTHOUSE WAS QUIET BY TEN P.M. Everyone had retired, including Iris Zarene, who slept in a room off the first-floor landing. It was the only room on that level, and its window was a gable above the front porch. Because she was wary of Iris, Canny decided to go out her bedroom window and edge along the porch roof to the fire escape. She was pretty sure the two children were in the room beside hers. She'd only have to pass their window, and they'd be fast asleep. Canny was very tired. She'd been up since six-thirty, with only one decent night's sleep in the five days before that. She'd rather stay in bed but felt that, before she got upset and ran away from Ghislain, she'd promised him she'd be back.

As she plaited her hair, which was so long and thick that it was still damp with river water, she thought, "I can always go to sleep once I get there." The idea seemed natural. If she was with Ghislain she wouldn't have to worry about being prevented from being with Ghislain, at the heart of the magic. Ghislain would teach her. When Ghislain talked to her, he was talking to the real—secret—Canny. It was exciting, and also strangely restful. He wasn't really trustworthy—after all he'd tied her up—but yet somehow she trusted him.

Canny trimmed the lamp and opened the window. She was ready to leave, but for a moment she stood, as if in a trance, remembering how, when Ghislain helped her from the veranda roof, he'd had his arms around her. At the time she'd been surprised and alarmed (and puzzled by the strange absence of odor in the air around him), but looking back now she could see she'd been quite safe, possibly safer than she'd ever been in her life.

Canny came to and practically floated through the window. She slid the sash closed and walked nimbly along the porch roof to the corner and the painted timber ladder fixed to the wall of the house. She clambered down it and made for the river path.

13

THE GIRL TURNED UP at around eleven, in time to see him prying dribbles of lead sign from the clay tiles. He'd left the window open for her. The lights were on, and although it was summer, he never had to bother about moths. Insects respected the spell and wouldn't usually cross any of the house's thresholds. The girl did though. She came in blinking, her eyes already half-mast. She settled in an armchair near the hearth and watched him work at detaching the ideograms from the dried clay, then peeling the remaining ripples of melted lead from his quartz crucible. When he was done Ghislain turned to her and saw that she hadn't moved. She was slumped and knock-kneed, and her face was soft with sleepiness. "Hey," he said.

She made a friendly, throaty questioning noise.

"The thing I want you to see—you have to pay attention to the preliminaries."

Again that little purring noise.

He went to the kitchen and took a couple of plates from the cupboard. He stopped in the front hall and only leaned through the parlor door to say, "This should wake you up." He raised one plate over his head. Her eyes moved to follow it and, when he smashed it on the hall rug, she flinched. He smashed the second plate. One fragment of porcelain lodged in the floorboards.

The girl got up and joined him. She said, "Why are you making a mess?"

He pulled the shard out of the floorboard and ran his finger over the white scar it had left. "Come and sit with me on the stairs," he said. He took her hand. It was fine, but not small. *She* wasn't small, she was tall and lean and strong. Ghislain moved closer to her to check their relative heights. He tilted his chin and rested it on top of her head. He was tall, but she must be something like five foot ten.

She suddenly leaned against him and sighed. He put his arms around her and they stood that way for a time. Ghislain could feel her shaking off sleep—or simply shaking and waking up. He put his hands into her hair, covered her ears, and raised her face to his. Her hair was dry but smelled of river water. Her dark skin was flushed, her mouth a rosy bruise.

Ghislain had never kissed anyone before. He'd imagined it would be exciting to kiss a girl, but not that it would be like breaking free. He pressed his lips to Canny's and seemed to pass through her, and be faraway, and yet at the same time he was still there, touching her. For days he'd been thinking about her, wondering who she was—and now, near to her, he couldn't get past her surfaces. Her hair, her skin, the long wands of her forearms, her high cheekbones, her throat, her smooth, firm upper arms. Her skin was silky and supple, like his own, but it wasn't his own. How *strange* that was. Ghislain lifted her shirt a little and put his hand on her ribs. He felt them expand and shrink. She was taking deep breaths. Her mouth tasted of toothpaste and apple crumble—apple, sugar, cinnamon.

A number of minutes went by, then Ghislain felt the midnight, like a slack tide about to turn. He didn't want to let Canny go, but knew he must. The girl would go, not at midnight, like Cinderella, but sometime, sooner than he wanted.

Ghislain hardly ever had visitors, and he *only* ever had visitors. No one stayed. No one was his to keep. Snatching a moment like this—it wasn't enough for him. His young body might be shouting, *"Now!"* Demanding, *"Right now!"* But his old heart was telling him that to give in to what he wanted would only bring him pain. *"You can't do this,"* he counseled himself. *"You can't stand it."*

Ghislain took Canny by her shoulders and turned her. "Look," he said.

The shards of crockery lay scattered on the rug, glowing in the soft gaslight. Then it was as if there was a breeze in the hallway, a wind stirring the smallest splinters. It wasn't a breeze from one direction, but from all points of the compass, and the patch of broken plates was a compass rose. The splinters stirred, then twitched and skidded inward. Then, with a stealthy tinkle, all the shards slid together, turning themselves over or around, to fit back together and seal seamlessly. The plates were whole again.

If there was ever any dust that settled on furniture, books, window ledges, it too was whipped away. The dried clay slip splattered on the desk in the parlor lost its cohesion and flew away as fine dust, and the cloud of dust posted itself out under the front door. The bright brass doorsill grew momentarily dull as the dust, dirt, crumbs of food, and a few long black hairs gathered together and went out over it.

Midnight was past. The waiting stillness gone, and replaced by an accomplished peace. The house seemed pleased with itself.

"Oh," said Canny, then, old-fashioned, "In all my born days!"

"Yes," said Ghislain, pleased too. Then he offered to show her what he was making.

The Hidden House had a locked room. Ghislain unlocked the door and pushed it open. Canny stopped before the black oblong of darkness while Ghislain went on in to turn up the gas. Canny heard the flint strikers spitting, and the light came, at first burning blue.

Canny thought of the locked rooms in fairy tales and what those rooms held—a little man at a spinning wheel, spinning straw into gold; or just the spinning wheel and a spindle with its wicked point, waiting for a cursed princess; or the bodies of Bluebeard's former wives hanging from hooks like sides of lamb in a meat locker.

"Why are you standing there?" said Ghislain. "Come on in."

The floorboards were bare. There were no curtains on

the bay window. The windowpanes were all rippled glass, so that no one would be able to see in. There was a long window seat in the bay. There was a fireplace with an empty grate, and in the center of the room, a roughly man-size form draped with a sheet.

Canny's footsteps echoed. So did Ghislain's voice. "Mind the rope," he said.

She stopped. A rope was coiled at her feet. It had a hook at one end and a loop at the other.

Ghislain pointed up at the ceiling. "There's supposed to be a sturdy hook up there, for the loop, but I have to keep drilling a hole for it over and over. Midnight mends it. The rope is actually too big for the job anyway. But now that I have you"—he laughed—"I thought perhaps we might unravel one of your sweaters and plait a wool cord. Something lighter."

Canny could see that Ghislain's "sturdy hook" was supposed to fit into the hub of fanning spokes of ceiling beams. The beams were all intricately carved with ideogrammatic sign. They were too big for the room. "Is that structural?" she said.

"Magically structural? Or structural in terms of engineering?"

"I suppose it must be magical," Canny said.

"It's the final phrase of the Great Spell."

"The spell that keeps the house perfect? Or the one that hides it and keeps you prisoner?" Canny asked.

"The first—the builders' spell, which keeps the house perfect. There are four foundation stones—two matched pairs. They're underground. The Great Spell is founded on them. Most of the carving and stained glass only refine the terms of the spell." He gestured at the joined beams. "But this and the clock in the library are a bit more important."

Ghislain carefully lifted the sheet on the shrouded form and let it fall to the floor. The revealed object was a kind of cage—one cage inside another. Both were entirely made of lead filigree, thousands of Ghislain's melted toy soldier ideograms, soldered together to make two forms with dimensions similar to those of a dressmaker's dummies, one inside the other. But, unlike dressmakers' dummies, these shapes went all the way to the floor.

Canny couldn't read the spell, or spells, because her eyes weren't able to separate the two layers. It was like looking through two pieces of overlapping lace and trying to distinguish a pattern. She said, "There's a way into this, right?"

Ghislain produced some pliers from his pocket and used them to bend back several flanges of lead. The outer cage split and opened. The second cage was already unfastened. On the floor of the inner cage was an inverted bowl of lead filigree. Canny saw that this cap thing was meant to go on top of the outer cage, that there was a smooth open ring around its top that the cap was meant to slot into. The inner cage was already closed on top. There was a lead loop jutting from the center of the cap where a hook could latch on, the hook tied to the rope.

"That's the crown," Ghislain said. "It's still missing several sections. Once it's lowered into place it closes the outer cage. The crown will activate the spell."

It had been this crown Ghislain was working on. Every sign forming the outer cage was the same. They all said: "Go now." They were meant to be read from the inside, Canny saw. The "Go now" faced inward, which was why the dust sheet draping the cages hadn't torn itself to shreds.

"Is the crown like an on switch?" Canny said.

"Yes."

"This is all one spell?"

Ghislain nodded.

Canny's eyes roamed. There was so much language on the inner cage—minutely detailed instructions. She couldn't see how it could be only one spell. She glanced at Ghislain. She must have looked nervous, because he took her hand. "I don't understand this," she said.

"But you can read it?"

"Bits of it," she said. "The words are facing inward. It's like trying to read the writing on a shop window from inside the shop."

"Harder than that, I think."

He was right. It was like trying to make one picture from the pieces of thirty different jigsaw puzzles all thrown together in a pile.

"It's an exhaustive list of what I don't mean when I say 'Go now,'" Ghislain said. "It's like all the 'Quiet Please' and 'No Smoking' and 'Wrong Way' signs in the whole world. You know how in grammar there are words called 'qualifiers' that modify adjectives? For example: 'you are *quite* tall, and *very* pretty'?"

Canny blushed.

Ghislain touched the gleaming gray lacework of the inner cage. "This is a bunch of qualifiers."

"So, someone gets in the cage. Then what happens?"

"Someone climbs into the inner cage, closes the outer cage, then the inner, and then unties the cord knotted near their hand and lowers the crown into place. Then the spell does its work."

She looked up and into his face. "You get in the cage?"

He nodded.

"The inner cage says what not to do?"

"Where not to go."

"And the outer cage says 'Go.'"

He nodded.

"The inner cage says, 'Not here, or there, or that other place.'"

"Et cetera, ad infinitum. But the outer cage doesn't just say 'Go now,'" Ghislain said, then his chin lifted and he added softly, but with terrible pride, "It says: 'Go from now.'"

"What? Like, 'Keep going from now on'?"

He shook his head.

Canny had a moment of innocent confusion, then the realization came—and it was as if someone had pumped her head full of water, till it felt cold and full. Tears leaked out of her eyes. "Go from this time?"

GHISLAIN LEFT HIS CONTRAPTION uncovered and the door to the room open. He took Canny into the kitchen. The range was still warm from when he'd cooked his dinner. He made lemon mint tea (herbs he could grow), and offered her some pie (it was made of last year's preserved apples and crumbly cornmeal pie crust. He'd grown and ground the corn). He folded the girl's hands around her warm cup and held them there. "You're shaking," he said. "I don't know why you're so upset."

"People can't travel through time."

"Are you upset because the idea is offensive to you? I don't know why. Do you think people can *refuse* to travel through time? You're a time traveler. You were living in last year, and now you're living in this year."

She pulled a face and told him to stop being so literal-minded.

"I'm not. This house isn't traveling through time like everything else. In this house every midnight is the same midnight. What belongs to the house is put back together and back in good order. The books even reshelve themselves. If I'm reading in bed I have to chase my book back to the library after midnight and retrieve it. The house is a house, and it's a 'Renew, Restore, Repair' spell."

"But the house only resists wear and tear, not time itself," Canny said, then freed one hand and leaned across to pluck a hair off his collar. "If you shed hair, you must grow it too. The house lets you do that."

"True," he said. "It isn't as minutely managing of me, but I'm not actually *of* the house. I wasn't born here. And the only reason I've been able to build my Spell Cage is because the lead I'm using isn't of the house either. My little cousin Felix left a battle set up here on the billiard table the week before—" Ghislain broke off.

The week before the explosion at Bull Mine. A storm had been brewing, and the light was yellow, the light coming through the skylight over Uncle Talbot's billiard table. The green baize had looked toxic, and Felix fiendish as he leaned over and moved his lead cannon and artillerymen with a billiard cue. It was a long campaign, and they had been playing it every evening when they came home from their shift in the mine.

Ghislain had just said "my little cousin" because he was looking down the wrong end of the telescope at that day in 1929, so long ago, when they'd been there together, fourteen-year-old Felix, and him, Ghislain, seventeen years of age, and about to stop traveling in time, like everybody else did no matter what this girl thought.

She seemed to be near to tears as she said, "It's a desperate idea." She was so troubled that her masklike face had managed to form a clear expression.

Ghislain put up a finger and stroked the crease between her brows. "And you imagine I'm not desperate?"

CANNY WENT AROUND THE TABLE and edged Ghislain half out of his chair so she could share it. She put her arm around his waist. She wanted to comfort him, but she also wanted to bring him to his senses. Perhaps she should kiss him some more. Appeal to his senses by investigating his body. She did place a kiss on the soft skin under his ear. Then she slid one hand inside his shirt. Their mouths came together again, wide, lips moving against each other as if they were trying to trap air and eat it. His tongue touched hers and their mouths pressed and clung. His heart was banging against her palm.

"Wait," he said, breaking off. "Look. People don't usually pet madmen to keep them calm."

"I didn't call you a madman, I only said your plan was desperate."

"I think it was implied, Canny. Poor man—you were thinking—driven mad by being kept so long in his lonely prison." He looked annoyed. But his mouth wouldn't harden, it seemed to have a mind of its own.

Fascinated, she touched it with her fingertips.

"Aren't you even interested in the magic?" He sounded pleased and indignant at once. Then he jerked his face away. "No, please stop. I'm getting a horrible feeling of having been here before, which probably means I'm in the room with myself and, believe me, once I'm gone I'm never coming back here, not even in spirit."

"What?" said Canny, startled.

Ghislain then patiently explained to her how his contraption was meant to work, and what he hoped it would do for him.

"The mistake you're making is to think I mean to shut myself into the two cages, lower the crown into place, and then *disappear*. That's not how it works. Nobody can travel through time, as far as we know. I mean no *body* can. So, what will travel will be my consciousness. Or maybe my spirit. The spell makes it impossible for my consciousness to go anywhere but back in time. It can't float off and hover over, say, the marshes near Metternich or the Temple in Founderston. It can only go back in my own time, within my own life. That's the plan."

Canny could see now that this made sense. That his spirit couldn't leave the cage, leak out into the room, and fly free in space. It had to go the only place it could—where it had been before, its own past. But, to her, it still seemed that he was planning to abandon himself. "But your body," she protested. She held him tight. "What about your body?"

"The house won't let me die."

"Your plan is suicidal. You must be able to see that."

He laughed. "Do you imagine I've been shut up here by myself for thirty years and not, at some time, tried to destroy myself? Sure I was scared—of the gas, the razor, the rope—but I did it. I did it over and over. After a while it was like a pastime. No one else I hated was within my reach. I had only myself to take it all out on. My body. And, come midnight, the house would repair me, like a broken plate. And it shouldn't have. I'm not of the house. And the Great Spell doesn't reform my cousin Felix's soldiers when I melt them down. So why did it choose to put me together? To put me back together again and again?"

He was furious. Canny found the only way she could be near him and not feel afraid of him was to cling even closer. She held on, and he held on, and he shouted at her, the house, the world, his fate. And then they were both quiet, holding on, holding hard, and trembling with effort.

Canny came back to herself—her reasoning self—long before he did. She had to talk him out of it, but she didn't want to argue with his pain, or his thirty years of captivity. "What can I do?" she thought. And then, for some reason, her mother came into her mind. Her mother in the outrigger with two feverish airmen. Sisema, in the hour when she lost her way because the whales went on ahead of her.

"Let's go sit somewhere comfortable," Canny said. "Or even lie down."

"Canny." He was tired. He was telling her off.

"What?"

"Stop caressing the madman hoping that's going to fix him."

"You need to discuss this with someone. And it's going to have to be me. Look, how long do you think you'd stay alive in the cage?"

He shook his head.

"Even with the Great Spell in place?"

Again he shook his head.

Canny thought for a bit, then said, "I just realized that that's why you said you wondered whether you felt strange because you were in the room with yourself. Presumably once you get in the cage and go, then this is your past too— this moment—and your spirit might be here, with us, watching us."

"Yes. That is what I meant."

"But how do you know that's what it feels like when your own spirit is in the room?"

"This has been done before. People have reported back," Ghislain said. Then, "Let's lie down, like you say, and I'll tell you more about the magic."

GHISLAIN'S GREAT-AUNTS, Rowan and Joanne Zarene, were twins. They were adept very early, and imaginative too. And, because they were twins, they were able to push the boundaries of the magic much further than others in the family.

"Before I talk about the great-aunts, there is stuff you have to know. For a start, this. There are four types of the Alphabet. The first is Basic, which doesn't get anyone anywhere, but all Zarene kids have to learn it in order to go on to the Tabular."

Ghislain told Canny that, with the Tabular Alphabet, she should think of the periodic table of elements, and how each element had its place, its valence, and its atomic weight. "Tabular Alphabet is about the relationships between signs. A Zarene child who masters the tables will at least be able to recognize when they're being worked on by someone else's magic. They can see magic if it's built into something, like the carvings in this house. They can't exactly read it. They can get general impressions, sometimes quite the opposite of the spell-maker's intentions. For example, imagine reading 'deserving' or 'repentant' or 'possible,' when what was meant was 'undeserving, unrepentant, impossible.' With those three words there are two different prefixes that make the negative—'un' and 'im.' But there are hundreds of modifiers in the Alphabet. It's very complicated. Kids who learn Tabular can't necessarily do magic, but they can guess when magic is around and can get the gist of anything visible. A few Zarenes have the brains to study the Alphabet's Ideogrammatic form. There are endless possibilities of combinations, and a spell that is made with Ideogrammatic sign is very hard to unravel. The carvings in this house are enormously complex. They're not like words. They are like one long song made up of words that were never heard before. Which is where they came from, but I'll get to that. Ideogrammatic magic has to be performed quickly and accurately if it isn't made solid—like the wood carvings, or my lead latticework. Magic made quickly, in the moment, is what we call 'warm sign.' If sign isn't made solid, or if it isn't performed with physical contact—like when you drew the pain rune on the surface of the water in the rain barrel—then it almost always has to be magnified. Something has to carry it, and make it linger a little bit longer."

"Smoke," said Canny. "Steam."

"Yes!" Ghislain laughed in delight. "How did you know?"

"I was watching your uncle Cyrus at his beehives." She didn't mention Cyrus's test—she guessed Ghislain would be worried if he knew that Cyrus was onto her.

"Cyrus isn't my uncle, he's my cousin. And the kids you've met may call him uncle, but he's their great-uncle, maybe even their great-great-uncle. He was twenty-five in 1929. I was seventeen."

Canny shivered. She put her face against his throat. "You're a grownup," she said.

"Yes, and no."

"That's why you're not all over me like a rash," she said.

"Oh, you mean I'm showing mature restraint? Or perhaps you imagine I think it's indecent to kiss you? You know, Canny, my body is seventeen as yours is sixteen. And I've been shut up here alone."

"Okay," she said.

"Stop shaking," he growled. "I'm not going to hurt you."

"Or anything else me," she said, which made him laugh.

Canny found she was both relieved and disappointed.

"You're going to leave," he said. "You come from

Castlereagh, and you're going back there. You're on your summer break and summer will come to an end. That's why I'm not all over you. Just because you're an opportunity, that doesn't mean I'm going to grab on to you. Carpe diem doesn't mean a damn thing when it's always the same day—the same Goddamn perfect day!" he finished, fierce.

Canny let go of him and took a deep breath as if she were coming up for air. She sat up and did ferocious things to her pillow to get comfortable. The pillow bashing disguised her sad little sniffs.

"Canny," Ghislain said, uncertain.

"Shut up!" she said. "You're right—of course. And I'm not much of a girl anyway. I'm just here. Just being here doesn't mean I'm an opportunity."

"For sex," he said. "You're talking about sex—you know that, don't you?"

"No I'm not! It doesn't have to be—*humping*!" She used the rudest word she could imagine herself using. "I just—" She was about to tell him how much she liked him and how unused to her own feeling of liking someone she was, how she wasn't in solitary confinement in paradise like he was, but she was alone, alone—

—and then she remembered Marli. Marli's fingertips making misty spots on the thick green glass of the portholes of her iron lung, wanting to touch something. She remembered Marli and realized that hours had gone by and she hadn't once thought of her friend.

And then she was really distressed.

"What is it?" Ghislain was worried. "Canny?"

What was wrong with her? Was she such a coward that

she could only attach herself to people who couldn't walk away from her?

"You're both trapped," she said.

He looked very puzzled. The single candle was on the dresser behind her so she could look at him, not he at her. He had to lean up on his elbow and roll her onto her back to peer into her face. "What do you mean 'both'?"

"My friend Marli is in an iron lung. I visit her. I walk onto the ward, and sit down, and talk to her, and listen to her, then I get up and I walk away." She began to cry. "I was saying that I wasn't an opportunity, but then I thought that maybe that is all you are to me—someone else I can walk up to and look at and then walk away from, like a tiger in the zoo."

"Grrrrr," said Ghislain tenderly.

"What's wrong with me?" she cried.

"Maybe you can only imagine someone wanting your company if they really, really need company," Ghislain said.

She thought about this for a moment. Then nodded.

"But why?"

"My mother says I'm not interested in the same things that interest normal people," Canny explained.

"And you've stumbled on a whole valley of magic-loving Zarenes."

"Yes," she said. "But I don't care about that now. It's you I care about. Or it was, till I remembered Marli. Now I'm confused."

"Well, you can visit my body. You can push a grass stem through the Spell Cage and tickle me," he said.

She clenched her teeth. She wasn't going to start crying again. After a moment she said, "Isn't there some other way you can escape?"

He flopped back down. "I haven't finished explaining," he said. "Becoming an incorporeal tourist in the scenes of my own life—that's just the *least* I can expect, if my spell works at all. But I'm going looking for something. If I find what I'm looking for I might be able to solve the problem of how to get back to my body without an anchor."

Canny said, "You're going to have to explain the anchor bit."

GHISLAIN TOLD CANNY ABOUT HIS GREAT-AUNTIES, Joanne and Rowan. Because they were twins they served as anchors for each other. They made a spell, something like his lead filigree cages, but theirs was a wide sheet of hand-made lace. A Spell Veil. Great-aunt Rowan had wrapped Great-aunt Jo in the lace and, after twenty hours in some kind of coma, Jo had stirred and talked again. Then she got up and spent the next months doing nothing but sleeping, eating, and sculpting a block of limestone into a certain, secret shape. The shape was that of her Master Rune, she said, which she had seen when she went back to the moment of her own conception. Or rather to that first moment of division when the fertilized ovum that became her and her twin split to grow into not one body, but two. Jo had also glimpsed a ghostly print of her sister's Master Rune and had seen enough to recognize that Rowan's was similar, but distinct. Jo told her sister—and other Zarenes—that having her rune, she now had the whole of the magic.

So, of course, Rowan wrapped herself in the Spell Veil too and traveled back to find her own Master Rune.

"Have you heard about photographic memories?" Ghislain said.

Canny nodded. She didn't say she suspected she might have one.

"The great-aunties only ever had to get a glimpse. I mean, a soul can't carry a camera, can't carry *anything*, so the great-aunties had to be able to remember perfectly what it was they saw."

"What's the difference between a soul and a Master Rune?"

"A Master Rune is like a codex of all the possibilities of each person's life, and their relationship to the magic."

Canny was irritated, tickled by the loose threads of his explanation. She understood this Master Rune business in principle, but every time he said "the magic" she felt confused. That was silly, because she'd witnessed the magic, and even practiced it a little. The Zarene magic was as real and solid as a stone, or as real and forceful as the wind. But any stone was once an infinitesimal fraction of the vortex of matter, fire, and gravity that became the planet Earth. A vortex that began as an eddy in a whirlpool of hydrogen atoms that, pressed together by a great gravity, began the aeons-long fusion reaction that was the sun. Wind came from changes in air pressure, because sometimes the air was light and dry, and sometimes full of vapor from perpetually evaporating oceans. So, that was a stone. That was the wind. Things that had scientific causes, that *came from somewhere*. But where did the magic come from?

Ghislain was listening to her busy silence. He asked her whether he should go on.

"I'll save my questions."

"Great-aunt Rowan found her own Master Rune. Her soul went wandering and was brought back to her body by the ballast of that other soul, Jo's, so like her own, standing guard over her body. The great-aunts made foundation stones out of their runes—two of each. They never let anyone see them. The stones are buried at the four corners of the house. They made all the carving and stained glass to tell the house what they wanted it to do, which was look after itself, do its own maintenance, stay clean, and look after its own possessions. The house took about ten years to build, with my grandfather and great-uncles pit-sawing the timber and doing all the basic carpentry. When I was little I remember being fascinated—and revolted—by Rowan and Joanne's hands. They were scarred and twisted, crippled by holding tools to do all this." He gestured around at the paneled walls.

His hand made a breeze and the candle flame fluttered, the candlelight flickered on the carvings.

"People can do that?" Canny said. Ten years seemed nothing compared to what they had achieved. "What did you call the spell? The Midnight Mending—people can just do that?"

"Hmmmm," he said. *"People."*

"All right—Zarenes."

"The spell has gotten stronger," Ghislain said. "When I was a kid you'd have to glue the broken plate back together and then leave it for a long time till the cracks were sealed.

The house only resisted wear and tear, and helped its occupants stay healthy. It didn't stop time, or resurrect the dead. The great-aunts both lived to see ninety, even if they couldn't button their own clothes. But the spell wasn't anything like it is now. The way it is now—that's not actually possible."

"Um," Canny said. "But it is, though. It's a fact."

"Yes."

"Why did they choose to make a 'Repair, Restore' spell, rather than something else?"

"I think they hated housework. And their childhood home had been washed away by a flood. They must have wanted something that would last."

"It's not your great-aunties' spell that's keeping you prisoner though, is it?"

"No. My cousins Cyrus and Iris and my brother Lealand made that one."

Lealand was his brother. Canny thought of that watchful, saturnine face. Those pouched, faded eyes. "Is he your older brother?"

"Nine years. Or thirty-nine. Take your pick."

"And is the imprisoning spell stronger too?"

There was a gloating smile in Ghislain's voice when he answered. "For nearly twenty years Zarenes have had to leave the Valley when they grow into their magic, even if they've only a small talent. If they stay, the strong ones lose their magic and get very sick. The weak ones simply fail to thrive. They catch too many colds, or get dental cavities. They lose their hearing and walk with a limp. So, Zarenes come to the valley to learn from Iris and Cyrus and

Lealand once they're school-age, though not all of them; some of their parents hang on and refuse flat-out to send them. Or at least now they do. Now that they're tired of waiting for a solution to the problem. Iris has been promising a solution for decades, but she hasn't found one. In fact the problem is worse with each passing year. I ask Cyrus about it when I see him. He hems and haws, but now and then he talks to me."

Canny remembered Lonnie Zarene's miserable hunched figure, standing on the steps of the train. His panic when he realized his tattoo meant nothing to the guard.

She picked up Ghislain's right arm, pushed up his sleeve, and turned his tattoo to the candlelight. Lonnie had three ideograms. So did Cyrus. Bonnie had two, the little children only one. Ghislain had four.

Canny touched the blue-black marks. "Is each of these the name of a form of the Alphabet?"

"You're so clever," Ghislain said, pained, as if she was pinching him. "Where did that come from?"

"You mean because I'm not a Zarene?"

"Yes."

"What a snob," she said. Then, "My mother is very clever, but mostly she uses it to manage people. Not nicely either. She is like a big cat with a nest of little mice. The way in which she's most clever is that she remembers absolutely everything that people say."

"What's that like?"

"What do you mean?"

"I mean, it must be tough having a mother like that. Is she scarier than Iris?"

Canny remembered that Iris Zarene also had four marks on her right arm. "There are four types of the Zarene magic and you've only told me about three of them," she said.

"I told you about the great-aunties. They had the fourth kind. Found magic."

"Yes. But you want to find your Master Rune. You haven't already found it. And yet you have four marks."

Ghislain studied his own arm. "Well," he said, and then didn't say anything else.

"Well, what?"

He sighed. "I don't want to tell you. After all, I'm not being kept prisoner just because the rest of my family are brutes."

She seized his arm again and held it still, raised between them. "Is the reason you're being kept prisoner to do with why you have four marks?"

"Yes."

"Iris has four marks."

"Yes, she does."

"And she's not being kept prisoner."

"No, she isn't."

Canny shook him. "Tell me," she said.

"No." Then, "Don't grind your teeth, you might chip them."

"All right—tell me where the magic comes from."

Ghislain reared back to get a better look at her.

"Don't look so surprised. It's not really a surprising question. The magic is a kind of energy. An energy that is systematic. Either that, or it's a system for controlling energy. It's like the relationship mathematics has to the rules of the universe—but mathematics is only descriptive, whereas the magic is instructive."

"You're good at mathematics—I remember that."

Canny sighed. "I've early entry into a postgraduate university mathematics course, though I have to do a degree too, in other things. When I was fifteen I invented a logarithm that people are now using in cartography. I wrote a paper about it with a mathematician from Castlereagh University. Both our names are on the paper. It was published in the *Journal of Applied Mathematics*. Everybody knows that math is my thing. They've built a little fence around me with a label—*Genius Mathematicus*—and a reminder about not feeding the animals." She seethed. She was always being made to feel exceptional, and misshapen.

She had stiffened and moved away from him. He remained still and listened, then said, "You have a horrible talent." He sounded more thoughtful than hostile.

Canny rolled over and curled up, let him have her bony spine. She tried to quell the tremor in her voice. "I know what I'm like. Don't think you're telling me something that hasn't been impressed on me—forcefully—by teachers, and snotty boys, and nasty girls, and even my own mother. I have a great talent with limited usefulness, and it is 'unbecoming.'" She used one of her mother's words. Her mother would say, *"Don't interrupt. Don't talk out of turn. Don't straddle that chair. Don't raise your voice. Don't show off. It's unbecoming."*

Ghislain went on being mean, in a musing way. "But you're generally very clever too, aren't you? Sly, like your mother?"

Canny wiped her eyes. She would stop crying. She wanted to shout at a whole lot of people, "See, I can cry!" But more than that she wanted to stop crying.

Ghislain went on. "You have more rat-cunning than anyone I've ever met. It's a kind of strength. And it makes me hopeful. It is warming somehow. And you keep making me laugh. Your brain is so surprising. I'm talking to you, and walking in step with you, then it's as if you vanish and reappear several steps ahead of me. It's exciting!"

Canny sniffed (unbecomingly) and sat up. She said, "I thought you were being mean to me."

He eased up too and took her hands, and they stayed like that for a time, hands twined, leaning on the bed's carved, be-spelled, headboard.

Ghislain was so right about her. She was sly. She'd been manipulating Sholto all week, and she should be ashamed. But the more she stood back and studied people's feelings, and played on them, juggling others' ideas about how people should behave and feel—understanding the ideas, but not behaving or feeling the way other people did—the more she did that, the stronger she felt. "We're both bad people," she said cheerfully.

He laughed. "I wish you could stay with me so we could be bad people together."

"But—" she said.

"You don't belong here, Canny. And I'm going to go off on my desperate quest."

Canny bent her face into his neck and nuzzled him.

"I'm afraid for you," he said. "You need to go."

"But I can stay," she said, then remembered Marli again.

Ghislain was shaking his head. The sparse two-day-old stubble on the underside of his chin sandpapered her brow. "The longer you stay the deeper in the magic you'll get; then, when you do have to leave, the more you'll lose. The magic is fundamental to you. It's instinctive. It's tied up with your other talents, like math, and I'm scared that, the longer you stay, when you do finally go and the magic retracts from you and goes back into the imprisonment spell, it'll pull out some of your strength and vitality."

"I want to stay," she said. "But I have a friend I can't leave. At least not forever."

"Marli."

"Yes." Canny had another sober thought. She'd hoped to use the magic to do something for Marli. But she couldn't bring Marli to the Zarene Valley, and the magic couldn't leave it. "Oh, what's the use?" she said to herself.

"Does your friend have family, and other friends?" Ghislain asked.

"Yes." Unlike Ghislain, Marli wasn't wholly alone. Marli would miss Canny, but she had her big brother and little brothers, her mother and father and uncles and aunties and cousins. Canny said, "I should just decide that I'm going to stay with you. But you're not going to give up your plan to abandon your body, are you?"

"I could postpone it for as long as you stay," Ghislain said, tentative.

"Then I'd always have that hanging over me. I'd know that, as soon as I was gone, you'd climb into your sarcophagus."

"That's another good name for it," Ghislain said. "My

Spell Cage." He sighed. "I know it's too much to ask—for you to stay. But you know, Canny, you're not supposed to think it all through. You're supposed to be swept away by romance, not coolly examine the problem from all angles."

"I can't help it. And it's not as if we can just carry on like we've never met."

"No. That would be irrational," Ghislain said, straight-faced.

She slid down the bed again and rested her head against his hip. She said, "I just *do* think. I'm sorry." She was very tired. She'd be even more tired tomorrow. Then, "But it is tomorrow," she thought. She closed her eyes and saw the smashed plate come together, then fly apart, as if it were an opening valve. She fell through the space between the jagged white teeth of broken crockery. She landed, and jolted awake. She made a little grunt as if someone had punched her. The candle was an inch shorter. "What time is it?"

"About three."

Sholto had said he'd get her up at seven-thirty. She moaned.

"Go back to sleep."

"I mustn't."

He leaned over her and kissed her hair, and then her mouth. His hand cupped her bent knee, then slid slowly to the back of her thigh. For a moment she was only there in those two places, mouth and thigh, where he was touching. She was there and she wasn't Canny Mochrie, who was unbecoming. She was alive *now*. Now, now, now.

But he stopped caressing her, and when she looked at

his troubled, reluctant face she saw he was being sensible and that it was difficult for him. He drew back.

"No. No," she said, reaching.

He caught her hands, and said, "You wanted to know where the magic comes from?"

She did want that. And she wanted to be kissed. Two very different sorts of satisfaction. She heard raindrops ticking on the window glass, but she didn't want to listen to that. Didn't want to imagine the slippery mud of the pig path, or how wet she'd be by the time she got to the foot of the hill.

Ghislain took a breath and began: "The Zarenes were one of the five Ephrun families who ended their long wandering in Southland. The island of Ephrus was destroyed by a volcanic eruption in—do you know this?"

"1715."

"And the people of Ephrus arrived in Southland?"

"1730. I'm good at dates too. Sholto is always telling me snootily that history isn't all dates."

"No, it's currants and raisins too."

Canny laughed.

"I think I'm not going to like your stepbrother."

"He'd hate you," Canny said, with satisfaction.

"And what did the people of Ephrus bring with them to Southland?"

"I hope you're not going to test me all the way through telling me this," she said, then gave the answer. "The people of Ephrus brought the bones of St. Lazarus. They're kept in a jeweled casket behind the altar of the temple in Founderston."

"They brought the bones of St. Lazarus—and a song the saint heard when he was in his first tomb."

Canny stared at Ghislain. He reached out and gently closed her gaping mouth.

"A song made up of words in demotic Greek, and an unknown tongue."

"All right," said Canny, drawing out the words.

Ghislain told her that she shouldn't start from a point of skepticism. Then he turned his head and stared intently at the window. The sash slid smoothly up. The lace curtains stirred inward, and Canny heard the rain falling softly on the veranda's tile roof. Ghislain turned back to her. "Just to remind you how real the magic is." Then, "You said it must come from somewhere. Why not from God?"

Canny frowned.

"Don't you believe in God?"

"I don't know," she said. "My mother does. I used to go to church with her. Now I go for the Sunday morning services at the hospital. There is one at ten a.m. on Marli's ward. Marli believes in God, and I've prayed for her, many times."

"Lazarus heard a song in his tomb. He remembered it in his second life. After the crucifixion, he left Palestine and settled on the island of Ephrus. He married, had a family, and taught his children the song. They taught their children. After fifteen hundred years everyone on the island was a descendant of Lazarus. They all knew about the song, and some had memorized it. Those who could repeat it word perfect could somehow use it. John Hame, who led the survivors from the island after the volcanic eruption, used the song to make a creature out of volcanic ash and mud. Hame's creature helped him excavate the caves on the island where people had hidden, and the ruined chapel where the bones were." Ghislain glanced at her. "Do you believe me? You must, after everything you've seen with your own eyes."

"I don't know," she said. "A language that doesn't just describe nature but commands it is one thing, an animated mud man is quite another."

"That would be found magic. My fourth mark stands for found magic. John Hame called a mighty spirit—he *found* it—and he put it into an earth puppet and taught that puppet to be human enough to help him. Hame animated the earth. The song is a reanimation spell, but we've always thought it works with time too. Our Savior didn't just recall Lazarus's soul to his body, he moved Lazarus's body back to when it was still alive. Or reached back in time and pulled the body's life forward. It's impossible to say which. But the song is all 'hear you me' and 'rise up!' And 'be as you were.' Those are the magic's core utterances, which is why the house's 'Be as you were' is so strong, backed up by Rowan and Joanne's Master Runes, their never-dying whole selves. But, if you take Lazarus's song apart, its parts can be used for almost anything. So—that's where the Zarene magic comes from. Only it isn't sounds, like the song."

IN THE EARLY DAYS OF SOUTHLAND—GHISLAIN said—when the people from Ephrus had settled on the damp streets on the east bank of the Sva, there was a woman called Geli

Zarene. She was the only daughter of a prosperous baker.
Geli Zarene had a strange mind. "I don't know whether
you know this, but there are people in the world with a
very odd gift, one that looks like crossed wires. These people
firmly believe that every number has a color, and every
color has a smell, and every smell has a sound, and every
sound a shape. They have strange insights, and strange ir-
ritations. They are bedeviled by unintended connections
and meanings. Someone tells them a birth date and blue
fog bursts around their heads. Most of it is like that—pretty
pointless, just unmeant meanings. Imagine a straightforward thing like a price tag coming with lots of sensory information. One dollar fifty equals brown-orange. It's a
silly way to experience the world, and Geli Zarene was
having a pretty silly, overstimulated life. Then some elder
taught her the Lazarus song. And every sound, every one
of those unknown words, came to her as a figure, a glyph.
And that's where the Alphabet came from. It's Geli Zarene's alphabet. Everything that entered the magic later
was found by twins who could anchor one another and
leave their bodies."

Canny said, "You mentioned a Hame. The dreamhunter . . ."

"Yes. I'm sure none of *that* was a coincidence. But by the
time Tziga Hame came along, the Zarenes had left Founderston and settled here. We made magical wards to keep
the other four families out, or at least warn us if they tres-
passed. One of the other families was up to something
evil, and the Zarenes had packed up and fled. The ward-
makers were twins too, by the way, Aron and Elek Zarene.

Their headstones are in the graveyard, if you want to verify at least that bit of my story."

Canny said she hadn't looked at the valley's graveyard.

"The wards must be pretty weak by now," Ghislain said, musing.

"So that's why Iris asks all her guests questions about their ancestors before she lets them sign the register," Canny said. "She's trying to weed out any direct descendants of the other four families. She looked very strict when my brother said his mother was a Tiebold. Iris said, 'Not those Tiebolds who married Hames?'"

"So that's how they do it now. I didn't know," Ghislain said. "The wards were still working in 1929."

Canny remembered then that she'd seen the Zarene Alphabet melting like fire in the dark air after something had knocked her down in a farm paddock on the far side of the Palisades. She gripped Ghislain's arm. She told him about that night and what had happened to her. She said, "That means I'm one of them, doesn't it?"

"A Hame, Magdolen, Vale, or Eucharis? Possibly. But your name is Mochrie, and your mother is a Shackle Islander."

"And my father was American, I believe. A marine who died at Tarawa."

"Named?"

"Creech, I think. He never knew about me."

"Having a grandparent who was a Hame, Magdolen, Vale, or Eucharis wouldn't be enough to get you knocked down."

"But, Ghislain, the magic isn't blood, it's knowledge. How could the wards know what anyone was?"

"It's blood and knowledge. Not because it is in our blood, but because the ward is made out of the magic, and the magic has something to do with time, and the magic recognizes something coming all the way down from Lazarus. A bit of time set aside by the song, or by Our Savior, or by God. The bit where Lazarus was *dead*. It's recognizing the four days that were taken back. It's recognizing the thing that happened and was undone. I'm pretty sure that's what the ward is made to sense."

"So then I *must* have the blood. Or was there something else apart from the other four families that those wards were guarding against?"

Ghislain bit his lip and considered. Canny realized she could see his face quite clearly now, not just highlighted and outlined by the light of the candle, which had guttered and gone out, but in the radiance of the silvery, rain-washed twilight coming through the open window.

It was late. She had to be going.

"Well," Ghislain said, tentative. "It wouldn't be much of a ward if it wasn't meant to guard against the Hames' earth servants too, if any Hames happened to be still making them, and one happened to come this way."

"I'm not made of earth."

"No." Now he was looking at her with troubled speculation. "What are you made of?" he said.

She made a small sound of sleepy displeasure, and he gathered her to him again. Canny muttered that he wasn't doing a very good job of letting her go. Then she dozed for a while. She was roused by the first peeps of the dawn chorus—late, because of the rain. She lay doped with sleep and an unfamiliar ease of heart that warmed her from the inside out. Then she moaned and extracted herself from his grasp. "I have to go. I'll be missed. The only way I can keep my freedom is to keep sneaking around." She wouldn't think about Cyrus Zarene and his testing bees and what he now knew. She was going to see Cyrus today—she'd have to act fearful and reproachful and try to make him grateful that she was keeping his bad behavior secret. Yes, she'd have to act—some more.

The floorboards were cold. Canny found her sneakers under the bed and crouched to lace them up. Her eyes were blurry and her fingers clumsy. Ghislain got down and helped her. Then he held her ankle and kissed her knee.

She waited, dumb and still, like a horse being shod. He let her go and followed her downstairs, out the door, and as far as the edge of the perfect lawn.

14

SHOLTO HAD FINISHED his porridge. Canny's was cooling and forming a skin. "But I called her half an hour ago," he complained to Susan.

"You go. I'll chase her up," Susan said, and watched him put on his oilskin and stomp off through the wet fields to the river path.

Susan went upstairs. She couldn't hear the shower running. No one else was up. Even their hostess's somehow forbidding door was sealed shut.

Susan found Canny still in bed and deeply asleep. The girl's usually dry, witchy hair was stuck to her cheeks and neck as if it had been soaking wet when she'd climbed into bed. Susan lifted one long hank of hair so that she could see Canny's sealed eyelid. She shook the girl.

Canny moaned.

"Did you have a bad night?"

"Mmmmf," said Canny.

"Sholto's gone to Massenfer. He'll be back this afternoon and he's going to expect to find you hard at work."

Canny attempted to open her eyes. She squinted, then threw her arm over them.

Susan said, "Tell you what. I'll make a start on the transcription, and as soon as you're up, you can hurry to the apiary and take over from me."

"Thanks," Canny muttered, and heaved over, wound in her sheets as if these too had adhered to her overnight.

"Canny?" Susan said, wanting to ask the girl why she was wearing her clothes in bed. But Canny had gone under again.

CANNY DIDN'T GET TO THE APIARY TILL NOON. She kept a wary eye out for Cyrus Zarene as she crept into his house.

From the living room, she heard a magnified clunk and then Lealand Zarene's voice.

"We pressed on to crosscut nine, which was about half a mile from the working face. Water was still seeping through from the shaft flooded in '26, and the gateway was wet for about four hundred yards down from there. That wet patch was where we found the first intact bodies . . ." *Clunk*.

Canny peered around the doorframe. Susan was sitting at a highly polished table. The tape machine was before her. She was writing.

Canny went into the room. "Where is Mr. Zarene?"

Susan leaned back, laced her fingers together, and stretched. She said, "I expected you before now. Mr. Cyrus was heading over your way. You and he must have taken different paths. I've finished transcribing his interview.

This is Sholto's tape from late yesterday, of his interview with Mr. Lealand." Susan got up. She tapped the pages. "When you finish with him, wind the tape all the way back and do Flossie Santini."

"There's a coal miner called Flossie?"

"Florentian Santini. Flossie. He still has his accent and is a bit exhausting to transcribe, so I thought I'd leave him to you."

"Fine," said Canny. She didn't mean to sound surly, but it came out that way.

"Were you asleep all this time? Do you think you're coming down with something?"

"Don't worry about me."

Susan flipped the rewind switch and let the tape spool back. "Just go from where I left off." She pulled out the chair, inviting Canny to sit.

Canny sat and stared at Susan's neat handwriting.

Susan said, "What are those marks on your neck?"

"Bee stings."

"Maybe that's why you're off-color."

"Could be." Canny seized the opportunity that came her way—excuses were like a fog she wrapped around herself.

"That mead was delicious, thanks," Susan said. "When you went to bed we finished the bottle."

Which was what Canny had been counting on, inattentive chaperones last night and a late start this morning. She smiled at Susan. "I'm glad you liked it."

When Susan had gone, Canny picked up her pencil and flipped the switch.

". . . The shaft was wet for about four hundred yards down from there. That wet patch was where we found the first intact bodies. My father, Colvin, Uncle Talbot, my cousin Felix, and William Young, the union representative. They were all kneeling. They hadn't even managed to get their breathers off their belts. They'd been stifled by chokedamp and had gone down where they stood. Or they had gone down defensively to brace against the blast—it would mostly have missed them, since they were just inside the crosscut."

Canny paused the tape and scribbled down what she'd heard. Then she started again.

"Farther on the going was harder. There was burning debris and thick smoke funneling up the shaft. We found a shattered compressor. Its tank had ruptured and the kerosene had mixed with water, and although there wasn't much air in the mine, the kerosene kept igniting periodically. Blue fire would run across the black water, then flame out. The bodies in that section were in a bad way, but we were able to retrieve three. Men kept going back with the stretchers, so eventually it was only—"

Canny paused the tape again. She found she been holding her breath. She wrote down what she remembered, then rewound to check that she'd got it all correctly. She had.

"—eventually it was only Mews and me. We went as far as we safely could. The bodies were hard to find. Hard to see. One was only recognizable as human from its thigh bone."

Sholto's voice. "But you brought what you could out?"

"Our stretcher held what was left of four bodies. Though we only knew it was four after the autopsy."

"Mews told me that you insisted on going back in."

"We were both pretty cut up at not being able to. Gas was building up in the mine again by that time, and it was deemed too dangerous to continue. I was off my head. The deputies slapped cuffs on me, put me in the back of a paddy wagon, and I spent the night in the cells in Massenfer. I was dozing in the cell when the vibrations of the second explosion woke me up. That was five hours after the search was called off, so another team could have gotten in and out again safely."

Canny paused and caught up with the story. Then she turned the tape on again.

"There were two more explosions before they finally sealed the mine off, with eleven men still inside. Eleven bodies," said Lealand.

Canny listened to her brother's businesslike noises of sympathy. She imagined Lealand staring coldly at Sholto. He must have, because Sholto quickly went on to something else. "You won't take offense if I spend a few minutes checking various discrepancies in the accounts I have already?"

"Don't you mean inconsistencies?"

"That's a better word, yes."

"'Discrepancies' is an accountant's word."

"Sorry. Okay—there was a storm raging at the time, but people in Massenfer report feeling the vibrations of the first explosion when they were sitting down to dinner."

"That's a discrepancy?"

"I'm just checking the timing. I don't think any of my interviewees are being dishonest, obviously. Only—it's thirty years ago now."

"The storm was more over this end of the gorge. Also, I'm sure you can tell the difference between your house flexing in a westerly gale and in an earthquake."

"Point taken," said Sholto. "Okay. This next one is tricky. I don't want you to take offense, but Mews got me wondering about the insurance policies. Apparently every Zarene in the mine had a large life insurance policy, taken out shortly before they all signed on."

"Which looks suspicious since most of them died?"

"No. I don't imagine a Zarene would insure Zarenes then arrange an accident." Sholto sounded embarrassed.

"I'm glad to hear it," said Lealand. "After the flood we were very aware of the possibilities of accidents. The Zarenes who signed on to earn money to pay lawyers and fight the dam project were insured so that, even if there was another accident, the rest of us wouldn't lose the valley. It was cold-blooded caution. We had enough money to pay the premiums, but not enough for really good lawyers. My uncle Talbot was pessimistic. He was just seeing the possibility of calamity heaped on calamity. He didn't want to lose everything."

"Who were the beneficiaries of the policies?"

"A family trust."

"That makes sense," Sholto said, sounding a little disappointed. There was the rustling of papers.

Canny knew she should pause and try to work out what to write down. Did Sholto want his questions included?

She should flip back and see what Susan had done. But she couldn't stop listening.

Sholto's voice. "I'm interested that, like several other people, you've mentioned the wet patch in the mine. Why do you think the fire didn't flame out there?"

"It did. Nothing in the wet section was burned. My father and uncle and cousin Felix were all untouched. Dead, but untouched."

Sholto cleared his throat. "In the disaster inquiry papers—which I reviewed again last night—Appleby, one of the accident inspectors, said that the mine burned from the working face to crosscut fifteen. Then the shaft was untouched by fire in the wet section, but burned up beyond that. Your cousin Cyrus was within a hundred yards of the mine's entrance. He was blown up the gateway by the shock wave. His horses were killed, but not burned. But only a short way down from the dead horses there were signs of fire. The shaft was scorched from South Main, the big junction near the downcast, all the way down to the wet patch."

"So?"

"No, wait, I'm not finished. The blast blew things up the gateway toward the surface. Appleby says the bodies and debris along the gateway from the wet section to the junction at South Main were as you'd expect, blown up the shaft, but they were burned as if the fire had come *down* the shaft."

"The fire came up the shaft. The explosion was at the working face."

"I have four different witnesses talking about two fires."

"There couldn't be two. The second explosion was nine hours later, once the gas had built up. It happened at three in the morning, while I was in Massenfer jail."

"I said two fires, not two explosions. My four witnesses swear there were two fires, almost simultaneous, one traveling up the gateway from the working face—coal dust ignited by exploding methane gas—the other racing down the mine from the junction at South Main to the wet patch."

"Impossible. Any explosion would consume all the methane and then would start a coal dust fire, which would rapidly use up all the oxygen, leaving carbon monoxide. That's what killed most of the men, carbon monoxide. Chokedamp. Everyone in side tunnels untouched by the blast or fire—the chokedamp got them too. The men in the wet patch were killed by chokedamp. Two fires—that's impossible, you must be able to see that."

"If they were simultaneous—"

"How could they be?"

Sholto cleared his throat. There was more rustling. The creaking of someone wriggling around on a couch stuffed with horsehair. "Well," he said nervously. "There would have been timers, I expect."

"Timers?"

"Explosive devices," muttered Sholto. "Dynamite."

There was a silence. Canny looked at the tape. It was still spooling. There was tape hiss.

"Or perhaps," said Lealand Zarene in a peaceful, mocking voice, "one of us was a foster child of fire, and when coal dust fire broke out in the mine after the explosion, the foster parent fire answered it by leaping forth and rushing to meet it headlong—like two rams on a hill."

More silence, then, *"What?"* said Sholto.

"Two fires, with a wet patch between them, so they never locked horns."

"What?" said Sholto again.

Then, "Explosive devices my arse," said Lealand Zarene with dismissive contempt.

Canny listened to the little bit of tape after that. Sholto had tried to recover. He'd stammered and apologized and Lealand continued to sound scornful. Then Sholto had turned off the machine.

Canny wound back to listen again and this time kept pausing to faithfully transcribe every word. Question, answer, question, answer. Then she took a break. She went to the kitchen and filled a glass with water and drank it leaning against the kitchen bench. There was a bowl of apricots on the table. They were ripe and tempting, some overripe, with bruises that made their skin transparent. Canny plucked several out of the bowl and went back to her papers. She rewound the reel to its beginning and found Flossie Santini.

Mr. Santini, despite his unusual name, was not so interesting. He'd had some disagreement with management about the half-pie changes to safety measures after the flood in 1926. He'd survived the disaster because, like Lealand, he was on a different shift. He hadn't been part of the rescue efforts, so his testimony was all about life in the mine before the disaster.

Canny dutifully transcribed what she heard and then

spitefully added every cough and shuffle like stage directions. That would teach Sholto.

One of Flossie Santini's stories made her laugh. He was
complaining about how the Zarenes had come in and taken
all the good jobs. One Zarene was promoted over his head,
after only two years' experience.

"Do you recall the name?"

"Cyrus, he was a chain runner. He survived, so I'm not
speaking ill of the dead. Oh, and the other survivor, the
kid, he was useless. He usually stuck by his uncle and
father—Talbot and Colvin Zarene. He never lifted a pick, I
swear. He used to walk around with a stick of chalk scribbling marks on the timbers and rock bolts. A zany. Baked
in the head."

"But he was drawing a wage?"

"Exactly. I'd come to the mine from Westport. I'd been
a miner for six years. But the Bull Mine was a funny opera-
tion. Funny about the Zarenes. A mate of mine said they'd
bring the mine luck. Said it with a perfectly straight face.
Some luck!"

Canny rewound and scribbled, smiling to herself, imagining Zarenes turning up to sign on and flashing their tattooed forearms at any locals. And she imagined Ghislain
with his chalk, standing guard over the Zarene patriarchs,
and almost certainly telling the roof to stay in place.

SUSAN CAME BACK AROUND FOUR. "The rain's stopped," she
said. "We won't move the equipment today, but you can
carry the transcripts back to the guesthouse."

Susan picked up the stack of papers, straightened its

edges, and slipped it into a satchel. "I'll box up the recorder and be along shortly."

SHOLTO'S DAY HAD GONE QUITE WELL at first. He got to his appointment in good time, despite the greasy gorge road. The wife of his interviewee had kindly made him lunch. The interview was good, and unproblematic. Later he found what he was looking for in the county council records. He wasn't being bamboozled by science, or strange stories.

Sholto had saved up his one unpleasant task for the end of the day. He had to place a call to Calvary in the Shackle Islands and tell his stepmother how Canny'd been out overnight.

He waited by the phone booths in the post office till his one lit up—the operator had gotten through.

When Sisema came on the line she didn't sound alarmed, she sounded skeptical. "Whatever can be the matter?"

"This is a courtesy, really," Sholto said. "Nothing is the matter. How are you and Da? I understand you had your picture on the front page of the *Clarion*?"

"You called to chat?" Sisema said.

"No. I called because I thought you should know that, a few days ago, Canny was out overnight."

"Sholto!"

"Something upset her, and she stalked off, then got stuck up a rough hill in the dark. She chose to stay put, which was probably sensible. She's fine now."

"Did Susan upset her?" Sisema said.

"No. Of course not. There was an injured animal. She had to put it out of its misery."

Silence. Then, "I can't imagine Canny doing that," Sisema said. Then, "And that's what she told you? Might there have been somewhere else she was instead?"

"No. Where we're staying there are only three houses. And there are no boys, if that's what you're worried about."

"There are always boys."

"Here in Massenfer maybe. But where we're staying there aren't any. Besides, Canny isn't interested in boys."

"True."

"And, Ma, you've seen the boys in Massenfer."

"That miserable little town with the memorial to the miners? The one your father insisted we visit, and where we had to catch a train all the way to Westport to get there?"

"That's the place—the rail line goes to Westport because the coal goes there."

Sisema chuckled. "If Canny had been on that trip, she really would have dug her heels in about being made to go with you."

Sholto was pleased that Sisema wasn't going to hold it against him that he'd temporarily misplaced his sister— though he was disappointed at how little she knew about what he was up to. Anyway, she was being understanding, so that was a relief. But then she seemed to think of something. "Canny wasn't lost in the bush, was she?"

Southland's climate was a maritime one, never too hot in summer and, in winter, only snowing in the high country. But Southland's rain forests were dense, damp, chilly, and famously unforgiving.

"No. There's no bush except on the hill at the head of the valley. Canny has been into it, but it's not very big and you'd be safely out of it if you went downhill in any direction."

Sisema was silent for a moment, then she said, "Where is this?"

"The Zarene Valley."

"I've never heard of it."

"It's along the Lazuli, which flows into the Taskmaster, the gray river that runs through Massenfer."

"Oh yes, that's right, you took the car."

"Da's car. For the recording equipment. How is Da?"

"Sunburned. The silly man. Sholto, where does the road go? The road into this valley with the bushy hill? I suppose it must go over the mountains?"

"The Palisades. Yes."

Silence again. Then Sisema asked, "There's a town before the mountains?"

"A little country town with strawberry fields, called Oatlands. Then the pass, then Massenfer."

"We went by rail," Sisema said, in a pinched voice. "On that trip where your father took all the photographs for his book, we went by rail."

"Yes, you said. And I remember, I was there. What's the problem, Ma?"

"That valley. Is there a road into it from the top of the pass?"

"No. There's a road through the river gorge."

"Oh, thank goodness," Sisema said.

Sholto had never heard his stepmother sound watery. It

was unnerving. Then he remembered. "Wait. There was once a road from the hilltop. It's a walking track now. Canny would have gone up it before getting lost. She's fine, Ma. You don't need to worry. I just thought I'd better tell you now rather than have it come out later."

More silence on the other end.

"Mother?"

"Sholto, I want you to take your sister back to Castlereagh today. Forget about your father's little job. I'll deal with your father."

"You're not making sense."

"Do what I ask." Imperious.

"No—this is my work too. If you want me to drop everything I'm going to need more explanation."

"I don't have to explain anything to you. I trusted you to take care of Akanesi and that's what you're going to do."

Sholto recalled all the niggling concerns he'd had about Canny and her behavior, and the slippery sense he had that she was never quite where she was supposed to be. "This is silly," he said. "The Zarene Valley is a lovely place full of perfectly hospitable people."

"Sholto!" Sisema said sharply. "You had better oblige me." Then, "I'm coming home right away."

"It's five days by sea from Calvary to Westport," Sholto reminded her. "And, if I remember right, you don't sail till Wednesday night."

"I will send a telegram when I arrive in Westport," Sisema said. "Here is your father." Then, aside, "Gordon, tell your son that he must do as I say."

The Professor came on the phone. "She really has a bee in her bonnet, doesn't she?"

"I don't understand why she's insisting we remove ourselves, Da."

"We can sort that out once we're home," the Professor said.

"In seven days."

"Precisely. Sometime within the next six days you can do what your stepmother asks and remove yourselves immediately." The Professor chuckled.

Sholto thought that he could actually hear the nudges and winks. He wasn't going to get an explanation, he was only going to get orders from Sisema and this conspiracy of naughty boys stuff from his father. "How about you do something for me, Da," Sholto said. "How about you find out what she is actually upset about?"

"She is just throwing her not inconsiderable weight around, son. Best to let it blow over."

The Professor had stopped whispering. Sisema wasn't in the room anymore.

"It might be important," Sholto said. He felt feeble. His father wasn't giving him any useful clues about what he should think and do. "It's bizarre," he said. Then, "Da?"

"This is costing," said the Professor. "It's a collect call, I presume."

"Yes. I was sure you wouldn't mind paying."

"It was you who made the call. So that means it was you who put her in this state."

"No. I mean—yes, I called, but—"

"Sholto, can't you manage for yourself for a month? Isn't that girlfriend of yours any help?"

"Oh forget it," Sholto said in disgust. "I'll deal with it all at my end."

"It's too late to make that decision now, isn't it? You *had* to call. You just *had* to say something."

He had inconvenienced his father.

Sholto said goodbye and put the receiver back in its cradle. He left the post office, fuming. Why was he always being made to feel incompetent? The Professor and Sisema had no idea what he was dealing with. Canny had never been placid, but she'd always been predictable. Now Sholto had the impression she was up to something she shouldn't be every time he closed his eyes or turned his back. Even yesterday evening, when Sue and he had been drinking the mead and having a good time, Canny had sat watching them and smiling in a distant, kindly way that was very civilized, and very unlike her.

Sholto got back in the Austin and hurried back to the Zarene Valley. When he reached the meadow that sloped down to the Lazuli he was met with a very surprising sight.

Two tents were draped on the lilac bushes. They were wet and molded to the branches, as if they'd been hanging there for days. And when Sholto hauled them off he saw that the foliage underneath them was yellow.

Sholto bundled the tents up. He left one in the Austin for the time being. The other he carried, with difficulty, because it was soaked and heavy, along the track back to the guesthouse. He spread it over the clothesline behind the house, where it could dry and he could keep his eye on it.

CYRUS HAD BEEN AT THE GUESTHOUSE, touching up some paintwork in a place the twelve-year-olds were too short to reach. He'd taken note of the arrival of Canny Mochrie. She'd come in, glanced at him, then rushed upstairs, taking the steps three at a time. A short while later Susan arrived, paused, greeted him, and said she'd left the recording equipment in his parlor. She'd thought Sholto would be back to help her move it, but he was running late.

"I could lend a hand," said Cyrus.

"Thank you for the offer. But Sholto will be back soon."

A few minutes later, Sholto came in, nodded hello to Cyrus, and hurried upstairs. Cyrus finished his touch-ups and got down from the ladder. He was rinsing his paintbrushes when Iris appeared and offered him tea. Cyrus wanted tea, but he didn't want to sit and have a visit with his sister, who was probably missing her latest protégé, Lonnie. Lonnie would be the last talent for some time, and Iris knew it. But it wasn't Lonnie himself Iris was grieving for, though the boy had been in her care for most of the seven-year period he'd lived in the valley. What Iris was missing was the faint hope she'd been nursing that, one day, things would be the way they'd been when she was a young woman and the Zarenes had lived at one with the magic. Cyrus didn't want to talk about this, and he didn't want to sit feeling as if his thoughts about Canny Mochrie were fish in a pool, lurking in the waterweed, hiding from the prick-eared shadow of a watchful cat.

As it turned out Iris eyeing his hidden thoughts wasn't something he had to worry about. As he followed her into the kitchen she stopped suddenly, and he nearly stepped on her heels. She was staring out the window, transfixed by the sight of a tent draped on the clothesline.

"Oh, the tents were finally found," Cyrus said, then saw what had his sister so riveted.

The marks on the dirty white canvas had streaked, so were no longer fully decipherable. They'd been painted in some black pigment, probably ink. All the lines were bleeding, and Cyrus couldn't tell what the spell had been—but he recognized its remnants as Ideogrammatic sign.

He stepped up beside Iris and looked at her, curious. She only glanced at him, her eyes blazing. Then she swung on her heel and marched to the foot of the stairs. She called, "Mr. Mochrie! Might I have a word with you?"

SHOLTO HEARD HIMSELF CALLED. He said, "Hold that thought," to Susan.

They'd been talking about what might be going on with Sisema.

Sholto went downstairs and said politely, "Yes?"

Iris's face was pale, with two hectic spots on her cheekbones. Her eyes were hooded, but hot with life. "I would like you to fetch your sister. I have some serious things to say to her."

"What has she done now?"

"I mean to speak directly to her about what she's done. I don't require a go-between."

"Oh Lord, it's my day for this," Sholto said, impatient,

and stomped upstairs. He hammered on Canny's door and then flung it open.

Canny was lying on her stomach, head bent over the now thin pad of her fancy writing set, furiously filling page after page of another letter to Marli. This reminded Sholto that he'd picked up a letter for her at the post office before he put in his call. The letter could wait, he decided. If Canny was about to be told off by their hostess, Marli's letter could be her consolation.

"Miss Zarene wants a word with you," Sholto said. He turned at a touch on his shoulder. It was Susan, looking concerned.

Sholto said, "You may as well stay out of this, Sue. I'm going to too, as much as I can." Then, "Get up, Canny, and come hear what Miss Zarene has to say."

Canny slipped her feet into her muddy sneakers and followed Sholto downstairs. Or rather, they reached the head of the stairs and he let her walk ahead of him. He saw Canny falter when she saw Cyrus—falter and then square her shoulders as if shaping up for a fight. She turned to Sholto and whispered, "Susan has seen my bee stings. But I didn't tell her what really happened." She sounded a little breathless. She grabbed his arm and held him so he'd stop to hear her.

"Whatever it is, Canny, let's first listen to what our hostess has to say." Then, "We've got her where we want her, you know. I found the tents, returned to the place we put them. I suppose she now means to tell us we didn't look hard enough."

Canny dropped his arm. She looked at Cyrus and Iris,

waiting in the dining room doorway. Her gaze flicked to the front door.

Sholto was very surprised when his sister launched herself down the stairs, hitting only one step, then the carpet of the hallway. It slid under her foot and bunched up against the stairs. She came down on her knees and then staggered up. She didn't look at Cyrus, only made a fist and fended in his direction as he tried to grab her. Her fist connected with his shoulder and he reeled back.

Iris Zarene had both arms up, her wrists swiveling and hands making fiddly movements as if she were finger-knitting thin air. Sholto watched, his mouth hanging open, as Iris stopped gesturing and thrust her hands forward as if shaking off something sticky. Canny ducked and leaped out the front door. The vase of flowers on the reception desk flew into the wall and shattered. A painting dropped off its hook. Sholto would have sworn that his sister hadn't touched them, was nowhere near them. Had Iris Zarene flung something at his sister? "Hey!" he protested.

Iris shot him a poisonous look and hurried out onto the porch.

Sholto ran down the remaining stairs and rushed after her. He jostled roughly with Cyrus, and for a moment they were ridiculously jammed together in the doorway. Then Sholto was free.

Canny was pelting across the children's garden—the shortest way to the river track. Sholto shouted her name. Iris set her cupped hands to her mouth and hollered, "Boys! Come here right now."

Some boys arrived from the door behind Sholto, one saying, "Excuse me," to Susan as he knocked her aside.

"Hey!" said Sholto again—this time in a thunderous roar.

The boys looked searchingly at Iris, followed her pointing finger, then just took off, without asking anything or having exchanged a word. They gathered into a pack and ran flat-out after Canny.

Sholto saw his sister look back, hesitate, and then cut away across the fields, running parallel to the river. She put her hand on a fence post and vaulted over it, pushed through the birches planted along the fence line, and disappeared from view.

The kids paused too, looked back at Iris, who, with hand signals, directed some to follow Canny and others to take the river path—though Sholto couldn't see how, by going that way, they'd have any hope of heading her off.

Sholto couldn't see *anything*—why his sister was being chased, or why she'd fled.

She had reappeared, over the horizon of the windbreak, running through a field of kale toward the next fence.

Sholto suddenly realized that her change of direction and Iris's instructions to the children to make a flanking movement both pointed to one thing: Canny wasn't aimlessly fleeing, she was headed toward some particular place of sanctuary, and Iris and the children knew exactly where that place was.

Cyrus put his fingers in his mouth and let out an ear-splitting whistle. In another minute Sholto spotted some more big kids converging on the field Canny was aiming for. They spotted her and sped up.

"What the hell is going on?" Sholto said, then, very self-conscious and embarrassed—because he was a well-behaved young man—he grabbed Cyrus Zarene's arm and tugged on it. "Talk to me!" he demanded.

But the two adult Zarenes only watched the progress of the hunt. They didn't spare Sholto a glance.

Susan came up beside him and took his hand.

Canny was floundering a little now. Not all in, but out of breath. Her shadow was long—it was late in the day—and rippled, because the field had just been mown but the hay hadn't been raked up yet and was still lying heaped in long rows. Sholto had thought his sister was limping, but she was only slithering on the two different surfaces of stubble and piled hay.

Susan gasped. Three boys had emerged from the trees Canny was heading toward. They weren't the same ones Iris had sent to flank Canny, they were bigger boys, twelve-year-olds from Orchard House. Sholto saw that Canny was trapped, with three kids before her and five behind. Iris gave a sigh of satisfaction and said, "Mr. Mochrie. You and I are going to have a serious talk."

Susan burst out, "I'm not going to stand by and watch a pack of kids hauling that girl back by her hair! I'm going to get my walking stick and go beat the shit out of them if they lay one finger on her!"

"They won't catch her," said Cyrus softly.

Iris looked at her brother as if he was being preposterous.

Canny had come to a halt. She dropped her chin and re-garded the boys. Then she jogged toward them, once glanc-ing back to check on the progress of the younger kids. As she came up to them Canny put out her hands and began to do something—something like Balinese finger-dancing. Sholto had a strange recollection of a statue he'd seen, a brass altar statue of the Hindu goddess Kali, with her four arms, dancing in a circle of fire. He shook his head.

The boys in front of Canny all tottered to a standstill. They stood rigid and seemed to quiver, as if buffeted by wind. Then one by one they turned, stiff and reluctant, and began to march away from her. They didn't go together in one direction, but dispersed, and plodded away in three different directions.

Sholto had no idea what he was seeing.

Susan, trying her best to make it make sense, said, "What could she have said to them?"

"That's the 'Go,'" Cyrus said, in a hushed way.

"What's the go?" Sholto demanded. "What the hell is happening?"

And Cyrus Zarene told him, "Your sister is using magic like an accomplished magic user with decades of experience, that's what is happening."

"It's impossible," Iris said. Then, accusing, "You *knew*."

"As of yesterday I knew," Cyrus said. "I know she's been watching our every move. I know she's evaded the Liars' Trap at Orchard house. I know she has adapted Lealand's spell against codling moths and your great misdirection spell from Fort Rock to hide her brother's tents so she could stay in the valley and continue her efforts to reach the house on Terminal Hill. I'm pretty sure she's been up there. She has the black light of love in her eyes."

Sholto stared at Cyrus, and then at Iris, who was also

staring at Cyrus. Iris flushed, and her gaunt face seemed to swell. "Stop her!" she screamed. "Send your bees. Call some to tell the others. I can see dozens in the children's garden." She pointed.

Cyrus's eyes widened. "Surely you're joking."

"Do I look like I'm joking? We have to put a stop to this now. Once she sees the bees she'll go hide in the river. She's not stupid."

Cyrus wavered.

Sholto staggered back from the Zarene siblings. "You're mad!"

They ignored him.

"Make her go to the river. Call your bees." Iris's gaze was terrifying, compelling.

Cyrus went and stood between the rows of lettuces in the children's garden. He produced a cigarette case from the inside pocket of his vest, took out a cigarette, and tamped its end on the lid of the case. To Sholto, Cyrus looked like a man pausing to weigh what had been asked of him—taking a moment and having a smoke. Then Cyrus lit the cigarette and began puffing quickly and blowing clouds of smoke among the children's bean vines. Once the still air was full of smoke, Cyrus closed his eyes and raised his hands. He seemed to be conducting an invisible orchestra.

Within half a minute he had around fifty honey bees crawling on him, tapping him with their feelers while he continued to make a series of slow, complicated, deliberate gestures.

All at once the bees lifted away.

Sholto saw them go off, like light little bullets, over the trees and toward the apiary.

Cyrus put his fingers in his mouth again and issued another earsplitting whistle to recall the children from the fields.

"The children on the river path will be near the swimming hole by now," Iris said. "They'll know to go in the water."

Cyrus looked at her sternly. "I told my bees there's a mouse in the hive. That the valley is the hive, and the girl the mouse. Iris, I sincerely hope your other guests have gone. They were due to leave today, weren't they?"

"Yes," Iris said.

Susan jumped off the step, paused to give them all a look that said she had no idea what she was looking at. Then she set off after Canny.

"Get going," Iris said to her brother. "I'll follow you."

Cyrus told Sholto he should catch his girlfriend and rein her in.

Sholto was cold all the way through. He was very confused, but he recognized something in Cyrus's expression, some authority he thought he might be able to trust. He wanted to stand there and rage, and demand answers, but—

—but the bees among the squash and pea blossoms in the children's garden had flown toward Cyrus all at once, landed on him and dabbled their antennae on his skin, before taking off together and passing from sight. A retriever would race off at a sign from its master, a falcon would fly from its handler's glove, but *bees*?

Sholto set out after Susan. He looked back and saw Cyrus

hurrying after him, as fast as his limp permitted. "Sue!" Sholto called. She came to a stop. Then Sholto did too.

Up the valley the air over the trees was filling with smoke, a black vapor like that from burning oil. But as it became more dense, Sholto saw that it wasn't smoke, because it writhed and reformed rather than dissipating.

Streaks of black came from all over the valley and wound in to make not a swarm, but a *storm* of bees. A sleek, dark whirlwind that spun over the apiary. Bees skimmed past Sholto's head. He looked back to see that Cyrus was still walking but was covered in them, his shirt invisible under bee bodies, his arms dripping bees, his face bearded by them. Between this cloak and the vast cloud was a thin filament of insect bodies, traveling back and forth, carrying messages.

Sholto stood frozen. Susan came back to him. She was shaking and crying. He put his arms around her. They stood dumbly and watched the apparently entranced Cyrus Zarene walk past them. His body was humming. The far-off cloud was humming too, like an electrical substation.

Farther off Iris Zarene's normally deep-pitched voice had risen to a shriek. "Now, Cyrus!" she shouted. "Do it now!"

CYRUS WAS NOT GOING TO DO ANYTHING MORE till he could see the girl and check how close to the river she was, and till he was completely sure of the whereabouts of the boys Iris had sent along the river path. He was aware too of the gardens out at the wide end of the valley and the children at work there, weeding the vegetable beds around the derelict houses their grandparents had lived in. And he was aware of the children at this time of day shut up in Lealand's schoolroom learning their Alphabet.

The bees were heavy and warm. He wasn't being stung. The swarm gathered over the apiary wasn't angry—only ready, waiting to be shown the way, the task, the enemy.

Cyrus passed Sholto and Susan and plodded on. He didn't turn his head to see if they were following him, though he could hear his sister, nearer now but no longer shouting, no longer daring to, so near to his cloak of bees. Then she was beside him. "Quickly," she hissed, "before she makes herself invisible. You know she can do that."

Bees didn't need eyes to see. Iris understood that. But Cyrus needed to see with his own eyes the swarm frighten the girl into the Lazuli. He needed to see her safely underwater.

The swarm was nearer now, the filament that tethered them to him was shorter, the messages were flying faster.

"You don't mean to do anything, do you?" Iris hissed. "It's all a big show. You think you can fool me?"

Cyrus opened his mouth to answer her. But he didn't dare speak. He could feel the furry bodies gathered around his lips. He shut his mouth again. Not one of the bees stung him.

Then Cyrus spotted Lealand, hurrying toward them. Lealand hesitated once, under the shelter of the row of cherry trees that hid the path to Orchard House. When he stepped out from the shelter he glanced up at the swarm like someone considering a thundercloud.

Cyrus climbed carefully over the fence and began across the field of kale. When Lealand reached them they were all halfway across. Cyrus glanced at his cousin. He wanted to say to Lealand that it was so far, *too* far to the river.

"Whose idea is this?" Lealand asked.

"That Mochrie girl has been up at the House," Iris said. "She's been plotting with Ghislain."

"What do you imagine they're plotting?"

"His escape, you fool. And he *hates* us."

"Are you all right, Cy?" Lealand said, ignoring Iris.

Cyrus moved his eyes to meet his cousin's.

Iris said, "Cyrus has to stop the girl. He has to make her go into the river."

Cyrus saw Lealand look behind him—no doubt at the young couple. Sholto and Susan would be there still—terrified, intimidated, but following him because they knew he too was hunting Sholto's sister.

Lealand moved out of Cyrus's line of sight. Iris immediately leaned in close. She wasn't at all afraid of the bees. Her eyes were stretched wide and seemed to have skins of light over them. "I suppose he's going to style himself as some sort of peacemaker, but you just wait till he finds out what you've been keeping from us, brother."

LEALAND ZARENE FELL INTO STEP with Sholto and Susan. He looked at the rock in Sholto's hand. "Are you thinking of braining Cyrus?" he asked.

Sholto dropped the rock.

"That would make things worse, not better," Lealand said.

Sholto believed the man. He didn't know what to ask, what to do.

"Stop this!" Susan pleaded.

"Mr. Mochrie, this is about your sister, isn't it?"

Susan said, "Iris sent kids out after Canny when she ran away. It was about our tents. They turned up. I don't understand her—Iris's—" Susan searched for a word.

"Rancor?" Lealand suggested.

Sholto couldn't believe how cool the bastard was—with his own cousin ahead of them, covered in bees, and looking for all the world like someone walking the last mile to a place of execution. "Please!" Sholto said. "Do something to stop this."

Lealand left their side and hurried to catch up with his brother.

Sholto seized Susan's hand and got her to pick up the pace till they closed the gap between themselves and the others. They caught up in time to hear Lealand say to Cyrus, "Send the bees over the river to the feeder calves."

"The calves won't know to run into the water," Iris protested. "And even if they did, if they go in where they are, they'll all get washed down into the gorge."

Lealand looked frostily at Iris. "I'm sacrificing the feeder calves."

CYRUS CAREFULLY NEGOTIATED THE NEXT FENCE. He didn't respond to Lealand's suggestion.

Sholto scrambled over after him and rushed around to intercept him. He stood in Cyrus's path, bullish, flushed red, and quivering with fright.

In the lowering sun, the trees by the river were a semitransparent barrier. Cyrus caught sight of the girl when she swerved onto that path and began to sprint again. He saw the first lot of Iris's children, ahead of the girl and backing away into the shadowy forest at the base of Terminal Hill. They meant to lie in wait and ambush her.

If he sent the bees now, the girl would see them coming and go into the water. She was closer than all the other children, so the bees would concentrate on her. Iris's other children were in the forest, and when they saw the swarm attack they'd go deeper into the trees and dig in somewhere. They were Zarenes and lived with hives and understood what to do.

Cyrus watched the girl, her floating gait, her black plait beginning to unravel and lift behind her. He saw her glance back and falter. She broke stride and dipped her head so that she could peer between the trees. She had spotted the swarm. Cyrus saw the dark O of her mouth. She had seen what was coming. The Lazuli was beside her, its slow bend where the willows trailed in the water. This was possible. He could do it. It would be all right.

Cyrus showed the girl to his bees. *This is the mouse in your hive.* The billowing sail of the swarm consolidated itself into a sleek vortex and turned to the river.

Cyrus felt lighter, his bee shirt had shredded and gone. But he was worn out. He lowered himself to the ground. As he did, a shadow fell across him. He heard Lealand gasp and looked up.

The girl was standing directly before him. She was hard to see, because the low sun was right above her head. But it was her—Canny Mochrie—in her dirty shorts and blouse, her hair loose and smoking around her head.

Iris cried out in rage.

The swarm paused momentarily, then tore in two. The two clouds hung in proximity, slowly drifting apart, though they each boiled, the insects furious. Cyrus could feel their massive distress. He finally saw the cause of it. He saw the long brown limbs of the girl running along the river path, once more heading toward Terminal Hill. And he saw the same girl standing several feet from him. He heard her brother say her name, in an uncertain, wavering voice.

Cyrus's shock sabotaged his command of the swarm. All at once the bees lost the idea that had governed them. The clouds began to dissipate. Some of the bees couldn't deal with where they found themselves, or the energy they'd expended, and Cyrus watched a slow peppering of bodies dropping down from each cloud even as they grew thin, then came apart. The substation hum had gone. So had both the girls. The one on the trail had passed into the forest. The other one, the one in the field, had simply vanished.

15

GHISLAIN HEARD CANNY BURST through the front door
of the house and rushed to meet her. He had only a moment to take in her face. It was clenched with misery and
terror. He gathered her to him and stroked her hair, his
fingers snagging on tangles, broken twigs, and leaves.
"What happened?" he asked, and kept asking, but whatever it was she was too shaken to speak.

Ghislain sat down on the lower risers of the staircase
and pulled her into his lap. He soothed and murmured, not
really listening to himself, but he was saying her name, and
"Love" and *"My own."*

Eventually Canny managed to get something out. She
said, "He knows."

"Who knows what?"

"Sholto knows I've been lying to him." This admission
made her shiver.

"I'm sure it won't be a big deal to him. Older brothers

must know they're obstacles." So, he thought, this Sholto knew she'd been sneaking off somewhere to see a boy. Canny had been so resolute about her bad behavior that Ghislain was surprised she was upset at being caught out. This Sholto must have a very sharp tongue.

But of course, it wasn't the whole story.

"The rain washed my spells off our tents and he found them and brought them back to the guesthouse and hung them on the clothesline. Iris could see there'd been spells. She sent the boys to chase me. Then Cyrus sent his bees."

Ghislain only just managed not to throw her off him. He had been working with melted lead in his locked room. The windows were open because of the fumes. If anyone came, anyone following her up the hill, they could look in and see his Spell Cage, his escape plan. "Do you think they're coming up here?"

"I don't know," Canny said. She lifted her face from the blotched patch on his shirt. "They're old people, and it's not easy."

"They're not that old, and it's not as hard for them as it is for you," Ghislain said. He set her on her feet, circled her waist with an arm, and carried her off to the locked room. There he let her go and jumped up onto the window seat to close the windows. He put the fireguard back over the fireplace, leaving his tools in the grate. He gathered Canny up again, locked the door, and dropped the key in his pocket.

Once he'd done all this, Ghislain's panic relented. Everything was secure, and no one would dare set foot in the house. His dread gave way to exaltation, and he felt himself flush all over. They were on their way up the hill—his jailers, his enemies. He said to Canny, "Was it all of them? Iris, Lealand, and Cyrus?"

"And Sholto and Susan and some boys. They were all coming after me."

Ghislain hadn't seen Iris or his brother for nearly twenty years.

"You're shaking," Canny said.

He turned to her and saw her eyes grow wide. "How did you escape the bees?" he asked.

"I don't know." Her voice went pinched and desperate. She seemed to shrink in his embrace, drawing herself away from him. "You're *excited*," she accused. "Actually happy about it all."

He shook his head and tried to lead her back to the open door. They would go out onto the porch together. They'd face his family together. This girl—she was his advocate. If she stood beside him, she was on his side. Canny didn't know it, but she would argue his case, she would speak on his behalf.

But Canny wouldn't come with him. She pulled herself out of his grip. "No," she said, and backed away from the stretched sunlight on the polished floorboards of the entrance hall. She melted into the shadows by the staircase. The shadows seemed to wrap her as Ghislain's arms had a moment before.

Ghislain felt the sudden excitement, splitting, and polite bow of the imprisonment spell as two of its three makers passed through it and came to him. They climbed into sight, then stopped at the top of the steps and clustered there. Three people—Iris, Lealand, and a stranger. There wasn't enough room for them to stand shoulder to shoulder. The long, gold, angling light was behind them, and the shadows of the hills at the rim of the valley were slicing up through the lively summer air. As the shadows advanced, that air grew still, the fizzing midges becoming invisible again.

The sun became a white spark, then went behind the hills. It was instantly twilight. The air went cool. Ghislain could now see his visitors properly, two aging people, gray, but not yet bent. But old—old on the outside too.

The young man with them was gingery, freckled, very ordinary apart from his wide-set hazel eyes, which were as soft as the eyes of a young deer. Ghislain looked at Sholto and promised himself he was going to do his best to be polite to this one.

"Where is the girl?" Iris said.

"Getting right down to business, Iris," Ghislain said. "When it's been so long since we've seen each other."

Iris made an impatient, dismissive gesture. "You were mad. Who needs to see that more than once."

LEALAND DREW A LONG, STEALTHY BREATH. His heart was deafening him. If asked, he too would swear that he'd last seen Ghislain in 1939 when Iris and he had gone up to the house together to try to see if they could get some sense out of his brother about why the Great Spell was steadily getting stronger. And why the imprisonment spell was sucking all the magic out of any Zarene who hadn't been involved in casting it. Cyrus, who'd volunteered in '29 to be the one to see to Ghislain's needs, had been saying for some time things like "Ghislain is not himself" or "Ghislain doesn't really talk to me these days." Vague stuff. And Cyrus was depressed after each visit. Lealand and Iris were used to Ghislain's arrogance, his haughty sense of his own power, and despite Cyrus's not-quite-warnings, when they went up the hill in '39 they thought they'd find the boy they'd known. Angry, yes. Bitter, almost certainly. Full of arguments and accusations and all the old excuses—absolutely. Gloating and unhelpful—probably. But they didn't expect to find a shambling, barely mobile, half-starved seventeen-year-old.

They'd discovered Ghislain sitting just inside the doorway, next to a black patch on the wall. He had made an outline of his own sunrise shadow on the east-facing wall of the portico entrance hall. He'd filled it in with layers of thick, silky charcoal. It was nearly a day's work. Apart from the charcoal blackening his fingers and his face where he'd been scratching himself, and the bits of bloody scalp where he been plucking out his own hair, he didn't look like someone capable of anything so designed and deliberate. He just sat, biting his bottom lip, and looking through them and through the last of the day, as if everything were transparent.

Ghislain only ever had twenty-four hours to get his body into a bad way, but that's what he'd been doing, taking it out on himself, and making a picture of his own shadow, perhaps to say, "I'm still here."

When she saw this, Iris had said only, "Oh, he must have known we were coming. He was always such a pretender." She even said, "The house is tidy, so how bad can he be?" as if she had no imagination.

But—and no one knew this—that wasn't the last occasion

on which Lealand had seen his brother. He had seen Ghislain again in 1942, the morning after he'd noticed an unfamiliar light up on the hill and gone up to investigate. The lights were the headlamps of a Marine Corps jeep that Lealand found downhill from the old garage, resting at a wild angle, front bumper sunk in a patch of tree ferns, its driver dead at the wheel.

When Lealand got there mid-morning, the jeep's battery was dying and its lights were dim. It looked as if the driver had managed to switch his headlamps on, hoping to be found. The driver's door was closed, but the passenger door was open.

There was a rope attached to the jeep's back bumper, but it seemed to have been thrown forward downhill. Lealand pulled on the rope, hauling in what was tied to its end. As he hauled he could already see what had happened. The marine had been using the jeep to pull something free, some stuck object. One end of the rope had been tied to the jeep's back bumper, and the other to the thing he'd wanted to move. The thing had come free suddenly and unexpectedly, causing the jeep to leave the road and crash into the forest. Lealand could see the snapped branches on one of the overgrown pear trees on the first terrace. The stuck object had catapulted through the branches and broken them off. There was a reek of rye whiskey all around the vehicle. Lealand spotted a twelve-slot crate in the back of the jeep. Moonshine made on the Peninsula always came in unlabeled jars. The crate held one remaining jar. Lealand retrieved it and put it in his pocket, then went back to hauling on the rope.

He reeled in a horror. As soon as he saw what was on the other end of the rope, he ran up the hill to find his brother.

Ghislain's body was hanging over the rock wall between the cultivated terrace and the wild one. From the way the blood was wiped about the rocks, as well as soaking the ground at the foot of the wall, Lealand could see that Ghislain had tried to help himself, tried to at least raise his body and lift his face from the stones. He'd perhaps even been thinking. Lealand deduced that from the gouge marks behind his brother's bare feet. Ghislain had dug his toes into the soil of the garden. He had been trying to pull himself back and turn himself over. But there isn't much a man hanging head down over a wall can do to right himself if he has no arms.

Now, seventeen years after that morning, Lealand looked at the beautiful young man standing on the porch, flushed with triumph, and tried to remember that moment—the moment when he'd finally had the power to properly punish Ghislain for Bull Mine and those kneeling, stifled miners. Because the house couldn't reach all the way down the hill into the untamed, *unspelled* tangles of forest and retrieve the missing fifth of its human chattel—Ghislain Zarene's arms. If Lealand hadn't carried the grisly objects up the hill, then carried Ghislain too, and put both Ghislain's body and his arms down indoors, then the Midnight Mending wouldn't have been able to put his brother back together. The house had been full of those whiskey jars— all empty. Everything else was cleared away, because everything else belonged to the house.

So that was that—a jeep crashed in the forest, a dead

marine at the wheel, Ghislain in three pieces, blood in the garden, empty whiskey jars, a forage cap belonging to a Private First Class, USMC, Division II. And the house itself, full of wounded silence.

Lealand had a good look around but there was nothing to be learned, since the house always tidied up after its occupant. There were a few new things—Ghislain had been whittling, making human and animal figures from wood: a boy in overalls, a girl in a ballet dress, a horse, a train engine, and a rowboat. The carvings were dry, splitting, so the work was old. Possibly Ghislain had made the figurines sometime in his first ten years alone, before he went mad. Or he'd made them to stop himself from going mad— whittling, whiling away the time.

Lealand had left at eleven thirty p.m., before the Midnight Mending. But not before he'd carried the dead marine up the hill too and put his body and the bloodied rope into the window seat of a downstairs room. Midnight might mend Ghislain, but sooner or later he would smell the body and—if he was still even a little mad—he'd think he was responsible for yet another death. And then perhaps he'd think again about why he deserved to be where his family had put him.

IRIS SAID, "This is a new low for you, Ghislain—getting your hooks into a young girl."

"Do you imagine I care what you think?"

Lealand said, "It's better not to speak to him, Iris. We must concentrate on helping Mr. Mochrie extract his sister."

317

"I don't see my sister," said Sholto. He started forward. The Zarenes each grabbed an arm.

"Not a good idea," Lealand said. "He can be very dangerous."

GHISLAIN TOOK A STEP BACK across the bright brass lintel. He held out his hand to Canny. She came to him reluctantly. She whispered, "Sholto looks so upset."

"Don't show him you're sorry," Ghislain said. "It never makes any difference. Thirty years ago I sat for a whole week where I'm standing now and watched them come and go, winding their spell around me. I kept saying sorry, which they only took to mean that I accepted responsibility for everything. I sat still and let them have their feelings. I waited to be forgiven."

Canny peered out the door. "They're afraid of you," she said.

"They should be." Ghislain drew her into his arms. He turned her so that her back was to the open door. He put his chin on the top of her head and looked over her at Iris, Lealand, and Sholto.

"Canny!" Sholto called.

She clung tight to Ghislain.

"Dear?" Sholto said.

Ghislain raised his voice to say, "Go on, Mr. Mochrie; put your case."

"I'm speaking to her, not you," Sholto said. Again he tried to move forward and again was caught. Iris began whispering fiercely in his ear.

Ghislain said to Sholto, "You're going to let Iris caution you, are you? After the bees, how can you listen to anything she has to say?"

"We know the bees were a mistake," Lealand said.

"Oh—so people *do* make mistakes?" Ghislain said.

Sholto shook Iris off, but Lealand still held him. The young man was clearly not sure enough of his safety just to take a chance on approaching Ghislain.

"Dear," Sholto said again. "You know as well as I do that you shouldn't be out all night with a boy. You don't need me to tell you that. Which isn't to say you can't see—this person. You just have to take things more slowly."

Ghislain laughed. "He's pretending this is a normal situation." He smiled at Sholto, mocking and amused.

Sholto's chin jutted, and his brows came together. "No matter what you think—*mate*—there's normal in it. You're a bloke. She's my sister. The normal rules apply."

Ghislain pointed at Lealand. "And that's my brother. Do you think I have much faith in family feeling?"

"Canny," Sholto said, dismissing Ghislain. "Look at me."

Canny turned, wiped her eyes, and looked at him.

Sholto slipped his hand into his pocket and pulled out Marli's letter. "You have a letter," he said.

Canny said softly, too softly for anyone but Ghislain to hear, "Marli can't tell me much because, to write a letter, she has to get someone else to take dictation." Then she began to cry. "I can't," she sobbed. "I can't go on with it. It's always the same. I hurry in because I have things to tell her, but I hate the place. I hate the smells."

• • •

CARBOLIC FLOOR CLEANER, boiled food, vomit, and the fruity-smelling white polish the nurses used on their shoes. The hair smell of Marli's hair, which was only washed once a week.

Ghislain always smelled of the outdoors, even indoors he smelled of rain, and rosemary, and the perfume of the forest.

"Girl," said Iris Zarene. "Has he told you he's a murderer?"

Sholto waved the letter, as if he hoped to fan away Iris's words before they reached her. "Canny. Look."

"I want to come and go as I please, Sholto," Canny said. "I know I shouldn't have lied to you. But I only want my freedom."

"You've been free at school, and free with Marli too," Sholto said. "When classes are done, or visiting time is over, you walk out and hop on a bus and come home. Freedom is being able to come home when you want to. Everything doesn't have to be a pledge. You don't have to man the barricades and die at your post."

Canny only heard: *Come home.* "No," she said, and then couldn't talk for a bit. She was too busy fighting tears. Ghislain said something about going in and closing the door, and how that would show them—but he sounded exultant, not sympathetic. Her eyes were swimming. She could scarcely see Sholto. In the dusk, the white square of the envelope in his hand seemed to have a light in it. It looked like a glass of milk used to when she was smaller, and Sholto would pour it out for her. That was back when

Sisema and the Professor were first married, and Sholto and she were shy of one another, and when he came in from high school, an hour after she was home, he'd pour himself a glass of milk and get her another too. He'd sit down with her and, every day, say the same thing. It always made her laugh. "Can you help me with my homework?" he'd say. And it was funny because she was seven and he was fourteen. And even funnier because she *would* help him with his math.

Finally Canny managed to choke out, "I kept it secret because I wanted to steal some—" then, with an effort, "magic."

Iris Zarene said, "Girl, just because you got up the hill to this house, that doesn't mean the magic has chosen you."

Canny ignored Iris and gazed intently at the blur that was her brother, and the envelope, that white bull's-eye. She took a hitching breath and said, "I wanted to steal some magic to make Marli better."

SHOLTO'S HAND SANK TO HIS SIDE. Tears came into his eyes. The only thing he understood, of everything that evening in the valley, was his sister. The man and woman beside him were wolves. The man Canny was clinging to was probably a mad wolf. But Canny was faithful. And because she was a kid she was waiting for her faith and patience to be rewarded. She was like that bloody elephant in the book she'd used to love so much, though, at seven, she was already too old for it. She used to get him to read her that book, though she could read herself and it took her courage to ask him for anything. She got him to read it to her because, for some reason, she wanted to share with him—her new brother—what was essential to her. Her faith. And it should be, it should be, it should be like that—

—but it wasn't. Yet how was she supposed to understand that there were things that were impossible, when she was brought up hearing over and over how you could set out in a canoe, with a compass and green coconuts, and save people?

Sholto turned to Lealand Zarene and said, "Bugger this. I'm going up there to talk to them. He won't hurt me if he cares for her." He wrenched his arm free of Lealand's grip.

"Wait," Lealand said softly, then followed Sholto a step to murmur in his ear. "Tell her to look in the window seat. He keeps it locked. But the key will be on the board in the kitchen with all the rest of the keys."

Sholto eyed Lealand distrustfully, then gave him a curt little nod.

As he walked away Iris said, "You're a fool." Then she raised her voice to address Canny. "Girl. If the house didn't mend Ghislain, what is inside him would show on the outside too, and he wouldn't just be old, like me, he'd be ugly."

"No," Canny said. "He bakes bread and keeps busy like a—like a busy grownup," she finished. She ground her fists into her eyes to wipe away tears. "What do you know anyway? You haven't spoken to him for years."

"We've all changed," Ghislain said to Iris and Lealand. "Only I stayed young. And I didn't get my sentence reduced because there wasn't a sentence. The term of my natural life wouldn't work for me, would it? I look like the kid who made mistakes, so you can have the pleasure of punishing that kid forever."

"Come off it, Ghis," Lealand said, sounding like an older brother telling off an irritating younger one. "You've threatened to kill us countless times. We'd be stupid to let you go."

"And besides, we couldn't undo the spell even if we wanted to," Iris said. "And that's your fault. You were always going to eat up everyone else's magic. You pulled it all in, and it has set hard around you. You were always a greedy, greedy boy."

"You're your own prisoner," Lealand added.

Then Iris again. "And now you want to feed on young Agnes. You can't bear to think of all her ability out of your hands."

Sholto climbed the steps. He kept his eye on Ghislain, watching him react to this. Sholto was sure that what they were saying was true, even if it seemed heartless. Ghislain was drawing Canny away toward the door and seemed prepared to let Sholto follow them inside. But then Canny put her mouth to Ghislain's ear and whispered something, and Ghislain pulled the door shut instead. As it closed, air puffed out of the house's dark interior—it smelled of molten metal, a sour scientific smell.

Sholto put his arms around his sister. He said, "We'll figure this out."

Ghislain moved away from them.

"Come," Canny said. "Let's sit for a bit." She led Sholto around the veranda to the kitchen door, where there was a bench. She sat him down and settled beside him. Ghislain leaned on a veranda post and regarded them. Sholto looked at the rabbits in the hutch. The hutch had been moved to a fresh patch of grass and the rabbits were busy, clipping it close with their sharp incisors.

"I want to apologize properly," Canny said.

Sholto took his sister's hands. "There's no need. You just have to let me get you out of here." He was whispering.

Canny wiped her eyes again and gave a little gleeful laugh.

Sholto's gaze wandered. Everything looked brand-new. The timber was freshly dressed and painted. "This place," Sholto said. He heard himself sounding disgusted and bitter. Then because it seemed he'd promised, he handed Canny Marli's letter.

She took it, then put it down beside her. "I'll read it later."

"Once you've gone, Mr. Mochrie," Ghislain said. "She can't possibly have you and her sick friend working on her feelings at the same time."

Sholto tried to stay calm and focus on what he should do. It was difficult. Ghislain stayed in one place, but he kept crossing and uncrossing his ankles, fidgeting like someone who wanted a fight.

Sholto decided to face Ghislain and deal with the only thing he did understand. "You were responsible for the second fire in the mine, in 1929?"

"Yes."

"1929?" Sholto repeated. He swallowed bile.

"Yes. I had something inside me. It wanted to protect me. It mostly knew how to mimic. It felt the explosion, thought, 'Fire!'—thought faster than people can—and it turned itself into fire."

"You didn't *do* anything," Canny said, in wonder. "You're not to blame. It wasn't deliberate."

Sholto was alarmed to see the love in her expression of relief. Love was pouring out of her, aimed at that not-young, youthful man.

"I shouldn't have been carrying it with me," Ghislain said. "It was too dangerous to take near people. I knew better."

"It was trying to protect you," Canny said. Then, non-sensically, "The ewe running to save her lamb turned into fire. I saw that. This thing—you're its lamb, you're its child. It was trying to show me that."

Ghislain looked like he had no idea what Canny was talking about. But Sholto did—at least a little. Lealand had said in his interview, "Perhaps one of us was a foster child of fire." That's what Ghislain was—or had been—the foster child of something that could turn itself into a miles long, speedy dragon of a coal dust fire.

"I was a thoughtless, egotistical kid," Ghislain said. "If I hadn't been down there with my secret friend then there'd have been more survivors."

"Where did it come from?" Canny asked.

And Sholto looked at his sister's expression of wonder and avid curiosity and thought, "How will I ever get her away from this place?"

WHAT CANNY HAD SAID TO GHISLAIN when Sholto joined them was "Don't ask Sholto in. The house is our place."

The idea that they were together, and excluding someone, was hard to resist. So Ghislain let her lead her brother around to the kitchen door, and they sat down on the sun-warmed bench while he leaned on a post. And, after a bit, he told Canny and her brother a little about the Found One he had carried into the mine.

Then Canny asked him where it had come from, and he was about to tell her, when Cyrus came around the side of the house and climbed onto the porch. "Ghislain," Cyrus said. Then, "Agnes. Mr. Mochrie. I found Miss Miller and took her back down to the river path. She kindly agreed to see those poor pain-racked boys back to Orchard House."

Canny said, "They were waiting for me in the forest. I had to use Lonnie's pain rune on them."

Cyrus said, "Can your brother talk you into leaving?"

"You sent the bees so it wouldn't have to come to talk."

Cyrus said, "At this minute you and your brother are completely in Ghislain's power—you do know that, don't you?"

Ghislain said, "And you, Cy, you're completely in my power too."

"Not that you're going to start showing off. Remember, the less Mr. Mochrie knows the better."

"What about me? I know so much now," Canny said.

Cyrus looked at her with sympathy. "What you know is entirely subject to what you are, Agnes. Everything you understand is like a hook in you, attached to what has to stay here. You can't leave here and keep it. Your brother, on the other hand, will remember a bit more. He may even remember that there were two of you."

It took all of Ghislain's willpower not to turn his head and stare at Canny. He heard her say, "What?" Baffled.

Sholto muttered that he didn't know what he'd seen. Then he said, "Canny, will you come with me now?"

"Because you've seen me one last time, he's saying," Ghislain said. "And that has to be enough."

"That's not what I'm saying," Sholto said.

"Because there's no future in me," Ghislain said.

Cyrus said, "Agnes, I can't just leave you here. Not with a clear conscience."

"I'm not to be trusted," Ghislain said.

Canny told him to "Shhhhh."

"I'm not moving," Sholto said.

"And *we're* not asking you in," Canny told him.

Sholto looked at her bleakly.

Canny took Ghislain's hand. "It's getting a bit chilly out here. Ghislain and I are going to make ourselves something to eat."

Sholto got up. He fixed his eyes on Ghislain and said, "I'm asking you to behave"—he blushed—"like a gentleman."

"I don't give promises," Ghislain said.

Sholto turned to Canny. "Don't forget your letter." Then he seemed to think of something else. He came right up to her and put his mouth to her ear—just as she had to Ghislain a little while back. He whispered something, met her sharp look, and stepped away. Then he went past Cyrus and stomped off around the front of the house. Cyrus made to follow, but Ghislain grabbed his arm. "There were two of her?"

"Yes."

"But I don't know anything about that," Canny said. She sounded aggrieved. "I didn't do anything!"

"And you're sure you don't have a twin?" Cyrus said.

"No, I don't!"

The dusk was now no longer blue, but gray. Cyrus's face was indistinct under his phosphorescently white hair. Ghislain couldn't make out an expression in either Cyrus's face or voice when he said, "Be very careful with her," and then extracted his arm from Ghislain's grasp and followed Sholto.

THEY WENT INDOORS. Ghislain picked Canny up and sat her on the table. He lit the gas mantle over her head, and, as the soft mist of white light bloomed above her, he kissed her cheeks and then her mouth.

He got busy packing handfuls of kindling into the range. Then he lit them and crouched at the open hatchway blowing on the flames. He fed the fire more substantial bits of wood, then a shovelful of coal. He filled a pot and put it on to boil, then opened a cupboard to look for the new potatoes he was keeping there. "Boiled potatoes and salt," he said. "I'm getting low on salt."

"Next you'll have me running messages. Doing shopping."

"I won't."

"Admit it, you keep thinking what use I can be to you."

"You've been useful. You stood with me."

"I'm not hungry," she said.

Ghislain closed the cupboard and came to sit beside

her. They stayed silent for a few minutes. She gazed into the middle distance and he gazed at her.

"You left your letter outside," he said.

"My own letters won't have had enough time to get to Marli. Or she'll have the first one now, but this letter has come too quickly to be an answer to that one, or to any of the stuff I've told her about the magic, and you. Marli's letter will be all stories about things that are happening on the women's ward. She likes the plots. The nurses and orderlies come and talk to her, to tell her their side of things. Because she's always there, and she's a good listener." Canny made her explanation and then fell silent again. Ghislain waited, watching her face. She looked quenched, and broken.

"Even if my first letter has reached her—the one about the thing that slapped me on the other side of the ranges, then—" She sighed. "I forgot to tell her that I wasn't just trying to entertain her. She'll think I'm making up a story, that we're having a game. So her letter will have a story in it, about something magical that happened to her."

Canny leaned against Ghislain. She nestled, warm. "I'm not ready to have to choose," she said, "whether to stay or go. I'd rather go on sitting with you than open Marli's letter."

He kissed her hair. "We could go lie down on the big sofa in the library."

They did that, went to the library, kicked off their shoes and lay down, he wrapping her so that even her feet were tucked between his lower legs. She shivered for a time. "I'm going to feel homesick everywhere now," she said. "I can't go home. But I shouldn't be here either."

Ghislain thought that if he kept kissing her, he could make it so that she wouldn't think of leaving him for a very long time. And when she did finally go, there really would be nothing for him to stay for. It would make everything easier. Even after his planning and work, he needed a decisive moment—like the moment this girl turned her back on him for good. If he kept kissing her, she'd become life for him. Then she'd leave, and that would be life turning its back on him, not the other way around.

"You should stay as long as you like," he said. "We don't have to do things to anyone else's timetable. This is our house, and time means nothing here."

She didn't answer.

"I love you," he said. "If you stay, I'll stay."

She continued silent, but still pressed against him, warm and pliant. "What did your brother whisper in your ear?" Ghislain asked.

"Nothing important."

"Something trivial, private, embarrassing?"

"Yes." Canny sat up and freed herself from his arms and got off the sofa.

"Where are you going?"

"I'm getting my letter."

He stretched out a hand, relaxed, graceful. "Leave it a little while longer. Let me tell you how I acquired my Found One."

Her face opened and lit up and she came to lie beside him again, in the loose circle of his arms, so that, as he talked, she could watch his face.

16

"ONE DAY, WHEN I'D BEEN working in the mine for about a year and was tired of it, tired of the family's plan to tediously accumulate money for legal fees, I went in search of a quick fix for all of us. I went in search of some new, powerful magic.

"I broke into the linen press at Orchard House and stole the great-aunties' Spell Veil. I thought I could go get my Master Rune. In other words, I didn't believe what I'd been told about anchors. Of course I couldn't go back to my own beginnings and find my Master Rune, but I did get out. I got out *somewhere*.

"When the family built this house they cleared the whole summit of the hill. It took years for the trees along the boundary to grow back, so that their tops hid the house from the view of people on the valley floor. When I was a boy what you used to be able to see was a skirt of old growth forest all around the base of the hill. And above that the garden terraces and the house. All the trees that are big now, like the black beech and golden ash, were just saplings.

"Anyway, when I wrapped myself in the great-aunties' Spell Veil and left my body, I found myself still in the valley, as it was then, when the house was clear of trees. Only, in the place I found myself, the top of the hill was an island. The valley was full of water, a lake without a shore. The lake had scoured away the sides of the hills so that, instead of a shore at the water's edge, there were bare, undercut bluffs.

"I was in a dinghy, but it had no oars. I had to paddle with my hands, kneeling up on the seat in the bow, scooping the water behind me. The dinghy waggled slowly forward, bow down and stern up. All the time I was paddling I was looking at the island. It was just the top three terraces of the hill. Actually, I think its shores were the farthest reaches of the Great Spell, where the imprisonment spell now begins.

"It was taking some time getting to the island. I paused for a rest and, without my hands agitating it, the water grew smooth, and I could see into it. It was clear, like resin. I could see far down, to drowned trees, their leaves yellow but still fixed to the branches. There was fruit down there too, rising like bubbles in the water, drifting up and bumping against the hull of my boat. Apples and pears and apricots and peaches, some full of holes, fruity caves where the wasps had burrowed because everything had been left to ripen too long.

"I finally got near the island. At the lake's edge the surface of the water wasn't smooth anymore, but rough with what I thought was a layer of dead leaves. But when I put my hand into the floating matter it felt all wrong; light and resilient. I grabbed a handful and lifted it to my eyes, and found that what I held was a handful of dead bees. The water all around the island was covered in a carpet of drowned bees.

"The boat bumped up against the stone wall of the lowest terrace. I stood to step onto the waterlogged garden, and someone came rushing out of the tangle of raspberry canes. And I saw that it was *me*—which I'd heard happened sometimes and is normal. After all, I was supposed to be going back within my own lifetime in order to get to the moment of my own conception and discover my Master Rune, bursting into the universe with every other possibility of my life. I was supposed to be in my own past, and I could expect to see myself. But I should have been seeing my younger self in a world I recognized.

"This me wasn't any younger. He looked exactly like me then—in 1929, and now—seventeen years of age.

"He got down on his knees on the terrace wall, put his hands together, and scooped up a big handful of dead bee bodies. Then he went like this—"

Ghislain demonstrated, crushing the palms of his hands together so forcefully that his arms trembled. "And then this," he said, and flung out his hands. "The ball of dead bees flew toward me, I yelled, and the whole mass flew into my mouth and down into my chest and stomach. Then all the bees came back to life and stung me. A fiery pain spread out into my whole body.

"I didn't see what happened to that other me, because right then the bow of the dingy bumped up as someone climbed into it over the stern, out of the lake."

Ghislain stopped. He smiled at Canny, his smile mirthful.

"Who?" Canny said. "Who climbed into your boat?"

"Iris, of course. She climbed in and told me that we had to go, immediately, if we were ever going to get back to our bodies. She took my hand and pulled me out of the boat and into the lake. We swam away from the island, then dived down into the lake's perfectly clear, glassy depths. We swam over the tops of the trees to the house you know as the guesthouse.

"There was a long curtain billowing out the window of my room—the room with the northwest-facing dormer window."

"My room," Canny said, soft and wondering.

"It was a long, lace curtain," Ghislain said. "And when I saw it I realized it was the great-aunties' Spell Veil. Iris shoved me through my bedroom window and pulled the drifting length of lace in after us. She pushed me down onto my bed and held me there.

"And everything was *real*, Canny. You know how hard it is to hold someone in place when you're both underwater? That was how it really was. The only unreal thing was the length of time one breath sustained us. Everything else was faithful to the facts of the world. The mattress was pulpy and waterlogged, and trapped bubbles came out of the bedclothes and floated up to the ceiling and joined there to form a silvery skin of air.

"Iris reeled in the Spell Veil and wrapped it around herself, then drifted down onto me so that I was wrapped too.

And then I came back into my body with a sickening crash to find myself cocooned in the veil with Iris."

"She had climbed into it after you did?" Canny said.

"It was the only thing she could think to do. You see, people don't go and come back, not without an anchor. Iris had left her right hand free. She had covered it in pain runes, written with that kids' invisible-ink recipe—egg white, lemon juice, water. She'd set two lit candles between her spread fingers. The candles burned down, and their heat and glow had brought out the invisible-ink pain runes, then once they burned lower, they actually scorched the skin of her hand. It was the agony that brought her back to her body."

Canny let out a little sigh. "Iris saved you."

"Yes."

"But she hates you."

"That came later, when she'd lost her father and uncles and cousins, and her fiancé, a guitar-playing coal miner from Massenfer who was a friend of Lealand. Imagine the valley's women. The methane explosion and choke-damp killed most of their men. The second fire—my Found One's fire—took the rest. By my reckoning, another eight men might have survived if it wasn't for what I carried."

"The ball of bees. That was it, your Found One?"

"Yes, that was it. And maybe the other me was it too."

Canny frowned and glanced away. There was something she should remember.

Ghislain went on. "Iris might not have *hated* me then,

but she was always competitive, and envious of me. She was even more envious once she realized I'd brought something powerful back with me."

Canny had forgotten to close her mouth, her lips were parted, soft, red with heat and sleepiness and excitement. She stared at him through slitted eyes, and then kissed him, passionately. She opened her mouth and drew his tongue into it. The taste of her was marvelous, but he broke away. "No," he said.

"But—why?"

"You're too young."

"You might be older than me, but not all that much has happened to you."

"I've been sequestered, that's true. But I have the patience of a fifty-year-old."

"A friend of the Professor's who's a neurologist says teenagers aren't just adults who haven't had as much time under the sun. He says teenagers' brains are actually different. It's physical. If you're seventeen, Ghislain, you have a seventeen-year-old brain. Your patience is just a habit."

"I know that," he said.

Canny pushed her fist into his chest, for emphasis, and said, "I don't want to grow out of my courage!"

"But there are things I'd love to grow out of," Ghislain said.

"Don't say that! The Professor and Mother are always telling me I'll grow out of things. And if my grandma Mochrie is in the room she always says sarcastically, 'Oh, she'll grow out of hips that work properly too.' And, 'Growing out of things isn't all it's cracked up to be!' "

"I think I like this Grandma Mochrie."

Canny stopped glowering. "Yes. Me too. She's been very useful. And my other grandparent, who I don't see very often, he's useful too. He taught me how to scale a fish, and make cloth out of flax." She patted Ghislain's cheek. Apparently she was over her moment of self-abandon. "Granddad Afa," she said affectionately.

CANNY WAS COMFORTABLE IN GHISLAIN'S ARMS—until she said something, her grandfather's name, and Ghislain gave a seismic jolt and she actually felt his skin go cold.

"What's the matter?" She could feel him trying to control his breathing. "Do you hear the others? Are they coming back?"

He was wrestling himself back into composure. He said, "I think there might be someone coming. I was worried about your letter. You left it out there, sealed, so they'll know you haven't read it. They might remove it. To bait their hooks."

Canny rolled off the sofa and landed with a thump on the floor. Ghislain sat up and helped her to her feet, and she rushed outside.

No one was out there. Dew was falling and the boards of the porch were damp under her bare feet. The lawn was visible in the squares of lamplight shining from the library windows. The garden and forest were invisible. There was no moon, only the thick skein of the Milky Way, thousands of stars in a black sky.

Marli's letter was where Canny had left it, its envelope dimpled with damp. She took it indoors.

Ghislain was waiting for her in the kitchen. He was nursing the fire in the range back to life.

Canny opened the envelope. It held only one page.

GHISLAIN WATCHED CANNY unfold the letter. Her fingers shook. He was shaking too and trying to hide it from her.

When he first caught her spying on him under the cover of Iris's revised spell, he thought she was part of a plot. Iris's plot. He was thinking it again—she was part of a plot, a grand and patient, mad and mysterious plot originating he-knew-not-where. But, whatever kind of plot it was, she wasn't in on it. And he loved her.

Canny was reading. She looked up at him and passed him the page.

> *This is Sione writing for Marli.*
> *Dear Canny. I have a cold so have to wait to write to you. Can you remind me when you are coming home? I would get Sione to ring and ask but there is no one at your house. I will write as soon as I feel a bit better. All my love, Marli*
> *This is Sione again. It is a bad cold and her breathing is not good. I think you will not mind me telling you that.*

Ghislain folded the letter and returned it to her. He said, "You have to go."

338

"I'll go tomorrow morning," she said. "Sholto can put me on the train."

ONE OF GRANDMA MOCHRIE'S FAVORITE SAYINGS, which she'd come out with when Sisema was trying to do something like make a trifle with shop-bought sponge fingers instead of homemade sponge cake, was: "If a thing is worth doing it's worth doing properly." Canny sat at Ghislain's kitchen table and watched him doing things properly. He said he was starving and was going to boil potatoes. But it seemed that boiling something wasn't going to keep him busy enough. He found some walnuts. There was a walnut tree in the garden, he said, and these were last summer's nuts, seasoned, but still oily. "I don't have butter. But I can make walnut butter."

"You're playing host," she said to his back. "Because you're scared I won't come back."

He didn't answer.

"I will."

He stayed quiet.

"Please don't doubt me."

He glanced at her. "I don't," he said, then continued to concentrate on cracking walnuts.

"Are you angry at me for going? You said I should."

"I'm not angry." He put the walnut meat in a mortar and began to crush and grind. "I don't often have butter or oil," he said. "It's great to have some oil. My rabbits have no fat on them and I don't keep a goat anymore. So I scarcely get any fat, animal or vegetable." Then, "We are going to sit down like civilized people and share a meal."

"I'm not a civilized person, and I don't want you to be," she said, petulant.

"Yes you do."

He set out his potatoes, his precious salt mixed into the walnut butter. Canny discovered she was hungry, and the food was very good. She ate like a sixteen-year-old who has been rushing up and down hills for days. He picked at his food like someone facing an ordeal. She didn't notice. She'd stopped watching him because she was hatching another plan.

She had to leave Ghislain, but there'd be no point in doing that if she couldn't find a way to save Marli—to steal magic as if magic was medicine she didn't have enough money to pay for.

After she'd eaten she went to the bathroom and brushed her teeth with her finger. Then she said they should lie down together again. "And at least talk all night."

He said, "All right," and went to get a rug. She lay down on the big leather sofa—and fell into a stuffed, exhausted sleep.

WHEN SHE WOKE, the only light in the room was the red glow of coals in the fireplace. The flames had died down and the coals were cooling and making a hollow tinkling. Ghislain was slumped in a chair he'd pulled up beside the sofa. He was asleep, holding her hand.

Canny freed her fingers from his grasp and got up. She stood over him for a time, and then very stealthily searched his pockets. A warm metal object rolled out into her searching hand—the key to the locked room.

• • •

CANNY MUFFLED THE LOCK WITH ONE HAND and turned the key. The hinges were silent, in perfect working order, of course. The door didn't creak, or the floorboards.

She stood in the doorway of the room and waited for her eyes to adjust. The windows had no curtains, and, sometime in the last little while, the sky had clouded over and it had begun to rain. Maybe the moon was behind the cloud, because the sky was radiant, and the rain magnified its light.

Ghislain's Spell Cage stood in the center of the room, in a patch of light from the window. It was making a lacy shadow on the floor. It looked sinister and secretive and semihuman. Its first layer was open, flanges bent like beckoning fingers. Canny went to it and pushed the hatch wider. It scraped on the floor. She peered at the door to the inner cage. She found its two catches and picked at them, trying to pry them open. The lead was soft, and she was easily able to.

She looked about and found Ghislain's final piece of the spell—the latticework crown of the outer cage. The rope was already tied to it. But of course the hole for the hook on the ceiling beam would have filled itself in at the last Midnight Mending.

Canny unfastened the crown from the rope and carried it to the Spell Cage. She couldn't reach the top of the cage, so she dragged a chair over and stood on it. She lifted the cap into place. It fitted perfectly into the open ring at the top of the head portion of the outer "body." Canny performed this coronation, then stepped back and looked at the space—mansize, Ghislain-shaped—which was waiting for her to fill it.

Ghislain had said that he'd been arrogant and foolish to go into his great-aunties' Spell Veil with so little hope of coming back (and none of coming back safely). He'd said that, without a twin, it couldn't be done. If she climbed into the Spell Cage, who knew what would happen to her? The Spell Cage wasn't a Spell Veil, with enough flexible length to wrap the body of anyone brave enough to send his soul after hers—and she knew that Ghislain would do that, if he could.

Ghislain was planning to go, unanchored. To go one way. But the house would keep him alive. Canny wasn't "of the house." She'd die of thirst. She could be grappled out of the contraption, but what would she be like? A soulless, floppy puppet, a glazed mute. What she was considering was impossible. Still, looking at the space inside the sarcophagus, Canny had the feeling she got whenever someone asked her a really difficult math question. Not a Math Competition question, but one like those that clever men in the mathematics department at Castlereagh University asked her when they were examining her for her scholarship. Canny never worked through the steps to find her answers. She just fished them up, as if she were looking down into a dark pool knowing that the right fish was lurking there. A number, or a value. She could almost see it now.

Rain ran down the windows. The room was full of trickling shadows. Canny stepped into the Spell Cage. She turned to the hatches and put a hand on the outer one. She hesitated, and then broke into a cold sweat. Her heart started banging so loudly it seemed to be trying to bash its way out both of her ears. The cap was in place, and if she had closed the outer cage and activated the "Go from now" spell without all the meticulous fine print of the inner cage, then she'd probably already be dead.

After this stupid near miss, it took some time for Canny's hands to be steady enough to pull the door to the inner cage closed and pinch its soft lead flanges to fasten it. Nothing happened of course. And nothing would happen, because once she was fastened in the inner cage she couldn't close the door to the outer one. That was why Ghislain was going to use a rope to lower the cap into place *after* he was encased in both cages. The cap would activate the spell for him. If Canny wanted to do that now she had to find some way to close the outer cage from inside the inner one. But she couldn't. Here she was, being bold, and planning some crazy leap of faith, and it wasn't possible.

Canny laughed with relief. Then she just stood for a bit feeling a little bored and a little silly, like the last kid waiting to be found in a game of hide and seek.

Ghislain appeared in the doorway of the room.

Canny said, "Um. I was just trying it for size." She felt embarrassed. Not that she'd been caught doing something dangerous, or that she'd picked his pocket for the key, but because he'd know she meant to try to use the Spell Cage, and that she'd failed to understand how it worked.

He came up to the cage and looked at her through the open hatch of the outer layer. His eyes were as black and as gleaming as the lead the cage was made of—mineral black, as they'd seemed the first time she was this close to him, when he'd manhandled her down from the veranda after she'd escaped out an upstairs window.

He smiled at her; a small, confiding smile. Then he pushed closed the outer door and, with his clever fingers, pinched its fasteners shut.

17

IN THE HAY FIELD the first crop has been cut but not raked and boxed in bales. The sleek dry grass is lying in long mounded rows. Canny knows how slippery it is to walk on. Hasn't she already gotten to the end of this field?

But here is Sholto, with Susan, and Iris, and Cyrus Zarene. Cyrus looks exhausted and is slumped on the ground. Canny knows she should say something to Sholto. She's had him running from pillar to post. (Such a silly saying that, pillar to post.) Sholto, Susan, and Iris look stiff and frozen, like posts and pillars. Like Lot's wife in the Bible, whose story has always puzzled Canny, since the wife's only sin seems to have been a nostalgic desire to look just *once more* at the city where she'd spent a whole life and raised her children, before being hustled out of it by Lot and a bunch of stern angels. A last look—that's a natural wish.

Sholto, Susan, and Iris have turned into pillars of salt. Canny studies them and looks around. Everything seems to start as soon as she turns her head. The trees begin to move in a slight breeze. And there are a group of children between the trees, running along the river path.

Canny looks down at the cut hay. Someone should gather it up now. It will rain tonight (the locked room was filled with glimmering rain-light).

Canny tilts her head and looks up into the sky at its one dark cloud, a cloud made of roiling, weaving bees. The swarm divides, one half hovering uncertainly over her head, the other drifting after another Canny, the one fleeing along the river path ahead of the pack of children.

"Oh!" thinks Canny. She now understands what is going on. She drops her chin and meets Sholto's eyes and tries to say something. But there isn't time.

BY HER SECOND JUMP CANNY UNDERSTANDS that she'll never be able to go back. That she has no business being where she is, standing over herself and Lonnie Zarene, who are sitting together on a bench at Massenfer Station. Lonnie is scribbling his pain rune over and over on the front page of the *Castlereagh Clarion* and Sisema Mochrie's self-satisfied face. Voyaging Canny casts no shadow and can't linger, even if she wants to.

SHE IS STRETCHED THIN AND FLATTENED OUT, standing under the oaks in their early summer green. She is on the road that runs between the back door of Castlereagh Women's Medical ward and the hospital parking lot. She tries to find her feet, and run, run, run.

The Austin is parked just up the road, a figure in its

driver's seat. It is Sholto—Sholto, who asked her to come home. Canny has to get to him to say sorry, she won't be coming home, and goodbye. But she should also turn and go back down the hill to the ward and sit with her friend, who has a cold, her friend whom a cold can carry off forever. She should be in the car seat beside Sholto, who will drive her home. She should be with her friend. She is homesick—torn in half by homesickness.

THEN SHE IS SOMEWHERE ELSE. It's summer and she is walking along the Westbourne waterfront on a windy day. There are two girls going along in front of her. They are carrying their swimsuit bags over their shoulders and are wearing shorts and halter neck blouses. They both have long, crinkly, cloudy black hair. One girl's hair goes down to her hips, the other's to her shoulders. It is herself and Marli, and she—voyaging Canny—is walking behind them, as if she is the wind.

The wind is waiting for its moment.

The beach is crowded—a city beach on a sweltering day. The little kids all have red flannel sun bonnets. People think the polio is discouraged by the color red.

The wind pounces, a gust makes Marli's hair fly forward and wrap itself around her ice cream cone. Canny watches her younger self go into fits of giggles. Marli is trying to pull the ice cream out of her hair, and her hair out of the ice cream. The cone is her favorite flavor, tutti-frutti. But voyaging Canny recalls that it wasn't very good that day. Both Marli's tutti-frutti and her orange chocolate chip had been full of splinters of ice. That meant the ice cream had thawed and been refrozen.

This is their last outing. Tomorrow Marli will have a sore leg, then a headache.

Voyaging Canny can't catch up with them—yesterday's girls. She can't make herself heard, can't say, "Drop that cone, Marli. Bin it!" She wants to shout, "It's the ice cream. Don't eat the ice cream." But she is a weak, gusting summer breeze. She can't knock the smeared cone from Marli's hand. Marli is going to go on and eat it and its imperfections, because those girls have spent all their spare change and this is the day's last treat, and they've only got enough for the ferry ride back across the harbor.

Here is the ferry now, sliding into the long pier. The fishermen are reeling in their lines. There is no time.

It's a school day in the gym, and a hateful lesson in folk dancing. Folk dancing is a craze the young teachers straight out of Training College have. They use the word "ethnic." Canny and Marli think "ethnic" means dolls in national costume, and folk dances.

Marli and Canny are in the same circle. Voyaging Canny remembers this dance. She waits for the circle to break, to become a spiral, then divide into two circles, one within the other. When it does, she slips her hand into the hand of the boy who is last in the chain of dancers. It's Jonno; he's dragging his feet. As she takes his hand, he turns and looks at her, aghast.

(Canny remembers that, the day after they did folk

dancing in physical education, Jonno suddenly blurted out that his nana said that if you got between a person and a person's ghost it meant that one day that person was going to save your life. He said that to her, and she didn't know what he was talking about, and told him, "You're off your head, boy.")

Canny must maneuver herself in this dance so that Marli is between her and that younger Canny, the one in a daggy knit top and cotton rompers. (The boys get to wear shorts, but the girls must wear these things with elasticized cuffs on the thighs. Rompers can't ride up too far and are therefore *decent*. Girls must never forget decency.)

The two circles split and partner up and spin around, the dancers' hands crossed to grip. Voyaging Canny is on her own, drifting like an electron dropped by its atom. Without the other subatomic particles, she is about to turn into a different element. That must not happen. She tries to line Marli up between herself and herself. It's like lining up a tough pool shot. Her left hand finds the real, clammy, sour, dirty hand of a boy. Once again she enters the figures of the dance, and someone else is cast out. She *is* going to be able to carry this off, after all.

But then the dancers all turn to paper, a chain of paper dolls being danced between three mirrors, above Marli's head. Marli is in the iron lung. Schoolgirl Canny is standing beside her friend, her scissors put aside, dancing paper-chain people back and forth to illustrate a story about this year's fiasco of a folk dancing lesson.

She is saying that the boys had played up so badly this year that the teachers split the class into boys and girls.

And of course boys were never going to hold hands with other boys.

Marli's laugh is like someone playing a harmonica, it sounds as her breath goes out and as it draws in again.

Voyaging Canny is standing behind both girls, watching all this. She wonders if Marli can see her reflection in that left-hand mirror, the one that shows the windows full of brown oaks and yellow sycamores. But voyaging Canny can't see her own reflection. She has no body and never will again.

Goodbye, laughing girls. There isn't any point in lingering here. She can't maneuver her friend between herself and her ghost, or hold up her end of anything even as light as a paper chain.

SHOLTO AND A SMALL, DARK GIRL are nursing their glasses of milk, sitting side by side at the kitchen table. Voyaging Canny watches them from the doorway. Little Canny is doing Sholto's math homework while he makes her an origami crane. Little Canny hears Sisema before voyaging Canny does. Voyaging Canny is shocked by her mother's force, her physicality, as Sisema breezes past and bangs into the room. "I hope I'm not interrupting anything," Sisema says.

Little Canny: "Sholto is helping me with my subtractions."

Sholto looks at his small stepsister with admiration. Butter would not melt in her mouth.

CANNY KNOWS HER MOTHER'S HERMIT CRAB story by heart, so she isn't surprised to find herself hovering over the street and the figure sitting on the high, white-painted curb, feet in the gutter. She is surprised to see herself there too, her small five-year-old self, half asleep, head resting on her mother's arm. A poor, tired, sticky child in a too short frock and with purplish scars on her legs.

(The scars are from boils. Canny had forgotten her boils. It was the mosquito bites. Sometimes she'd wake in the night to hear the bright chirping of a pink lizard clinging to the breeze-block wall behind her head, catching the mosquitoes attracted to her ripe little body.)

So—she was there in her mother's great moment of insight.

The palms are silent. There is no wind. The roaring is the reef beyond the palms, the park, and the strip of crab-grass that is as green and groomed as a golf course. The palms are still, so Canny can hear the glassy chiming of the tree frogs.

The crab is an ambulatory shell balancing on six pointed feet. Then you see the eyes, swiveling to look down the vast gulf of the gutter, and the claws nervously clipping the air like a bored ticket collector coming along an empty train carriage.

"We're not going to get anywhere this way," thinks voyaging Canny. There is somewhere she's supposed to be.

(Her mother went the very next day to Arahura's shipping office and bought a single one-way ticket to Southland—children under seven could share their parents' berth.)

One way. Voyaging Canny is plagued by this thought. There is something she has to get—something like a return ticket. Maybe then she can go back.

The crab on the curb is perhaps thinking that the sea is down there, and if he can only find a safe way—

He tests the drop, sidles farther along, tries again.

Sisema watches him. She is a handsome young woman. Her face is all shapely planes, the hollows of her cheeks are pitted by acne scars, and that change of texture makes her face more sculptural and dramatic. Sisema's face is hard and disenchanted. It isn't the haughty one her daughter knows now.

Canny looks at this young mother and remembers being the sticky girl, always trying, and failing, to make her beautiful mother laugh.

But even as Canny watches, Sisema's expression is changing. She is looking at the crab tenderly now. She nudges her sleeping daughter and says, "Shall we help this fellow?"

Little Canny comes awake, sees the crab and, encouraged by her mother—"Careful, Akanesi"—she picks him up by his shell, puts him down in the gutter, then quickly lifts her bare feet out of the way as he scuttles off toward the drain. Sisema laughs, and little Canny sees she has permission to laugh too.

The crab with the cockleshell house has found the drain. Little Canny says, "Not down there!"

Voyaging Canny can only just understand them, her mother tongue is very rusty now.

"Well, that's his lookout!" her mother says. Sisema gets up and hoists little Canny to her feet. "Come along, baby." Then, "What do you think of the crab? He carries his own house. Clever, eh?" Then, "You know, baby, that's what I liked about traveling with your daddy and his friend. We went off with just as much as we needed and no more. We had to keep washing our clothes. But I liked that. We'd park up somewhere sunny. I'd string a line between the top of the windshield and a tree. I'd hang out our clothes and make us some shade."

CANNY FINDS HERSELF UP BY THE RAFTERS of the church in Arahura, floating on billows of music. The hymn is less melody than chant. The overlapping choruses of bass and baritone, of tenor, contralto, and soprano all swell and fall like surf. Canny is looking down on the men in their white suits and white shirts and white ties, and the ladies' hats, made of bleached flax in lacy weaves. On the center of each crown is a flat, glossy shell. The hat brims are covered in flowers, or gathered white ribbon, or coronets of pale seashells. From where she is, the body of the church looks like a lawn covered in fallen blossom.

Sisema is sitting by herself in the gallery. She has a hat and a shawl. She is nursing her baby beneath the shawl. All the babies and small children are up in the gallery where they won't be too noisy during the sermon. Among them is a little prince in a burgundy suit and bow tie. He looks like a pageboy from a fancy wedding. He is howling and will still be heard once the singing stops. All the women are trying to quiet him. All except Sisema, who isn't sitting anywhere near the rest of them. Her seat is so far toward the front of the church that she will be behind the minister once he climbs up into the pulpit. She and her baby won't be visible to him. Better *not* to flaunt a fatherless child in front of the congregation.

• • •

THERE'S A PATTERN. THESE ARE PIECES, not fragments. They fit together.

CANNY IS BACK IN THE VALLEY, and she thinks for one moment of wild relief that she will be able to find her body. But the woman beside her is her mother, not herself.

Her mother is wearing a silk blouse, worse for wear, with missing buttons. Sisema is showing too much smooth, polished mahogany skin. Her khaki shorts are gathered with a belt at her waist, and her legs are long and strong. Her hair is pinned into rolls over her ears, loose at the back and ironed straight.

Sisema is standing, unsteady, on the bottom, messy terrace of Ghislain's garden.

Ghislain is on the wall above her. He is giggling. His skin is glossy with sweat, and if voyaging Canny had any sense of smell she'd smell the whiskey fumes coming off the both of them. They are swaying and laughing because they're drunk and what they are doing is very funny—even though one of them must know what will happen.

Ghislain has a rope around his wrists, tied in a capable knot. The rope has a bit of slack. Canny can't see what is at the other end of it, but from a little way down the slope, through the mass of overgrown rhododendron bushes, she can hear voices, men with American accents. And she can hear an engine revving.

"Ready?" calls one of the Americans, laughing too, shiftlessly, drunkenly.

Sisema goes to the edge of the wall and tries to peer

through the trees. She puts a hand around the rope. She says, "Slowly off the clutch, James."

There is a hoot, lewd laughter, a teasing voice. "Hear that, Alex? Sis wants us to go slooooooowwwwlllly."

Chortle, chortle. "Right. I can't go slowly *enough* for Sis."

Sisema's hand is lifted by the rope as it grows taut. Ghislain is laughing harder and she turns to look at him, uncertain. His laugh is too wild. He is not amused, he is mocking fate.

The engine revs. Ghislain is pulled forward. For a moment it looks as if he is braced against some invisible, slanted barrier, then his bunched fists burst through it. His feet are still on the lip of the wall, then only his toes. He is apparently resisting the pull of the jeep.

(The jeep, *of course*, thinks voyaging Canny.)

Sisema is baffled, because if Ghislain was resisting, he'd have planted his feet and leaned back and flexed his arms. His body isn't in the position of a man resisting, but of a man whose feet are tied. The rope is far above Sisema's head now and out of her reach. It is twisting gradually, and growing thin.

The jeep revs. Ghislain is screaming with laughter. His fists are blue and red with trapped blood. The rope is so taut that Canny can hear it creaking. Then there's a fibrous "pop." Ghislain's screaming laughter becomes a scream.

Sisema shouts, "Stop! Stop!" She jumps at the rope, but can't reach it. She runs to the wall and clambers up far enough to grab Ghislain's feet. She tries to free them, to see how they're caught, what's holding them in place. Her hands scrabble in the dirt, but she can't find anything.

Ghislain is stretched out along the air. Downhill the engine howls. Sisema leaps back down, turns, about to plunge through the bushes to stop those deaf, mischievous men. Then Ghislain gives a grunt, and there is a series of popping and rending noises and his arms are pulled from their sockets, trailing quivering strips of muscle and tendon, ball joints suddenly exposed, clean and white and coated with healthy gristle. Blood spurts out in two streams and splashes Sisema. The bound arms crash through the trees, snapping branches. Down the hill there is a metallic rattle, a gravid thumping, and a very loud crash. The forest quivers, and all the birds leave the canopy in a panicked cloud.

Ghislain has been pulled onto the lower terrace, finally. He is facedown over the wall, by Sisema's feet. She looks at him, not seeming to notice the streams of gore dripping from her head onto her cheeks and joining beneath her chin. Her face is utterly empty, so frozen that Canny sees how like *her* her mother looks. They could be twins. Perhaps Canny's frozen face has always been a memory of this moment.

Everything is silent. The frightened birds have disappeared. Downhill there is only the long dying gasp of steam from a split radiator.

Canny keeps her eyes away from the anguished, flopping form at her feet. She tries to make herself noticed, but her mother is gone, flinging downhill, making a horrible sound that's not scream or groan or whining, but a bit of all of them.

Canny floats up toward the house. The sun swings back

across the sky, and stops still. It is earlier in the same day. The bench by the kitchen door is occupied by a man in unpressed sage green cotton pants—United States Marine utilities—an undershirt, and dog tags.

On the bench beside him is a nearly empty cup of coffee with three soaked cigarette butts in it. He has another lit cigarette between his shaking fingers. He looks up at her, shades his eyes, says, "Morning, Sis." Then, "Where did you get that horrible outfit?"

Canny opens her mouth to answer, but nothing comes out. She slips by him and goes indoors.

All the curtains are drawn. There's a little more light in the front hall from the stained glass around the door. A jacket is draped on the banister, cotton twill, with buttoned pockets and a corporal's stripes.

In the parlor the chairs and sofa are no more or less worn than they were. Another man is lying on the sofa. He is wearing shorts and undershirt, sweat is gathered in the hollow of his clavicle. He has a thin, yellow-tinged face and lank blond hair. The whisky jar by the sofa is empty and lying on its side, no sign of spillage, perhaps because it overturned before midnight and all mess is cleared up at midnight and all the house's own things gathered up and returned to their rightful places.

Canny would like to open the curtains and let in the morning sun. She'd like to get a better look at the sleeping man, but she knows she can't alter anything, can't even twitch a drape, and even if the man on the bench outside did see her, he only mistook her for her mother.

Canny goes through into the library and discovers

Sisema standing before the huge gilt-framed mirror above the mantelpiece. The mirror reflects the room, but not Canny in the doorway. Sisema's arms are raised, her elbows cocked. She is rolling her forelocks and pushing hairpins in under the rolls to fasten them. She licks her palms and flattens the loose locks in the back, frowning with savage displeasure at the black, crinkly mass.

Sisema is wearing a pretty, flounced blouse with sweat-stained armpits. Her arms are thicker and stronger than Canny's, her breasts rounder, more attractive. Her skin is darker, but not the strip of midriff that is exposed when she lifts her arms to wipe more spittle as lacquer across the frizz on her crown, trying to tame it. Sisema is sun-darkened, stronger than Canny, and older too, by a few years. More curvaceous, and her eyebrows are plucked into thin arches. But Sisema is so like her that Canny is amazed she hasn't ever noticed it before. (She hasn't wanted to. The Sisema she knows is thirty-five, buxom, and schoolboys turn their heads to check her out as she sails by them. That Sisema is heavy and handsome, snooty and sly, and of course her daughter wants to be nothing like her.)

Canny studies the rumpled hearth rug and bunched blankets. She thinks, shouldn't she have gone back earlier? But she is glad to have been spared the sight of her mother naked—naked and drunk like Noah in the Bible, and look where seeing Noah naked got the son who cared enough to creep into his father's tent and cover him up. *Cursed.*

("Really," Canny thinks. "I've got to stop thinking of those Bible stories where it's always the person in the story who I most understand who gets punished. The person who actually does something *human*." Ghislain had told her that the Zarene magic originally came from God—and if she's about to plunge her hands into the fountain of the magic and drink, she should be God-fearing.)

"Shouldn't I be here earlier?" Canny wonders. "To be in at the moment of conception?"

Then she remembers biology lessons. Castlereagh Tech was a practical, progressive school. Her biology teacher had used words like "coitus," which was more scientific than "sex."

("The word 'sex' covers a whole range of behaviors," said her biology teacher. "We are to speak of coitus. The actual act of procreation." And then he cracked his ruler down on the chart and its cross section of the reproductive parts of a sheep. He ran his ruler back and forth from "vulva" to "uterus," and then traced the wiggle of the fallopian tubes. The chart is definitely nothing to do with sex—Canny and Marli's idea of it—which is Jimmy Stewart's face the moment he wakes up and finds Grace Kelly leaning over him. Canny and Marli's biology teacher proceeded to describe the meeting of spermatozoa and ovule, and how fertilization takes place a number of hours after coitus.)

Sisema finishes fussing with her hair. She searches in the blankets for a packet of smokes, pulls one out and puts it in her mouth, finds matches in the pocket of her belt-cinched men's shorts. She slides the box open, fishes out a match, and strikes it.

The moment the match ignites, another light bursts into being. A spark, as bright as the flame of an arc welder,

passes out through the bare skin of Sisema's midriff, unnoticed by her. Something momentous has just happened
inside her, and she isn't aware of it. She touches the match
to the tip of the cigarette and purses her lips to blow smoke
up into her hair.

The spark lifts free of Sisema. It seethes, diminishing in
brightness as it grows in size. It floats, white, ectoplasmic.
It is frozen ectoplasm, no longer mobile, but caught in the
shape of movement.

The burning shape hovers before Canny like a crack-
ling ball of St. Elmo's fire. She recognizes it, and knows it's
been with her her entire life. It was always present. It *is* the
present.

18

IT WAS AS IF SHE'D BEEN in a decompression chamber, set
to several atmospheres above normal air pressure, and that
chamber had suddenly come apart at the seams. Everything flung itself off her, even the air. She felt the tiny hairs
all over her body stand up and, at the same time, there was
a wrenching, bursting noise, and a series of loud thumps.

Canny opened her eyes. It was still night, the light
around her was coming from a splattering of small fires.
Molten lead had embedded itself in the walls, igniting the
wood and wallpaper. The ceiling, walls, and floor were splattered with silver fluid. Some of the lead ideograms were
still intact, but semimelted and curling up like dying spi-
ders.

Canny didn't dare move. She didn't have her shoes on,
and the fragments of destroyed Spell Cage were still smoking. As she waited, the soft lead began to set and cool, and
the flames on the walls died back, turned blue, and then

went out. The room filled with a thin haze of smoke that stank of molten lead.

Canny discovered that she was clutching a key. It wasn't the key to the room—the one she had taken from Ghislain's pocket. That was still in the door. This was a small, ornate key, something a cabinetmaker might use. Canny studied it, and then turned her gaze on the window seat.

Before Sholto went back down the hill he had whispered in her ear, "You should look in the window seat. Lealand says Ghislain keeps it locked, but that its key is in the kitchen."

Canny stepped over the jagged circles of lead that were all that remained of the Spell Cage and picked her way through the smoking debris. She stroked her fingers along under the lip of the window seat till she found the embossed lock-plate that matched the decorative key. She inserted the key, turned it, lifted the lid, and stood poised over the shadowy interior.

Since the fires were out the only light in the room was from the window, a trickling rain-light. As her eyes adjusted, Canny caught sight of a small, pooled gleam. She reached in and picked up a watch and fob chain, gold by their weight. The watch had been lying with a coiled rope, on top of a puddle of dull-colored clothes. Canny moved the rope and touched the clothes—heavy cotton over something stiff. She moved her hand and the texture beneath it changed. Now she was touching something that felt like beef jerky. She bent close. The puddled clothes were revealed as not-quite-flat pants legs and a stuffed, lumpy jacket. Then her eyes made out a clump of hairlike fiber.

She bent still closer. The smell of mildew and corruption rose into her face, and she saw that her hand was resting on the browned, shrunken cheek of a mummified body.

Canny jumped back. The lid of the window seat came down with a loud clap. She turned and fled, left her shoes—again—stumbled to the front door, out it, and onto the soaked lawn. There she stopped. The watch fob was still in her hand. There was more light outside, though it was before dawn and raining hard. Canny's fingers were wet. She fumbled, but finally snapped open the watchcase.

Something was crawling on its white face. Canny nearly dropped it. Then she saw that the crawling thing was an arrow, and that the object on the fob chain wasn't a watch, but a compass. The compass arrow swam to orient itself. It pointed ahead of her, due north, down the valley. It seemed to be showing her the way she should take. She raised the compass to her eyes to make out the inscription on the inside of its case.

Thomas Afa. Harbor master.
Arahura. Lost Link

There was a splashing behind her, then Ghislain was on her. He wrapped his arms around her, and as she fell to her knees, enfolded her with his body. The compass case closed in her hand with a bright little "click."

The stink of molten lead had followed Ghislain out the door. It mixed with the wet-garden, cold-earth smell of night. Ghislain was weeping. "I agreed, I know," he said.

"But you can't just go and not say—" But he couldn't say it either.

Goodbye.

The rain increased. The lawn was sizzling, and the wormholes audibly bubbled. Canny and Ghislain knelt inside a silvery capsule of drenched air. His mouth was warm against her neck. It was the only warmth in the world. Canny wept too. She choked out, "After everything you said, you closed me in the cage."

"I don't know what you mean."

"You said even you'd die in the cage if the house wasn't in the habit of keeping you alive."

"Canny, I don't understand what you're saying."

"You said it was impossible. You said that, without an anchor, I'd be lost."

"We've both been asleep," he said. "You must have been dreaming, love." He got his arms under her sternum and pressed her to him as if he meant to incorporate her body into his.

Between sobs she said, "Didn't you look in your locked room? Didn't you see what's happened?"

He raised his head. Cold rain leached off her hair and washed away the warmth where his mouth had been. "What's that smell?" he asked.

"Molten lead." She opened her hand and showed him the compass. "I looked in your locked window seat."

He touched the compass, but didn't take it from her.

"You must have known all along," she said. She freed herself enough to turn around and look at him. "You must have known who I was. Who my mother was."

363

His face was gray in the twilight, his eyes dark, liquid, miserable. His expression told her that he understood what she was saying, and knew what she suspected. He said, "I was badly hurt. Or I was dead, and death left a hole in my memories. The house restored everything, including my peace of mind. I went back to my everyday—I hadn't any other option, except madness. *More* madness. I tried not to think about things. It was too horrible. I didn't really consider what had happened until weeks later, when I was finally able to trace the source of the horrible smell. I found the compass with the body. It belonged to that woman. Sis. I read the inscription, but I didn't make a connection till tonight, when you said your grandfather's name."

"So you're telling me you didn't kill the man in the window seat?"

"I don't know. Not with any certainty."

Canny tried to shake him off. She struggled violently. "You're a liar! You tried to kill me!"

Ghislain tried to calm her. "Canny, I don't know what you think I've done."

"You shut me in the Spell Cage!" Canny burst out of his grasp. The ground was so wet that her feet couldn't find traction, and her flight was inefficient and slithering. But he didn't follow her, and the rain came down in curtains between them. Before long she was in the forest. She let herself be washed down the slot of the pig path, sometimes skidding on her feet, sometimes stumbling with water pushing up around her, and plastered with leaves and mud.

• • •

WHEN CANNY AND GHISLAIN WENT INTO THE HOUSE and closed the door, Sholto followed the Zarenes down the hill. He soon discovered he couldn't get back up it again. He tried and tried, and sometime before midnight Susan joined him. She had coats, umbrellas, apples, and a big flashlight. They made a mutual, unspoken agreement not to try the hill again and just waited, only once shifting to a higher section of the path as the river rose and the rising stream tugged at the green fronds of the willows.

They waited all night on the river path, huddled in the figure eight of clear air under their kissing umbrellas. They didn't say much, having already exhausted all their information and arguments.

By sunup they could actually feel the river under their feet—a constant quiver in the earth. "I've heard that the Lazuli Gorge road sometimes closes," Susan said, sounding fearful.

"We'll face that problem if we have to."

At that moment Canny stumbled out of the forest, her clothes coated in mud, her feet bleeding, and her hair as wet as waterweed.

They rushed to her. Sholto hugged her, while Susan shook open the blanket she'd held all this time, its dryness preserved by her oilskin and umbrella. She wrapped the blanket around Canny, then Sholto picked his sister up and strode off downriver.

Susan pattered through the puddles after him. "Are we going straight to the car?"

"No," Canny said, in a quiet, definite voice.

"There are our bags to think of, Sholto," Susan said. She

tried to catch up and come alongside so she could check on
Canny. The girl was pale and scratched, but her mouth was
set, and she was looking at her brother with knitted brows.
"I am not going to run off without getting dry and warm,"
she said.

Susan couldn't understand how Canny could keep doing
this—putting terrifying and strange stuff behind her and
forming a new plan. She could see that that's what the girl
was doing—see the calculating mind at work under all the
physical and emotional distress. But that was Canny—
Sisema Afa's daughter, whether she owned it or not. Her
whales had gone, so she was going to steer by the stars.

"I'd be better off for a bath and bed," Canny insisted. It
sounded sensible, though Susan knew it wasn't. The problem was that what Susan and Sholto now knew they still
didn't understand. And they couldn't seem to hold it in
their heads like ordinary information, the sort that leads
to practical decisions.

"We're not setting foot in the guesthouse again," Sholto
said. He was obviously doing better than Susan with the
strange circumstances.

They squelched on. In Sholto's arms, Canny began to
shiver, then to quake. Her teeth chattered uncontrollably.

Susan grabbed the back of Sholto's coat. "Stop! We can't
go on like this. I'm freezing. She's freezing. Before I came
out with the gear, I slapped eighty bucks down on Iris Zarene's pretentious guest book. We are fully paid up, with
one more night up our sleeves. Let's use it."

Sholto stopped. He swung around and glowered at
Susan through his dripping hair. "Haven't you got the

sense to be scared of them? God knows what they're capable of."

"I'm more afraid of the weather, Sholto. The rain and the river."

Canny joined in, her voice tremulous. "I feel sick, Sholto. I can't seem to get warm."

"Don't you remember what they did?" Sholto asked Susan.

"I don't know what I remember. They sent the boys to chase Canny, and the bees got stirred up. That's what I remember. They said weird and threatening things." Susan stuck out her lower lip and glowered.

"So *cold*," Canny moaned.

Sholto looked from one female to the other, then heaved Canny to change his grip and turned away from the flooding river and toward the guesthouse.

CANNY WAS SITTING IN THE BATH while Susan knelt on the bath mat, gradually adding hot water and pushing it down the tub with her hand. She froze when she heard Sholto intercept Iris Zarene at the bathroom door.

"No," Sholto said, then stiffly, "My sister requires some privacy."

Iris said, "I packed your bags and put them on the porch, Mr. Mochrie. Your money is in one of them. I don't want your money."

"You can bring those bags back indoors, thank you very much," Sholto said.

"This is my house, Mr. Mochrie. I decide who gets to stay under its roof."

"I'm sure there's some law against chucking people out in bad weather. Something about reckless endangerment."

"Oh, you're so clever." Iris oozed contempt.

Canny hugged her knees, apparently mesmerized by the water flowing from the tap. Susan turned it off, the better to hear.

Sholto was saying, "I'm sure the sheriff will be very interested in some of what has been going on here."

Iris gave a bark of laughter. "Report us. Please do." Then her voice changed pitch to pierce the closed door. "You lying little monster," she said. "This won't do you any good. That magic you've so cleverly cultivated is going to stay where it belongs. And when it leaves you, it's going to turn you inside out."

"Get out of here!" Sholto yelled.

There was the sound of two sets of footsteps going along the hall, and on the stairs. Sholto was stamping and shouting, chasing Iris off.

Susan began to soap Canny's hair. Canny sneezed. "I'm almost deaf. My ears are stuffed," she said.

"Did you catch any of that?"

Canny said, "It doesn't matter what Iris says. The air she is using to talk is my air."

"Fine," Susan said. She dug her fingers into Canny's scalp. "At least your grandiosity isn't as nasty as hers."

Susan washed, then rinsed Canny's hair with a fat sea sponge. Canny let off an impressive volley of sneezes and her nose began to bleed. She pinched it closed. Blood dripped off her wrist into the soapy water.

"Stay still while that clots." Susan got up and began to gather Canny's muddied clothes.

"Leave those," Canny said, nasal. "Could you find me my pajamas?"

Susan dropped the clothes back on the floor. Something in the wet mass went "clink." Canny met Susan's look, challenging.

"Are you stealing stuff now?" Susan asked.

"No."

"Okay then." Susan went off in search of pajamas.

Canny's bag had been spitefully put out under the dripping eaves. Sholto had retrieved it, emptied it, and was hanging various damp garments over the top of the wardrobe door and the foot of Canny's bed. Susan saw that the bed had been stripped. She went in search of bedding, found another guest room empty, and removed all the quilts and blankets. Canny would have to do without sheets.

Susan reassembled Canny's bed with one under-blanket and several quilts. Sholto showed Susan the room keys. "I have these. And I raided the drawer of Iris's desk and found her spares too."

Susan laughed.

Sholto laid a fire in the grate of Canny's room. There was a coal box in every room, all of them full. He said they should be able to keep at least this room warm and dry.

Susan was still in her wet clothes and felt clammy but not chilled. "It's cold for summer, but mostly it's just wet."

"Canny's sick, so she's feeling it," Sholto said.

"She's not as bad as you think."

"I thought you were the one who was worried that she was at death's door."

Canny appeared then, wrapped in a towel, her hair still sopping.

"Dry yourself," Sholto scolded. Then he muttered, "I don't know what we're still doing here."

There was a quick flash of movement in the hallway. One of the big girls hurrying past. Susan darted out and grabbed her. It was Bonnie. Susan said, "Can you find Canny some dry pajamas?"

Bonnie looked at Canny with a kind of thrilled terror, then gave Susan a little nod.

Susan let her go. She could hear one of the adult men downstairs—she thought it was Lealand, his voice was deep and heavier than Cyrus's. "The forces are gathering," she said to Sholto.

"They can gather as much as they like. We are not shifting till we're ready," Sholto said. Then, to his sister, "Take that wet towel off and get into bed."

Canny waited till he'd turned back to the hearth and then obeyed him. She dragged the quilt up to her chin and lay shivering.

Sholto put an arm around Susan. "Can you get her cocoa or something? Are you brave enough to go down and do that? I think you're less likely to end up in a confrontation."

Susan nodded.

"Then you can get some sleep. I'm going to guard the door."

Susan went downstairs. She stood for a moment in the hall, steeling herself, then boldly strode into Iris Zarene's kitchen. "Blessings be upon this house!" she said, loud and droll. That earned her a startled look from Lealand Zarene. She immediately began searching the cupboards.

"What are you doing?" Iris said.

"Making Canny a hot drink. She is tired and sick and sore." Susan found cocoa and a cup. She went to the safe for milk. Its enamel pitcher was cooling in a bucket. She lifted it out and carried it dripping across the floor to the bench.

"That's not the way we do that," Iris said.

"I'm sorry. *My* house has a refrigerator," Susan said. She wouldn't look at them. She found a pan and poured milk into it and set it to heat on the always-hot coal range. She carried the pitcher back to the safe, then stood at the stove, stirring the milk so that it wouldn't form a skin. Her own skin was crawling.

"This one studies folklore," Iris said informatively to her cousin. "She has been asking the kids all sorts of awkward questions about local legends concerning witches."

Lealand laughed dryly.

"The other one is a history student. I had a snoop at his papers to see what he was saying about us. He writes things like 'Humans are animals made of memories.' Fine sounding, soap-bubble thoughts."

Susan felt breathless. The milk was steaming. She poured it on the cocoa powder and stirred.

"You'll forget, you know," Iris said in a cool, conversational voice. "All those bubbles will pop and you'll be left with empty air."

Susan picked up the hot cup and carried it out of the kitchen.

• • •

WHEN SHOLTO WENT OUT AND SHUT HER bedroom door, Canny bit down on the rustling quilt and cried, stifled, silent and hopeless. She didn't stop till there was a knock. It was Susan with cocoa. "Where is that girl with those pajamas?" Susan said, impatient. Then Bonnie appeared behind Sholto's barricading chair.

Canny turned her wet eyes on Bonnie. "Thank you," she said, then, "Do you have a moment to speak to me?"

Bonnie glanced at Sholto, who moved his chair to let her by. She hovered, uncertain.

"Please," Canny said, with deep and desperate intensity.

Bonnie came nervously in and laid a nightdress on the end of the bed. It was Victorian, floor-length, embroidered cotton.

"That's an antique," Susan said.

"Sorry," Bonnie whispered.

"No, I don't mean *old*, I mean that it's exquisite, and it seems a shame to use it."

"It's all I could find," Bonnie said.

Canny sat up and raised her arms like a helpless infant, and Susan slipped the garment over her head, pulled it down, and buttoned its cuffs, pushing the tiny mother-of-pearl buttons into their loops. Canny said, "Thank you, Susan. You go get some sleep."

Susan looked quizzically from one girl to the other. Canny patted the bed, inviting Bonnie to sit beside her. Bonnie sat. Susan threw up her hands in exasperation and went out. Sholto closed the door.

"You're in such trouble," Bonnie said.

Canny leaned back on her pillow and sipped her drink. She thought how she'd averaged one meal a day for days—and maybe two hours' sleep. Each sleep had been recuperation from a terrible illness, and every meal a communion.

"Bonnie, I need your help. There are a few odd, but not terribly complicated things I need brought to me. I'm not going to be allowed out, so someone else has to do it for me. I'm sure you can manage."

Bonnie shook her head.

"*And* you can manage to say you'll help me."

"What do you want these things for?"

"I'm not going to tell you that. But I will tell you something I know, to prove I'm not a dabbler, and I'll make you a promise, a very, very solemn one."

Bonnie's eyes grew wide.

"Okay. What I want is some chicken wire, some pliers, quite a lot of newspaper, a jug of water and a glass, a packet of corn flour, and some tissue paper. Do you need to write this down?"

Bonnie gave an impatient flip of her right hand that made her forearm slip free of her sleeve. Canny looked at the tattoo. "Oh, that latest one means you've mastered the Tabular Alphabet."

Bonnie blinked. "Yes." Then, "On your first day here you told me you could see the house on Terminal Hill. I could have told Aunt Iris and Uncle Cyrus and Lealand. I should have, but I didn't."

"I know, and I'm grateful, but you had a good reason for not telling. You're like Lonnie. You don't want to have to leave the valley and never come back."

"And lose what I've learned," Bonnie said, her eyes filling. "Either I stay here and get sick, or I go and lose what I've learned. It isn't much of a choice."

"You won't have to do either. I'm going to try my very best to change things. That's my promise."

Bonnie nodded. "Okay. I'll help." She jumped off the bed. "It'll take me a while to get everything. I have to wait till the coast is clear. But I can just give some of it to your brother."

"I'd rather you delivered it to me yourself."

"The chicken wire is hardest," Bonnie said. "I can hardly cut it from the chicken coops."

"There's a cylinder of it protecting a sapling next to the guesthouse sign," Canny said.

"So there is." Bonnie studied Canny carefully. "Do you remember everything?"

"Pretty much."

"You must be a Zarene!"

"There are people who remember everything who aren't Zarenes," said Canny. "But I think I may be a Zarene, though, believe me, I'm not as happy about it as you seem to be."

WHEN BONNIE MADE HER FIRST DELIVERY—the water jug, glass, and corn flour—she found Canny sitting up in bed, crying bitterly and unself-consciously, and catching her tears in her cupped hands. Canny signaled with her chin at the water glass. Bonnie brought it over and Canny dribbled the small pool of salty water into it.

"Is that magic?" Bonnie whispered. "What kind of magic is it?"

"I'm just going to do whatever seems right," Canny said. "And I hate this crying. It has to be of some use."

"Why are you crying?"

Canny's face crumpled. She tried to control herself. "The thing that mattered most, I got wrong," she said. "And I had to give up what I wanted. Now my friend Marli is ill, and I should be at home."

Bonnie touched her arm. "It'll be all right, you'll see."

The last thing Bonnie delivered, after discarding her raincoat at the back door of the house, was a whole sack full of tissue paper, most of it pristine filmy squares. "These are the tissues we use to wrap the export apples," she said. "I stole a whole packet. There are some discards in there too. They're the scrunched ones."

Canny put her nose in the sack and took a whiff. The tissues had a faint apple scent. "Perfect," she said. "You can go to bed now. And thank you. Thank you very much for your help, Bonnie."

"Your brother has nodded off. He didn't wake up this time when I slipped past."

"Good. Try not to wake him."

Bonnie paused with her hand on the door handle. "I don't think you're a Zarene," she said.

"Why not?"

"I don't know. You just seem like a stranger. Don't take this the wrong way, but you seem like the strangest stranger I've ever met."

"And brown," Canny said. "Very, very brown."

Bonnie looked worried, then remembered and laughed. "Good luck," she said and went out.

CANNY CLIMBED OUT OF BED and spread her materials on the old rag rug. She looked at what she had, then closed her eyes to measure the object she had seen, the hovering, turning, coruscating shape. She picked up the pliers, pressed the twanging sheet of chicken wire flat, and began to cut. Now and then she stopped to push her hair behind her back—it was drying and gaining volume.

Three hours later she had the base of her shape, a wire cage with wriggly strands teased out of it to make several curling arms. These had only to be in the right attitude, curved so deep and no deeper; the actual shape she could refine as she built it up with layers of paper. Inside the cage she'd hung the compass, its fob chain anchored so that it could swing in the space, not rattle around loose.

Canny turned to making her glue, a mix of corn flour, fresh water, and salt tears.

FIVE HOURS LATER she was smoothing on a final layer of apple tissue. Some of the tissue paper was faintly pink, stained by blood from the cuts she'd gotten while shaping the chicken wire.

Canny set the finished shape by the hearth. She felt its weight shift as, inside it, the gold compass swung. She stayed by the fire, her eyes periodically drooping then flying open again.

The model of her Master Rune slowly dried and

whitened. Its tissue skin didn't crack. She'd made it carefully, and absolutely faithfully, so that it was at once a fragile papier-mâché sculpture and an adamant, ageless thing that expressed every particle of her magic and possibility of her life.

Iris Zarene had promised Canny that she'd lose her magic once she left the valley, that it would be torn out of her. Ghislain had said something similar, suggesting that the roots of her magic, when ripped free, wouldn't come up clean, but with the stones and soil of her essential self clinging to them. Canny was afraid that she wouldn't just forget the Zarene magic, but the valley itself, the river, orchards, hives, hidden house—and Ghislain. It seemed that nothing she could do would spare her from the pain of loss. But, though she wouldn't be spared, perhaps she might be saved (so that she could save Marli). If only she could smuggle her Master Rune out of the valley.

"Out of the valley," Canny thought, *"where I was only last night."*

The marine sitting by Ghislain's kitchen door, smoking a cigarette, had seen her. He'd mistaken her for her mother. Shading his pink-rimmed eyes, he'd said, "Morning, Sis. Where did you get that horrible outfit?"

Even without her rune, Canny had somehow managed to be visible to him, and perhaps to Jonno too when, in the folk dance, he'd reached for her ghostly hand. The question was, *with* her rune, would her hands be less ghostly? Would they be solid enough to carry this papier-mâché sculpture for just five seconds, and a single step? Ghislain had insisted that a soul couldn't carry anything. So why

377

did she have the feeling that what was impossible for him and all his powerful Zarene ancestors was, for some reason, possible for her?

At dinnertime Susan knocked on the door and asked Canny if she wanted something to eat. "I've shamelessly raided Iris Zarene's kitchen again."

Canny called through the door, "I just need to sleep." She was surprised at how croaky her voice was. Susan went away, or perhaps took her turn guarding the bedroom door. Canny didn't know, because for a time she fell into a feverish, shallow sleep, curled around her sculpture.

About an hour before dawn she climbed stiffly to her feet and stood for a time listening to rain dripping from the eaves. The fire was dead, the grate cold. Canny turned to face the fireplace and stooped to pick up the now dry sculpture. She stood straight, squared her shoulders, and, after a slight breathless hesitation—during which she blushed, as if deeply embarrassed—she took one step across the rag rug.

Canny's body came to a standstill a foot from the hearth, her hands held out before her, empty.

But her spirit floated forward to settle slowly onto the polished floorboards of the upstairs hall of her home in Castlereagh, right outside her brother's bedroom door, in a hall brightly lit by moonlight shining through the claret, amber, and lilac panes of stained glass on the landing.

Canny carefully set her Master Rune down on the hall runner. She looked at the door. "Knock knock," she said, then stepped back and leaned on the wall opposite, her torn hands concealed behind her.

After a moment the door opened and Sholto poked his head out, looking a little bit like a grumpy turtle.

"Sholto," Canny said, calmly, but with all the love she felt.

He peered blearily at the Rune. "What is this?"

"An artwork," Canny said.

"You're giving me an artwork?" He sounded doubtful.

"Yes," Canny said.

"Why are you giving me an artwork?" He sounded suspicious, as if he thought she'd gone to all this effort only to tease him.

"So you can look after it for me," Canny said simply.

"In the middle of the night, you're giving me an artwork so I can look after it for you?"

"Yes."

"And," said Sholto, with immense sarcasm, "does this mean I'm supposed to take it with us? Do you think I should put it in the back window of the car, with our sun hats?"

"No, that wouldn't do at all," she said, mild. "I want you to keep it here, at home."

Sholto's eyes strayed from hers to the Rune. For several long minutes he just gazed at it, lost to himself. Then he said dreamily, "Where am I?"

"Home," said Canny. "It's Thursday morning, on the day before we set out, and I've brought you this artwork. It's a papier-mâché sculpture, made of chicken wire, and strips of newspaper, and the tissue used to wrap apples. I want you to put it away somewhere and keep it safe for me."

She watched Sholto pick the Rune up, fumbling a little when the suspended compass shifted inside it.

"Thank you," Canny said. "I know I can rely on you."

"You can go back to bed now," he said, impatient. "I'll take this—Lady Senator's fancy hat—and find a corner for it."

Canny's brother went into his bedroom and used his foot to close the door. "Thank you, Sholto," Canny said again, then pushed off the wall and stepped forward—

—and back into her body. She stumbled and just caught herself by seizing onto the warm mantelpiece above the fireplace with her empty, lacerated hands.

THEY LEFT THE GUESTHOUSE VERY EARLY, before anyone else was up. Sholto was carrying both Canny's and his own pack. It was still raining and he led them an indirect way, along a track that went from ruin to ruin through the gardens. He picked some tomatoes, skins split from too much rain. He passed a couple to Susan, who ate them greedily. He held one under Canny's nose, which was all he could see of her face under the dripping hood of her coat. She shook her head. She was going slowly and dragging her feet, but she stayed upright and kept on.

Cyrus Zarene was waiting for them in the meadow. He was standing beside the Austin, enveloped in a stiff old sou'wester. He had a wheelbarrow with him, a tarpaulin covering whatever it held.

Sholto unlocked the car. Cyrus pointed at the trunk, so Sholto unlocked that too. Of course what Cyrus had was the anthropology department's precious reel-to-reel tape recorder.

Cyrus and Sholto carefully transferred the machine to the dry trunk.

Cyrus said, "I'm sorry for everything that happened, and everything that's about to happen."

Sholto looked at him in disgust. "Can't you people open your mouths without issuing threats?" He stepped closer, thrust his face into Cyrus's. "If my sister ends up with a teenage pregnancy I'll slap such a lawsuit on you, your heads will be spinning."

"How strange," said Cyrus. "You're already forgetting."

"I'm forgetting nothing, mate. I might not be able to cast spells, but I can pay lawyers."

Cyrus stepped back. "If you really want revenge just start reminding people of the Lazuli Dam project."

Sholto was outraged. Why would the man say that! Sholto was incapable of doing anything like that. He might want to discomfort Lealand, Cyrus, and Iris, but the idea of drowning the valley's apple and apricot and cherry orchards made him sick to his stomach. "What do you think I am?" He turned and squelched over to the driver's door and got in.

Unfortunately Sholto wasn't going to get his graceful exit, or the last word. He had to climb out again and ask Cyrus's help in pushing the mired Austin back onto the road, both of them laboring side by side while Susan steered and Canny waited, silent, swathed and dripping.

Once the Austin was safely on the gravel, Sholto said, "Look. Thank you. And thanks for bringing our stuff."

"Look after her," Cyrus said.

Sholto fired up again. "Of course I'll bloody look after her!"

THE GORGE WAS VERY GREASY and visibility poor. Sholto drove hunched over the wheel. The windshield wipers labored, throwing water about and only making brief quarter-circle transparencies through which the road ahead could sometimes be seen.

Canny was in the back with their packs. Now and then Susan checked her in the rearview mirror, but the girl hadn't removed her wet coat and was almost indistinguishable from the packs and soggy, bundled sleeping bags.

Once Susan craned to look out the passenger-side window. She saw the Lazuli, its water a wicked, opaque caramel color; the current humped and sinewy. She quickly looked away.

They came around a tight bend and there, before them, was a slip. Rubble and clay blocked most of the road. The mass of earth must have come down hard, for the road had a long crack in it a few feet inside the crash barrier.

The Austin slid to a stop.

There were lights beyond the slip. Headlights, flashing amber warning lights, and the red revolving light of a patrol car belonging to the Massenfer Sheriff's Department.

As soon as they came to a stop, cold air came into the car. The back door was open. Sholto and Susan swiveled to look into that not quite so full backseat, and then spun forward again to see Canny climbing, picking her way up the unstable slope of the slip.

"God!" said Susan. "What the hell is her hurry?"

"Marli," Sholto said. He jumped out of the car and shouted his sister's name.

Above Canny, a drooping sapling came free, with its footing of roots and earth, and tumbled down the slope. Canny stepped back and let it go by. It bounced on the crash barrier, fell into the current, and was whipped away downstream, traveling at an impossible speed.

Sholto set off after his sister, turning back a second to say, "You stay there, Sue. Promise you'll stay there."

Susan stayed put and watched her boyfriend struggle up the slope after his sister.

He caught Canny at the top. She slithered and fell to her knees. He teetered and righted himself, keeping his grip on her coat.

Then, with a shift and sigh, the whole edge of the road broke away and slipped as a single mass into the river. A great wave washed up the far side of the channel, scooping another large hunk of earth loose. Sholto and Canny were now balanced at the edge of a clean cliff face of rock, the river below them. Sholto leaned back and began to kick up the slope, away from the edge, pulling his sister with him. Canny didn't resist, or assist him. Her heels dragged and her free hands made little gestures at the drop.

The crumbling edge froze and re-formed, as if invisible hands were patting the sods back into place.

SHOLTO REACHED THE CREST of the humped landslip and let himself slither down the far side, his sister partly on top of him, as if his body were a sled. He could hear Susan shouting his name.

A deputy and a couple of husky men in plastic rain slickers came and picked them up and brushed them off. "You were nearly gone there, son," one man said. He guided them toward the lights. Sholto found he was quaking with shock. Then someone climbed out of one of the cars, shook a dry umbrella open, and said, "Akanesi. Sholto."

It was Sisema.

SHOLTO DIDN'T COME WITH THEM in the sheriff's car. He wouldn't leave Susan. Once Susan had seen that they were safe she'd gotten back in the Austin and carefully reversed it around the corner, away from the crumbling road. They could see she was still waiting there, because of the raindrops shining in the cones of light cast by the hidden car's headlamps.

Two road repairmen and Sholto eventually trod a thin track back across the middle of the landslip. The men returned without Sholto and, a moment later, he reappeared, hurrying head down around the corner. A little after that the lights of the Austin withdrew as one of them, either Sholto or Susan, continued to drive, in reverse, back along the gorge to find a wider section where they could turn and head back to the valley.

ON THE RIDE INTO MASSENFER, Sisema told Canny that she'd gotten the SAF to send one of their B-52s to fly her from Calvary on the Shackle Islands to Ardour Air Force Base on the southern end of the Peninsula. "Massenfer Valley is too twisty for a long runway. Those planes are big, but that means we were able to do the trip from Calvary all in one hop."

Sisema seemed pleased with herself. She said she'd called in the debt they owed her.

Canny felt dull, as if a warm cloud were settling in around her head: something overpowering, hot, and perfumed, like steam from a commercial laundry.

Her mother said, "Didn't Sholto tell you how worried I was?"

"He didn't tell me he'd spoken to you."

"Well, you hearing that your mother wanted you ferreted out of that place probably wouldn't have helped his case," Sisema said. "Sholto may be lackadaisical, but he's not stupid."

Canny slid sideways and rested her wet head on her mother's shoulder. Sisema put up an absentminded hand and stroked her face. She raised her voice to talk to the sheriff. "If my stepson comes to complain to you later just bear in mind that he has a tendency to exaggerate. He likes drama."

"Yes, ma'am," said the sheriff.

"Why would you say that?" Canny muttered.

"Straight to the railway station, if you would be so kind," said Sisema to the sheriff.

"Whatever you say, ma'am," said the sheriff.

"And I'm surprised this man isn't asking more questions," Canny said, as if to an invisible audience. She saw the sheriff's eyes flick to meet hers in his rearview mirror. He looked wary, then he looked wooden.

"Oh," said Canny, still to herself. "He's scared of them."

19

SISEMA HAD PURCHASED a first-class compartment on the Peninsula Express, destination Westport. She had a porter at Massenfer Station run for blankets and tea and then sat Canny in the least drafty corner of its decayed waiting room. "I wanted to change trains at Kinnock Junction, but they told me that the first train to Castlereagh wouldn't come through for two hours, and it was a slow local. So I've wired ahead to arrange another first-class compartment from Westport."

Did she expect her daughter to congratulate her? Canny was too tired to form a sentence. She'd sprung a leak, and the dry matter in her head was liquefying.

Sisema pulled off one of her lilac cotton gloves and laid a soft palm on Canny's brow. "It's just a cold, I hope," she said.

"You rushed back because I had a cold?"

"No, darling." Sisema got up to help the porter with the tray. He apologized that the tearoom was closed.

Sisema said, "This will do very nicely." She tipped him. He beamed and asked did she need anything more. Another blanket perhaps?

"Is the train on time?"

"Yes, ma'am."

Sisema smiled and sent him off with a wave.

Canny couldn't taste her tea, even when it had cooled.

As soon as they were on the train Sisema had the attendants make up one of the beds. She got Canny out of her clothes and into it, then sat on the red leather seat opposite. Canny stared at the decorative ironwork on the station awning and then flinched as the train shuddered and began to slide out of the station. The station clock sailed by overhead, midday looking like midnight.

"I mustn't sleep," she said. If she stayed vigilant how could this thing creep up on her? She could feel it coming, softening the edges of the world.

"If you're not eager to sleep then perhaps I ought to start now," Sisema said. She wasn't looking at Canny. Her gloved hands were folded into her lap, though she'd unpinned her hat and placed it on the seat beside her.

The brick walls of the rail-side warehouses slid past, and the valley opened up. The train followed the curve of the river. All Canny could make out through the rain was the top of the black coal tailings on the slopes above the Taskmaster.

Sisema said, "I was afraid the people in that valley would find out who you were. I was afraid that someone had seen me, all those years ago, and would put two and two together.

You see, my grasp of geography is very bad. I'm sorry about that. You'll see what I mean when I explain."

Canny fixed her eyes on her mother, who it seemed was finally going to tell her something.

"WHEN I FIRST CAME TO SOUTHLAND," Sisema said, "people were very kind to me. The people in the know, that is. They kept an eye on me and set me up on dates with groups of nice young people. Groups, so there'd be no poor fellow having a brown girl foisted on him. Sometimes I felt like I was the only brown girl in Castlereagh. The people from the archipelago never ventured farther north than Pitt River, and my own people hadn't started coming here. I was different—a bit of a hot potato. And though there was goodwill, none of the folks being nice to me knew what the goodwill was about, so they were kind of thinking, 'We'll see,' about it all. People don't have faith without having the story.

"So I was lonely. And there was this man. A very funny, attentive man. I worked for him, and I was in love with him, but he was married. In the summer of 1942, late November, I said yes to this man's suggestion that I go off on a trip with him. He'd booked a hotel in Esperance, on the tip of the Peninsula. We took his car. He'd been hoarding gas. Anyway, we got there, and I couldn't go through with it. I spent the night in the hotel lobby. He was very cross with me. The manager's wife came and threw me out before breakfast. She said, 'Go away. We don't want your kind in this establishment.'

"So, there I was, standing by a phone booth on Main

Street, looking at the coins in my purse, when a jeep pulled up. Two marines were in it, a private first class and a corporal. Alex and Jim. They offered me a ride. Said they were going back to Castlereagh *slooooowwwly*. So I got in. We spent the next few days driving, and swimming in rivers, and lying around in the grass. We'd park in the afternoons, and I'd string a rope between the windshield of the jeep and a tree, and I'd do our washing. Then I'd hang it out to dry; I'd make shade. We'd lie about in the shade of our laundry and drink. The marine boys had purchased a whole crate of that moonshine they sell in jars on the Peninsula. Those boys weren't really sleeping. They'd been popping bennies. The military used to give them drugs to keep them awake during battles, and they'd gotten a taste for it. James especially. He was a little crazy from too much. Amphetamines—never go near them, Canny. Alex went a bit easier on the drink and pills. He wasn't well; he had a parasite from the jungle. He was a mess, really. They'd seen some terrible things. Pill-popping lushes, that's what they were, but they were also real gentlemen.

"We got into a bit of trouble at Massenfer and were chased out of town by the sheriff. The boys' jeep was a match for the sheriff's car and we got ahead and cut down a side road near the summit of the Palisades. We switched off our lights and waited for the sheriff's car to go by. James wanted to turn back the way we'd come, but Alex thought he could make out a road going down the hill. There was one, very bumpy and overgrown. It took us all the way down the narrow head of a valley, then up a kind of driveway that went in a spiral around a forested hill.

ELIZABETH KNOX

"The driveway stopped by some old garages belonging
to this gorgeous house. We could see the lights of other
houses down in the valley, but there was only one person
living in the house on the hill, a guy about my age who said
he was there because he couldn't leave. He was very hospitable even if he was a little strange, so we cracked a jar with
him and kept drinking.

"I've thought about it, and thought about it—and I
think we were there two days and one night." Sisema fell
quiet and brooded.

"Ma?"

"I don't remember when it was he told us he couldn't
leave." She looked at Canny. "There are things I have to
get right so you'll understand everything. One of those
things is that I forgot to tell you that no one knew James
and Alex were gadding about together. James was the driver
for some major, an officer who was on furlough and holed
up in a posh Peninsula holiday home with a local lady. This
major had said to James, 'You push off, and be back on the
twenty-second.' Alex had been on medical leave and was
mooching about in Esperance. He'd only just hooked up
with James before they found me. So, no one knew they
were together. The other thing I have to try to make clear
is that we thought there were two perfectly explainable
things going on with that boy. Possibly he was a bit neu-
rotic and scared of leaving his home. Either that, or he was
telling that story about himself because he was nearly of
age and should have been thinking of signing up."

Canny was listening to her mother, but every joint in
the track the train clattered over was a number. Canny was

390

counting backward, away from the sum. It wasn't a simple process of subtraction. All the numbers and symbols were being obliterated. A storm was coming, and it was snowing on the graph paper. The signs, sines, and cosines grew dim. The grid was fuzzy, furred with white, and then the page was blank. She was losing something. It was leaking out of her. It was as if she were bleeding to death.

"Anyway," Sisema said. "The house was in great shape, super clean and tidy, and it was obvious to me that the boy's family were only off for a week or so and would be back any minute. That made me nervous. I kept washing the dishes and mopping the kitchen floor.

"The one night we were there was very hot, though it was still a month off high summer. It was the kind of weather when it's really difficult to sleep. Anyway, when I did finally, I had a dream in which I was trying to make a cord for a very complicated whalebone carving. The carving didn't have a hole drilled in it, so I had to weave a kind of cradle for it. You know how I taught you to make thread from combed flax and beeswax? Well, in the dream I had honeycomb, but I had to use my own hair instead of flax. In the dream, my hair was long, like it was when I was a young girl, and like yours is now. I was plucking long strands and tying them to a chair leg so I could wax and plait them.

"My hair wasn't strong enough by itself, so, in the dream, I took off my blouse and began to search for a loose thread. I couldn't find one, and when I looked again the hair was gone too. So, in the dream, I unclasped your grandfather's fob chain and compass from around my neck and tried to use that. That must have been when I lost it. I think I took it off in my sleep. In the dream, I got up and went around the room trying to peel the decorations from the walls. They came away like corn silk, sleek and strong, and then turned brown and shriveled up, like withered corn silk. Anyway, I was so long at it—trying to find thread for a cord—that I lost the carving. I was standing stupidly looking about when I realized I was awake, and the young man was in the room too, asleep on the rug.

"I went out to check on the marine boys. They had started drinking again. James hadn't even slept. They were hatching this plan to tie the young man to our jeep and pull him down the hill. They said he had to stop telling stories and making excuses. They were half mad from booze and bennies and the things they'd seen, and they meant no real harm. They thought they'd only yank him off the terrace garden. He was going to make a big leap. At worst, if he lost his footing, he'd land in the bushes—big rhododendrons smothering some fruit trees. It was going to be a laugh. The young man thought so too, when he woke up and we put it to him. Then he had half a jar of whiskey for breakfast, chugging it down like it was cider.

"James was the one to tie the boy, with some clever seaman's knot. He and Alex went down to the jeep and I tossed the other end of the rope to them over the bushes. They fastened it to the jeep and started its engine.

"All the men were carrying on like it was hilarious. And James and Alex only got more wild and amused. When the rope went tight and nothing budged, all they thought was that I'd untied it and then attached it to something they couldn't shift, like one of the trees. But that wasn't what happened. This is hard to explain."

Sisema rubbed her forehead. "There was an invisible wall. Really—there was. We could pass through it, but that kid couldn't. He didn't seem surprised by it. He just kept shrieking with laughter. Then—I heard later, because he told me—Alex kicked James's foot off the clutch and the jeep leaped forward and, before it stalled, it dove right off the road and ended up wedged against a tree, bumper down, on an almost vertical slope. It fell, and stopped suddenly and—"

Sisema went quiet for a moment, and then continued in a strangled voice. "James broke his neck. And that boy—his arms were pulled out of their sockets. They were torn off.

"I couldn't think. I just rushed downhill and dragged Alex out of the jeep, and we ran away through the forest. We left everything. Hiked down from the summit to that little town, Oatlands, and caught a bus. We didn't report what had happened. And Alex went back to the camp outside Castlereagh, early, to the astonishment of his friends who couldn't imagine why anyone would waste their leave.

"And I went back to Castlereagh too, and my job. I saw Alex only once more, shortly after, when the rumor went around that the marines were all shipping out—the whole division. There was the strike on the waterfront—the waterfront workers were out for more pay, and the wharves were locked. The marines were loading their own supplies, so some of them were still on land, not already on the ships out in the stream. There was a blackout, of course. So, there was a thin new moon, the dark harbor, and ghostly gray ships, and all these people, mostly women, crowded at the big iron wharf gates waving messages and whispering to the marines doing the loading up—whispering names, and have you seen this one or that one. Alex found me and we hugged through the gates. We didn't say much because he was so wrecked by what we'd done.

"This isn't important for you to know, Canny, but I'd like you to anyway. What I thought about myself changed so much in such a short time. I'd had to keep it secret—the brave thing I'd done for those airmen. But I'd known I was a hero, so I was hero in my own heart too. I had a kind of steadiness about myself. But it wasn't public, and by the time it was, and people wanted to know me, I'd left those two men dead on that hill. Then when the Shackles were liberated and my story came out, people made a fuss of me. But by that time I was starting to show, starting to bust out of my clothes, so I went home.

"Then, three months after that, when you were a little baby, I found out that Alex was gone too. Killed at Tarawa. I read about it in the newspaper. The navy had the wrong maps of the atoll and put some of those boys out of the boats in full battle gear in nine feet of water."

Sisema pulled a handkerchief from her sleeve and touched it under her eyes. "Alex died, and there wasn't anyone to tell on me. Or anyone to talk to either."

Canny tried to think—think and speak. "You said my father was a marine who died at Tarawa. You also said his arms came off. Ma, which one of those men was my father?"

Sisema thumped her hands on her thighs and cried, "I don't know! I didn't *do* anything. I ran away from the married man. James and Alex were honorable and treated me like a little sister."

There was a horrible sensation of loosening in Canny's head, as if someone were gradually severing every anchoring strand of a great web in her mind, so that it was drifting in and sticking to itself and becoming not a gleaming catchment of light, but a dusty, clumped cobweb full of desiccated insect bodies. *Desiccated bodies*—that should mean something. There was a reason those particular words had come to her, only she couldn't recall what the reason was.

"What about the boy in the house?" Canny said.

"I did kiss him once," Sisema said. "I was in the bathroom and he came in behind me and I told him he was cheeky. But he wouldn't say anything, so I kissed him to get a reaction. But it wasn't like kissing a boy. His lips had no flavor, and his body no smell, and all I could hear was this twittering, like birdsong. Or like a hearth fire when the flames have gone from the coals and they squeak and tinkle. That sound. And I've heard it ever since. The doctors say it's tinnitus, but it started back then. It's why I sometimes talk too loud—because I have this endless tweeting and buzzing in my ears."

Canny jolted, as Ghislain had when she spoke her grandfather's name. Her mother put a hand on her to quiet her. "Darling, you have a fever, so don't throw the blankets off."

But Canny was trying to throw herself off, her body, so

she could go back and be with him. *"Ghislain!"* she thought, shouting his name in her mind. In her mind's eye she saw the other one—the one who looked like Ghislain, but wasn't Ghislain—the one Ghislain had seen on the shores of an island in the drowned valley. The one who had tossed the ball of dead bees at him. The one—she knew now— who had helped her down from the veranda roof when she'd climbed out a window while Ghislain, the real Ghislain, was around the front of the house saying to Cyrus, *"What would I do with a girl?"* The one who had smiled at her, before shutting the door of the Spell Cage. She remembered how, both times, on the veranda, and in the locked room, she'd been eye to eye with him. She could still see his hard, inhuman, mineral black gaze. Black like coal. Black like a sealed mine shaft. Black like the windows of a house gutted by fire.

And then the train plunged into the Palisade Range, entering a tunnel. And as it went in, the lights momentarily failed. They flickered, and the carriage went black. When, only seconds later, the lights came on, Canny looked about her and wondered where she was, and what she'd been thinking. She freed her hands from the blankets and raised them to her face. They were hurting. She unclenched her fists, slowly and painfully pulling her fingernails from her palms. The little shuteye shapes filled with blood.

"Canny!" Her mother snatched a towel from the rail by the basin and folded Canny's hands into it. "I'm sorry," Sisema said. "You shouldn't listen to me."

Canny let her wounds be stanched. She gazed at her

mother, puzzled. "Was I listening?" she said. "What were you saying?" Then an invisible ax struck the top of her skull, cracking her head and letting the cold air in on her brain.

The pain was so great she thought it would kill her.

THE CURTAINS WERE CLOSED, but there was a strip of light between them. The light was a blade that kept coming for her. Then, whenever the blade withdrew, she could see what the gap illuminated—a patch of lemon yellow paint. So, she was in her own bedroom. She'd been trying to sleep somewhere strange and it hadn't worked, and someone had had the sense to get her home.

The light beside her trembled. It was a water glass. "This will help," someone whispered. It was her mother. Her mother was being uncharacteristically muted.

Canny thought she should try to manage some last words at least. But she couldn't think what to say. After all, what do you say to your own mother when you're about to die? But her mother eased her upright and tilted the water glass to her lips. The water was wonderful, but she threw it all up again. Her mother washed her face with a warm flannel and folded a clean towel over the spill of bile on the quilt. Then she went away and Canny was able to stay still—to quail at the sight of a hoop of light that rotated, blazing, before her closed eyelids.

Later—she knew it was later because she couldn't see the strip of light anymore—someone came in and turned on the pink-shaded lamp on the vanity. Its soft radiance was magnified by the vanity's three angled mirrors.

A man sat down on the edge of the bed. He opened his big black bag and produced a stethoscope and a thermometer.

Canny tried to cooperate with the doctor. She thought that if she was good and helpful and gave the right answers, perhaps she'd live. But it turned out there were many questions she couldn't answer, because the answers were simply unavailable to her.

"When did you last eat?"

". . ."

"Have you been sleeping?"

". . ."

"Have you had a lot of sun?"

After the last question the doctor said to Canny's mother, who was craning over his shoulder, "Does she seem sunburned to you?"

"No," Sisema said, then in irritation, "Dark skin shows red too, you know."

"Mrs. Mochrie, I served in the Pacific, and I know very well what sunburn looks like on all shades of skin. I only mean that Agnes is your daughter so you should know how she usually looks."

"I'm sorry, doctor. The fact is that Canny's never had enough color. She's not sporty, and she has been an indoor girl since her friend went into the hospital. What I can see is that she has lost some weight."

"Much?"

"No. A little. Her stepbrother is held up by the flooding on the Peninsula. He'll be able to tell us if she's been skipping meals."

Canny tried to say that she thought she'd been doing a lot of running. She remembered running, climbing, scrambling.

The doctor pulled the covers all the way back and began squeezing her legs and arms. He had her move them for him. Tears came into her eyes.

"Does that hurt?"

"My head," she said. When he moved her body her head was jostled. "It's only my head," she said, with effort.

"She hasn't a temperature. It isn't polio, Mrs. Mochrie. I know that's your concern."

"They're only immunizing the small children so far."

"Soon everyone will be immunized." The doctor put his palm on Canny's face and prized one eye wide open. He shone a light into it. She thought he would see only a cavity. She was empty; something had smashed its way out of her.

The doctor held his hand up before her face. "How many fingers am I holding up?"

Canny could see his fingers, quite clearly. They were a number. But she couldn't even say the number. Numbers were her air, and her air had turned poisonous. "I can't say the number," she said. She had to tell the doctor that. It was important.

"Have you forgotten the word for the number?" He sounded perplexed.

The number related to other things, and it wouldn't let itself be thought, or named. How to explain that?

The doctor tested the grip of both her hands. He asked her what day it was. She didn't know. He had her say

"Around the rugged rocks the ragged rascal ran," and "Peter Piper picked a peck of pickled peppers." She did that without any trouble, but for a moment wondered if she'd have managed the second tongue twister if she'd known how much a "peck" measured.

"You know what," the doctor finally said to Sisema. "I think we'd best treat this as a migraine. Migraines can present like strokes when they're very bad. But she's a healthy young girl, and there's nothing wrong with the grip of either of her hands. So I don't think there's any reason for us to suppose she's had a stroke."

The doctor gave Canny a sleeping pill. He moved off with her mother and gave his instructions.

Canny was on a rail and was traveling slowly backward away from the door to her bedroom, till the doorway was only a little slot, like a keyhole with light shining through it.

SOMETIME LATER THE OPEN DOOR ZOOMED IN AGAIN. The light was blazing in the hallway, and Sisema and Sholto were having an argument in ferocious whispers. Canny tried to catch some of it, but only managed to hear Sholto say, "We have to tell her."

SOMEONE WAS STROKING HER FOREHEAD. Their hand was heavy and warm. The curtains were open. Canny found her own hands under the covers and made them move. She shoved the other hand away and covered her eyes. The hand returned to her hair.

There was perfume, farther away than the hand. Canny

told the people in the room that she couldn't open her eyes until they closed the curtains. A moment later there came the hawking noise of closing curtains, and the clamorous brightness went away.

Sholto was sitting on the edge of her bed. He was wearing a jacket and tie, and his hair was darkened with hair cream and combed into a sleek quiff. Sisema was standing by the window. She was wearing a dark gray dress, high-heeled pumps, and a hat with a half veil.

Sholto said, "We have some very bad news." He sounded tender, but self-conscious. He waited a moment. For Canny to prepare herself, she supposed. But she didn't need to hear him say it.

After he had said it, Sisema said, "There's a vigil. For the traditional period. She was home for one night with her family. Now she's at a community hall in Congress Valley, and her schoolmates are being encouraged to visit."

Sholto stroked Canny's hand. "We know you're family, Canny, not a schoolmate. But you couldn't have moved last night."

WHEN CANNY HAD REACHED the Austin in the soggy meadow at the end of the Zarene Valley, she had thought, "Now I can sleep. And, at the other end, I'll go straight to the hospital." Marli would be there, in her iron lung, smiling insouciantly, like the magician's assistant about to be sawn in half. There'd be a nebulizer fizzing away near her head, like there was the last time she had a cold. And, really, there'd be nothing to be alarmed about. There would be the smell of menthol, and Marli's whispering voice telling her how the doctors and nurses had all made such a big fuss, and how she was going to be fine. Just fine.

THE HALL IN CONGRESS VALLEY was one Canny had been to before, once to play badminton and once to listen to a pipe band. It was cold, the building was in the shadow of a hill and there was an unseasonable anticyclone messing up the summer for the whole Southwest.

Marli's family were ranged along the wall behind a low barricade of floral tributes. They were sitting on mattresses, their backs against the wall. They had coats or blankets over their legs. There always had to be a respectable group of watchers sitting with Marli, so they weren't free to move about and get their blood going.

Marli's casket was in the middle of the group, its head against the wall and two mattresses abutting it. Marli's mother was on one side of the casket, with Sione and his daughter, her first grandchild, pressed against her. Marli's father was on the other side, leaning over, his elbows on the edge of the casket and his hands inside. He was gently stroking his daughter's cheek.

Canny went to them, and then stopped short. The casket was lying on a finely woven, bleached flax mat, trimmed with pale green and white wool. Canny knew how much work had gone into that mat, and she didn't want to put her feet on it.

Sisema came up behind her and leaned on Sholto so that she could kneel. Her corset creaked. She unbuckled Canny's shoes and pulled them off her feet.

Canny went forward. Sione scrambled up and actually

caught her, because she fell over. She couldn't keep her feet under her.

Marli was so still. Her lips were dark and sealed. The casket was quilted like a movie star's bedroom furniture, in gleaming white satin. Marli had a satin coverlet drawn up to her waist, and she was wearing a white organdy dress with orange and blue crisscross embroidery. Her hair was in a French plait with green and white ribbons braided into it. The casket was crowded, full of flowers, but it was as if Marli had fallen very far down, and Canny tried to look *through* her friend to see her. But she couldn't see her. Marli was there, and not there. She was her, and not her. Canny kept saying her friend's name as if impatiently prodding for attention, "Marli? Marli?" Then sharply, "Marli!" She sounded like one of their teachers. *When I talk to you please pay attention.*

Sione helped Canny crawl to Marli's side. She slumped there, her elbows on the casket, opposite Marli's father. He reached out and touched her hair and nodded at her. Nodded, and nodded. Tears were dripping off his chin. "She couldn't," he said. He was finding it difficult to speak. "She couldn't. Eh."

"Yes," Canny said kindly.

She couldn't live.

Marli's mother said, "You look like you've been in the wars, darling. Are you better now?"

"It's just a migraine."

"Migraines don't scratch you up."

Canny looked at the scabs and bruises on her arms, and the scratches visible under her sheer tights. Her hands were the worst—all cut up, and hovering, trembling above Marli's carefully braided hair. Marli's hair felt exactly the way it should, but the give in her scalp was all wrong, her skin no longer elastic and resilient. Marli really had changed; had *been changed*. She really was gone.

THEY STAYED FOR A FEW HOURS till the pill Canny had taken, the one Sholto had warned would make her floaty, wore off. Her head didn't hurt, but it felt as if it was hatching plans to start. When she came out of the cloakroom someone tried to put a plate of food into her hands—the kitchen was full, bustling, the tables at the far end of the hall were covered in paper tablecloths and paper plates piled with roast chicken and slices of taro cooked in coconut milk and sausages, buttered bread, fairy cakes, lamingtons.

"No thank you," Canny said. "I'm just waiting for my mother."

Sisema was at the end of the hall, rearranging the wreaths to make room for their own. Canny drifted over to the windows and leaned on one. The glass was cool.

Outside some of her classmates were sitting around a picnic table. They were the girls who used to play netball with Marli. They were lighting up, touching their cigarette tips to light as many as possible off one match, though that was said to be unlucky. Canny watched one girl swing herself up onto the bench to plant her bottom on the tabletop. Her Ma'eu teammate came up and slapped her legs, and Canny heard her say, "We don't sit on tables. We *never* sit on tables."

Canny had sat on a table herself, recently, although she knew never to do it. She remembered feeling stunned to find herself sitting on a tabletop—remembered being uncomfortable. But how had it happened? And why did she remember being startled, and *delighted* too? Because she'd been lifted up and put there. But when had this happened? And who had lifted her?

By the time her mother joined her, Canny's eyes had clouded and were pinched at their corners.

"Is your head hurting again?" Sisema asked.

Canny didn't nod or move her jaw. She didn't answer. She just followed her mother stiffly out to the road. Sholto had fetched the car—they'd had to park hundreds of yards up the street. Sisema turned on the tap on the outside wall of the building and held her hands in the stream till her fingertips turned pink. Canny came and did the same. They were both clean, but the ceremonial second washing felt right. Sisema said, "You have to keep doing things like this. Just one simple thing after another." She shut off the tap and shook her hands. "Life is all steps, but sometimes it's only stepping-stones. This is a stepping-stone time for you. But I'm here with you."

THE FOLLOWING DAY, Canny attended the funeral. It was a blur of noise and nausea. The interment, at least, took place out in the open air.

Everyone went to the cemetery. Marli's brothers and uncles carried her casket from the hearse to the grave, and put it down, not on the cold ground, but on that same finely woven mat that had been laid ready. Then, when it was time to put the casket in the ground, Marli's mother put out a hand to Canny and, gently whispering the few necessary instructions, she had Canny help her wrap the casket up in the flax mat. They made a parcel of it. "That looks warmer," Marli's mother said. Then, with great difficulty, because its handles were now hard to find and hold, Marli's menfolk picked the parcel up and carried it to the big cradle of straps, the wet edge of the grave wheezing as they trod carefully along it.

By that time there were seeds of shining blackness appearing in what Canny could see, black seeds that became streaks, then bottomless holes in her field of vision. She leaned against her mother and shook.

She couldn't see, but she heard the quiet engine of the undertaker's hoist start up. And then the singing, the long, rolling swells of melodic chanting.

Sione caught up with them before they got to the car. He said, "Canny? We understand that you couldn't make it in time. We know you were sick. We don't want that to trouble you, so you need to know this. In the morning of her last day when we came to visit Marli, before she got very bad, she told us that you had been there during the night. She told us that you had come into the ward and braided her hair. You saw how her hair was in a French plait? It must have been one of the nursing sisters who did it, but Marli thought it was you. She told us, 'Canny came to visit me. She was wearing a beautiful dress. She fixed my hair.'"

As Sione told his story he let the tears run on his face.

Canny couldn't answer him. She was blind with pain,

and crying. But she heard her mother say, "It's very kind of you to tell her that. God bless you, dear."

DESPITE THE BARBITURATES SHE'D TAKEN, Canny came awake in the middle of the night, driven up from sleep as people are by the memory of a thing that has to be done, a task, a duty that is theirs alone.

After a moment she understood that she'd woken because it had begun to rain. It was raining, and Marli was out there, beyond comfort, with the rain falling on her.

20

January 1963, Castlereagh, Southland

IT WAS THE FORMLESS TIME after the ceremony and the photographs, the toasts and speeches, the first dance, the cutting of the cake, and tossing of the bouquet. In the begonia house, where the wedding breakfast had been served, the piles of meringues had been reduced to rubble. The white tablecloths were stained with red wine and Fanta. The children were floppy and glazed, or were still grimly eating cakes. One flower girl had been sick, and her mother was in the washroom rinsing her hair ribbons.

The band had packed up. The dancing was over, but not before the clot of a bridegroom had stood on the bride's train and torn a hole in it. The bride and groom had gone off to put on their "going away clothes." The wedding party was only waiting for them to come back for final farewells and congratulations.

Some of the guests had already departed, others were nosing around a long table covered in presents. Those who'd maybe had a bit too much to drink were picking up parcels and shaking them. The mother of the bride issued warnings. "Don't you separate that gift from its card. There's nothing worse than having to guess who to write a thank-you note to and resorting to faking it, writing 'Thank you so much for your beautiful gift' to someone who's given you a garden hose."

The best man and groom's younger brothers had taken off their jackets and rolled up their shirtsleeves. They were doing handstands on the lawn between the conservatory and the beds of roses.

One of the bridesmaids had two bouquets, hers and the bride's. She was giggling with her girlfriends about being *next*.

The other bridesmaid had slipped off her pearl-gray shoes and was plucking the flowers from her crown of plaits. The day had been hot and the flowers were wilted. After she'd done that, she was coaxed up to pelt around after some of the sugared-up kids, until one of them got into the fountain and flung water at her. She went off, shaking drops from her bias cut fawn satin dress. She showed the other bridesmaid the grainy streaks of damp, and the other bridesmaid pointed out the holes in the toes of her stockings.

The bride and groom returned, he in a cinnamon-colored sports coat, she in a cowl-necked burnt orange dress, with a yellow hat and gloves. Everyone crowded around. The couple's car was tufty with streamers. The groom had tried to tear off some of the decorations but had forgotten the "Just Married" sign in its back window.

The bride went around kissing everyone and had a

little cry with her sister, the bridesmaid who'd caught her bouquet. The other bridesmaid was wearing her shoes again but had a pencil behind her ear because she'd been helping the bride's mother make a preliminary list of the gifts. The clot of a groom tried to pull the pencil out and managed to free a long loop of hair. He tried to tuck it back and about five people said hastily, "No, it looks fine, don't try to fix it." The bridesmaid held his hands down and kissed him on his freshly shaven cheek. She and the bride hugged, and held on for a long time. The bride shed a few tears. The bridesmaid said, "You look really lovely in that color, Susan."

The bride said, "Thank you for everything, Canny. Get one of these oafs to drive you home. Don't think of walking."

Canny laughed. "So close to home, and in daylight, of course I'm going to walk."

"But no one's waiting for you at home."

"My key is in my purse. At four o'clock on a Saturday, University Hill is as safe as houses."

"Not all houses are safe," said Susan darkly. But that didn't mean anything to Canny.

"Come on, my sweet," urged the clot of a groom. "We'd better hit the road."

More kisses and hugs and backslapping and teasing jokes, then the couple got into their car and wavered away over the speed humps.

CANNY WASN'T, THESE DAYS, particularly prone to embarrassment and was happy to walk out of the gardens in her long bridesmaid's dress. She picked up its hem and began to climb the ten flights of steps that zigzagged up University Hill. People she met coming down looked delighted to see someone in wedding finery. One old man struck his walking stick several times on the ground, like a formal herald, and said, "What a vision of loveliness!"

She stopped at the top to take in the view. It was a windless day and the harbor was like silk. The Westbourne ferry was halfway across, its decks crowded with day-trippers. The wharves were busy, the cranes in stately motion. The light was clear, the air pure, and everything faraway looked close.

Canny went along the street and through the gate in the arch of the hedge. She found a car in the driveway. It wasn't one she recognized.

Sisema and the Professor were away at a conference in Founderston, and Canny had the house to herself. So when she found the strange car, and the house unlocked, she didn't close herself in straightaway. She stood in the hall and called out. "Hello?"

"Hello," came back. It was Sholto.

Canny ran upstairs. Sholto was standing at the window of his old bedroom, which faced the Botanical Gardens. The rose gardens, fountain, begonia house were all completely visible.

"Could you make her out?" Canny said.

"In orange, at the end," he said. "I haven't been here long enough to see her in her wedding dress."

He turned around and studied Canny's outfit. She did a little twirl.

"Beautiful."

"Yes. Some brides put their attendants in nasty colors."

"Sue always was very generous."

Canny looked at him soberly, then sighed and said, "Well, you know what I think."

She thought he'd been an idiot to let Susan go. To decide that their small differences were important. To not try to change, even a little. To not see the warning signs. To take things for granted. All the usual stuff.

"How was the clot?" Sholto said.

"Blissfully happy. A great lummox. And sweet," Canny said, knowing she was being unkind to Sholto. Then, "What happened to your car?"

"I sold it. That's a borrowed one. Sisema sent me a letter saying she wanted me to clean out my room, and she preferred me to do it when she and the Professor were out of town."

Sholto and his father had had a bad falling out, a year ago, when Sholto's book came out.

Sholto said, "I think they even expect me to take all the dusty sports trophies. The stuff parents usually keep."

Sholto's room smelled musty and unused. There was a sad little crowd of cricket, swimming, and debating trophies standing on the carpet, ranged like a circled wagon train, with empty cardboard boxes looming around them.

"You've hardly made a start," Canny said. She sat on his bed and once again slipped off her shoes.

"I'm sorting. Making it clear what it's okay to throw away. I'll give them the pleasure of doing that."

"Purging the house of Sholto," Canny said.

"The Professor was making a big, scrupulous fuss about what I was going to take and keep, like he always does about family things," Sholto said. Then he repeated with the right emphasis, "Family *things*." He pulled a face. "As if the family having things and passing them on with due ceremony represents family to him." He turned away and opened the wardrobe. Empty coat hangers rattled. He said, "I've bought a berth on the SS *Arcadia*, sailing to England. I'm off on Wednesday. I hate this place. There's nothing for me here."

Canny said, "You have ideas about Southland, and it's your ideas you hate. All you see is smug, timid, insular Southland, instead of gentle, reserved, dignified Southland. It's both. You should stay, Sholto, and keep asking questions."

"Oh sure," he said. "No one needs a twenty-six-year-old thundering from the pulpit. And anyway—who are you to say I shouldn't cut and run? *You* were supposed to be doing something better."

After a time he noticed that his rummaging was the only sound in the room. He came to sit with her, though he didn't apologize, because he thought he was telling truths she needed to hear. But he took her hand and held it.

What Canny remembered was that the thing she'd been best at—math—became lethal to her. She remembered it in her gut. It wasn't just a story others told about her, or an explanation she sometimes had to give. Her deep, irrational gut memory of severing and sacrifice was too mysterious for any explanation to make sense of it.

Her mother's story came closest. Sisema's take on what

happened to Canny was this: Canny's grief for Marli was so great that it was like a serious illness. Canny had a kind of breakdown, where she persuaded herself that her sorrow-induced illness should cripple her, as Marli's illness had crippled Marli.

The summer before, Canny had been on her way down the ten-flight shortcut to the city when she'd met Jonno on his way up, carrying a smart new houndstooth coat over his shoulder. They stopped to talk, and when she asked why she hadn't seen him lately on campus, he told her he'd left. "I didn't fit in," he said, and then he winked at her because she was supposed to know why. "University isn't for us, eh."

Jonno said he'd gone and done a bookkeeping certificate and was working for an importing firm. But he'd just applied for a job at IBM in Founderston. "They have these giant computers that can calculate the average of sets of up to two hundred numbers, in a fraction of a minute. If I get the job I'll be the first person from my family to go north in five hundred years."

Jonno's "five hundred years" made Canny forgive his "not for us" remark. "I love it that you can say that," she said.

Jonno gave her one of his "I'm testing you" looks (she always failed his tests) and said, "You know, we all read your brother's book."

"Your family?"

"No. All of us."

He meant the Faesu, the people of the archipelago, Southland's first people, who had twice settled, and twice abandoned, the mainland.

At the time of the conversation, Canny made a mental note to tell Sholto what Jonno had said next time she saw him. Then she forgot. She'd become a forgetful person. She'd stood on the steps that day, chatting with her old Math Competition teammate, and feeling like he'd let her down. No doubt he felt the same. It was meant to be different for them. They were expected to put up with feeling uncomfortable at University—surrounded by white students. They were supposed to put up with feeling out of place so that their kids *wouldn't*. (That was one of the many sensible things the Professor had said to Canny.)

So—Sholto reminded her that she was supposed to be doing something better. Then he felt remorseful and came to sit with her and held her hand.

After a moment she said, "Never mind about me."

"No! I'm not going to listen to that. You could have made some useful contribution. Proved or invented something new."

"I mean it, Sholto, never mind about me. Now I'm going to argue with you using your own thesis, the one from your book."

Sholto's book was called *The Forgetful Land: An Immaterial History of Southland*.

"Your thesis is that Southlanders are afraid of the immaterial in our lives, and that makes us lose our feeling for the material too so that, as a people, we're a vague and soggy lot with no passion or conviction. An example of yours that I liked was how no one here can talk seriously about justice without trying not to call it 'justice,' because 'justice' is too grownup and grand for us. So that, when they were trying to ban the use of convict labor at the beginning of the century, we had senators saying they wanted to fix 'inconsistencies in the application of our laws.' Can't you see that you did the very same thing just now? You said I'm a tragic loss because my brains were *useful*."

"I'm a hypocrite," Sholto said. "Or I know when I'm beat. Take your pick. But I guess I should have said that you're a tragic loss because your brains were yours and yours alone. You were the one who could pull the sword out of the stone. And you gave it all up."

"Not on purpose," Canny said. Then she sighed and added, "I'll miss you."

Sholto glanced at her, almost shy. Then he recovered. "The old Canny wouldn't have said that."

Canny reflected that the old Canny might have said that she'd be lonely without him. The new Canny wouldn't be lonely, not with her fellow students at the Teachers Training College and the hiking club. She said, "The old Canny was a cold fish, apparently. One of my friends decided to tell me that the other day. She was congratulating me on how much I'd changed."

"You were never a cold fish."

"No. I was a proportionality symbol, the one that looks like a fish."

"I'm amazed to hear you mention something mathematical."

Canny's head felt tender. The afternoon was hot and dry, but there was a thunderstorm feeling in the room. That would be her last mention of anything mathematical. "My teachers tried to tell me to pay more attention to what other people wanted. But I remember watching others only so I could work out how to outwit them. I had no time for anyone but Marli. I clung to her from the moment we met, and when she ended up in the hospital, I think I made myself see *only* her. As if by visiting her every day, and thinking about her first thing in the morning and last thing at night, I could make her stay alive."

"You were trying magic. Performing a ritual so that something miraculous would happen. That's what Susan would say."

Canny squeezed his hand. "Susan is interested in what goes on *under* what we all think. And while she was with you she encouraged you to look deeply too." Then she quoted his book at him. She could still quote from memory. "*'We have floated our material culture over a sea of folktales and ghost stories nobody respectable will tell.'* The Professor and snarky Founderston book critics tried to turn you into that 'nobody respectable.' The Professor thought he was mocking you when he said that you were so in love with the big questions. But that was a *good* thing."

She left him to think about that. She went downstairs and poured two glasses of milk and carried them and a bowl of ripe apricots back up. She broke an apricot open for Sholto and showed him the stone, clean and untouched in its capsule of air. "I love it how apricots practically stone themselves," she said, and flicked the stone free. Something about the sight of that apricot pit—hidden, essential to the fruit, but no longer even touching its flesh—moved Canny and meant something to her, though she couldn't think why.

Sholto spat out his stone, then pulled a chair over to his wardrobe and stood on it. He began rummaging through piles of old clothes and comics. He said, "The Professor didn't like my spoiling his work with the little questions either. Like how did Ghislain Zarene escape from the Bull Mine without a speck of soot on him?"

"I don't know that story," Canny said, and put down her partly eaten apricot. She had the blurry feeling she got when one of her migraines was coming on. The room was beginning to look as if she were seeing it through frosted glass.

Sholto was peering at her. "Are you all right?"

She rubbed her forehead.

"Mind your makeup," he said.

Canny closed her eyes. When she got scattered like this, as a preliminary to the pain she'd find herself making puns, as if she'd lost the ability to take words as they were actually meant. She said, "My makeup is like numbers— one of those mysteries I've learned not to ask questions about."

"You don't mean paint and powder."

"I mean my parentage."

"The clay and the fire," Sholto said, and Canny heard his feet thump as he jumped off the chair. "Hey, Canny?" he said. "How offended would you be if I didn't keep this? It was the only artwork you ever made me." He held something out to her. "It'd be pretty hard to pack." The thing made a dry, papery sound.

Canny opened her eyes.

It was yellowing a little, and almost certainly no longer

smelled of Zarene Valley apples, but there, in Sholto's hands, lay Canny's Master Rune.

Sholto knew his sister had never been a sentimental person, so he was surprised to see tears. Tears, a tremulous smile, then, "Thank you, Sholto," she said, and accepted what he held out to her, that odd artwork he'd thrown up on top of his wardrobe three years ago and forgotten about. "You kept it for me." Her voice was shaking.

"Mmmm," he said, ashamed.

She got up, and he took an involuntary staggering step backward. It was as if she had turned into a cascade, a waterfall that flowed upward, or a big bright Founders Day firework. She looked exactly the same as she had a moment before, tall, shapely, dark, very good-looking—but that was just her outside. Just her clay. He had handed her the old artwork, and she caught fire.

The room was quiet. The evening was hot, the birds stunned by heat. The traffic was still light because the day was long and no one had to hurry home. The world went on as usual. But Sholto took another step back. The first step he'd taken was from fear, the second was to give her room, as if she were about to break into dance, or wind up for a shot-put throw. But she only continued to stand, straight and still, with the artwork between her bookend palms.

Then something happened. Sholto thought there was a flash of light so bright that he was forced to turn his face away. When he opened his eyes, still looking away, he could have sworn he saw, for a moment, the room as it might look in fifty years if no one bothered to look after it. He saw a water-stained ceiling, and wallpaper sagging off the walls. He was dizzy, so he covered his eyes.

Canny said quietly, "I only needed to be reminded. I don't have to keep this. What it represents—I don't know how to use it yet. But I do know I won't be making foundation stones." There was a clink, and more papery rustling.

Sholto made himself look. His sister was rotating the artwork in her hands, as if seeking a way into it.

"I guess I'll need pliers," she said. "I have to retrieve Granddad Afa's compass from inside it." She gave a little merry laugh and met his eyes. "I don't want to keep secrets from you anymore, Sholto."

Sholto was covered in cold sweat. "Not even if I want you to?" His voice was tight with nerves.

"Pliers?" she said.

"You'll find some in the toolshed. But, Canny, what is that thing?"

She put the artwork to her ear and shook it. "It's a kind of codex. A key to all my magic. I made it on our last day in the Zarene Valley. It was the only thing I could think to do. I sent my spirit back in time and gave it to you for safekeeping. It's made from Granddad Afa's compass, which Ma lost in 1942, and newspaper, tissue paper, and galvanized chicken wire from around a sapling by the sign to Iris Zarene's guesthouse."

There was a bit of silence, made mostly of Sholto's speechlessness. Then Canny said, in quite a different voice, and not a pleasant one, "Ah yes—Iris Zarene."

21

IT WAS AFTERNOON, and most of the children were shut up with Lealand in the schoolroom at Orchard House, learning their Alphabet. Cyrus had been building some new beehives out of dismantled apple crates but was interrupted by Iris, who had walked over to seek some of his bee venom ointment.

They were in his kitchen. He'd made nettle tea and was spooning some of the waxy ointment out of the big crock he kept it in, into the crystal container Iris had brought with her. The container had been a present from their mother, on the occasion of Iris's twenty-first. It was meant for jewelry, but in the life she'd lived, Iris hadn't had any use for jewelry.

"You really should have electricity put in," Cyrus said. "And get a washing machine with a wringer. You can't keep using that old-fashioned mangle with your rheumatism."

"It's the first time my hand has troubled me in summer," Iris said. "So it'll be arthritis, not rheumatism."

Cyrus put the crock away and sat down at the table. He scooped a dollop of ointment out of the crystal box and began massaging it into Iris's scarred hand.

"Hello?" someone called from the front door. It was a young voice, but not a child's.

"Why can't those hikers keep to the trails?" Iris muttered, exasperated.

"The beehives usually discourage them," Cyrus said, and got up to see what the hiker wanted—honey, honeycomb, or mead.

The hiker was a young woman. Cyrus took in her hiking boots, khaki shorts and white polo shirt, and her movie star sunglasses. Then she removed her glasses and he saw that it was Agnes Mochrie.

It sometimes happened that young Zarenes would venture back. The less talented ones could manage a short visit before falling ill. And they could tolerate another bout of withdrawal when they left again. The real magic users never returned. But here she was—the girl who should have lost so much of herself that Cyrus would have sworn that she wouldn't even know where to go looking for what she'd lost.

"Hello, Cyrus," she said. "How are you keeping?"

"Ah . . ."

"You are *keeping* at least, aren't you? It's what jailers do."

"I see. I'm going to get sarcastic wordplay rather than thundering wrath. That's a relief." Cyrus was really annoyed—and elated. She'd beaten it somehow, the thing none of them had been able to beat. He felt frightened and, at the same time, absurdly proud, as if she were his protégé, not Ghislain's.

"May I come in?"

"Can I stop you?"

"I'm not a brute," she said, offended. "If you tell me to leave I'll just go straight up to the house. I only came here to give you a heads-up. I'm going to free Ghislain, and you might like to start thinking about how you're going to handle that."

Cyrus saw she'd grown up—and it wasn't just a matter of the three years that had passed. He stepped aside and invited her in. "We're in the kitchen," he said. "Do you remember your way?"

"*We?*"

"Myself and Iris."

"Iris," said Agnes Mochrie. "Good."

ALL THOSE YEARS of being awkward and on the outside of things stood Canny in good stead. She wasn't embarrassed, self-conscious, or nervous. She turned her attention outward to absorb the moment and savor it.

Iris Zarene stared, then levered herself up from the table, knocking over her chair.

"Easy," warned Cyrus.

Iris's burned hand glistened and made a sticky whisper as her fingers flashed. Her other hand was faster, and silent.

The dust motes in a shaft of sunlight were suddenly funneled into a transparent tube of air, and then became invisible, moving in a speedy vortex as the air formed into a force rope.

"Oh, come on," Canny said, and began mimicking Iris.

Before Iris could throw her force rope—casting off first, as if it was a bit of knitting, Canny saw—Canny had finished her own. Hers wound itself around Iris's like a big constrictor around a smaller snake. Silvery-blue light crackled in the ropes like a thunderstorm contained in a snow globe. The surrounding air gave a few glassy screeches, and then the shaft of sunlight was empty of movement and dust. The vacuum between Iris and Canny collapsed with a thump, and Iris's crystal box jumped a foot sideways, its lid suddenly covered in starbursts of cracks.

Cyrus seized his sister's arms and forced them down to her sides. "Would you both just cut it out! This is my kitchen."

"Sorry. But she drew first," Canny said.

Cyrus pulled out a chair for his sister, and another opposite for Canny.

She didn't take it. "I'm going on up the hill. I only came to let you know."

Iris was pale and wavering. Cyrus helped her into her seat. She managed one word. "How?"

"Ghislain had built a Spell Cage," Canny told them. "Something like your great-aunts' Spell Veil. He knew the house would keep him alive. He planned to escape back into his own past, presumably not the parts when he was a suicidal solitary prisoner." Canny spoke in a flat, bored way, then paused to study Iris. She was looking for some sign of remorse but saw only self-righteous fury. "In other words he'd just got to the point where slow starvation and atrophy seemed better than what he had."

"We couldn't release him," Iris said.

"Because you were afraid of him."

"No!" Cyrus protested. "Because our spell had become so strong we hadn't any hope of breaking it."

"He deserved what he got," Iris said.

Her brother rounded on her. "He'd served his time! The only thing that made it bearable to me that he was trapped there was that the house was so peaceful and beautiful." Cyrus looked pleadingly at Canny. "He's been in a kind of heaven."

"*Alone* in a kind of heaven," Canny said.

Cyrus dropped his face into his hands.

"So, you're his champion," Iris said to Canny.

"It wasn't like that. At first I only tried to get up the hill because the hill tried to stop me. I was just solving a problem. And then I realized it was magic, and I wanted to do something for my friend Marli, who was trapped too, in an iron lung. I wanted to cure her."

Iris had her color back, and her haughtiness. Her voice was acid. "That's your story. That you didn't steal anything. You didn't trespass and poke your nose in where it wasn't wanted. You simply found something you were looking for—for *unselfish* reasons. Well of course that's your story."

Canny looked away. She pictured her Master Rune—saw it clearly, the beautiful, lunar smoke of it. It was every part of the life she'd lived so far, open to every other part. It held all that and could hold much more. Every passing

425

minute gave her more places she could go. Go back, see, learn, understand everything better. But that was all she could do—better her understanding. Oh—and be there. She could be there.

ONCE CANNY HAD PULLED the model of her Master Rune apart and retrieved her grandfather's compass, she knew there was a first thing she must do. To do it, she didn't even need to take off her beautiful bridesmaid's dress. She just left her body, standing in the dress, as inanimate as a dress-maker's dummy, and floated to the door of Marli's ward.

She waited there, watching a nurse working in the light at the head of the iron lung.

The nurse slipped a straw into Marli's mouth and en-couraged her to drink. Then she washed Marli's face with a steaming flannel and dried it for her. She spread a salve on Marli's cracked lips. She promised to be back in a min-ute or two, and then went out past Canny without seeing her.

Canny floated into the room. One thing that she'd par-ticularly loved about her dress was the sound it made when she walked. Now Canny discovered that the spirit of a dress made no sound.

Marli saw her of course. The blanched, sweat-beaded face reflected in the chrome-edged mirror lit up on seeing her. "Canny!" Marli whispered.

Canny had to concentrate in order to pick up the hair-brush. But taking hold of the brush was inevitable—because she'd done it already—and so she reached for it, and closed her immaterial fingers on its handle. And there it was, in her hand. "Would you like me to brush your hair?"

"Yes." Marli turned her head one way to let Canny start on that side, and to watch her in the mirror.

"I've brought some hair ribbons, I thought I'd weave them into a plait."

"That really is a beautiful dress," Marli said, gazing at Canny in the mirror. "Though Mum would say 'Do you need to show quite so much of your lungs?,' meaning breasts."

They both giggled; Marli wheezing.

Canny fanned her friend's hair out and brushed it till it was sleek. Then she began to make a French plait, weaving the ribbons into it—green and white. Marli closed her eyes, basking while Canny worked. Once Canny was done, she opened them again and said, anxiously, "Will you come tomorrow?"

Canny carefully put the hairbrush back on the tray on the top of the iron lung. Her hands didn't tremble. Only bodies suffer the poisonous venom of fear. She'd lied so often, and none of the things she wanted to say could be said. This couldn't be a valedictory visit, only a loving fare-well. She said, "I'll come the day after tomorrow."

"Okay."

Canny stooped and touched her lips to her friend's hot cheek. "Sweet dreams, dear. Try to get some rest."

Marli obediently shut her eyes again. Through the thick glass of the porthole in the wall of the iron lung, Canny watched as Marli's good right hand found her crabbed and atrophied one and gripped it tight. Marli held on to herself.

Canny left her friend. The way she went—the way that worked—there was no place where she could pause and look back.

IN THE KITCHEN OF THE APIARY Cyrus Zarene said, "Agnes, telling us why you went up Terminal Hill still doesn't explain how you come to be here, memory, magic, and all."

Canny laughed. "Well, I used Ghislain's Spell Cage. I thought he shut me in it, as if the only real use he had for me was as a guinea pig."

Cyrus drew breath to ask another question, and she held up a hand. She was pleased to see Iris flinch. "I had an anchor," she said. "So I went all the way back to my beginning, found my Master Rune, and returned."

"You're lying," Iris said.

"No. Look. You'll understand at least as much as I do once you know that, all those years ago, when Ghislain was sitting on the veranda of the house waiting for you to shout at him, or beat him about the head, and then begin to *forgive* him—all those years ago, while you and Lealand wound your imprisonment spell around him, he wasn't alone. His Found One was with him. After it caused the second fire in Bull Mine it didn't burn out and disappear. It wasn't consumed. Fire was just something it mimicked. That's what it does best—mimic.

"Remember when I was missing overnight and everybody was looking for me? You came up to the house, Cyrus, to ask Ghislain if he'd seen me. While you were out in the front talking to him, I was around the back climbing down from the veranda roof. I got stuck and was helped by someone I thought was Ghislain. And a few days later someone I thought was Ghislain shut me in the Spell Cage. But both times it was the Found One, mimicking Ghislain. If I'd had any idea how strong Ghislain was supposed to be I'd have been more suspicious. Ghislain could tie me up with, well, with one of those force rope things we just made. But I was twenty yards away from the person I thought was Ghislain when he caught hold of me to make sure I didn't take a hard fall off the first terrace. He—it—held me and put me gently down. The reason that the great-aunties' 'Repair, Restore' spell can actually resurrect Ghislain, and your imprisonment spell leaches the magic from everyone who didn't make it, is because Ghislain's Found One is there, making the magic stronger. It's the stone in the fruit—and the next tree in the stone."

Iris looked furious and tearful, but Cyrus was smiling at her.

"Why are you smiling at me?"

"You understand the magic. What it means."

"I understand that, at its heart, it's resurrection magic and has something to do with time," she said. "Ghislain told me all that. But when you climb in a Spell Cage and close its doors and go back, it's even easier to understand. I don't just have a past, present, and future. I have an always-present present that's made up of my whole life so far. At the end of my life I think all that rolls back into the magic. The twin Zarenes are still there, in the magic. I can feel them. They're the stone in the fruit."

"She hasn't explained herself at all," Iris said to Cyrus, aggrieved. "She just says 'I had an anchor'—but *how* could she have an anchor?"

Cyrus got up and started opening cupboards and assembling tins and packets. Canny saw that he was putting together some stuff that she could take to Ghislain. She could smell coffee beans. She said, "Don't grind those. There's a grinder on the wall by Ghislain's bench."

"I know," Cyrus said. "And it's always better freshly ground."

"You're both being ridiculous!" Iris said.

"It's my specialty," Cyrus said. "You've always said so."

"That, and being a turncoat."

Cyrus paused, didn't turn around, but when he replied his voice was hard. "You and Lealand made all the decisions. *I* made all the visits."

"So," Canny said, "you must know about the jeep crashed in the forest?"

"It appeared in 1942. It's a U.S. Marine jeep. The road down from Fort Rock was still drivable then, at least to a jeep," Cyrus said.

"One of the marines died in the crash. A guy called James. Lealand put the body in a window seat in the house, just to play spiteful games with Ghislain."

"Lealand never said anything about that. He's a dark one."

"He told me," Iris said.

Cyrus heaved a sigh.

Canny said, "Don't give me too much stuff, Mr. Cyrus. I may be magical, but I'm not a mule."

Cyrus began judiciously removing a few things from the flour sack he was giving her to carry.

"My mother, Sisema Afa, was with those marines," Canny said. "Perhaps Ghislain's Found One saw a female and seized its opportunity. It made twins. Not me and a sister. It copied my mother—but inside her, as a baby. Copying was something it knew how to do. So I'm my mother's twin. My mother was my anchor. I've thought about it and thought about it, and that's the only thing I can come up with. Maybe the Found One *meant* to make an anchor—but then how could it know I'd come back? I think it might just have wanted to escape by sending some of itself out beyond your imprisonment spell. By becoming a kind of father. But it wasn't human, so instead of being half my mother and half my father, in the normal way, I'm almost all my mother—her twin—with just enough Found One so that the magic answers me. That's how the magic works for me. I might understand the Zarene Alphabet because I'm a math genius, but it answers me because the Found One is my father."

Canny paused and watched with great satisfaction as Iris's eyes grew wide and her face pale.

Cyrus said, "I must say, Agnes, you're taking this very calmly."

"I've had some time to think about it, and it makes sense of things that have troubled me in the past. I always felt misshapen. Now I understand why. I'm much happier to think that I'm not completely human than to go on feeling that I'm a human being with something missing. And, believe me, it's better to think I'm not completely human than the alternative. When I learned that my

431

mother had been in the house in 1942 I had a moment where I thought that *Ghislain* might be my father. You can imagine how that made me feel! But he's not. If he was, I wouldn't have a twin, and my spirit could never have found its way back to my body."

Cyrus shook his head and then laughed. "It got lucky, didn't it? The Found One."

"Yes! I might never have come to the valley. If my mother had known I was coming here she would have absolutely forbidden it. She never really got over what happened to her here. She was partly responsible for two deaths—the marine, Jim, and Ghislain. And the other marine died shortly afterward, at Tarawa—Alex Creech." Canny gave his full name as a way of honoring him. "When Alex died there was no one left in the world who shared the blame for those deaths. But of course it was only ever *one* death. Ma wasn't to know that Ghislain has probably lost count of how many times he's died."

"Ghislain makes things up," Iris said, dismissive.

Cyrus rounded on her. "One day you're going to have to face that it was a terrible thing we did to him. We should have released him years ago, when we still could."

The siblings glared at each other. Then Cyrus said to Canny, "How are you going to free him?"

"I don't know. He and I can work it out together, with the Found One, I guess. And"—she smiled—"you can keep us supplied with coffee."

WHEN CANNY CAME INTO THE LIBRARY of the house on Terminal Hill, Ghislain barely glanced at her. His face was sad, resigned, and vulnerable. He immediately looked away, at the book before him on the desk, and didn't say anything to acknowledge her.

Canny said, "It really is me."

No answer.

"But I guess that's the sort of thing your imagined Canny would say."

He shook his head. He wouldn't look at her.

"And that's probably another thing your imagined me would say. That is, if you're really imagining me properly."

He gave her a shy look. "I couldn't have imagined that," he said. "That's too convoluted for me." Then, his voice shaky, "*Please* let that really be you."

She went to him, draped her arms over his shoulders, and laid her cheek against his.

His body remained tense. "My imagined Canny can sometimes make herself felt," he said. "Though, when she does, she never speaks, only sings like the dawn chorus." Then, apologetic, "I'm quite mad, and my hallucinations are very strong."

She kissed the hair at his temple. "When you see me, it might not be a hallucination, Ghislain. It might be your Found One taking my form to try to comfort you. It's been with you for thirty-three years, and it has learned a lot about being human. But there are still things that it just can't understand. When it makes itself look like me I'm sure it means well, even if it makes you crazy."

The library clock whirred and a larger number appeared in the little window at the top of its blank face.

Canny could only see the side of Ghislain's face, but

she thought she detected the beginnings of relief, if not hope.

"Why didn't it do it before now?" he said. "Not pretend to be you but—say—pretend to be Cyrus, who has been visiting regularly for a long time. How come it perfected you, when it would have had much more practice at Cyrus?"

She said, delicate, "Maybe the last time you felt this desperate it hadn't got the hang of having a believable body—being seen and felt."

Ghislain turned to take her in his arms and pull her down into his lap. He held her hard, buried his face in her hair, and inhaled deeply. "You have your own scent," he said.

Canny brushed back his free-spirited forelock.

"You left me lying on the lawn and melted away through the bars of rain. I think that was the moment when my prison was most visible."

"Your Found One shut me in the Spell Cage. I thought it was you. And you had Granddad Afa's compass. I put two and two together and got four when, all the time, there was another number in the equation that I couldn't see."

"But, Canny, I *know* I'm not your father. I'm not *anyone's* father. I may have had a bad moment, and horrible suspicions, because of all the holes in my memory, from all the times when I was dead. But I know you're not a Zarene." He shivered and looked into her eyes. "Beyond that, my imagination fails me."

"The other number," she said, trying not to sound school-teacherly. She didn't quite manage it.

He drew back more to get a better look at her. She watched it dawn on him. "That explains a lot."

She nestled close to him, and patiently and happily explained the rest of it. How one of her parents really was some kind of monster.

When she'd finished and was waiting for questions, he surprised her. He asked, "What happened to your friend, Marli?"

"She died, three years ago." Canny put her hand on his cheek. "Thank you for remembering."

"I've gone over every moment of our time together. Every touch, look, conversation. And at night when I get into bed I leave my shoes beside yours."

"I was always leaving my shoes behind." She laughed, and then said, very gently, "I'm not going anywhere now, Ghislain. I'm going to stay here with you, and we're going to discover how to break the imprisonment spell. I don't think it'll be too difficult since I have my Master Rune. Getting up the hill would have been easy this time, except they've killed the pigs and the paths are overgrown. But the spells all gave up the ghost when I got near them. It wasn't violent. It was just like—'Okay, Boss, over to you now.'"

"Leaving isn't urgent. At the moment I just want to be alone with you."

"Yes."

He kissed her again, a long, lingering, caressing kiss.

LATER, WHEN THEY WERE LYING in the sun on the lawn, Ghislain drawing aimless squiggles (or possibly runes) on her bare stomach, he asked, "Does Iris know you're here?"

"Yes."

"How are we going to deal with her?"

Canny was glad he'd thought to ask and grateful she'd have weeks, and maybe even months, to work some changes in him. She sat up and he did too. He began idly pulling grass out of her hair.

Canny said, "Before I left Castlereagh I looked in the phone book for Middleton and gave Lonnie Zarene a call. He's the boy who was forced to leave the valley when I was last here. He was grief-stricken about it, and I promised him I'd do something to fix things for him and the other Zarene kids. I called him to tell him that I was setting off to try. We were talking about Iris, and I realized that he's very fond of her. That made me change my mind about what she deserved. Who loves who—that has to be important. I mean, it must be anyway, no matter what we think and feel, if there are things in nature just *longing* to be spoken to. Things that, when you call them, respond with love, like your Found One."

"Are you sure it's love?"

"Yes, love, I'm sure it is."

"When the spell is broken do you think it will leave us?"

Canny considered. "It made me and loves you, so I think it'll stay with us. But if it does go—if it wants to, or needs to—how much can that matter? You and I have enough strength to live our lives, don't we?"

"*Love* enough," Ghislain said. "I'm tired of strength."

GO FISH

QUESTIONS FOR THE AUTHOR

ELIZABETH KNOX

What did you want to be when you grew up?
When I was about six I announced to my parents that I wanted to be a jockey— not that I'd ever been on a horse! Not wanting to let me know too soon what the world was like (then), my father said, "But darling, you'll grow too big!" So I put it out of my mind. I never did get too big, and by the time I was fifteen New Zealand had its first female jockey. Of course by then my plans had changed.

When did you realize you wanted to be a writer?
When I was sixteen. I'd started writing letters between the characters in an imaginary game I played with my sisters and friends. I remember lifting my pen from the page and thinking, "This is what I want to do with my life."

What's your first childhood memory?
I was eighteen months old. It was night and I was buttoned into my father's coat with my head poking out of his collar. We were on the deck of the Lyttelton ferry. I remember looking at the lights of Seatoun and Breaker Bay as the ferry sailed out of Wellington Harbor.

What's your most embarrassing childhood memory?
I was eleven. It was the end of year school performance. The girls of my class and the class above ours were doing a fashion show of the clothes we'd made in what they used to call Manual Training (the girls did cooking and sewing, and the boys did woodwork and all made Taiaha—Māori spears—and caused one another injuries). I was the announcer of the show. My friend Denise hadn't given me her notes so, when she came on stage, I said, "And Denise is wearing . . ." then, hissing, *"Denise, what are you wearing?!"*

As a young person, who did you look up to most?
My father. He was vivid, flamboyant, opinionated, and very handsome.

What was your worst subject in school?
Math.

What was your first job?
I had a holiday job with my father, who was the editor of a New Zealand encyclopedia. I had to make a photo library. I mischievously filed photos of the Prime Minister of the day under Disasters.

How did you celebrate publishing your first book?
I bought a pair of boots.

When you finish a book, who reads it first?
My husband, Fergus, who is also my New Zealand editor and publisher (though only of my adult books).

Are you a morning person or a night owl?
Hoot!

What's your idea of the best meal ever?
Fresh mozzarella and sliced tomatoes drizzled with some grass-green olive oil and followed by black Otago cherries.

Which do you like better: cats or dogs?
I have three cats—a ginger boy, a beige boy, and a black girl. They are from the same litter and still sleep in a warm, furry pile.

What do you value most in your friends?
Warmth and optimism.

Where do you go for peace and quiet?
The Wellington Botanic Gardens are at the bottom of the street where I live, so I go there.

What makes you laugh out loud?
I laugh so often it has to be inappropriate some of the time!

What's your favorite song?
Hoagy Carmichael's "Stardust"—a very old jazz standard.

Who is your favorite fictional character?
Camille Desmoulins in Hilary Mantel's *A Place of Greater Safety*. Of course Desmoulins is a historical figure (French Revolution), but Mantel's Desmoulins is wonderful and strange, and tragic and loveable.

What time of the year do you like best?
Late summer.

What is your favorite TV show?
This is difficult! I'm going to have to say *Buffy the Vampire Slayer*. But *Deadwood* is a close second.

SQUARE FISH

If you were stranded on a desert island, who would you want for company?
My husband Fergus and sister Sara. I'd like my son Jack to be there too, but I'm sure he'd much rather be on a nearby island with his many friends.

If you could travel in time, where would you go?
Tata Beach, Golden Bay, New Years Eve, 1975. It would have to be the kind of time travel where only your consciousness travels and you enter your younger body. I remember being sent to fetch my grandmother for the family barbecue (my mother's family at that time had three houses on the beach). We walked along the track by the lagoon. Grandma said she was wearing her "plum gown." We saw a weasel and a weka. I'd just like to do it again, that walk with Grandma Douglas, then the meal with my parents and sisters, aunts, uncles and cousins.

What do you want readers to remember about your books?
How they felt and who they were when they were reading them.

What would you do if you ever stopped writing?
Well, I guess I might stop burning the coffee!

What do you like best about yourself?
My ability to forget myself completely for long stretches of time.

What is your worst habit?
I'm a very bad networker—too solitary, shy and uncommunicative. You'd think it would be okay for writers to be like that, but not anymore, not really.

What do you consider to be your greatest accomplishment?
My novel *Black Oxen*—deemed a failure by some. When I do a talk, there are always people who come up to me afterwards, look left and right, lean in close, and say, "Of course the book I really love is *Black Oxen*—I've read it six times!" I feel that way about it too. Hooray for the minority!

What do you wish you could do better?
All the women in my mother's family are gardeners. I love gardens. But . . . well . . . the thing about the cats and husband and son is that, when they're hungry and thirsty, they come and tell me. . . .

Laura's world is next to the Place, an unfathomable land that fosters dreams of every kind and is inaccessible to all but a select few—the Dreamhunters. Now, fifteen-year-old Laura and her cousin Rose will be tested to see if they qualify for the passage. Nothing can prepare them for what they are about to discover.

Keep reading for a thrilling peek into
Book One of the **DREAMHUNTER** Duet.

1

ON A HOT DAY near the end of summer, Laura Hame sat with her father; her cousin, Rose; and her aunt Grace against the fern-fringed bank on a forest track. She watched as her uncle Chorley and the rest of the picnic party passed out of sight around the next bend.

Chorley turned and waved before he disappeared. Laura stared at the empty, sun-splashed path. She saw black bush bees zipping back and forth through the air above the nettles and heard the muffled roar of Whynew Falls, where the rest of the party were headed.

Laura and Rose; Laura's father, Tziga; and her aunt Grace were sitting under a sign. The sign read, *CAUTION: YOU ARE NOW ONLY 100 YARDS FROM THE BORDER TO THE PLACE.*

"The falls are loud today," Tziga said. "It must have poured up in the hills."

They listened to the cascade pound and thump. Laura,

who had never been allowed near the falls, tried to imagine how they would sound up close.

Her father said, "Think how startled Chorley would be if one of these girls suddenly skipped up behind him."

Aunt Grace squinted at Laura's father. "What do you mean?"

"Come on, Grace. Why don't we just get up and wander along that way?"

"Tziga!" Grace was shocked. Laura and Rose were too. The family had owned a summer house at nearby Sisters Beach for ten years, and at least once a year they would go with friends for a picnic up in the old beech forest. Every summer those who *could* would continue along the track to see the falls. And every summer the girls were forced to wait at the sign with their dreamhunter parents. Tziga Hame and Grace Tiebold couldn't go and view Whynew Falls themselves because, one hundred yards from the honest and accurate warning sign, they would cross an invisible border. They would walk out of the world of longitude and latitude, and into a place called simply the Place. Tziga and Grace could no more continue on to Whynew Falls than Laura's uncle Chorley could walk into the Place. Uncle Chorley, like almost everyone else, couldn't go there. Tziga and Grace were part of a tiny minority for whom the rules of the world were somewhat different.

"Come on, Grace," said Tziga. "Why should we make the girls go through all the ceremony of a Try? It's only for the benefit of the Regulatory Body, so they can see their rules enforced. Why can't we just find out *now*, in a minute, in private?"

Rose wailed, "It's against the law!"

Tziga glanced at Rose, then looked back at Grace. He was a quiet man, self-contained, secretive even—but his manner had changed. His *face* had. Laura thought that looking at him now was like peering into a furnace—its iron doors sprung open on fire. Her father was a small man. He was a mess, as usual, his shirt rumpled and grass-stained, his cream linen jacket knotted around his waist, his hat pushed back on his dark, springy hair. Laura's aunt Grace wasn't any better turned out. Both dreamhunters were thin, tanned, and dry-skinned, as all dreamhunters became over time. Rose was already taller than her spare and weathered mother. She was white and gold and vivid, like her father, Chorley, and like Chorley's sister, Laura's dead mother. Laura had, unfortunately, not inherited her mother's stature or coloring. She was little and dark, like her father. But—Laura thought—her father, though small and shabby, still had the aura belonging to all great dreamhunters. She liked to imagine that the aura was a residue of the dreams they'd carried. For when Tziga Hame and Grace Tiebold ventured into the Place, dreams were what they brought back with them. Dreams that were more forceful, coherent, and vivid than those supplied to all people by their sleeping brains. Dreams they could share with others. Dreams they could perform, could *sell*.

Laura's father was saying, "We were pioneers, Grace. You didn't 'Try,' you crept past the cairn beyond Doorhandle early one morning when there wasn't a soul on the road. Do you remember? That moment was all your own. There wasn't anyone standing by with a clipboard and contracts."

Laura saw that her aunt had gone pale. Grace stood up. Laura thought Grace meant to walk away, back toward the road, to go off in a huff and put an end to Laura's father's crazy talk. But then she saw Grace turn to look up the track toward the border.

Laura's heart gave a thump.

Her father got to his feet too.

Rose didn't move. She said, "Wait! What about our Try? You've even bought us outfits—our hats with veils."

"Rose thinks she's a debutante," Laura's father said.

"I do not!" Rose jumped up. "All right, I'll go! I'll go now! I'm not scared. I was only trying to follow the law. But if you don't care about it, why should I?"

"Good," said Laura's father. He offered his hand to Laura. She looked at it, then took it and let him help her up. She busied herself brushing dry moss from her skirt. The others began to amble slowly along the path. Laura caught up with them and gave her hand to Rose, who took it and squeezed it tight. Rose's hand was cold, much cooler than the air, which, even in the shade of the forest, was as marinated in heat as the open paddocks, the dusty roads, and the beaches of Coal Bay. Rose's hand was chilly, her palm coated with sweat.

Around the first bend was another, very similar. The track was flanked by black beech trunks. The sun angled in and lit up bright green nettles and bronze shoots of supplejack.

"I guess we won't see the Place until we're there," said Rose.

"That is right," Grace said. "There's nothing to see. No line on the ground."

Tziga said, "The border is around the next corner."

They didn't slow, or hurry. Laura felt that their progress was almost stately. She felt as though she were being escorted up the aisle, or perhaps onto a scaffold.

She didn't want to know yet. *It was too soon.*

In two weeks Laura and Rose were due to Try. Any person who wanted to enter the Place for the first time had to do so under the eye of an organization called the Dream Regulatory Body. The Body had been set up ten years before. It employed rangers—those who could go into the Place but couldn't carry dreams out of it—to patrol the uncanny territory and its borders. The dream parlors, salons, and palaces in which working dreamhunters performed had to obey laws enforced by the Regulatory Body and its powerful head, the Secretary of the Interior, Cas Doran. The parlors, salons, and palaces were businesses and had to have licenses. Dreamhunters, too, had to have licenses. A Try was the first step on the road to a license, and a livelihood.

The Body held two official Tries a year—one in early spring and one in late summer. Each Try found hundreds of teenagers lined up at the border. It wasn't compulsory to Try, but many did as soon as they were allowed, because dreams represented a guarantee of work and the possibility of wealth and fame. Any children who showed an inclination—vivid dreaming, night terrors, a tendency to sleepwalk—were thought, by hopeful families, to have a chance at the life. A dreamhunter or ranger in the family was another indicator of potential talent. More boys than girls Tried, since parents were more permissive with boys, and the candidates were, by and large, in their midteens. The earliest age of a Try was legally set at fifteen.

Rose and Laura had celebrated their fifteenth birthdays that summer.

Walking along the Whynew Falls track hand in hand with her cousin, Laura felt desperately unprepared for an impromptu Try. Every night that summer as she'd put her head down on her pillow, she had mentally ticked off another day—the time narrowing between her and her life's big deciding moment. She had felt as though she were hurtling down a slope that got steeper and steeper the farther she fell. For Laura knew that, after her Try, she would either be in her father's world or remain at her school— Founderston Girls' Academy. She would have a calling or be free to continue her education, to travel, to "come out" when she was sixteen and appear at every ball that season. If she was free, Laura knew she'd inherit the Hame wealth— but not the Hame glamour. And, free, she would lose Rose, because *Rose* fully expected to walk into the Place, fall asleep there, dream, and carry back her dreams intact, vivid, and marvelous. For Rose had already been into the Place, had been a number of times, because Grace Tiebold had gone on catching dreams when she was pregnant with Rose. (When her sister-in-law Verity said to her, "Did you ever think that you would go there and leave the baby behind?" Grace had put a hand on her stomach and laughed at Verity—also pregnant—saying, "Oh! Darling! What a bloody thought.")

As Laura approached the bend around which her father had said the border would be, she began to drag her feet. Rose gave her hand a sharp tug. "Come on," she whispered. "Stick with me."

"Tziga," said Grace. "Just tell me this—why now? We could have tried last year, or the year before, or when they were only ten. We could have whipped them across quickly when they were really tiny, and they wouldn't even have known where they were. We would have learned whether they could cross or not, and just waited to make it official."

Laura saw her father shake his head at Grace, but he didn't answer her.

"Why do you need to know *now*?" Grace asked again.

Laura gave a little sob of tension. Then she crashed into her aunt, who had suddenly stopped in her tracks. "Jesus!" Grace said. They all stepped on one another. When Laura righted herself, she saw a ranger approaching along the path.

The man came up to them. He looked, in quick succession, surprised, suspicious, and polite. "Mr. Hame, Mrs. Tiebold," he said respectfully. "Good day to you. Are you going In?" Then he looked beyond the adults at the two girls. He stared pointedly.

"No, of course not," said Grace. "We are just waiting for my husband and our friends. They went along to the falls."

"I see," said the ranger. He stood blocking their path. He cleared his throat. "Perhaps it would be wiser to take these young ladies back to the sign."

"We do know exactly where the border is," Grace said, frosty. "It isn't as if it moves."

"It *is* very well marked," Tziga said, neutral. "We're not likely to make any mistakes."

"But you can't always keep your hand on your children near the border—best not to go too near." The ranger was quoting a bit of the Regulatory Body's official advice, saying something he no doubt had to say to many people on his patrols. But because he was addressing the undisputed greatest dreamhunters—one of them the very first—he at least had the decency to blush. "I'm very sorry," he said.

"We're not dopes, you know," Rose said, indignant. "Laura and I are Trying in two weeks, for heaven's sake. Why would we spoil that by sneaking across now?"

"It is better to be careful," the ranger said. He focused on a point above Rose's bleached straw sun hat and composed himself into a stiff state of official dignity. He looked blockheaded.

"Come on, girls," Grace said. She turned Rose and Laura around and propelled them back along the track.

Laura swallowed hard to suppress her sigh of relief.

The ranger hovered for a moment. He seemed to realize that Tziga Hame meant to stay put, so he followed Grace and the girls.

AT WHYNEW FALLS, LAURA'S UNCLE CHORLEY Tiebold filmed the other picnickers as they requested. He shot them pointing up at the waterfall, wet from spray. He filmed them jostling and giggling at the pool's edge.

When he was finished, Chorley packed up his movie camera, hoisted it onto his shoulder, and followed his neighbors back along the track. He was itching to return to his work-shop in Summerfort, the family's house at Sisters Beach. He wanted to see whether he'd managed to capture on film the scales of shadow pushing down the white face of the cascade. Chorley picked up his pace to catch up with the others. He passed the orange-painted circle of tin tacked to a tree trunk—the border marker. He went on a few steps, then for some reason glanced back. He saw the track, tree ferns, gray, knotted sinews of a red-bush vine. Then he saw a flicker of color and shadow in the air, and his brother-in-law, Tziga, materialized on the track behind him.

Chorley flinched. He had filmed this phenomenon—people passing into and out of the Place on its busiest border post, the cairn beyond Doorhandle. It was Chorley's best-known film; he'd sold copies to all corners of the world. Everyone wanted to know just what it looked like—and that it didn't look like trick photography. It didn't. It was a quiet, unfussy, terrifying sight. The only time Chorley had seen it and hadn't felt frightened was when, shortly before they married, he and Grace had played a stalking game in the long grass on the bluff above the river at Tricksie Bend. Grace, inside the Place, hadn't known where Chorley would be outside of it, and he hadn't known where she would emerge. She jumped back and forth, sometimes startled to find he was close by and could grab her. It had made Chorley anxious, made his heart ache to see Grace come and go like that—go where *he couldn't follow*. But it was magical too.

"There you are," said Tziga. "You always come last when you're carrying your camera." He stepped around Chorley and walked ahead of him, turning back now and then to speak. Looking up, for Chorley was quite a bit taller. "You know—there's far too much interest in Laura's and Rose's Try," he said.

Chorley couldn't remember anyone mentioning the girls' Try at the picnic. Not even Rose, who grew more excited the nearer the event came. He said, "I may be following you, Tziga"—he poked his brother-in-law with the legs of his camera—"but I don't follow you."

"There's too much interest in the *outcome* of their Try. That's all I'm saying. I don't want them besieged with publicity, or contracts."

"That's why we've bought them hats with veils, to keep their faces out of the newspapers," Chorley said. "To keep it all as private as possible. We could, at least, all agree to do that much. You *do* realize that I've been trying to talk to you—and Grace—about this for months now?"

"I know. But there was never any question that they'd Try as soon as the law allowed."

Chorley took one hand off his precious camera to grab Tziga's arm. "*I* questioned it," he said. "The law can say what it likes, but I think they're still too young."

"They *want* to Try," Tziga said. He looked very unhappy.

Chorley said, "Rose wants to—Laura just doesn't want to be left out." He watched Tziga's face go remote. Even Chorley, who knew his brother-in-law better than anyone, couldn't tell whether Tziga was offended, angry to be told something about his own daughter that he should know himself, or whether he had just dropped down into a colder and deeper reach of his usual sadness. "Tziga," Chorley said, and gave the arm he held a little shake. He was annoyed with himself for poking the chisel of his complaints into this crack in his brother-in-law's certainty. "Look," he said, "it'll soon be over. It'll be decided one way or the other."

"Yes."

Chorley told Tziga to get a move on. The others would wonder where they were. "You do know it will be all right whatever happens," he said as they went along. "I'm not a dreamhunter, and I'm all right. Grace and you are dream-hunters, and you are too—all right, I mean. Aren't you?" He gave Tziga yet another chance to confide in him, to tell him why, lately, he'd seemed so *hunted*.

Tziga just made a faint affirmative noise, then asked Chorley if this was the camera Chorley wanted him to take into the Place.

Chorley immediately forgot his worries. "Yes," he said. "Are you saying you will? Finally?"

Tziga said yes, he'd take Chorley's camera In tomorrow.

Chorley was rapt, and for the next hour, long after they'd caught up with the others, he talked. He gave instructions, advice, almost gave a shooting script for the film he most wanted to make but couldn't make himself.

Tziga interrupted only once, when they reached the cars, which were parked at the gate of the farm beside Whynew Falls Reserve. He said to Grace, "There he is," and tilted his head in the direction of a man in a duster coat, a shadow against the tangled trunks of the whiteywood forest.

"He's seeing us off," Grace growled.

"Who is it?" Chorley asked.

"A ranger," said Rose.

Chorley saw Grace give Rose and Laura a sharp look.

The girls got into the car. Chorley said to the dreamhunters, "Do you think that ranger is watching you?"

"Of course not," said Grace.

"Yes," said Tziga. "I'm being watched. The Regulatory Body has a big investment in me. Contracts. That sort of thing." He made one of the gestures peculiar to him—seeming to crumble something in his right hand and cast it away into the air. Then he went around the front of the car to crank it for Chorley.